Hope you enjoy!

Hayden
Nicholas

EZEKIEL'S
CHOICE

Hayden Nicholas

WESTBOW
PRESS
A DIVISION OF THOMAS NELSON

WestBow Press books may be ordered through booksellers or by contacting:

WestBow Press
A Division of Thomas Nelson
1663 Liberty Drive
Bloomington, IN 47403
www.westbowpress.com
1-(866) 928-1240

Because of the dynamic nature of the Internet, any web addresses or links contained in this book may have changed since publication and may no longer be valid. The views expressed in this work are solely those of the author and do not necessarily reflect the views of the publisher, and the publisher hereby disclaims any responsibility for them.

Any people depicted in stock imagery provided by Thinkstock are models, and such images are being used for illustrative purposes only.

Certain stock imagery © Thinkstock.

All scripture taken from NIV version of bible.

ISBN: 978-1-4497-7714-2 (sc)
ISBN: 978-1-4497-7715-9 (hc)
ISBN: 978-1-4497-7713-5 (e)

Library of Congress Control Number: 2012922266

Printed in the United States of America

WestBow Press rev. date: 2/14/2013

ONE

Zeke Allenby opened his eyes and saw the first rays of sun peeking through the tent flap, casting a wedge of orange light on the canvas wall. He reached for his hiking boots at the foot of the sleeping bag, rubbed Billy on the head, then left the small tent. He knelt by the campfire—now nothing but smoldering embers—and stoked the fire back to life while examining the morning: sunrise in the clear eastern sky; the surrounding canyon terrain of oak, mesquite, juniper, and pinyon; towering Victorio Peak behind him with its higher-elevation tree variety of Douglas fir, Ponderosa pine, cypress, and madrone.

The Sierra Diablo Wildlife Management Area encompassed nearly eleven-thousand acres and had been organized more than a half-century ago, mainly to protect the Texas Bighorn Sheep population. Frank Whiting, a friend from Zeke's army days, owned a huge ranch nearby and allowed Zeke to camp and hunt on his property. Occasionally, Whiting arranged permission for Zeke to enter into the wildlife area, like now, where Zeke could explore the area where the Apache chief, Victorio was finally routed by Buffalo soldiers of the Tenth U. S. Calvary in 1881. The Tenth prevented the Apaches from reaching any of the springs nearby, including Rattlesnake Springs, near where Zeke and Billy now had their campsite. The routing of Victorio and his band of Apaches marked the end of the Indian Wars of Texas, forcing them into Mexico where Victorio was killed a month later. Zeke had a small collection of military artifacts ranging from arrowheads found in the American Southwest to a Taliban whip found in the Khyber Pass in Afghanistan. He had hoped to find some bullet casings, buttons, or other items relating to the Tenth Calvary but had been unsuccessful so far.

Zeke boiled a pot of coffee over the campfire's low flames as Billy patrolled the perimeter of the campsite, sniffing the ground where he'd marked his territory the night before. Two days from now they would return to their parked Jeep; a good three hour hike through mountain trails and canyons used by Apache and Comanche hunters centuries earlier. This area of West Texas was centered in Texas's wild mountain range: the Davis Mountains to the south, the Guadalupe Mountains to the north with its peak ranking the highest in the state at over 8000 feet above sea level. Then, as the plan went, they would drive back to Zeke's cabin a few miles north of Gold Tree, Texas, about a half-hour drive. Once at the cabin, Zeke would pack for the trip to Houston to leave Billy before catching his flight overseas. Zeke's sister-in-law, Ruth, would keep the dog for the entire ninety days, the term of his contract with a Central Asia-based NGO firm named *S-WORKS*. Ruth and the kids loved the dog but Zeke dreaded the separation from his beloved German Shepherd.

Zeke sipped his coffee and searched the sky overhead. He'd first noticed the anomaly four days ago. He remembered long ago, during the aftermath of 9-11, when the skies had also been devoid of aircraft. The distant rumble of a commercial jetliner high in the sky or a small single-engine Cessna buzzing about were so common most people never noticed the absence of them. But Zeke did. *A terrorist hijacking?*

The nagging feeling to return to his cabin became overwhelming. He poured some hard dog food into a fabric bowl and gave it to Billy before breaking camp. Soon he was packed, the large backpack straddling his shoulders as he surveyed the campsite, making sure he left the area as he'd found it.

Two hours later they stopped at a spot where the trail wound around a rocky cliff. Zeke decided to climb the cliff for a better view. He'd been noticing the strong odor of wood smoke wafting downwind the last half-hour or so. He focused his binoculars to the southwest, toward the vicinity of Gold Tree, a small outpost of a town not much more than a post office and a dozen stores. A slight brownish haze hovered in the distance but he didn't see any large plumes of smoke or other signs of a wildfire.

An hour later they arrived at Zeke's parked Jeep near the dirt ranch road that would lead them away from Sierra Diablo Mountain. He popped the Jeep's hood and reattached the battery cables to the battery, a habit of his for discouraging would-be car thieves, and also because he left his Jeep unused for long periods of time due to his overseas travel.

When they reached the fork of unpaved road leading to the cabin, Zeke switched on the Jeep's radio and heard nothing but static. He adjusted the tuner across the entire AM range and couldn't find one single transmission, hearing only constant white noise from the Jeep's speakers. He felt his heart rate increase slightly, realizing the serious implications.

When they finally reached the cabin, Zeke noticed Billy's sudden change in behavior. The dog's thick neck fur stood on end and a low growl vibrated his powerful chest. When Zeke saw the cabin door he knew why. The door stood wide open. Anger swelled within him, mixed with that gnawing feeling in the pit of the stomach that came with violation—that particular feeling you get when your world is invaded and your most precious belongings are senselessly ripped away. Yes, he knew that feeling well. The memories rushed forward: the late afternoon over five years ago when the police cruiser and detective sedan pulled into his Houston driveway, the cops walking slowly toward his front door while he watched through the living room window . . .

STOP! Zeke commanded himself to halt the memories. He stepped out of the Jeep. "Stay," he told Billy in a low voice. He drew his M9 automatic pistol from his holster and removed the safety. He heard Billy whine as he approached the opened door. When he stepped inside the cabin he saw piles of debris covering the kitchen floor. He made a quick security sweep of the small cabin's interior until convinced the intruder or intruders were gone. He whistled once and Billy came running into the cabin, instantly sniffing the floor from one end of the cabin to the other.

Mainly a one room layout, the cabin had a kitchen near the door and two bedrooms in back with adjoining bath. In the kitchen, the fridge's door stood opened, revealing its dark interior with a mound of trash and old food containers on the floor in front of it. He flipped several light switches on the walls to no avail while Billy sniffed the debris on the floor, picking up scents no human could detect.

After checking the fuse box and electric meter outside in back of the cabin, Zeke wondered if the power outage included the entire area surrounding Gold Tree or just portions of it. He feared he knew the answer. *No AM radio stations transmitting?* AM transmitted over a range of hundreds of miles, and if the atmospheric conditions were right, even farther.

Returning inside the cabin, he walked straight to the large pantry located in the kitchen. As he opened the pantry door, ambient daylight revealed empty shelves. Among the debris on the floor, Zeke searched for the flashlight he usually kept on one of the shelves. He couldn't find it so he went to the fireplace mantel and grabbed a candle and matchbox, apparently one of the few things untouched by whoever or whatever had trashed his cabin. He lighted the candle and returned to the pantry, stepping over the debris to pull a lever under one of the shelves in back. The back wall came ajar, revealing a secret storage room. The storage room was filled with stacked boxes of canned goods, bottled waters, bags of rice, various hardware items with ropes, cables, and assorted tools lining the walls—a survivalist's wish list of items. He focused his attention on a tall metal container standing against the back wall. He knew the storage room hadn't been discovered, but he needed to see the metal container's contents anyway. While the candlelight flickered in the dark room he opened the container door, revealing his collection of rifles, pistols, shotguns, and boxes of ammunition.

He left the storage room and began pacing the cabin while sorting through his thoughts. He thought of an animal invasion. He'd seen cabin kitchens ransacked by bears, even raccoons, but this was different.

Definitely not a burglary, he told himself. *Nothing's missing.* The small flatscreen TV near the wood stove looked untouched. His laptop, still plugged into the wall outlet, sat on the small chest-of-drawers near the breakfast table, his cell phone next to it. The only thing that appeared missing was food from the fridge and pantry. He wondered if a transient had stumbled upon the cabin and raided the food supply.

Zeke walked back to his bedroom with Billy following close behind. He went to the small bedroom closet. His jeans and shirts still hung on the hanger rod but were pushed tightly to one side. His dress jackets and a few windbreakers hung in their usual spots but one item was missing. He sorted through the hung items rapidly while looking for the gray cotton hoodie with ARMY RANGERS stenciled on it, a garment he wore when he'd asked Amber to marry him.

Gone.

The wave of emotion came quickly, surprising him with its speed and intensity. Billy whined and rubbed his snout on Zeke's legs. Zeke shut off his grief as quickly as it had come. He left the bedroom and headed back to the secret storage room in back of the pantry. He reached into a cardboard box and grabbed a pint bottle of Jack Daniel's whiskey. A moment later he downed a shot from a small glass near the sink and stared out the small window above it. He thought of something, then headed for the chest-of-drawers across the room where his laptop and cell phone sat apparently undisturbed.

Zeke grabbed the cell phone. The screen displayed the message: *searching for signal*. After thirty-seconds of waiting, he powered down the phone and restarted it. Same thing. He opened the lid of his laptop. The monitor screen displayed a blank gray screen for a second or two before shutting off completely. He removed the power cord from the back and tried to restart it from battery power. Nothing. He stared into oblivion, trying to come up with an explanation other than the one currently racing through his brain.

I should drive into Gold Tree right now. He scanned the interior of his small cabin. He had plenty of food and water, a wood-burning stove for cooking, but he really needed to get gas in the Jeep for the drive to Houston. He had a quarter tank, planning to fill up on his way out of town. And of course, gas station pumps used *electricity*. He was curious about the situation in town. He decided to go now.

As Zeke changed into some clean clothes in his bedroom, he thought more about the situation, wondering how widespread the power outage might be. Local power losses were common in this remote area, but the loss of *all* AM radio reception suggested something much bigger. His mind wandered: *What if this turned out to be bigger than just a local power outage; like a massive failure of the region's power grid, or national power grid.* It didn't take a genius to realize that society broke down fairly quickly when the basic essentials were gone. The importance of obtaining fresh water and a food supply seemed obvious to most people, but one crucial factor was seldom considered: protection. Not just protection to one's self and loved ones in the normal sense, but protection of those basics essentials needed to survive; defending your water and food supply from those less prepared for a catastrophic event. Decent, friendly, law-abiding people could become a pack of hungry wolves when food and water are impossible to obtain, especially as they see their loved ones slowly dying of thirst. Cities would be the worse. *Places like Houston*, he thought. *Ruth and the kids.*

Zeke grabbed a long, baggy tee-shirt from the closet to conceal the M9 and its holster. He fastened his sheathed K-bar knife around his calf to conceal it under the pant leg of his army fatigues. After feeding Billy some fresh dog food from the pantry, he filled a metal flask with the rest of the Jack Daniel's whiskey near the sink and stashed it into one of the many pockets in his army fatigues. A few minutes later and Zeke had a leash and harness on Billy as they headed out the door.

As Zeke drove the Jeep along the winding dirt road toward town,

Billy's long tongue lapped at the air while the wind blew through the fur on his head. About halfway down the road Zeke thought he heard the distant reports of rifle fire coming from somewhere in the distance. He brought the Jeep to a halt and shut off the engine. He scanned the rough terrain while listening for anything out of the ordinary. He heard nothing more so he started the Jeep and continued down the road.

A few minutes later the Jeep reached the intersection of 2060, the paved highway leading to Gold Tree to the north, and to the Interstate to the south. Something caught his attention perhaps a mile in the distance, on the southbound section of highway connecting Gold Tree to the rest of the world via the Mangas Bridge. He saw a group of people and vehicles on the road. *A car collision?* He didn't think so.

Zeke turned south onto the highway and eventually saw an army roadblock, complete with concertina wire and uniformed soldiers guarding the approach to the bridge. Zeke stopped the Jeep a distance from the roadblock and grabbed his binoculars. He looked past the roadblock at the Mangas Bridge spanning the steep canyon beyond. The road on the opposite side of the two-thousand-foot bridge also had a roadblock of concertina wire and armed soldiers. He heard shouts from the soldiers at the roadblock nearest him. He saw several soldiers waving their arms, trying to get his attention. He slid back into the seat and drove the Jeep toward the soldiers.

When Zeke got fifty feet or so from the roadblock, two uniformed soldiers with M-16s at the ready marched toward him. Zeke noticed their uniforms lacked any unit insignia. *A bit odd*, he thought. He guessed they were National Guard, or maybe MPs from Fort Bliss, the military base near El Paso. *But why no insignia?* He slowed the jeep and brought it to a complete stop. The two young soldiers divided, one approaching the passenger side and the other approaching the driver's side of the Jeep. Both soldiers were alert, keeping their eyes on Zeke and the German Shepherd in the passenger seat. Zeke held a firm grip on Billy's leash.

"This is a restricted area!" one of the soldiers shouted. The soldier approaching Zeke's side of the Jeep said, "You'll have to turn your vehicle around and leave the area, sir!"

"What happened, soldier?" asked Zeke.

"The bridge is closed," the soldier said. "You have to leave immediately."

Zeke saw no sign of damage on the concrete supports of the bridge or the steel cable structure above it. "Is it damaged?" Zeke asked, ignoring the soldier's command.

The young soldier cleared his throat and said, "Sir, I'm going to ask you again to leave the area . . . immediately."

Zeke saw an officer heading toward the Jeep, a second lieutenant with one hand resting on his holstered sidearm. This had to be the roadblock's commander. By the officer's appearance and macho swagger, Zeke figured the second lieutenant was as green as they come. *Probably a Walmart clerk when he's not doing time with the Guard.*

"There a problem here, Mista?" the second lieutenant barked.

"No, sir," Zeke replied. "I was just asking the Private here what was wrong with the bridge."

The second lieutenant's eyes narrowed. "It's got structural damage so it's closed to all traffic!" he said with a Boston accent. "Now turn your vehicle around and leave the area immediately!"

"May I take a closer look?" Zeke asked.

"Absolutely not!" The second lieutenant shouted, his patience gone. "Now—"

"—May I ask what exactly you are guarding?" Zeke interrupted. "I mean, a simple barricade with signs notifying the public that the bridge is closed due to structural damage would be sufficient, wouldn't it?"

The second lieutenant approached closer to Zeke's side of the Jeep. "That would be a first-rate idea," he said with a sarcastic tone in his voice, "except for the fact that most of you drunk cowboys don't know how to read! And we don't want you to get hurt when you drive your *pickemups* onto an unstable bridge that may fall down at any moment!"

Zeke smiled while nodding in an approving way. "Well done, Second Lieutenant. Is Colonel Bill Forney still running the command at Bliss? It may be *General* Forney by now."

The question side-railed the second lieutenant for a brief moment. "Never heard of him," he finally said.

"Thought so," Zeke said while putting the Jeep in reverse and backing away into a 180 degree turn. He shouted out, "Have a nice day! If I see any of 'dem *pickemups* in town I'll pass along you're warning!" Zeke revved the Jeep's engine and sped away, looking in his rearview mirror at the officer and his soldiers still standing in the road.

Zeke didn't believe there was anything wrong with the bridge. The question was: *Why are armed troops preventing anyone from entering or leaving the area by way of the bridge connecting it to the rest of the world?*

Zeke continued to drive north on the highway toward Gold Tree. As he entered the small town he saw a few cars and *pickemups* parked along the street, the same as any day. An old Chevy pickup drove by in the other lane, heading in the direction of the roadblock. *Where does he think he's going?*

When the Jeep reached Gold Tree's small town square, Zeke saw a small crowd of people cloistered in front of the one-story stone building housing the local sheriff's office *and* the post office. An American flag flew at half-mast in front of the building. Down the street he could see *Cactus Jack's Food Mart* with several of its large windowpanes shattered.

Zeke parked the Jeep on the street and walked his leashed German Shepherd toward the people gathered in front of the building. They were having a noisy discussion with Sheriff Morris Campbell, the only town official Zeke had met before, although not under the best of circumstances.

"Listen," Sheriff Campbell told the crowd in a tired voice. "I can't tell you anything. Until communication is reestablished, we are *all* in the dark."

"Can't you go out there and talk to em', again?" an older man asked.

"I've been out there twice," Sheriff Campbell retorted. "The commanding officer told me all he knows is the bridge is damaged so the road is closed. End of story."

"They are liars!" a Native American man shouted. "They are trapping us in here like rats!"

The crowd began muttering.

"We're not *trapped*, John William," Sheriff Campbell said.

"Oh, no?" John William shouted back. "So I guess it is just a coincidence that troops are guarding the mountain passes, too!"

Sheriff Campbell looked tired as he said, "I don't know nothing about that."

"They've shut down our power, Sheriff," another man in the crowd said, "and somehow disabled most of the vehicles in town. We're cut off from the rest of the world. I think that means we are *trapped!*"

More mutterings from the crowd.

"I bet them weirdos from Corn Ranch had something to do with it!" a grizzly looking man in a cowboy hat shouted.

Zeke had to smile. The area known as *Corn Ranch* had been bought years ago by an Internet billionaire from Seattle for his sub-orbital space exploration company. Complete with launch pads and research facilities located near the salt flats north of Van Horn, the company claimed it would eventually offer sub-orbital flights in its vertically propelled spacecraft; a sort of expensive high-tech joyride for *astronauts* chosen by the company. *More than likely, millionaire yuppies fulfilling childhood fantasies,* Zeke thought as he watched the angry little crowd confronting Sheriff Campbell.

"I'm telling you!" John William shouted. "It's the army! They did it!"

More muttering from the crowd.

"All right, all right," Sheriff Campbell said with a weary grin. "When I know something else I'll let you know." He turned and walked away.

"How am I supposed to get my medicine?" an older woman pleaded, causing others to join in, throwing another barrage of questions at Sheriff Campbell as he disappeared inside the building.

A young, portly shaped woman wiped tears from her eyes. She leaned against an older man wearing a John Deere ball cap, both of them looking scared and angry.

Another man in the crowd, probably in his early forties, bald as a cue ball and dressed in khakis and a button-down shirt looked out of place in this crowd. Cueball watched the scene without any comment, a kind and intelligent expression frozen on his face.

Zeke turned his attention across the street near a row of small shops with a liquor store nestled in the middle. More dark interiors. More broken glass and debris on the sidewalk. A woman with an infant in one arm and a garbage bag full of something in the other arm stood in front of a storefront, talking with a young man wearing a camouflaged hunting vest. Down the street from the row of shops, Zeke saw a small group of children playing at a playground located in Gold Tree's community park. A park bench facing the street sat empty. A filthy-looking man with long matted hair and a dirty beard shuffled toward the bench, mumbling to himself.

Zeke started to turn his attention back to Cueball when he noticed another man leaning against a tree in the playground. Zeke could have sworn the man wasn't there just a moment earlier. The man was tall and muscular, wearing military-style cargo pants and a dark-green teeshirt. Everything about the man spelled Special Forces, maybe a retired Green

Beret, if there really was such a thing. The brim of a ball cap shadowed the man's face, and although his eyes were hidden by a pair of aviator sunglasses, he appeared to be watching the crowd across the street. But for some unexplainable reason Zeke felt the man's attention centered on him.

Zeke crossed the street with Billy in tow. They walked along the sidewalk in front of the row of shops where the young couple stood, their conversation now turned into a full blown argument. As Zeke and Billy approached the couple they stopped arguing. Zeke tipped the brim of his ball cap as he led Billy on a wide berth around the couple. "Pardon me," he said while passing by, heading toward the park and the vagrant sitting on the park bench.

The vagrant was rummaging through a crumpled paper bag. Zeke gave Billy some length on the leash to sniff the grass at the park's edge while he glanced toward the man in the aviator sunglasses leaning against the tree. The children's laughter in the park's playground mingled with the mutterings from the crowd across the street. The vagrant looked up from his paper bag while eyeing Zeke and the leashed German Shepherd. "He a friendly mutt?" the vagrant asked in a hoarse voice.

"Can be," Zeke answered.

The vagrant's concerned expression melted into a wide grin, revealing a nearly toothless mouth. "That's good. I like dogs." He pulled a strand of greasy hair from his face and dug for something in the bag. He pulled out an opened package of cheese crackers and dug one cracker out with two soiled fingers. "Here you go, boy!" he said.

Billy immediately showed interest, tugging on his harness toward the cheese cracker. Zeke tightened his grip on the leash to slow Billy's advance. "That's okay," Zeke told the vagrant. "He's already had his dinner."

The vagrant appeared to be insulted. "Ain't gonna hurt him none," he mumbled. "I'd never give a animal anything bad to eat."

Zeke let out some slack on the leash. "Okay, boy."

The dog stretched his neck and gently took the cracker from the vagrant's outstretched hand. A couple of crunches, a swallow, then Billy licked his chops and wagged his tail, hoping for more cheese cracker treats.

The vagrant chuckled and patted the dog's head. "Good, boy! What's your name?"

Zeke smiled as he watched Billy rub against the vagrant's legs. The dog showed genuine affection for the homeless wanderer. "His name is Billy."

"Billy!" the vagrant exclaimed. "That's my name, too!"

Billy the dog stuck his wet nose toward the package with the cheese crackers.

Billy the vagrant laughed and said, "Sorry, Billyboy, but this is my lunch."

Zeke saw the vagrant's eyes dart back and forth and knew what came next.

"But if you had something to trade," the vagrant went on, "like, let's say, something to drink, I might consider it." More darting eyes in Zeke's direction.

Zeke removed the flask of Jack Daniel's from his leg pocket. He squatted next to the bench and handed the flask to the vagrant while keeping an eye on the man in sunglasses leaning against the tree.

The vagrant's eyes lit up with joy. He grabbed the flask, took a deep gulp, exhaled loudly, then remembered his end of the bargain. He started to remove another cracker from the package to give to Billy when Zeke stopped him.

"That's okay," Zeke said. "Keep your lunch."

The vagrant took another pull from the flask before reluctantly handing it back.

"You been here a while, Billy?" Zeke asked.

"Yeah."

"When did the power go out?"

The vagrant thought for a moment. "Monday," he finally said. "Around midmorning."

"Four days ago," Zeke commented.

"If you say so."

"Where were you when it happened?" Zeke asked.

"Over there," the vagrant said while pointing across the street toward the abandoned grocery store. "People started coming out of all the shops and whatnot, chattering like a bunch of field mice. Some cars stopped right in the middle of the road, blocking traffic. Then the drivers started getting out and talking to the folks on the sidewalk. Then those folks started helping 'em push the cars to the side of the road. That's when I knew what *really* happened."

Zeke studied the vagrant's haggard face for a moment before asking, "So what *really* happened, Billy?"

"Well, it's like I tried to tell 'em," he said, gesturing to the crowd across the street. "But they wouldn't listen . . . the fools."

Zeke didn't say anything while waiting for the vagrant to continue.

"Look at 'em now,"the vagrant said. "Won't be long before they'll look like me."

"What was it you tried to tell them, Billy?"

"I tried to tell em' what I saw."

"Well what did you see?"

"A UFO."

"A UFO," Zeke repeated.

"Around midnight," the vagrant explained. "The night before everything went nutty. I saw some lights moving real slow through the trees up there beyond the bend, must've been about fifty feet off the ground. It didn't make a sound but I could feel it vibrating or something. It finally moved into this clearing up there and I saw what it was. A genuine flying saucer."

"Uh-huh."

"The next morning's when the electricity went off and all them cars died," the vagrant continued. "These aliens have some sort of magnetism powers, you see."

Zeke continued to nod in understanding. "Yeah, I see."

"But I don't know why some of them cars were damaged and others weren't," the vagrant added. "I guess them aliens didn't like 'em."

"The cars?"

"No, the people," the vagrant said in a testy tone.

Zeke smiled and asked, "See anything else?"

"Saw the aliens themselves."

"Really."

"Really," the vagrant answered quickly. "They're probably all over the place by now. Seen one of 'em right here in town."

"What do they look like?"

The vagrant shrugged while starting to eye the flask again. "Kinda like us, but different."

Zeke glanced at the man in sunglasses leaning against the tree. He turned his attention back to the vagrant and handed him the flask.

The vagrant took a big swig before handing it back. "Anything else I can help you with?"

"When did the Calvary arrive to save the day?"

"Huh?"

"The army," Zeke said. "You know, the roadblocks at the bridge?"

"Oh," the vagrant said. "Yeah, I heard about 'em. Later the same day, I think. Where in the heck have you been, anyway?"

Zeke ignored the question. For some strange reason another question came to mind. "Have you seen anybody wearing a gray hoodie with the words *Army Rangers* printed on front?"

The vagrant scrunched his face while trying to think. "Nope," he finally said. "Don't recall seeing anything like that. But I'll keep my eye out for you."

"Thanks."

A long moment passed. The vagrant began eyeing the flask, again.

Zeke handed it to him. "Here you go."

"Man, that's good," the vagrant said after taking a large gulp of whiskey and reluctantly handing the flask back to Zeke. He wiped his mouth with a dirty sleeve. "Hadn't had a drop since this whole mess started."

Zeke gestured toward the row of shops where the vandalized liquor store stood. "Nothing left inside?"

"No," the vagrant replied in an angry tone. "They took every last bottle off the shelf! Took all the tobacco products, too! You gotta smoke on ya?"

"Don't smoke. *Who* took everything?"

"Oh, a bunch of young punks," the vagrant answered. "Hooligans living on the edge of town in that trailer park out there. They're trading the booze for weapons, you see. Pistols, rifles, ammo, gunpowder, or anything else that blows up. Bunch a mean rascals. I keep my distance from 'em."

Zeke looked toward the tree and the man wearing the aviator sunglasses. The man was gone. Zeke looked in every direction but the man was nowhere to be seen. Zeke had been facing the tree the entire time and never noticed any movement at all. *I guess I'm getting sloppy.*

Zeke saw the crowd across the street starting to disperse. He handed the flask to the vagrant. "Tell you what, Billy," he said. "You keep this as a token of good will."

"Hey! Thanks!"

"I'll see you later."

"Yeah, later!"

Zeke rose to his feet and tugged on the leash. "Come on, Billy."

Zeke and Billy trotted across the street as the crowd started going their separate ways, some meeting up with their kids in the park's playground. Cueball was walking toward a red '66 Ford Mustang parked near the abandoned grocery store. "Excuse me," Zeke called out as he neared him.

Cueball responded with a pleasant expression. "Yes?"

"My name's Zeke Allenby."

Cueball stuck out his hand for a handshake. "Paul Stover. How can I help you?"

"I've got a place not far from here," Zeke said, "and I've been on a hiking trip since the beginning of the week. I got back to my place earlier today and found the power off. I came to town to find out what's going on and saw the roadblocks at the bridge. I guess I'm a little confused. Can you fill me in?"

"Well," Stover began, "last Monday, November the ninth, at around 10:00 am central, we lost all power. What is more important, all communications with the outside were completely cut off. Phone lines, cellular phones, police and emergency band radios, all dead. Then the army shows up with roadblocks to guard the bridge."

"They told me it was damaged," Zeke said. "But I can't see any damage."

"You've been there?" asked Stover.

"Yes, just got back a few minutes ago," Zeke said. "I talked to the officer in charge."

"Army?" asked Stover.

"Don't think so," Zeke said. "Maybe National Guard, but I've got doubts about that."

"Why is that?" Stover asked.

Zeke shrugged. He didn't want to be the one answering all the questions at the moment. "You think the power outage extends outside of town?"

"I don't know," Stover said. "I hope it's just local."

"I can't get *any* stations on the AM band of my car radio," Zeke said. "That means we're talking about something a little more widespread than just Gold Tree. Perhaps the entire portion of the state, or even larger."

Paul Stover had a knowing look in his eyes. "Yes, that is possible."

Zeke thought about Ruth and the kids. *What's the situation like in Houston? Probably not good.* "You live around here, Paul?"

"No," Stover replied. "I work for a man that has a vacation cabin not far away. We happened to be here when all this happened."

Zeke struggled to keep Ruth and the kids out of his thoughts. He admired the '66 Mustang. "She's a beauty. Got gas?"

"Yes, almost full," Stover said. "I filled up over the weekend before the power outage. Actually, I don't think gas is the biggest problem here in Gold Tree. A lot of folks have already left town, trying to get through the mountains with their four-wheel-drives. With enough gas and a bit of luck they may get through, but who knows if things will be any better on the other side. If they can't drive through them, the mountains are going to be tough on foot. Water is going to be more important than gasoline, but I guess they'd rather die trying than to just sit here trapped like rats."

Since Highway 2060 dead-ended a few miles north of Gold Tree, and with the bridge being blocked to the south, Zeke realized the citizens of Gold Tree really were trapped like rats. The mountains surrounding them were tough to cross even in the best of times. "So you think there's still gas in town?"

"At the moment, there's quite a few disabled vehicles in town with plenty of gasoline in their tanks," Stover replied. "But like I said before, gasoline supplies aren't the biggest worry. Sure, gas is needed for generators to keep the refrigerators working, but that won't matter when there's no food left to put inside those refrigerators."

Zeke nodded in understanding.

"Hopefully, relief supplies will arrive before too long," Stover continued. "Maybe that's what the Army is doing at the bridge," he added, this time with a smile. "Maybe they're securing it in preparation for the truck convoys arriving with supplies."

Zeke returned Stover's humorous expression with a smile of his own. "Yeah, right."

Paul Stover laughed a short staccato chuckle which made Zeke want to smile even more.

After a short pause, Zeke asked, "Paul, why do you think some of the vehicles were damaged and others were not?

"Well," Stover said, "I've noticed that older model automobiles have the least trouble, some not affected at all. But the newer models are a different story. Many were shut down completely. What about you, Zeke? You have a car?"

"Yes," Zeke replied, gesturing at the Jeep down the street.

"It wasn't damaged?"

"No," Zeke said, still thinking about the differences between old and new model automobiles. "What kind of trouble are you talking about?"

"Most of the newer models' ignition systems got fried," Stover answered. "Some partially, some totally. The older vehicles's problems are more minor. Lights, turn signals, music players, things like that."

"And all this happened when the power went out?"

"Yes," Stover replied. "At *exactly* the same time."

Zeke remembered Billy the vagrant saying that some cars were affected and others were not. "You have any theories of why the older models did better than the new ones?" Zeke asked Stover.

"A few," came the answer.

Zeke waited for Stover to explain.

"I don't have time to explain right now," Stover said, "but I would like to talk to you again. Can you meet me back here tomorrow?"

"Well, I might decide to take a drive to Houston," Zeke said with a smile.

Stover smiled back and said, "You got gas for that Jeep?"

"A quarter tank," Zeke answered. "I had a business trip planned for next week, but it looks like that's not going to happen now."

"What kind of work do you do, Zeke?"

"I'm a contractor of sorts," Zeke said.

"Military?" asked Stover.

"Once upon a time."

"You work overseas?"

"Sometimes," Zeke said with a smile. "May I ask how you know all this?"

Stover laughed. "I assess people fairly quickly. Part of my trade."

"Human Resources?"

Stover laughed harder. "No. Lawyer."

Zeke nodded with a smile while wondering how Stover guessed his vocation so quickly and accurately.

"You know this part of the country well?" Stover asked.

"You mean Gold Tree?"

"No, I mean the mountains," Stover said, "Apache, Eagle, Guadalupes."

"Big area," Zeke said. "I've hunted and hiked out here for a while, so I know portions, but I can navigate most anywhere if I have decent topographical maps and a compass. A GPS doesn't hurt, either."

Stover nodded. "Will you meet with me tomorrow?" he asked. "I may have a business proposition for you."

Zeke shrugged, not really interested in any business propositions. His only concern at the moment was getting to Houston to find Ruth and the kids. And the only thing standing in his way was a contingent of armed soldiers at the bridge and the rough mountain terrain surrounding Gold Tree. Maybe this *business proposition* could help him accomplish that. "Sure, why not."

Stover opened the door of his Mustang. "Good. See you here the same time tomorrow."

"Tomorrow," Zeke said before tugging on the leash and crossing the street. He wondered how this lawyer had sized him up so quickly. It bothered him that he was apparently so transparent to a complete stranger, although he knew he had the same ability to size-up others. Zeke knew he could usually recognize military personnel out of uniform, just like earlier with Mr. Green Beret in the aviator sunglasses, the man leaning against the tree in the park—the one who seemed to vanish into thin air. *Probably a CIA spook*, Zeke thought. He chuckled to himself. *CIA Ops in Gold Tree?*

Zeke and Billy headed toward the Jeep, past the row of shops with the broken glass. He ran some questions through his head: *Why were only the newer models of vehicles the ones most affected by . . . whatever it was that happened?*

Straight ahead, the couple with the infant were now screaming at each other in loud, angry voices. The baby screamed, too. The man, slightly built with a dark mustache suddenly slapped the woman hard across the face at the exact time Zeke and Billy were almost upon them.

"Hey!" Zeke shouted at the man.

The mustached man turned to Zeke with a look of rage on his face. His eyes darted between Zeke and the German Shepherd several times, the anger in his eyes softening a bit. "Mind your own business, mister," he said in a trembling voice.

Zeke ignored him while keeping his eyes on the woman. He held Billy close with the leash. "This your husband?"

The woman, ashamed, looked down at her baby, trying to calm it with gentle whispers. She eventually nodded in response to Zeke's question.

"You okay?" Zeke asked her.

"I said mind your own business," the mustached man said, this time taking an aggressive step toward Zeke but hesitating to move any closer because of the dog.

Zeke looked the man squarely in the eyes. He wondered if a medium-force blow to the solar plexus or just a few simple backhand slaps would do the trick. Then, from out of the blue, a thought entered his consciousness. It felt like it came to him from some external source outside of his body. Suddenly and instantly, Zeke knew if he roughed-up the man in front of his woman, the resulting humiliation would only make matters worse for the woman and the child. Logical, of course, but he usually never thought that way during a confrontation.

A smile grew on Zeke's face. He spoke in a soft, even voice. "Why don't you just relax and try to work out your problems together?"

Did I just say that?

"Life's too hard," Zeke continued, "and it's probably going to get even harder before too long. Look at them. They're your *family*. They're all you really have in this world. They're going to need you in the tough days ahead."

The man blinked a few times, his anger subsiding a bit.

"Any moment could be your last moment together," Zeke said while giving a tug on Billy's leash. "Believe me, I know."

Zeke and Billy walked back to the Jeep. He'd surprised himself back there with the angry man. Before today he would've definitely hurt the man for getting in his face. But something changed inside of him. Something unexplainable but still very real.

"I guess I'm just a peacemaker at heart," he told Billy with a smile. He glanced at his dog and began laughing for no good reason—at least for no reason he could think of. *Weird but nice.*

Zeke was enjoying life for the now despite the current circumstances. *I'm alive,* he thought. *It's a beautiful day. I'm with my best friend.* As they climbed in the Jeep for the drive back to the cabin, Zeke felt happy. Happy for the first time in years.

*   *   *

TWO

The meeting with Paul Stover the next day became more than Zeke had expected. Zeke learned that Stover worked for Albright Data Services, a high-tech company located near Alamogordo, New Mexico and owned by one Steve Albright. Stover was a lawyer, but he insinuated that he did a lot more than just legal work for Albright. Zeke couldn't get a straight answer from Stover about the *type* of data they dealt with, but he suspected it had something to do with the plethora of domestic and foreign intelligence agencies infesting the world today. After their brief meeting in town, Zeke followed Stover's '66 Mustang to Albright's vacation cabin a mile or so from town.

Albright's '*vacation cabin,*' as Stover had called it, turned out to be a huge, hotel-sized log home with gigantic picture windows overlooking the scenic mountain landscape beyond. Albright must have been in his early forties, approximately six-feet-tall with curly, graying hair and a slight paunch hanging over his belt. Also there for the meeting was a rugged, rawboned, cowboy-type named Will Hobson, a notorious local who had been one of the townsfolk that tried to get out of town by crossing the rugged mountain terrain west of Gold Tree. On a winding dirt road several miles into the journey, Will Hobson and six other Gold Tree locals were apparently confronted by a squad of army soldiers. Before this, Will and his party had halted their little caravan so several of its members—including Will—could relieve themselves in the brush nearby. The soldiers loaded everyone into armored personnel carriers, presumably taking their *prisoners* to Fort Bliss or some other holding facility nearby. But Will, who told the story with a bit of comic flare, had ventured farther into the brush than the others because his relief was in the form of a bowel movement. He returned to the road just in time to see the army APCs hauling everyone away. After returning to Gold Tree on foot, Will ran into Paul Stover and told him the story. Apparently, Stover thought it important to have Will at the meeting for some reason.

Steve Albright sat at the head of a long dining table while staring at a large county map spread before him. Zeke and Stover sat opposite of each other on either side of Albright while Will stood nearby. Billy sat leashed on the large covered porch outside the entrance doors.

Zeke examined the room while Albright studied the map. The roughhewn log walls blended perfectly with the antique furnishings in the room, including the gigantic elk antler chandelier hanging above them. The dining table was an elegant masterpiece made of English oak and had probably cost more money than Zeke made in a year.

Albright pointed to a thin line on the map indicating a dirt ranch road cutting through the mountainous terrain. "So is this it, Will?" Albright asked.

Will leaned over Albright's shoulder to examine the map. "Yep," he said, tracing his finger along the road. "Right about here's where the soldiers arrived."

Albright pointed to another spot on the map. "What about here?" he asked. "Is this passable with four-wheel-drive?"

"I reckon so," Will answered, "if someone knows how to drive off-road, that is. There's some pretty steep drop-offs up there the further you go. Wouldn't want to get too close to the edge if ya know what I mean."

Zeke had been listening the entire time but no one had asked him anything yet. He was starting to wonder why they wanted him at the meeting.

As if he'd read Zeke's mind, Albright looked toward him and said, "Do you think any of these routes are passable?"

Zeke thought for a moment before answering. "I don't think the routes are the real issue."

"Then what do you think the real issue is?"

"I know we are all in the dark to a certain degree," Zeke said, "but I think you need to approach this by looking at the big picture."

"Can you be more specific?" asked Albright.

"We've not only lost electrical power," Zeke explained, "but also our ability to reach the outside world—both physically *and* through communications. Armed soldiers are preventing anyone from leaving town, not just protecting us from driving onto a damaged bridge but from escaping through the mountains as well. Why? *Why* have they sealed off Gold Tree, Texas?"

Albright shot a quick glance at Stover.

"You know," Zeke said, becoming irritated with the little secrets they weren't sharing. "I'm not a rocket scientist, but I'm willing to bet that this *electrical anomaly* we're experiencing was not an accident, and that the higher-ups in government believe whoever or whatever is responsible is right here in our little town."

No one responded.

"So," Zeke continued, "it really doesn't matter which ranch roads through the mountains are passable and which ones are not. If the big brass wants the area sealed, it's sealed."

For a second Albright looked like he was going to say something, but Stover took over and said, "We cannot stress how important it is that we get to El Paso. With your credentials, we know you can get us through, saying we're on official business or something."

Credentials? Zeke stared back at Stover. This meeting was getting weirder by the second.

"Are you with the government or something?" Will asked Zeke.

Zeke was about to answer when Stover answered for him, "Something like that."

"You don't say," Will said while turning his full attention toward Zeke.

Zeke stared back. *I don't say,* he said in his mind, sort of a telepathic message to the lanky cowboy.

"We hope you will keep this to yourself, Will," Stover added. "He doesn't want his cover blown."

"I understand," Will replied. "My lips are sealed."

Cover blown? Zeke struggled not to burst into laughter.

"So what do you think, Zeke?" Albright asked.

I think this meeting is a bunch of crap, is what Zeke wanted to say, but he was curious to find out what Albright and his lawyer were up to. He cleared his throat and said, "Certain government agencies, including various branches of the U.S. Army have the ability to *easily* secure an area the size of Gold Tree and its vicinity. They have armed soldiers with all types of modern detection gadgetry that can probably detect a carpenter ant carrying a leaf in the bottom of a canyon; high-tech satellite and aerial reconnaissance up the ying-yang with thermal cameras that can zoom-in on your nose hairs in the middle of night. And you guys are worrying about the road conditions of the mountain passes?"

The comment about the nose hairs got a chuckle from Will Hobson who was especially enjoying Zeke's rant.

Zeke was finished for the moment. Until he got more information from Albright and Stover he wasn't going to have anything to do with this little game *or* their business proposition.

Albright stood from the table. "Let's take a break," he said. "Stretch our legs."

"Yeah, I need to scoot along," Will said. "I gotta generator at home to work on."

Albright stuck out his hand for a handshake. "Thanks for your help, Will. I really appreciate it."

"Anytime, Mr. Albright. Good luck on your travels." Will turned to Stover. "See ya, Paul."

"Thanks, Will," Stover said before heading into the room next to the dining room.

Will tipped the brim of his cowboy hat at Zeke and winked with a sly grin. "Nice to meet ya."

"Same here," said Zeke.

After Will left, Albright grabbed a crystal decanter and a couple of tumblers from a cabinet in the dining room. He set them on the table and began pouring a measure of brown liquor into one of the tumblers. "Eighteen-year-old scotch," he said. "Care for some?"

"Sure," said Zeke.

They tapped the tumblers in a silent toast and sipped the fine scotch whiskey. "So how long were you in the army, Zeke?" Albright asked.

Zeke took another sip of scotch. "Ten years."

"See any combat?"

"Plenty," Zeke said while watching Stover return with a file folder in his arms.

Stover sat at the table and perused through the files. "Sorry about that phony bit back there, Zeke," he said, "but it was necessary."

I think I'm about to find out what's going on.

"I appreciate your patience, Zeke," Albright said. "I hope you understand that we don't want to discuss certain issues in front of Will Hobson."

"Why?" Zeke said before taking another sip of scotch. "He a Russian spy or something?"

Albright broke into a big belly laugh. "No, not hardly."

Stover said, "Will's a good old boy, honest to a fault, but he has *loose lips*, especially after he's had a few to drink. Before nightfall, anyone who is nosing around town will *think* we are going to head west through the mountains, toward El Paso, with our guide, an agent for the government."

Zeke began nodding his head slowly. "A disinformation diversion," he said. "Or what we covert government agent dudes call a *DD* for short."

Stover laughed that fast, staccato, chipmunk chuckle of his. It made Zeke want to laugh. Stover slid a file folder across the table to Albright.

Albright examined the contents for a moment. He finished the scotch in his tumbler and set it down on the table. "As you know, that little show back there was for Will Hobson's benefit. The truth of the matter is, we know a little about your military background. Army Ranger, SOF experience in Iraq, Afghanistan."

"Why does that *not* make me happy?" Zeke replied. "And by the way, if that file you're looking at doesn't say *'retired,'* you need to correct it."

Stover stepped in. "Don't take it personal, Zeke," he began. "We have background information on all residents of Gold Tree because of the sensitive nature of ADS's data."

"What type of data?" Zeke asked. "And I think I'm experiencing *déjà vu*, because I swear I already asked that question. Hopefully, I won't get the same answer."

Stover smiled and looked at Albright.

"You're a man of the world, Zeke," Albright said. "You're smart, and you've had plenty of experience in covert activities. You know as well as I that information goes out on a need-to-know basis, and much of that is for everyone's own good. You agree?"

"Yes," Zeke replied. "But one thing I've also learned is: not having the information you *don't need to know* can get you killed . . . or perhaps in this case, get you tried for treason."

Albright thought for a moment before saying, "How about I let you in on what Paul and I *do* know, the parts we can tell you, that is."

"Go for it," Zeke said.

"The *electrical anomaly*, as you aptly named it," Albright said, "is nationwide. This is the worst disaster our nation has ever experienced. Our entire infrastructure has been shut down, much of it the result of our own doing because of our dependency on computers. Communication, transportation, medical, financial, even defense, have all been brought to its knees."

"And how do you know this?"

"I had an open line of communication with certain government officials until recently," Albright said. "I'll be able to reestablish communication once we get to our intended destination."

"What caused all of this?" Zeke asked as he searched Albright's eyes for the *real* truth.

Albright leaned his arms on top of the table. "You ever heard of EMP, Zeke?"

Zeke nodded slowly. "Electromagnetic pulse," he said. "As in an EMP bomb."

"Do you know the ramifications of a high-altitude EMP explosion?" Albright asked. "Say, one that was detonated two hundred or so kilometers in our upper atmosphere?"

"In less than a nanosecond," Zeke began, remembering a particular Ranger RRD training manual he studied years ago, "the pulse would descend and travel by way of metallic pathways, especially copper wiring, but also including railways, bridges, and other surfaces with conductive properties. In our culture this means massive destruction of computer chips, chips that run our nation's power grids, transportation, financial institutions . . . you name it."

"You are correct," Albright said. "That's the situation America is facing."

"But what does that have to do with Gold Tree being quarantined?" Zeke asked.

"I don't know," Albright replied. "There's obviously many things we don't understand."

Zeke could buy the EMP part. Since scanning for AM stations on his radio and finding none, Zeke had been wondering about an EMP attack all along. But he knew there was more to the story than they were telling him.

"But what we do understand is that the problem is nationwide," Albright continued. "I can only imagine what the situation is like in major cities and urban centers, and what they will become in a few more weeks."

Zeke nodded, thinking about Ruth, nine-year-old Connor, and little Amy, almost four, all of them trying to survive in Houston, a jungle of a city in the best of times.

"Here's the deal, Zeke," Albright said, his voice firm and resolute. "My company, ADS collects a universe of diversified data, mostly from outside sources but some from our own R&D division. This division deals with innovations in quantum mechanics, in particular, quantum computing." Albright paused while glancing across the table at Stover. "Let me put it this way," Albright continued. "Our research detected communications from an unknown source. Not some ultrahigh frequency radio transmissions or anything conventional, but transmissions that don't operate in any radio wave spectrum. This is science fiction stuff, Zeke." Albright waited a moment, either to let this sink in or to decide how to proceed with his explanation. "We believe," he continued, "that the unknown source sending and receiving these communications are the ones responsible for the pulse, and I believe I have the data to prove it."

Zeke tried to digest all he was hearing. *What if this ADS company was involved in some type of illegal actions?* Maybe their reason for using him was to set him up as a patsy. *What was it Lee Harvey Oswald said? 'I'm just a patsy.'*

"I know this may be in the need-to-know-only category," Zeke finally said, "but who is this *unknown source?*"

"We don't know," Albright said. "We haven't even begun to decipher all the communications, but we have sufficient proof that they used an electromagnetic pulse or something similar to shutdown our nation. I also believe this data will eventually reveal their future intentions as well."

Zeke exhaled loudly. "So what do you want from me?"

"We need you to get us to Austin," Albright said very plainly.

"I thought your company was located in New Mexico," Zeke said, shooting a look toward Stover.

"That's where the main office and research facilities are located," Stover replied. "West of El Paso."

"So why Austin?" Zeke asked.

Albright and Stover shared another look. "I live there," Albright said.

Zeke leaned back in his chair. "Maybe right now is not the best time to travel," he said while taking a glance around the room. "You don't have it too bad around here."

Albright formed a small smile and looked at Stover.

"After the unknown source discovered their communications were intercepted," Stover began in a low voice, "they began a trace. We shut down the system before the trace was completed and deleted the data files, but not before we sent copies to Austin through a secure system that we developed ourselves."

"They will probably figure this out in time," Albright added. "Even though I keep my personal life private, it's probably no secret that I have a home in Austin. But hopefully by then it will be too late."

"And who did you say *they* were?" Zeke asked in a nonchalant way, getting tired of the cat and mouse game. "You know, the *unknown source?*"

"I don't know," Albright said in an earnest tone. "But I believe without any doubt that they will do anything to get their hands on the data."

"How do you know this?"

"Because a message accompanied their trace," Stover answered for Albright. "A repeated phrase that is definitely hostile."

Zeke noticed Albright giving Stover a look.

"We only want you to get us to Austin," Albright said, moving away from the subject of the deciphered message. "And I'll pay you generously."

Zeke became a little more curious. "So what makes you think the army is just going to let us drive out of here?" he asked.

"We have an ace up our sleeve," Stover answered for Albright. "Hopefully."

"Which is?"

"You," replied Stover.

"And also," Albright added, "we don't believe they know our exact identities. Not yet, at least. That's why we have to move quickly. Like no later than tomorrow morning."

If Albright and Stover were telling the truth, it was starting to look like the *unknown sources* already knew Albright's identity and location and were probably connected to the government which enabled them to quarantine Gold Tree with armed troops to guard the main exits. Zeke knew there was more to this story. Lots more. He stared at Albright while rubbing his chin, trying to think of all the questions he had swimming around in his brain.

Albright interrupted Zeke's thoughts and said, "Here's my offer, Zeke. I give you fifty-thousand dollars cash, right now, and another fifty when we get to Austin."

A hundred grand. That's more than Zeke's ninety day contract paid, especially now, since there wasn't going to be any ninety day contract. Most people think money won't be an issue during society's breakdown, but Zeke knew better. Cash will be king. Prices for essentials will be extremely inflated, but available to those with hard, cold cash. And the more the better.

Before Zeke could respond, Albright said, "I know you want to get to Houston, Zeke, and I can see in your eyes that it has nothing to do with a business trip. Am I right?"

Zeke didn't respond.

"You have loved ones there," Albright said, "and you want to get to them as soon as possible."

Zeke stared back, not liking what he was hearing.

"Listen, Zeke," Albright continued. "I'm not trying to talk you into anything. If you accept my offer, I want it to be your decision." Albright paused before saying, "One thing I promise you, Zeke, when we get to Austin, through the connections I have, I will help you all I can in getting intelligence about your family's whereabouts and condition, and any assistance possible to help you retrieve them. I give you my word."

Ruth and the kids were Zeke's priority. He narrowed his eyes, wondering what he was getting into. "Okay," he said. "We have a deal."

Albright and Stover smiled, obviously pleased. "Wonderful," Albright said, rising from his chair and pouring Zeke another measure of scotch, then more for himself. He extended his glass in a toast. Stover lifted his bottle of Perrier. All three clicked their drinks together, sealing the deal for the unknown days ahead.

So lets get to work," Stover said as Albright excused himself and went upstairs. "Tell me what you need, Zeke."

Zeke asked for all the topographical maps Stover could get his hands on. He also had Stover make a list of supplies they would need. This is when he learned that Albright's eleven-year-old son would be going with them. Zeke protested, saying that was not part of the deal. "I can't be responsible for a young boy," he told Stover. "This little excursion is going to be dangerous in many different ways."

"He can't leave his son behind," Stover insisted. "There's no one to leave him with. Besides, Matt's a good boy, mature for his age."

"Well, why didn't he mention this earlier?" Zeke asked.

Stover grinned. "Well, probably because he knew you wouldn't go for it."

Zeke exhaled loudly and shook his head. "Where's the kid?"

"He's upstairs," Stover answered.

"I want to meet him."

"Okay," Stover said. "Now?"

"When I get back from my place."

"We'll see you when you return then."

They agreed to meet back at Albright's that afternoon to finish the route planning and to go over the general rules Zeke required in order to lead them successfully to Austin. Their adventure would begin before sunrise.

*

The Jeep and the Land Rover crawled along the rugged trail. Zeke had the Jeep loaded with supplies gathered from his cabin's secret storage room: dog food, backpack stuffed with essentials, two cardboard boxes of assorted MREs (Meals-Ready-To-Eat), another box stocked with canned food and other cooking ingredients, and several boxes of bottled water. Zeke stored his M4 automatic rifle and an M2A1 ammo can full of 5.56 mm ammunition on the floorboard behind the driver seat.

The trip had started off badly. The dirt trail leading them to an old mining road found on one of the old maps did not exist, despite its marking on the old map. Using a compass, topographical map, and some dead reckoning, Zeke finally found an alternative route which eventually led them to the 'Old Mining Road,' a process which took over four hours.

Now, near midmorning, they'd traveled less than Zeke had hoped for as they made their way through deep canyon trails in the northernmost part of Sierra Diablo, the mountain used for their getaway. They climbed out of their vehicles often, sometimes using their winches to get out of large ruts on this so-called *road*. At this point, calling the *'Old Mining Road'* a road seemed highly optimistic. But no army troops were aiming their rifles at them. No helicopters with loudspeakers. Gold Tree's lockdown seemed increasingly like a sham to Zeke; a show performed by the army or those acting like the army. But for what reason he didn't know.

Albright's eleven-year-old son, Matt, rode with Zeke in the passenger seat of the Jeep while Billy sat on his haunches in the rear, his furry head held up proudly while searching for scents in the fresh air. Matt appeared to be a bright kid with grandiose plans for his future. "Dad wants me to get a college degree first," Matt said. "He says after that I can join the military if I still want to. But he's against it."

"What do you want to do in the military?" asked Zeke.

"Well, I want to get into one of their special forces units," Matt said. "You know, SEALs, Delta Force, Green Berets, something like that."

"I see."

Zeke followed the trail up a steep embankment, the Jeep's tires slipping occasionally on the loose rocks of the trail. He kept an eye on Albright's Land Rover in his rearview mirror. Albright and Stover seemed to be doing well so far. At least they hadn't driven off a cliff or anything.

As they crept onward, Zeke thought about the looks Matt had given him before they had left in the cover of darkness early that morning— that look of admiration certain boys give you when they find out you're a Special Forces soldier or something similar. Zeke knew Matt's dad and Stover had probably told the boy a little about his background. He remembered the way Matt's face lit up when Zeke asked the boy if he wanted to ride with him and Billy in the Jeep.

"You think I should go to college before joining the military?" Matt asked.

"Well," Zeke said, stifling a smile. "I think you should finish middle school first, then high school next."

The boy blushed. "I meant after that."

"All that's a long way off," Zeke said. "You may change your mind before then."

Zeke kept his eyes on the narrow road as he navigated a sharp turn near an outcropping of boulder. "You might decide to become a lawyer . . . or maybe a veterinarian or something."

"Veterinarian?"

"I don't know," Zeke continued, "maybe a game show host."

"A game show host!" Matt scoffed. "I don't think so!"

"You got a girlfriend?"

"Girlfriends," Matt replied with emphasis on the plural form of the word.

"Well, that alone is a good enough reason *not* to join the military."

"You sound like my dad." A moment later Matt confessed, "All I've ever wanted my entire life is to be one of you guys. You're heroes, you know."

"Heroes?"

"Yes, sir," Matt replied. "Heroes. You go out there risking your life for nothing in return. All you get for your sacrifice is low pay and a lot of pain and agony."

"You got the low pay part right."

"You live in constant danger," Matt went on. "You never know if today will be your last day on Earth."

Zeke had to laugh. "And all this sounds good to you?"

Matt continued to expound on the virtues of a special forces soldier's life. "And yes, that's who I want to be. To learn all the things you guys know about weapons and survival, self-reliant and not afraid of anything, going into remote areas of the world—"

"—Whoa, whoa," Zeke interrupted. "Hold on for one minute, Matt. Back up a second."

Matt had a curious look on his face. "What?"

"Don't take this personal, Matt," Zeke said. "But that part about being not afraid of anything is a bunch of baloney. Maybe that's the way it is in the movies, or on TV, but not in real life."

Zeke could feel the boy's attention centered on him. "First of all, fear is one of the key ingredients in survival, in everyday life or in combat," Zeke explained. "It's the sense that alerts you of danger, allowing you to flee if necessary in order to stay alive. It's how you *control* your fear that is important. In a combat situation, somebody who is not afraid of anything will most likely be killed in the first skirmish. Worse than that, he'll probably get the rest of his buddies killed, too. That gung-ho, charge-the-enemy stuff may be great in a John Wayne movie, but it usually doesn't work in the real world."

"Who's John Wayne?" Matt asked sincerely.

Zeke hesitated for a second, feeling his age a bit more. "He was an actor. Tough guy. Never mind." After negotiating a particularly rough spot on the trail Zeke said, "Can I tell you a story, Matt?"

"Sure."

"My dad's dad was a World War Two veteran," Zeke said. "Army infantry, D-Day, Omaha beach, all that. Twenty-five years after the war, Granddad and two other veteran buddies of his attended a monument dedication in Normandy, France, honoring the Allied troops who died on the beaches during the D-Day invasion. During the ceremony some government officials were giving speeches. In the middle of one speech the official got to a part where he said something like: 'these brave men who did not know the meaning of the word fear,' or something similar. Granddad and his two buddies became disgusted and got up from their chairs to leave the ceremony."

Zeke glanced at Matt to see his reaction. Matt looked confused.

"You see," Zeke continued. "Granddad and his buddies, along with *all* combat veterans know this is hogwash. They were offended by the official's words. They knew that the courage shown by all those fallen soldiers was due to their brave actions while *being afraid*. Eddie Rickenbacker, the famous flying ace of World War One, put it this way: 'Courage is doing what you are afraid to do. There can be no courage unless you are scared.' You following me?"

Matt nodded like he understood but Zeke knew that the only way anyone could truly understand was to experience it themselves. Zeke just hoped his words made an impression on the boy so when the day came that Matt felt ashamed for being afraid, as would happen sometime in his life, the boy wouldn't take it so hard.

"Bottom line," Zeke said. "After college, with a degree under your belt, and you still want to join the military, then great. That make sense?"

Matt smiled. "Yes, sir."

They remained silent for the next five minutes or so while Zeke concentrated on the rough trail and its tricky turns. Matt finally broke the silence. "You have a wife and kids, Mr. Allenby?"

Zeke hesitated for a brief moment. "Nope. Just me and Billy."

Matt reached behind his seat and gave Billy a quick rub on the neck.

"Where's your mom?" Zeke asked the boy.

"Mom passed away when I was four," Matt said. "She died of cancer. It's been just me and dad ever since."

"I see."

"We used to see my Aunt Becky a lot," Matt added. "She lives in Houston."

"My wife's sister, Ruth, lives in Houston," Zeke said, wishing he hadn't asked the boy about his mom.

Matt turned to him with a puzzled look on his face. "I thought you said you weren't married?"

"I'm not . . . anymore."

"You divorced?"

"No," Zeke said, wondering how much he should explain. "She died. Like your mom."

"Cancer?"

"No," Zeke said firmly. "There was an accident."

"What kind of accident?" Matt continued.

Kids were so honest and straightforward, a trait Zeke usually appreciated. "Car accident," he finally said.

"Oh," Matt said, his curiosity abated. "Sorry."

"Me, too." A moment passed. "Well, that's something we both have in common, Matt. We've both lost someone we really loved."

Matt turned his head toward Zeke, a small smile forming on his lips. "Yeah, you're right."

Zeke drove on. *So strange,* he thought. He felt a certain peace settling deep inside him. Something so simple as a few words exchanged with someone who understood his loss somehow made him feel better. *No, not better. Just a bit stronger . . . to go on with life somehow.*

On a level section of the trail both vehicles stopped. Everyone got out and stretched their legs. Zeke spread out the topo map on the Jeep's hood. "Let's break for lunch," he said while studying the map. The hidden *Old Mining Road* was becoming more difficult to navigate. He didn't want to spend the rest of the nearly five hundred mile trip to Austin on foot, but he didn't want anyone driving off the edge of a narrow section of trail and falling to their death.

Everyone agreed about lunch, especially Matt. Zeke removed a cardboard box from the rear of the Land Rover and brought it to a spot between the vehicles. He opened the box on the ground, revealing a dozen plastic packages inside.

Matt looked over Zeke's shoulder. "Are those MREs?"

"Yes," Zeke replied. He pulled out a few and read the descriptions printed on the packages. "We got Chicken Fajita, Meatloaf with Gravy, Meatballs in Marinara . . ."

"I'll take the meatballs," said Steve Albright.

Zeke handed him the package and continued. "Chicken with Salsa, and for you vegetarians, we have Vegetable Manicotti."

Paul Stover took the MRE from Zeke's hand. "That's me."

"What about you, Matt?" Zeke asked.

Matt studied the packages. "How about the Chili with Beans."

"Fine choice if you weren't riding with me," Zeke said with a smile. He grabbed another package for himself and joined the others sitting on the ground. "You know how to use these?"

"What do you mean?" Matt replied. "You just open them and eat, right?"

"You can do that," Zeke answered while opening his package of Chicken and Dumplings. "But they taste much better hot." He removed the contents from the package and sorted through the items. "Instructions are on the heating bag," he added, "but it's simple to do."

Everyone watched Zeke demonstrate the preparation of the Meal-Ready-To-Eat. "The carton contains your entree," he explained. "These other packets will have your desserts and snack items. This is an accessory packet. Salt, spices, hot sauce, a plastic spoon, stuff like that." Zeke removed his entree pouch from the carton then grabbed a folded, foot-long plastic bag with words and diagrams printed on its exterior. He tore off the top of the bag, explaining the procedure as he performed it. "This is the polybag. Set your entree in the bag next to the heater, that rectangular thing inside, then hold them together above the fill lines at the bottom of the bag. Pour in the water between the fill lines, then squish them together a bit before folding the top of the bag over like this. Now hold the bag horizontally and put the whole thing back in your carton, making sure the heater is under the food pouch. Leave the top of the carton open and lean it at an angle." Zeke set the carton on the ground, leaning the top against a rock to prevent the contents from sliding out the carton. He stood and said, "Now wait about ten to twelve minutes."

Zeke went to the Jeep as the others prepared their MREs. He grabbed his binoculars and walked to the top of the road to get a better view. Billy trotted beside him, marking his territory on the scrub brush bordering that faint depression scratching the mountain called the *Old Mining Road*.

Zeke studied the rough terrain ahead through his binoculars. He knew of several canyons south that were easy hikes even for novices, but that put them on foot, and also on private ranch land. Under the circumstances he didn't mind having to deal with a few irate land owners but he wanted to remain unseen as long as possible, and the best way to do that at the moment was to stay on course, on this less traversed and dangerous section of Sierra Diablo.

Zeke walked back to the vehicles and sat with the others. He removed the bag from the MRE carton and unfolded the top. Hot steam poured out. "Watch your fingers because it'll be very hot," he said while removing the pouch from the steaming bag.

The others did the same. Matt was amazed. "How does it do that?"

"The FRH, or Flameless Ration Heater," Zeke explained in a facetious official-sounding voice, "is made of powdered iron, magnesium, and sodium."

Steve Albright finished Zeke's answer. "A chemical reaction happens when they're mixed with water, which creates the heat."

"Sweet," Matt said while removing the plastic wrapper from his spoon.

"I'd like to say grace," Paul Stover said. "Can we bow our heads in prayer?"

Zeke stared at the ground as Stover said the prayer. After it was over, Zeke began to eat his MRE. He hadn't expected Paul Stover to be a religious man, being a lawyer and all. Zeke reminded himself not to stereotype anyone by their occupation again.

"What do you think about the food, son," Albright asked his son.

Matt shrugged. "It's okay."

"It'll keep you alive," Stover said. "That's the important thing. Right?"

"Roughly fifteen hundred calories per meal," Zeke stated. "But tonight we'll have some hot grub done the traditional way, over an open campfire if we can."

"What do you mean, Mr. Allenby?" asked Matt.

"I mean if we're not being followed," Zeke said, "or if there are any patrols nearby."

Albright and Zeke had discussed what Matt knew before they left Gold Tree. Albright said he had not told his son all the details but had told him it was important they get to Austin, also assuring him that they weren't breaking any laws. Zeke hoped Albright was telling the truth, especially regarding the breaking laws part.

"They're not bad," Albright said between bites. "Better than most of the TV dinners we've had. Don't you think so, Matt?"

"Uh-huh."

"Pardon me?" his Dad said.

Matt swallowed his bite but didn't look his father in the eye. "Yes, sir."

The rest of the lunch was spent in silence. After finishing their meals they all climbed back into the vehicles. Stover climbed behind the wheel of the Land Rover as Albright sat in the passenger seat, the same as before. They waited for Zeke to lead the way in the Jeep. "Back to what you were starting to tell me earlier," Albright told Stover.

Stover said, "I just wanted to tell you that if they find us, I'm you, Steve Albright."

"What do you mean?"

"Did you get rid of your IDs like I suggested?" Stover asked.

"Yeah, burned them in the fireplace," Albright replied. "Just like you said."

"Look in the glove box."

Albright opened the glove box and removed a leather billfold. He looked in the billfold and saw a laminated ADS identification card. The name on the ID read: 'Stephen H. Albright,' with Paul's photo next to it. "What's this, Paul?"

"If we get apprehended," Stover explained, "I'm you. That way, you and Matt can get away. It'll be you they want, meaning me. Understand?"

It took a moment for Albright to understand. "I really appreciate it, pal," he said. "But I'd never let them take you without me."

"I'm serious," Stover insisted. "You got to think about Matt."

The Jeep began rolling up the incline. Stover put the Land Rover in gear and followed from a safe distance. "Something happens to me, I won't be leaving any grieving loved ones behind."

"Oh yeah?" Albright said. "What about me? And Matt? You're Uncle Paul to him, remember?"

Stover didn't respond. He kept his eyes on the narrow trail and the Jeep ahead.

"We are family, Paul," Albright said. "So forget the sacrifice deal. If you go, I go."

"Then what happens to Matt?" Stover asked. "You still remember what you promised him when Liz passed away, don't you?"

Albright turned to look out his window.

"He needs you to look after him," Stover said. "A boy needs his dad."

Albright didn't respond, continuing to stare out the window while keeping his face hidden from Stover.

Stover tried to lighten the mood. "Look, Boss," he said. "Nothing's going to happen, but if something does, just remember that I'm you, okay? We got a deal, Mr. Stover?"

Albright wouldn't turn to face Stover. He gently placed his hand on Stover's arm and lightly patted it.

Stover wondered if bringing up the subject of Albright's late wife, Liz, was a good idea or not. *Yes, it was a good idea.* Maybe this reminder to Albright of his promise to Matt would do the trick. Maybe if they got apprehended, the father would remember the promise to the son and do the right thing. Stover blotted a bit of wetness from his eye. Given the chance, he would gladly give his life for this man and his son.

*

Zeke remained alert as he crept the Jeep along the pitted, rocky trail. When they reached the next rise he was pleased to find the trail still negotiable. He passed an area that would've made a decent campsite, but with plenty of daylight left he kept moving. He knew they should be close to a spring marked on the old map.

More steep climbs on loose rocks. More dry creek beds. More narrow turns near dangerous drop-offs. More rock-strewn sections of trail. In one spot the rocks were so large they had to roll them out of the way manually, a process that ate up more than two hours. They finally reached a small creek that had running water, probably from the spring marked on the old map. They chose a relatively flat spot near the creek for their campsite. Everyone agreed to call it a day. They unloaded their gear and gathered firewood, eager to eat a warm meal before falling asleep under the stars.

Zeke promised to show Matt how to start a fire without matches. He showed him how to make a tinder nest by collecting the inner bark of some juniper trees nearby. Zeke piled kindling of various sizes on the ground before roughing up the juniper bark in his hands until it resembled a bird's nest. Stover joined them to watch Zeke's little exhibition of *Fire Starting 101.*

Zeke set the juniper nest on the ground and leaned over it. "Flint and steel," he said while digging in his pant pocket. "The way it's been done for centuries."

Stover smiled at Matt's attentive expression.

"Preparation is the most important part," Zeke continued, gesturing to the piles of small twig kindling and progressively larger wood within his reach. He brought his fist to the clump of tinder and started flicking a blue BIC lighter.

"Hey!" Matt protested while Stover laughed heartily.

"What?" Zeke replied. "It's flint and steel, isn't it?"

Zeke reached into his pocket and exchanged the lighter for a small stone rectangle. The stone rectangle connected to a metal blade-like object with a small piece of nylon cord. "Lighters and matches are great but they won't last as long as these little babies. They'll work even if they get wet. You can also wear them like a necklace." Zeke pointed to the rectangle of stone the size of a stick of chewing gum. "This is magnesium on this side," he said before flipping the stone to the opposite side. "This side is flint. The little blade is carbon steel. Stainless doesn't work as well. When you scrape the flint with the blade you get big sparks."

Zeke demonstrated, causing sparks to fly off the flint. "You can shave some of the magnesium into a little pile on top. It burns really hot but fast." He scraped a small bit of magnesium into a tiny pile on top of the tinder before handing the flint and steel to Matt. "Here, give it a try."

Matt took the flint and steel, and with Zeke's guidance he scraped the flint a half dozen times until a spark caught the magnesium pile. Zeke told him to hold the clump of tinder in his palms and blow gently, keeping the embers red until a stream of smoke started pouring from it. "Keep blowing!" Zeke told the boy. The tinder nest suddenly burst into flame.

"Hey!" Matt shouted. "Look, Dad! I made fire!"

Albright wasn't there. Apparently, he was off in the brush relieving himself.

Matt placed the burning clump on the ground and began feeding it kindling. Following Zeke's instructions, Matt gradually added larger pieces as Stover left to continue setting up camp. A moment later they had a small campfire. Matt fondled the flint and steel fire starter Zeke gave him.

"So what do you like to do when you're at home?" Zeke asked the boy.

Matt gave him a curious look. "Huh?"

"I mean before all this happened," Zeke said. "You know, hobbies, sports?"

"Oh," Matt said before placing another piece of wood into the fire. His eyes brightened quickly. "I'm engineering a software platform!"

"Wow," Zeke said. "When I was your age I was reading comics or glueing model airplanes together."

"It's actually a computer game," Matt explained. "But I'm creating it from the ground up."

"What type of game?"

"Artificial Intelligence Civilization," Matt replied, pronouncing each word slowly. "But not like those old ones with little villagers running around fishing and gathering wood for their huts. This one is *much* more advanced. The AI models have complex personalities and talents, which will alter over time, just like real life. But the best thing about it is they will have *decision-making* abilities."

"Sounds kinda scary," Zeke said with a smile.

Matt gave him a funny look. "They can't hurt you," he said with a chuckle. "They're inside the software. You know, inside the computer!"

"I know," Zeke admitted. "I'm joking."

"The ability for them to make decisions is the key," Matt continued. "*That's* what will make the game interesting. You'll never know what they'll do next!"

"Just like real life," Zeke said while standing to his feet. "I think that's great, Matt. One day you'll probably make millions with this game."

Matt looked at Zeke, a surprised expression on his face. "You think so?"

"I do," Zeke replied. "Now, I need to go help Paul set up camp. Make sure you keep the fire going."

"No problem," the boy said while continuing to stoke the fire, a big smile on his face. *Wow,* he thought. *I never realized that I could make a fortune with my game. That is, if we ever get computers working again . . . or even electricity, for that matter.*

The men organized the rest of their supplies around the campsite. Albright eventually caught Zeke's eye. "Thanks, Zeke," he said.

"For what?"

"For showing Matt how to start a fire."

"No problem," Zeke replied.

"I appreciate it."

While setting up his tent Zeke thought about the software game Matt was constructing. Maybe he should have told the boy that this career route would be better than joining the military. Then, as Zeke thought about it more, he realized the military would probably be the organization *most* interested in a game like this. A platform to predict what the enemy will do next. *They may already have something like it,* he told himself. *They love stuff like that.*

Within the hour the sunlight faded away. The campfire popped and crackled, casting flickering shadows on the small canvas tents pitched nearby. Zeke had a pot of beans over the fire. Stover had a small Dutch oven of biscuits buried near the fire, the dough made from a boxed biscuit mix. While they waited for the food, Zeke took an empty metal throat-lozenge container and a small strip of cotton cloth to show Matt how to make *char tinder.* "Just place the strip inside, put the lid back on, and poke two small holes, one in the top and one in the bottom," Zeke said while poking the holes and setting the aluminum container in the campfire. "It'll cook in there without burning. At first you'll see a flame coming out the top hole, then it will turn to smoke. When the smoke dies down, remove it from the fire. I'll show you what it looks like tomorrow."

Everyone finished their dinner of beans and biscuits about an hour later. Zeke gave Matt one of the two flashlights he'd brought in his backpack, both loaded with fresh bulbs and batteries. Billy followed Matt as he carried the aluminum camping plates and utensils the short distance to the creek's edge to wash them in the cold water. Matt aimed the flashlight at the trees across the creek, then toward Billy as the dog sniffed the ground, oblivious to the flashlight beam darting back and forth.

Matt squatted on the ground near the creek edge and leaned the flashlight on a rock, giving him a small lighted area on the ground and free hands to clean the dirty plates and spoons. As he stacked the clean plates next to the flashlight, a movement caught his eye. He looked up and saw a ball of green light hovering in the sky. He watched it for a while before it vanished. While he searched for it in the night sky he suddenly noticed several treetops begin to sway. The treetops on either side of the swaying trees stood motionless, confirming that wind wasn't causing their movement. Then he saw the ball of light again, much closer now, hovering ten feet above the ground on the opposite side of the creek. At this distance the ball appeared to be a swirling mass of matter, like swimming green tendrils in a thick watery substance. The boy's body began to shake in fear. He saw Billy a few yards to his left. The dog stood motionless while staring at the ball, a low growl coming from his powerful chest. Matt stared at the ball, and for about a second, maybe two-seconds, he noticed something else. *What is that?* His heart rate increased dramatically. *Something, something shaped like . . . what? Not transparent, but not solid, either.* Only one word seemed to describe the image inside the ball: *Reptile.*

Matt felt paralyzed. The ball seemed to be drawing him in and he felt helpless to do anything about it. Then, as clearly as if someone had whispered in his ear, he heard a voice say, *"Run! Run away now!"*

Matt came back to his senses. He dropped the plate to the ground and ran away from the creek as fast as he could. He heard Billy barking and he wondered if the dog was putting up a fight. He needed to go back to help the dog but he was too afraid. *Get Dad now! Get Zeke! They'll know what to do!* Matt heard the barking stop. *Hurry!*

When Matt arrived at camp the men stopped their conversation. The boy was excited and out of breath. "Dad! Dad!" he exclaimed. "I saw something! It was green and bright! I had to—"

"—Hold up, hold up," Albright said while rising to his feet with the others. "Slow down and tell us what happened."

Billy came trotting into camp. He seemed calm and unexcited, apparently already forgetting the incident at the creek.

Matt reached down to pet the dog. The boy took a deep breath and started over. "I was cleaning the dishes and I looked up in the sky and saw a light above the trees."

"An aircraft?" Stover asked.

"I don't think so, Mr. Stover."

"Let's go take a look," Zeke said, his M4 carbine already in his hand.

They all headed down to the creek with Zeke leading the way, his flashlight beam fanning the area in front of them. Matt stayed close to his dad. When they reached the creek, Matt pointed to the location in the sky where he first saw the light. "It was way up there," he explained. "Just a ball of light in the sky."

"If an aircraft was far enough away," Zeke said, "it would appear to be barely moving."

"I know, Mr. Allenby," Matt said. "That's what I thought at first, but then it just vanished."

"Could you hear it, son?" Albright asked, trying to mask the anxiety he was feeling now. "Any sounds from an engine?"

"No, sir," Matt said, staring at the treetops that had been swaying earlier.

"What happened after it vanished," Stover asked. "Did you hear anything?"

Matt was thinking how crazy it all sounded. He decided to leave off the rest of the story. They weren't going to believe him anyway. Plus, he didn't want Zeke Allenby to think he was some nutty kid. "Not really. It happened so fast."

They all stared at the starlit sky for another long moment. "Sure you didn't see a shooting star?" Albright asked, apparently relieved that whatever his son saw was gone now.

"Yes, Dad," came the response. "I'm sure." *A shooting star? Are you kidding me? Like I can't tell the difference between a shooting star and . . . whatever it was I saw.* Matt was really mad now. *He never believes me!*

"Well, whatever it was," Stover said, "it's gone now."

"Let's go," Albright said, putting his arm on Matt's shoulder to lead him back to camp. "Maybe tomorrow night we'll all see what you saw."

I hope not, Matt thought, moving away from his dad's arm. *I hope only you see it and no one believes you!*

They all walked back to their campsite, never seeing a distant star above them grow in brightness before fading into the night sky. Matt yawned but he didn't feel sleepy at the moment. Paul Stover and his dad talked for a moment in quiet voices before heading to their tents.

"Better get some rest, son," Albright said while going inside his tent. He glanced in the direction of the sky above the creek, a worried expression on his face. "Gonna be a long day tomorrow."

Matt didn't say anything as he squatted angrily next to the fire.

"See everybody at daybreak," Zeke said from inside his tent. He was already in his sleeping bag.

Stover said goodnight and retired to his own small tent. "Goodnight all."

Matt sat by the fire for a few moments, staring at the flames, his eyelids getting heavy. Billy meandered over and Matt put his arm around the dog's furry neck. "You know the truth, boy," Matt said in a low voice. "You saw it, too."

Billy glanced at the boy speaking to him, his panting soft and relaxed. The dog yawned then went back to his panting.

"Yeah," Matt said, standing slowly to his feet. "You saw it."

Billy watched the boy enter the father's tent. He lowered himself to the ground, resting his head on his front paws, hearing the crackling wood, his eyes darting from the fire back to Matt's tent, to the sky above the creek, back to the fire, closing his eyes, his breathing quieter, more crackling wood, his breathing slower and steadier now, then he too fell asleep.

* * *

THREE

R uth Sennot checked on the kids in the bedroom for the third time
in twenty or so minutes. They were still asleep despite the noises
coming from outside their small three-bedroom home in North Houston.
Earlier, a gang of boys had been terrorizing a home across the street,
throwing rocks and other objects at the windows. They'd scattered when
Mr. Blankenship, the old widower who lived alone in the house, fired a
shotgun from his front door, some of the pellets peppering the front of
Ruth's house. The boys came back a while later, shouting obscene taunts
and throwing more rocks, but this time more careful as they took cover
behind the trees in Blankenship's overgrown lawn.

Ruth saw it all as she peeked between the curtains in her bedroom
window, through the burglar bars, and out into the moonlit street beyond
her house. She pulled the curtains tight and sat back on the foot of the
bed. A series of burning candles scattered throughout the house provided
light in the nighttime. The candles were her only source of light at night
these days. Her bedroom was warm and stuffy. She smelled the stench of
mildew coming from somewhere in the bathroom. A single siren howled
in the distance, probably from the highway nearby. Normally she would
have heard a half dozen sirens by this time of night, but this was the first
time in days that she heard any sign of an emergency vehicle. *We have to
leave,* she told herself for about the hundredth time. The same response
came: *Where?* The same answer: *Anywhere.* If only Zeke had called or
showed up on her doorstep like she'd dreamed about the night before.
But how could he?

Ruth's son, Connor, turning nine next month, had been so brave
while looking after his mom and little sister, Amy. Two days ago they
were waiting in line at small church in the neighborhood to get a couple
of used one-gallon jugs of boiled water handed out by volunteers of the

church. While they were walking back home with the water, a trio of young boys about Connor's age tried to steal the jugs. Connor fought the one grabbing for his jug, bloodying the boy's nose before they all ran away. Ruth remembered the way Connor walked home: his chest puffed out, full of confidence, telling her how he wished Uncle Zeke could have seen him *punch-out* the kid. She was just relieved the boys hadn't been armed with knives . . . or guns.

Ruth stood and left the bedroom. She walked into the small kitchen and examined the shelves with their future food supply. One can of Fruit Cocktail and a half box of apple fruit bars. The kids next and last meal. *Last Meal.* The words stuck in her mind. Then the flood of tears came. Uncontrollable sobbing. She hurried back to her bedroom, not wanting to wake the kids and have them see her like this. She collapsed on the bed face-down, crying into her smelly pillow and smelly sheets, unwashed for over a week now. *A week,* she thought. *Felt like a month.*

Ruth finally pulled herself together. She stood from the bed and wiped her eyes, a determined look growing on her exhausted face. They were not going to stay here any longer. Most of the few neighbors she knew had already left, either on foot or in cars if they still worked. There had been rumors of relief camps located somewhere north of them, where food, water, and medical supplies were being rationed to the needy. "Who isn't needy?" she had told Helen, a single-mom from down the street with four teenaged boys. Helen had begged Ruth to come with her, all of them piling into an old mini-van with a half tank of gas. "We'll drive as far as we can," Helen had said. "Do the rest on foot if we have to." Ruth had turned her down for several reasons. Number one: the boys were wild and unruly, two of them already with criminal records. She didn't trust them, especially around Amy, her not quite four-year-old daughter. Number two: she'd had enough food to last three or four days at the time, and maybe Zeke would show up, or power would be restored. Of course, she said none of this to Helen, just a "no but thanks anyway."

Everything was different now, though. Funny how just a few days could change the situation so drastically. Power had not been restored. *Or food in my kitchen cabinets.* The neighborhood was turning into a war zone. Things were getting worse. Much worse. She knew nothing about Zeke's situation but she knew one thing about her brother-in-law: he *would* come for her and the kids. Someway he would find them. She just couldn't wait here any longer.

By candlelight she gathered her children's warmest clothing into a pile. They would all get dressed when sunrise came, carry their remaining food and water with them, and head for the freeway that would lead them away from Houston and eventually to the supposed relief camp Helen and others had been talking about. *Where did Helen say the camp was? Somewhere near The Woodlands. Then we will walk to The Woodlands. Walk to Canada if we have to.* She refused to wait at home any longer. Fear of gangs turning their wrath on her and the kids looked like a certainty if they continued to stay. But none of that mattered with all their food gone. They *had* to leave.

Ruth found a pen and paper in the kitchen drawer near the dead-for-a-week phone. She started to write. After finishing the note, she stuck it to the refrigerator door with a U.S. Army Rangers magnet, a little gift from Zeke to Connor a few years back. The *pop-pop-pop* sound of gunfire came from somewhere outside in the distance. She ignored the gunfire and knelt on the kitchen floor, bringing her palms together in front of her face. She began to pray. She prayed harder than she ever had in her life. Even harder than she had the day everything changed, when her Toyota and hundreds of other cars died in the middle of Interstate 45 and she had to run miles to Connor's elementary school with Amy in her arms.

Ruth prayed for God to look after her children, to help them find food and water and shelter, things she never had to pray for before. She prayed that Zeke was unharmed and would find them somehow. She ended the prayer by giving thanks to God, thanks for keeping her and the kids safe and together. Yes, *still together,* so important during dark days like these with so much uncertainty ahead.

*　*　*

FOUR

They drove around the bend and saw it. Not only was the road not visible, the vertical slope before them dropped at least five hundred feet to the canyon below.

Zeke, Stover, Albright, Matt, and Billy, stood outside the vehicles and stared over the edge of the slope. "What do we do now?" Matt asked.

Zeke compared the topo map to the old county map. He hadn't been surprised to find the mountain road gone from existence. He'd been expecting it since that last couple of map readings.

"The only way now is on foot," Albright said with plenty of irritation in his voice. He aimed his words in Zeke's direction. "Right, Mr. Army Ranger?"

Zeke turned toward Albright for a brief moment before turning back to the maps, wondering where Albright's irritable behavior came from. Zeke had picked up on something earlier before they broke camp that morning. They had been loading their camping gear back into the vehicles, almost ready to leave, when Zeke remembered the *char tinder* he'd made the night before. He told Matt to come over to the campfire, temporarily delaying the boy's last minute packing. Zeke retrieved the blackened throat-lozenge box from the edge of the dying campfire and opened the lid. The cloth inside was in pieces, black and flaky. "It looks burned and useless but it's not," Zeke told the boy. "It's only charred. That's why it's called *char tinder*. It'll take a spark easy, to start a fire."

"Thanks!" Matt replied. "I can use it tonight when—"

"—Matt!" his dad shouted angrily. "You're supposed to be packed and ready to go! We don't have all day!"

"I was but Mr. Allenby wanted to show me this," Matt explained while showing his dad the box of char tinder.

"That's wonderful," Albright said in a sarcastic tone. "Now get your stuff packed. Now!"

The boy lowered his head and finished his packing.

Zeke told Albright, "Sorry. That was my fault. I asked him to come over."

Albright never responded to Zeke's apology.

Now, as Zeke stared at the steep slope before them, he wondered if he should respond to the *'Mr. Army Ranger'* comment, or just let it go.

Stover, always the optimist, spoke up just in time. "We just continue on as planned, guys. We talked about this, remember? We drive as far we can then hike the rest if we have to."

"Yeah, I remember," Albright said impatiently. "Let's get our gear together. We need to get moving if we're ever going to get there."

"What about the Land Rover and Mr. Allenby's Jeep?" Matt asked. "We just leave them here?"

Zeke was already unloading supplies from the Land Rover and organizing them on the ground. "Yes," he said. "Take what we need and leave the rest."

Stover started helping him. "What do we need to bring?"

"Let's get it all laid out," Zeke said, "then we'll decide."

Everyone assisted in unloading the vehicles except Albright, who said and did nothing, his facial expression revealing his foul mood.

"Are we going to have to walk the rest of the way, Mr. Allenby?" Matt asked.

"Just through the mountains," Zeke said while grabbing the last box from the back of the Land Rover. "We'll find some transportation after that."

"What type of transportation?" asked Matt.

"Whatever we find," Zeke said. "Car, truck . . . maybe even animal power."

"Animal power?"

"Yeah, you know, horses?" Zeke said while sharing a smile with Stover. "Maybe a team of oxen and a wagon, I don't know . . . camels maybe?"

Matt giggled. "Camels?"

Stover joined in the fun. "Actually," he said, "back in the 1800s, the U. S. Calvary experimented with using camels at a fort somewhere here in Texas. I can't remember where exactly, but I think it was near here."

"That's right," Zeke said while sorting the supplies into groups. "Maybe we'll find some of those camels roaming around out here."

Matt cleared his throat. "Hel-lo?" he said in a singsong voice. "That was over a hundred years ago and I think all the camels would be dead by now, don't you think?"

"Oh, yeah," Zeke said, smiling at Stover. He glanced at Albright who was unloading some supplies from the Land Rover's back seat. "Well," Zeke said. "Maybe we'll find an airplane full of fuel. That would be nice."

"You know how to fly?" Matt asked.

"No, but I think I can figure it out," Zeke replied with a wink toward Stover. "You'll ride with me, won't you, Matt?"

"No way!" the boy said with a chuckle. "I think I'll just walk!"

Zeke and Stover shared a short laugh, both of them standing above the groups of supplies piled before them.

Albright stood nearby, staring at them with an impatient expression growing on his face. "Are you guys going to clown around all day?" he said. "Because I'd like to get moving, if you don't mind?" He turned his attention toward Zeke after he said this.

Zeke ignored him while keeping the smile on his face. "The best way to approach this," he said while squatting near the supplies, "is for everyone to grab their backpacks and separate the items we need from the pile. Certain things we'll definitely leave behind, like the tents."

"Where are we gonna sleep then?" asked Matt.

"Under the stars," Zeke said. "Everyone will take their sleeping bag, rolled and tied to your backpack."

"Well, you can do what you want," Albright said, "but I'm taking my tent."

Zeke stood slowly to his feet and faced Albright. "And I say you won't."

Albright stood his ground, his hands on his hips as he stared back at Zeke with a defiant expression on his face. Stover and Matt froze, staring at the standoff between the two men.

Whoa! Matt thought, never seeing anyone stand up to his dad like this.

"Who gave you the right to give me orders?" Albright asked.

"You did," Zeke shot back. "Before we left. Remember? You hired me to complete a job and I told you we would do it my way. And you agreed. You actually gave your word. You keep your word, don't you, Steve?"

Albright's eyes narrowed. His face was getting red but he said nothing.

Stover intervened. "Come on, guys," he pleaded. "We don't need to do this." He waited for a response but got none. "He's right, Steve. We agreed to do it his way until we get to Austin."

Albright turned his glare on Stover. "Oh, so you're taking his side now?"

"I'm not taking anyone's side," Stover replied. "I'm just reminding you that we made an agreement. And I know you *always* honor your agreements, right?"

Albright pursed his lips and spun away, stomping over to the Land Rover where he leaned against the hood with his back to the others.

Stover gave Zeke an apologetic look before walking over to Albright. He stood close and asked in a quiet voice, "What's up, Boss?"

While Stover talked with Albright, Zeke returned to sorting the gear. Matt stood like a statue, staring at Stover and his father conversing in low tones near the hood of the Land Rover.

"Hey, Matt," Zeke said.

Matt turned his attention back to Zeke. "Yes, sir?"

Zeke offered something in his hand. "I'm going to start handing you some things to put in your pack. Here, take this."

"What is it?" Matt asked while taking the rubbery object that looked like a small, deflated pool float of some sort.

"It's a water bladder," Zeke said. "We'll fill it later. Now, I'm going to hand you stuff, and you set it all near your backpack. I'll show you how to pack it all in a minute. Okay?"

"Okay."

As Zeke handed Matt different items to load into his backpack, Stover and Albright finished their discussion.

"I didn't sleep all that well last night," Albright confided to Stover. "I think I had a bad nightmare, but I don't remember any details."

"It's okay, Boss," Stover said. "Let's just move on as planned."

Albright followed him back to the growing pile of supplies on the ground. He asked Zeke, "Can I talk to you for a minute?"

Zeke stood to his feet. "Sure."

As Zeke and Albright walked a short distance away, Stover sat next to

Matt and the various items piled on the ground. The boy stared at Zeke and his dad.

"Whatcha up to?" Stover asked the boy.

"Oh, about five feet," Matt said in an absentminded way. He was focused on Zeke and his dad, but he played the game he and Stover played occasionally.

"That's the same answer you gave me last week," Stover said while squatting next to the boy and examining the items.

Matt turned his attention to Stover. He smiled wanly and said, "That's because I'm still five-feet-tall, Uncle Paul."

"Oh, yeah."

Matt gestured toward Zeke and his dad. "What's Dad and Zeke talking about?"

"There just working things out," Stover said. "Everything's good. Your dad just has a lot of things on his mind, that's all. I'm sure he's apologizing for his bad behavior."

Matt smiled inwardly. He'd never seen his dad apologize to anyone before. Never! Matt wanted to grow up to be like Zeke. Maybe then his dad would have to apologize to him someday! *Wouldn't that be something!*

"So anyway," Albright was telling Zeke. "I've had too much on my mind, I guess."

Zeke nodded passively, thinking this was as close as someone like Albright would get to saying he was sorry. Successful, ambitious men like Albright seldom apologized to anyone because they seldom believed they were wrong. At the heart of the matter were control issues, usually deriving from their childhood where they felt underrated and unappreciated. *Listen to me,* Zeke thought to himself. *Talking like some geek psychologist overanalyzing everything.*

"So I hope you understand," Albright said, apparently through with his explanation—*his* version of an apology.

"I understand," Zeke said in a pleasant tone. "But I want you to understand something."

"Okay."

"Ordinarily," Zeke began, "if someone under my command did what you did back there, I'd either beat the crap out of them or cut them loose to be on their own." He stared intently into Albright's eyes. "But this ain't the army and I'm not in the habit of splitting up families. As a matter of fact, I'd never intentionally separate a boy from his father. Never. So, if you ever do that to me again, I'll hogtie you and drag you to Austin if I have to. You copy that?"

Albright blinked once, not bothering to hide his surprise. "Yes," he finally said in a humble tone. "I read you loud and clear."

"Good. Now let's get our gear together and get moving."

Albright nodded and followed Zeke back to the supplies where Stover and Matt gathered items. "So what do we have here?" Albright asked, his mood obviously better than before.

Zeke squatted next to Matt. "We keep anything that can come in handy and doesn't take up much room in your backpack. He leaned over and grabbed a box of large plastic garbage bags. He removed several folded sheets and rolled them into a small bundle. "These can be used for many situations," he said. "And they're light and don't take up much room. Shoe laces, string, wire, anything like that. Three changes of underwear, socks, and undershirts or tee shirts." Zeke removed the cardboard tube from a roll of toilet paper. He flattened the toilet roll and packed it into his backpack. "This is one of the most important luxury items to have in the field."

As Zeke continued his instructions of the items to be taken, everyone listened closely while packing their backpacks as he suggested. Forty-five minutes later they were finished. After loading the remainder of supplies into the vehicles, Stover and the two Albrights hoisted their packs onto their backs while waiting for Zeke to return from his Jeep. He was grabbing a few last minute items and placing them in various pockets of his camouflaged fatigues and vest.

Stover was pleased. Steve Albright had apologized and Zeke Allenby had handled the situation professionally by letting Albright's bad behavior go aside. Things were good.

Zeke approached the trio as he slung his M4 carbine over his shoulder. "Everyone ready?"

Billy was pacing around anxiously, eager to begin whatever they were beginning.

"Let's get moving, then," Stover said. "We're burning daylight, boys."

"What movie did that come from?" Albright asked with a smile.

"*The Unforgiven*," Stover replied. "Or was it *Lonesome Dove*? Probably both."

As they followed Zeke on a narrow steep trail meandering through the junipers covering the slope, Matt scrambled up closer to Zeke to get a better view of the weapon on his shoulder. "Wow!" the boy exclaimed. "What's that?"

Zeke played it down. "An M4 carbine."

"Is it like a machine gun or something?"

"Something like that."

Matt stayed in step with Zeke. "What are you going to use it for?"

"Protection."

"From what?"

"Oh, I don't know," Zeke said, leading the group up the faint trail winding up the rocky incline. "Bears, mountain lions." He glanced back at Albright and Stover and almost added *'and bad guys armed with automatic weapons'* but for Matt's sake he decided against it.

"Mountain lions?" Matt said, his voice full of alarm. He regained his composure. "You think we'll see any?"

"Maybe," Zeke replied as he concentrated on the steep trail.

Stover said, "I hope not."

"Yeah, me, too," the boy agreed.

They all followed Zeke as he led them on a trail traversing the mountain. Billy scouted constantly, leaving the trail and rejoining it effortlessly. Two hours later they stopped on a ridge and took off their backpacks to drink water from their plastic bladder containers. Zeke used the compass to mark a new bearing on the topo map. "Two clicks that way," he said while pointing up to a gap in the ridge beyond the plateau. "We'll get a good view from up there."

They hiked on, enjoying the rolling terrain of the plateau, a relief from the steep, rocky inclines. Along the way Zeke told Matt how he could eat various wild plants certain times of the year. "The general rule-of-thumb is: if you don't know what it is, don't eat it. This applies especially to berries."

Zeke found some thistle nearby. He pulled it up from the ground and peeled the lower stalk before chewing on the tender root inside. "Not bad," he told Matt. "Here, give it a try."

Zeke laughed at Matt's facial expression while the boy chewed on the bitter tasting root. "Yuk," Matt said with a grimace. "That's awful."

Stover tried it. "Mmm," he said, trying to hide his distaste.

"It will give you plenty of nutrition," Zeke said with a smile. "You know, help you survive. That's the important thing, right, Paul?"

"Right," Stover answered before turning to Albright and offering him some. "Want to give it a try?"

"No thanks," came Albright's reply. "You're the vegetarian. You eat it."

After crossing the rolling plateau, they stopped at the foot of a steep incline leading to a gap in the ridge above them. They rested while waiting for their MREs to heat. A half-hour later they were back at it, following a steep trail winding its way toward the gap. At one point Albright lost his footing on some loose rocks and slid a few yards back down the trail on his stomach. He received a few scrapes and bruises but luckily no broken bones or twisted limbs. Zeke knew Albright and Stover were getting tired, which increased their odds of getting injured, but he wanted to get to the gap before sunset to surveil the terrain on the other side, and to find a good campsite for the evening.

By late afternoon they reached the gap. Zeke led them a short distance to a spot with a magnificent view of the terrain on the other side of the gap. He examined the terrain with his binoculars while the others removed their backpacks and sat on the ground near some boulders. They were exhausted.

Zeke searched for the highway he intended them to cross before continuing their journey. He wanted to maintain the high ground until finding a good spot to cross the highway in the cover of night. If anyone was attempting to ambush them, the highway would probably be the spot, but he wasn't planning on using it unless they found a working vehicle. With gas. And a working battery. Zeke marked a new heading on the topo map and decided to call it a day.

Mosquitos began to swarm as twilight neared. The small campfire seemed to help a bit but the insects were relentless. Zeke passed around some small, sealed packages of *OFF* insect repellant. Albright and Matt rubbed the exposed parts of their skin with the repellant-moistened towelettes. Stover had his own mosquito repellant—an all-natural citrus blend guaranteed to repel the insects in a *natural* way.

Soon the sky became dark except for the billions of stars overhead. The campfire flickered and sparked as they ate their MREs and drank water from their plastic bladders. The mosquitos had disappeared and a cool breeze crept through the gap. It didn't take long for everyone to sprawl out in their sleeping bags. Albright and his son fell asleep immediately. Paul Stover sat up in his sleeping bag and removed a ziplock bag of unsalted almonds from his backpack. He munched a few before looking at Zeke. "Want some?"

Zeke broke from his stargazing. "Sure," he said, turning on his side and leaning on his elbow. He took the bag and grabbed a few almonds. "Thanks."

"Matt told me earlier about your wife," Stover said. "I'm sorry."

Stover's words caught Zeke by surprise. "Yeah," he said. "And he told me about his mom. That's a hard one for a little guy. Hard on the big guys, too."

Stover nodded. "Steve has tried to do his best for Matt since Liz passed, but he's so busy, running the company and all. He's worried that a distance is growing between him and Matt."

"I think Matt's just at that age," Zeke said. "He wants to be grown up. Wants to impress his dad. I see it when they are together."

"Yes, I think you're right."

Zeke lowered himself back on the sleeping bag, his palms cradling the back of his head as he stared up at the stars. "I don't know anything about raising kids," he said. "I shouldn't be analyzing their relationship."

Stover said, "You'd make a great father, Zeke. Ever think of remarrying and having kids?"

"No," Zeke answered without hesitation, not wanting the conversation to head in this direction.

Stover thought for a moment, choosing his words carefully. "You've given us all some pretty good advice on this trip. Can I give you some?"

"Sure."

"You got to get it off your chest," Stover said. "I don't know how long you've been holding it in but you have to let it go. If you don't it will eat you up inside. I know. I've been there."

"Get what off my chest?" Zeke asked, feeling something inside him begin to stir.

"It's just like what Steve went through when he lost Liz," Stover explained. "He didn't want Matt to see his father break down in despair. So he kept his grief inside. I had to dig it out of him, one painful moment at a time. He eventually got better because he finally faced his grief, with me there to support him. I think having someone to share it with is very important."

Zeke sat upright and crossed his legs. He poked at the fire with a stick while staring into the flames. He didn't want to do this but he felt out of control. The memory was rushing forward now, impossible to stop. He surprised himself when he began to speak. "It was a couple of weeks before Christmas," he said. "We were living in Houston. I got home earlier than normal, around four that afternoon. Five minutes later, my wife, Amber, called from her cell phone, saying she and the baby had gone to the mall to pick up something she'd ordered."

'Oh, and Zeke? I got a chicken in the oven. Be sure to take it out if the buzzer goes off. See you in a little bit, baby. Josh says hi, too.'

"I poured myself a glass of wine and decided to use the time to wrap some gifts," Zeke continued. "I finished and put the gifts under the tree. An hour came and went. Then another hour. I called her cell several times but I only got her voicemail."

'Hi, this is Amber. Leave a message and I'll call back.'

Zeke stared into the fire, lost in his memories. "I called all her friends, then drove to the mall to search the parking lot for her blue Honda. Couldn't find it. It was around eight when I got home. I smelled the smoke and ran to the kitchen. I took the smoldering chicken outside to the patio and returned inside the house. That's when I heard the car door shut."

Zeke turned to Stover. "I thought it was Amber, and I had that weird feeling, you know, a mix of relief and anger, both at the same time. Then I heard *several* car doors shut . . . and I knew."

Zeke returned his gaze to the fire. "I looked through the living room curtains and saw the detective sedan in my driveway. A police cruiser was parking next to the curb."

'I'm Detective Morrison, this is Detective Sanchez. Is this the home of Amber Lynn Allenby?'

Stover gave all his attention as Zeke let the demons out.

"They told me that Amber and my nine-month-old son had been killed in a car accident. It wasn't exactly an accident, though. I learned the whole story later. A twenty-four-year-old man hijacked her in the parking lot. There were eyewitnesses. She had put Josh in his baby seat in back and was opening the driver's door when this man—an ex-convict released on parole just two days earlier—forced her inside the car at gunpoint. He got behind the wheel and took off with an HPD patrol car on his tail. A high-speed chase involving seven police cruisers ended when the ex-con lost control and careened off a freeway overpass at ninety miles per hour."

A long moment of silence.

"The funny thing is," Zeke said, "I never found out what she'd picked up at the mall. The Honda caught on fire after the crash. Everything was burned to a crisp . . . just like that chicken I pulled out of the oven."

"Dear God," Stover said under his breath.

"Any interest I had in God died that day, too," Zeke said, reaching into his backpack for a flask of whiskey. He took a big gulp and held the flask in his lap. "At first, I asked all those questions most people ask. If there is a God, how could he let something like this happen? I guess I quit thinking about it soon after."

"I used to be a nonbeliever," Stover said when sure Zeke had finished. "Actually, I considered myself an atheist, not wanting to waste my time on such abstract concepts of things like a supreme being; things that could never be proven in conventional methods. But then I learned something from a book that started to change my way of thinking. I can't explain it like the author, but he said that from the beginning of humanity it's always been about choice. When God created Man, God gave Man freedom to *choose*; freedom to choose to love and obey him, or to choose not to. In other words, God gave us freedom of choice instead of creating a bunch of mindless robots programmed to automatically please him."

Zeke wasn't making eye contact but he was listening.

Stover paused to organize his thoughts. "Okay, so we see on television all those starving children orphaned from wars, or we lose someone very close to us and we wonder how God could allow this to happen. I believe *part* of the answer is this: Because he gave *everyone* the freedom to choose. Sometimes those choices, intentional or not, can cause immeasurable pain and grief to others."

Zeke continued to stare into the flames of the campfire.

"Tell me if you've had enough of my little sermon," Stover said, "and I'll step down off my pulpit."

"No, I'm listening."

"Okay, here's something," Stover said. "One day I watched Matt playing this computer game he's building. He's improved it since, but this was back in its early stage of development. Anyway, this earlier version involved creating these little people characters inside a primitive world of stone dwellings with simple tools for farming, bows and arrows for hunting, stuff like that. Matt created the characters with different individual attributes; physical features, personalities, likes and dislikes, all with adjustable parameters of strengths and weaknesses, what he calls AI, or Artificial Intelligence."

"Yeah," Zeke said. "He told me about it."

"As I watched," Stover continued, "a thought came to me. Here was a world of beings unaware of their *creator* at the keyboard and mouse-pad. Matt provided the crops and weather for growing food but some of the people didn't help with the farming. They were too busy fighting each other over territorial boundaries between their towns and villages. Soon everyone suffered from not enough food. Matt would take some of the dead characters—at least the ones he liked—and place them in a program window where he could revive them later and put them back in the game if he wanted to. Using my limited imagination, I thought about the characters left behind in the game; how they would mourn the loss of loved ones, wondering where they went, unable to understand the complexities of the computer game and the human god controlling it."

Zeke began to smile. "And?"

"One day Matt returned from school and opened the game on his computer," Stover explained. "He became angry when he found the game in total chaos. There was a major war going on, entire towns destroyed and burned, nearly half of the characters dead or dying. Matt was furious at all the little people. He had his finger on the *Delete Game* button when I asked him why not program the characters to do what he wanted them to do. 'Where's the fun in that?' he'd said. 'It's too predictable.'"

"So what did he do?" Zeke asked. "Program a global flood? Or just hit the button?"

Stover smiled knowingly. "Neither. I mentioned a flood but Matt said he'd already done that, saying that disasters didn't change anything. When the new civilization was up and running, the characters would screw it all up again. Later, he told me he had a new idea but he didn't tell me what it was."

Neither man spoke for several minutes. Zeke offered the flask to Stover but the lawyer declined the offer. Zeke took one last sip from the flask and returned it into his backpack. "I still don't know how I'm supposed to deal with the anger."

"The old saying 'time heals all wounds' is not true," Stover said. "Wounds can deepen over time if you allow them. Time by itself is not enough. It takes something else to complete the healing."

"What then?"

"Forgiveness," Albright said.

"Forgiveness," Zeke repeated. "Me forgiving others or me asking God for forgiveness?"

"Both," Stover said. He paused for a moment before saying, "I believe it's like this: Say you are in the wilderness being chased by a ferocious Grizzly bear. Your cabin with its one-foot-thick log walls is only twenty feet ahead of you. The rational part of your mind *knows* you have plenty of time to reach safety but you are panicking with fear due to how you *feel*. Even once inside the cabin with a solid iron door dead-bolted shut, you are still scared out of your wits. Why? Because you are reacting to how you *feel*, instead of reacting to what you *know*. Forgiveness is like that." Stover leaned his face toward Zeke. "The way you *feel* about that man who took your family's lives will not change with just the passage of time. You think to yourself you could never learn to forgive him. But if you *know* that God wants us to forgive others like he forgives us, you can choose to forgive by giving your anger and hatred over to God. It's back to choice. You will never, on your own, *feel* forgiveness for the man who took your wife and child away from you without help from God. In your prayers, you must *choose* to forgive, giving it over to God and his judgment. This is how you *know* you have forgiven the man. Bottom line? You forgive the man for your sake, not his."

Stover's words were followed by a long moment of silence. Zeke tossed twigs into the campfire while thinking about everything. He finally said, "Can I ask you something, Paul?"

"Go ahead."

"Do you think God has already started to push the delete button . . . here and now in the real world . . . in America?"

"No," Stover replied without hesitation. "But I think some villager has shot a very sophisticated arrow at us. Maybe the first of many arrows to come."

"Who do you think the villagers are?"

"I don't know exactly."

"Do you think Iran is involved?" Zeke asked.

Stover didn't seemed surprised by the question. "Possibly."

"Anyone else?"

"Who would you guess?"

Zeke had to think for only a moment. "Russia."

"And why do you think they're involved?"

"They have the technical ability to develop something like you guys *tried* to explain to me back at Steve's cabin," Zeke replied. "And it's a well known fact they've been supplying the Iranians with technology and nuclear materials for a long time."

"That's a plausible assumption," Stover said.

"Well, many so-called *experts* disagree," Zeke went on, "because they have this misguided idea that the Russians became our friends after the Soviet empire collapsed. But they don't understand the basic Russian psyche regarding their pride. I know because I worked with them during operations in the Balkans when I was a fresh recruit in Uncle Sam's *'be all that you can be'* army. Maniacal pride. You saw it in the Russian infantry and all the way up the food chain to their *fearless leaders*. The thing that angers them the most is not western capitalist expansion around the globe, but being treated like they are insignificant, like they're not major players anymore." Zeke was tired but too engaged in his thoughts to stop. "Paul, do you think it's possible that one of these advanced nations could get some type of high tech weapon through our defense system?"

"That question may have been already answered," Stover said, lowering his voice as if someone might be listening. "Washington has been concerned about this for quite a while now. Their concerns aren't focused on the reliability of our missile defense system but rather on *new technology*, technology that could provide our enemies with the ability to sneak past our current defense shield in ways we haven't thought of yet, technology that ADS may have stumbled upon."

What type of technology? Zeke almost asked.

"It's possible that this tragedy was caused by an advanced nation or alliance of nations," Stover said with a faraway look in his eyes. "But I doubt it."

Zeke had to think about this for a moment. He asked, "You think this was an inside job? From what . . . domestic terrorists?"

Stover didn't respond.

Zeke tried again. "Maybe from those inside our government?"

After a short delay Stover said, "Possibly."

Zeke blinked. There was only one explanation left. He had a hard time asking the question. "Are you talking about something . . . extraterrestrial?"

Stover took his time to answer. "The word *extraterrestrial* suggests too many stereotypes of UFOs and little green men in flying saucers."

Zeke remembered the vagrant and his story of UFOs and aliens among us, in Gold Tree of all places. "If not extraterrestrial, then what?"

"Many quantum physicists believe," Stover began, "that we live in a *multiverse* instead of a universe. Like skins of an onion, we exist on one plane, or one skin of the onion, but there are many other planes that not only influence our existence but may have intelligent life as well. Another way to look at it is to compare life to a television channel. Everything we know and everything we have experienced in life and read about from others has all been on say . . . channel five. We're not even aware of channel four or six, except for the occasional interference during certain atmospheric conditions. That interference may explain some encounters with the unknown, or what we call *paranormal* or *supernatural*. You with me?"

"Yeah, I'm listening."

"So it's possible," Stover explained, "that the unknown source we're dealing with exists on channel ninety-nine—from a dimension so beyond our thinking and way of life that we can't even begin to comprehend it." Stover thought for a moment before adding, "To answer your question, maybe *inter-dimensional* would be a more accurate description than extraterrestrial."

Did Stover really believe that the zapping of our glorious computerized world was caused by aliens? Aliens not from another planet, but from another dimension? Zeke had to ask, "So they come from another dimension instead of another planet?"

Stover thought for a moment before answering. "Maybe they still exist in our dimension but from a planet very far away, and their method of traveling the vast distance through space is accomplished inter-dimensionally. I don't know."

Zeke understood Stover's answer but it didn't matter. He just couldn't buy any of it. He didn't believe in UFOs—extraterrestrial or inter-dimensional. He didn't believe in ghosts either, or vampires, or boogymen in general. He hoped any minute now that Stover would break into laughter, saying this was all a joke. The man was an educated attorney. He seemed precise and logical, not the typical MO for a new age wacko believing aliens from another planet or dimension had attacked our country—or the entire world, for all he knew. *If he's not playing an elaborate joke on me, that leaves two possible answers. Number One: He believes he's telling the truth because he's out of his gourd. Number Two: He's telling the truth and he's not insane.*

"So back at Albright's cabin," Zeke said, trying to ignore the thoughts running through his brain, "you and Steve told me that ADS uncovered some communications that didn't operate in the radio wave spectrum, but in a way that has something to do with quantum computing. Correct?"

"Yes."

"Correct me if I'm wrong," Zeke went on, "but I think you also eluded that through your accumulated data you were able to determine that whoever emitted those communications were also involved in this EMP attack, or whatever it is."

"Basically," Stover said. "Yes."

"And you believe *they* are after you for your data. Which means they knew you had intercepted their communications. How could they know?"

"We're not sure what alerted them," Stover said, "but we know something did. They began worming into our system. We shut the program down but it may have been too late."

"These *communications*," Zeke said. "What were they saying?"

Stover stared at Zeke for a long time, perhaps trying to decide how he should answer. "When put together in analysis form," he eventually said, "the data constructed a series of actions that predicted the present circumstances *exactly*. And it also showed that their technological abilities far exceed anything known on this planet."

Zeke didn't want to go back to the alien thing right now. "So who do you think is chasing us?"

"We're not the only ones exploring this new world of quantum computing," Stover said. "We may be the first to succeed in this particular area but others have been involved in the same field of research for quite some time now."

Zeke tried to digest everything. No matter how he processed it all, it came back to alien beings attacking the country, with or without the help of someone on this planet. "Does Steve believe all this?"

Stover chose his words carefully. "He's seen the data but he has a hard time with the otherworldly thing. Just like I do. But the facts are the facts."

"So you really believe we are under attack from beings from another dimension or wherever?"

"I don't want to believe it," Stover said. "All my brain cells have been rejecting the idea since the beginning. But the facts leave little room for doubt. Believe me, I've been searching for other explanations all along."

Zeke saw the sincerity in Stover's eyes but it was just too much for the rational side of Zeke's mind to buy into this theory of otherworld beings attacking the country.

"I have some interesting theories from a biblical perspective," Stover said while stretching out in his sleeping bag. "Just be ready to give a few hours of your time while I try to explain it. But right now, I'm bushed."

"I'm with you on that," said Zeke.

Both men tried to halt their thoughts. They were exhausted. Within minutes both were asleep. The only sound besides their snoring and the occasional crackling of burning wood in the campfire was some gentle rustling in the trees nearby . . . and Billy's low growl as he stared toward those rustling trees.

$$* \quad * \quad *$$

FIVE

With the first hint of sunrise cresting the eastern ridge, Matt awoke and noticed that Zeke and Billy were gone. He put on his hiking boots and approached the smoldering campfire while looking for signs of Zeke and Billy. The morning was chilly. He saw a small amount of frost when he exhaled. The boy added some wood on the coals and waited for the flames so he could warm his hands. Stover and his dad stirred in their sleeping bags. His dad woke first. "Morning, Matt," he said with a yawn. "Sleep well?"

"Yes, sir."

Stover sat up with his legs still in the sleeping bag. He looked around the campsite while putting a *Texas Rangers* baseball cap on his bald head. "Where are the early risers?"

Albright noticed Zeke's sleeping bag and backpack sitting near the fire, rolled, packed, and ready to go when they left camp later that morning. "Gone for a morning stroll, I guess."

"Maybe having his morning constitution," Stover suggested while sniffing the air. "I just hope he's downwind."

Matt felt some grumbling in his own abdomen. He opened his backpack and searched for what Zeke had called '*the most important luxury item*' to have in the field, besides water, of course. He found the roll of toilet paper, flattened as much as possible to conserve space. He found a spot in the trees not too far away, but far enough to not be seen, or even more important, to not be *smelled*.

The morning came alive with chirping birds and a cold breeze blowing through the canyon as sunrise arrived in all its glory. Stover, Albright, and his son heated their MREs as the campfire flames took some of the chill out of the air. Matt wished they had some of the beans and biscuits from their first night of the journey.

They were eating their hot MREs when Billy appeared from the slope near the campsite. Zeke followed, trudging up the hill with a flashlight in his hand. He raised the front brim of his ball cap as he approached the campfire.

"Hey," Albright called out. "Look what the cat brought in."

"Funny you should put it that way," Zeke said while removing the M4 from his shoulder and sitting down near the fire. He grabbed a collapsable fabric bowl inside his backpack and filled it with water from his plastic bladder. Billy trotted over and began lapping noisily from the bowl with his long tongue. "About a hundred meters east of here," Zeke said. "I found the remains of a doe. A fresh kill."

"From a hunter?" asked Stover.

"Yes, but not a human hunter," Zeke replied. "The paw prints lead up toward a bluff on the other side of that tree line."

"A bear?" Matt asked.

"Mountain lion," Albright said while looking at Zeke.

"And a good sized one," Zeke added, "according to the size of the prints. A hundred pounds, maybe a hundred-twenty."

Matt focused his attention toward the tree line. "Will he come back?"

"Not likely," Zeke said. "It knew we were here, but it wanted that doe, not one of us. More than likely it's long gone by now. Their hunting zone can cover a two-hundred-mile radius."

Albright glanced at his son. "They usually don't bother humans, Matt."

"Especially when we're together," Stover offered.

"I know," Matt said, trying to act unconcerned.

Billy finished his water and Zeke shook out the excess before replacing it in his backpack. "You always need to stay on your toes," he said to no one in particular, but his words were for Matt. "Be alert of your surroundings. There's a water source somewhere down the slope. That means wildlife will be near."

In a casual tone Matt asked, "More mountain lions?"

"Cats are pretty elusive," Zeke said. "Deer, elk, and smaller mammals most likely. Maybe black bears."

Matt blinked and asked, "Black bears like to eat berries, right?"

"Except for *blackberries*," Zeke replied with a smile.

"Huh?" the boy said before catching the wordplay. "Oh, I get it. Black bears. Black *berries*."

"So if they eat berries," Stover said, "they must be vegetarians . . . like me."

"Bears are omnivores," Matt said with a giggle. "Which means they eat about anything, right, Dad?"

"That's right," Albright said. "They're like me."

"Now that you mention it," Stover said while digging his toothbrush and toothpaste out of his backpack, "there is a resemblance."

Albright tossed a pebble at Stover. Stover responded with his rapid-fire, chipmunk laugh.

Zeke stood and hoisted his backpack over his shoulders. "I'm going to search for the water source," he said, slinging the M4 over his left shoulder. "Be ready to leave when I get back. Give me an hour, an hour and a half, tops."

Albright didn't seem to have a problem with delaying their departure. He was still tired and sore from the previous day of hiking.

Zeke and Billy descended the slope toward the canyon floor below, following a game trail until it forked in different directions. He took the right fork, feeling in his gut that it led to a small creek. A short while later he heard the faint sound of running water. He found a little creek rushing downhill over rocks polished smooth by the water. After a short walk upstream he found a good watering spot devoid of animal feces. Many hunters, hikers, and campers contracted *Giardia*, a parasite that infected the intestines. People often became sick from fresh streams where the water looked clear and tasted fine but was contaminated by the parasite.

Zeke drank from cupped hands and watched Billy scout the area surrounding the creek. He decided to lead everyone back to the creek to fill their water containers before continuing their journey eastward. As he and Billy headed back toward the spot where the trail forked, Zeke suddenly heard footfalls. He turned and saw a man running towards them on the game trail. The man looked terrorized, his heavy breathing and sobbing heard easily from the distance. Zeke called out, "Hey! You okay, Bud?"

The man turned his head in surprise toward the sound of Zeke's voice. He looked at Zeke with eyes full of fear and terror. With a loud moan he halted his running and started backing away but tripped in the brush bordering the trail. As Zeke approached him, the man began whimpering and pleading while trying to get back on his feet. "Please!" he begged. "I won't tell a soul! Just let me go, please!"

"Whoa!" Zeke said as he approached him, keeping alert to his surroundings and anyone pursuing the man down the trail. "I'm not going to hurt you. What happened?"

"You speak English?" the man said in surprise, more of a statement than a question. He eyed the German Shepherd approaching him.

As Zeke knelt beside him, the frightened man started showing signs of relief. "Who are you?" the man asked with a shaky voice. He glanced at Billy as the dog began sniffing his filthy clothing.

"My name is Zeke and this is Billy. Now what happened to you?"

The fear returned in the man's face. His eyes began darting back down the trail. "We gotta get out of here!" he said. "They could find me again!"

"Who?"

The man only shook his head in response, his eyes tearing up as he remembered something extremely awful.

Zeke stared down the trail, looking and listening for any signs of pursuers. He turned back to the man, amused by his shock of curly, almost white hair, incongruous with the man's weathered face. It was hard to tell his age, but Zeke figured he must be in his late-fifties. "Listen up," he told the man while patting the M4 slung on his shoulder. "If anyone comes down that trail with malice in their hearts toward us, they are going to be greeted by a hailstorm of bullets. You understand? You are safe now."

The man calmed a bit but he didn't seem convinced of his safety. He kept darting his eyes toward the trail as if someone would appear any moment. "Let's get out of here," he finally said, his voice revealing some return of self-control.

Zeke nodded. "Okay, me and some others have a camp not far from here. You look like you could use something to eat and drink."

Zeke helped the man to his feet and led him back to the camp. Stover and the two Albrights looked surprised when Zeke and Billy returned with the curly haired man in tow. "Get this man something to eat, please," Zeke said while ignoring their stares. "He hasn't eaten in a while."

Stover went to get an MRE while Matt squatted next to Billy, rubbing his furry neck and staring at Zeke and the stranger. Albright kept his distance and stared distrustfully at the man. Zeke removed his water bladder and offered the man a drink. After a long pull on the water bladder, Zeke took it back from him. "Not too much at a time," he told the man.

The man nodded and gave Zeke a humble look of appreciation. "Thank you."

After the man had begun wolfing down some hot food Zeke asked, "What's your name?"

"I'm Dr. Robert Margolian," he replied. "And your name was Zeke, correct?"

"Yes," Zeke replied, a bit surprised about the doctor bit.

Stover spoke up. "Are you a doctor of medicine?"

"Archeology," Margolian corrected him. "My specialty is Mesopotamia, the reason I've been in this part of the world for several decades now."

Zeke and Stover exchanged looks.

"Specifically, where are we?" Margolian asked, catching the look between them.

"Northern part of Diablo," Zeke said dryly.

"Diablo?"

"Diablo Mountain."

"Appropriate name, I suppose," Margolian said. "Is that near the border?"

"What border would that be?" Zeke asked.

"The Turkish-Syrian border, of course," Margolian said with a curious expression.

Zeke and Stover shared another quick look. They both wondered if this man was totally off his rocker, suffering from exposure along with the delusion that he was an archeologist working somewhere on the other side of the globe.

"Please tell me we are not in Iran," Margolian said, trying to read their expressions. "I'm without my papers at the moment."

"Why don't you know where you are?" Albright suddenly asked from a short distance away.

Margolian didn't turn to look at Albright but he said, "Forgive me, but my memory is a mess at the moment."

"You are not in Iran," Zeke finally said after giving Albright a look. "You are in a mountainous area of West Texas. That's Texas, as in America."

Margolian chuckled. "That's funny," he said. "And I thought I was only slightly lost." The smile dropped from his face instantly and was replaced by a look of fear and uncertainty.

Stover looked sympathetically at the man. "It's okay," he encouraged him. "You've experienced some type of memory loss but it will come back to you in time."

Margolian's confidence—almost a cockiness—came alive again. "Really," he said. "Where are we? I promise I won't reveal your presence to anyone, be it illegal or not."

When no one replied, Margolian said, "I have to admit when I first saw you, Zeke, I thought I had stumbled upon some type of American special forces operation, until arriving here and seeing the boy and the others. Are you tourists?" He glanced from face to face around the campsite. When everyone returned blank stares he returned to finishing his food, his face again revealing his confusion and loss of confidence.

Zeke raised his eyebrows at Stover who took over the conversation. "Dr. Margolian," he said. "My name is Paul Stover. Can you tell us what happened to you?"

Margolian didn't seem eager to relive any of it at the moment.

"You know," Stover went on, "the events leading up to when you ran into Zeke here?"

Margolian looked deep into Stover's eyes before dropping his gaze. He began to speak quietly. "My team and I were working the site as usual. As always, we left before sundown, but this time something happened after arriving back at the tents. I think I had just fallen asleep when I awoke suddenly."

"What awoke you?" asked Stover.

"A light outside my tent," Margolian answered. "Not a normal light, like let's say, a lantern or flashlight, but something larger and brighter. A large ball of light. Even through the canvas of the tent I could tell that it emitted color."

Matt had already focused his attention toward the man as soon as 'a ball of light' was mentioned.

"What color was this ball of light?" asked Stover.

"Green," Matt suddenly answered aloud. Everyone turned toward him. He felt his face reddening with embarrassment.

"That's right," Margolian said. "It was green, but of a sickly shade that made you almost queazy."

Matt understood perfectly.

"What happened after you saw this ball of light?" Stover asked.

"I left my tent to go investigate, of course," Margolian said. "Myself and the rest of the team saw the light disappear over a berm of rubble south of the camp. When we arrived at the spot where we had seen it last, it was gone."

"Go on," Stover encouraged him. "What happened next?"

"We all went back to our tents. Everyone was exhausted as always, but especially that evening. The current dig had drained us of most of our energy. I soon fell asleep, I think." Margolian's facial expression started to change. "I'm not sure." His previous state of fear was starting to consume him again. "I don't remember exactly what happened next, except that I was taken prisoner." Margolian's emotions took over. He began weeping with such intensity and despair it was difficult to watch.

Stover sat next to Margolian and put his arm around his shoulders. "It's okay. You're safe now. Just relax. Take a deep breath." Stover finally connected Margolian's name with his face and unusual head of hair. Years ago Stover had seen a *National Geographic* documentary about Dr. Margolian and his archeological work over the last several decades, especially in the Kurdish areas of Northern Iraq and Southern Turkey.

"Where, Dr. Margolian?" Stover asked. "Where were you taken?"

"I don't know. I just woke up and I was there." Margolian lifted his head slowly and said, "It was dark. So very dark. And very cold. I was bound. There were dark figures around me. At first I couldn't see them clearly—" Margolian started sobbing like a small child.

"It's okay," Stover said. "You are not alone now. We're right here with you."

Margolian regained a bit of control, "They were hideous," he sobbed before breaking down completely and crying into his hands. "They weren't human."

Albright made some type of sound from behind them. When Zeke and Stover turned to look, Albright made a circular motion with his index finger near the temple of his forehead.

Stover gave Margolian some more water as Zeke stood and walked a few steps away, wondering how he was going to continue their journey with a possible mental case on his hands.

A few moments later Margolian curled up in a fetal position and fell asleep. Zeke, Stover and the two Albrights huddled together a short distance away. Albright spoke first. "So what are we going to do with him? We can't take him with us."

"Why not?" Stover said.

"Because he could compromise us during the trip," Albright shot back. "I think he's insane."

"Why do you say that?" Stover asked.

"You heard him," Albright said. "He thinks he is an archeologist working in Turkey or Iran or wherever. Not to mention the part about being captured by *non-humans*."

"He is an archeologist," Stover said in a matter-of-fact way. "And a most famous one at that."

This got everyone's attention. "You mean you know him?" Albright asked incredulously. Stover didn't respond right away.

Zeke also waited for Stover to answer with an expectant look on his face. "Well?"

"Not personally," Stover finally said. "But I saw a television documentary about him a while back. He is one of the world's leading experts on ancient cultures in the Middle East. Mesopotamia, cradle of civilization stuff."

"You sure it's the same man?" asked Zeke.

"Absolutely," Stover replied.

Everyone turned to stare at the sleeping man who looked like a homeless person in ragged clothes. "He doesn't look like a famous person," Matt commented.

"What's he doing here in Texas?" Albright asked.

"You heard him," Stover said. "He thinks he's still in the Middle East."

"Well, if that isn't insane, what is?" Albright argued.

"He's got a point," Zeke said to Stover. "Famous archeologist or not, the man is obviously delusional."

"So what do we do?" Stover said. "Just leave him here?"

"Of course not," Zeke said.

Albright turned to Zeke and opened his mouth to say something but changed his mind after a few seconds of eye contact.

"Something on your mind?" Zeke asked him.

"Maybe we can get him some help along the way," Albright said in a quiet voice.

"My thoughts exactly," Zeke said. "We'll have to share our rations, but that shouldn't be a problem for long."

"Why is that?" Albright asked.

"Because you are going to feed us once we get to your home in Austin," Zeke said with a smile. "Right?"

Albright began to grin reluctantly. "Yeah, right."

*

After replenishing their water supply, they hiked for several hours along a faint game trail meandering through the rugged terrain. Margolian apparently now accepted the fact that he was currently in Texas and not in the Middle East, but he still seemed to be confused by how he got here. No recollection of recent global travel had surfaced in his memories, yet. They were hiking into a narrow valley, enjoying the downhill walk when a long-haired man with a bandana wrapped around his head stepped from behind a boulder with an antique-looking, double-barreled shotgun pointed at them. "Everyone get them hands up high!"

Stover, Margolian, and the two Albrights immediately raised their hands above their heads. Billy started barking and growling at the man.

"You better get control of the dog or he'll be the first to go!" Bandana said in a raspy voice.

Matt instantly called for Billy. The dog came to the boy and Matt held him by the collar. "Quiet, boy!"

Zeke called out, "Billy! Stay!" He saw that Matt's legs were beginning to shake with fear. "Hold him tight, Matt!"

Matt pulled the leash tight to him. The dog relaxed a bit but let out a whine.

Bandana turned toward Matt and the dog. "He comes at me and I'm gonna blow his head off, and then yours! You hear me, boy!"

"You're pretty tough with children," Zeke called out to get Bandana's attention away from the boy. "Why don't you try to intimidate me?"

Bandana grew angry. He turned away from Matt and Billy and came toward Zeke, his eyes full of rage and malice but something else, too. Zeke recognized it as fear. "Drop the backpacks to the ground!" Bandana shouted while keeping his eyes on Zeke.

Everyone but Zeke complied.

"You with the army gun," Bandana said to Zeke. "Remove it *slowly*."

Zeke removed the M4 from his shoulder and laid it carefully on the ground.

"Now the backpack," Bandana said.

Zeke dropped the backpack to the ground.

"Now move away," the man ordered. "And get those hands up!"

Zeke backed away a few steps, but kept his hands to his side, waiting for an opportunity to grab his M9 auto from the holster under his sweater.

"I said hands up!" the man shouted. "Unless you want to talk to Jihad here!"

Zeke reluctantly raised his hands above his head. "You have a name for your gun?" Zeke said, trying not to laugh. "Didn't that habit die out centuries ago?"

"Shut up!" Bandana said.

Another man, younger, also with long, scraggily hair came from somewhere behind them. He grabbed the M4 from the ground and strapped it over his shoulder with a proud look on his face.

"Search 'em, Kyle!" Bandana said, never taking his eyes off of Zeke. "Save army boy here for last!"

Kyle searched the pockets of Margolian, Stover, and the two Albrights, careful to keep his distance from the German Shepherd. He found nothing of interest in the pockets of the boy and Margolian, but he returned to Bandana with the wallets belonging to Stover and Albright. As Kyle went through the contents of the wallets, he sighed with disappointment at not finding any cash. "Man, there's nothing here but credit cards!"

Bandana started to say something when Zeke said, "What's the problem? Don't know where any ATMs are here in the wilderness?"

Bandana narrowed his eyes at Zeke. "Did I say you could speak, army boy?"

"I didn't know I needed permission from a loser like you," Zeke said, hoping it would rile the man into approaching him.

"Okay, tough guy!" Bandana said while striding toward Zeke. "Get on your knees! Now!"

"You want me to pray?" Zeke said before chuckling. "To you?"

Bandana, now enraged, marched closer to Zeke. He shoved the shotgun into Zeke's chest. "DOWN!" The sound and movement was enough for Billy to let loose a loud growl, causing Bandana to turn his head toward the dog for just a second, plenty of time for Zeke to force away the shotgun in an upward motion with his left arm while simultaneously driving his right fist directly into the bridge of Bandana's nose. Zeke jerked the shotgun out of his hands as Bandana fell backwards to the ground with blood already pouring from his nostrils.

As Zeke stood above groaning and bleeding bandana man, he turned to look at a panicking Kyle who struggled with trying to fire the M4.

Billy stopped growling and was now trotting in circles around Bandana while Kyle searched for the M4's safety switch. Zeke took his time in approaching him, knowing that even if Kyle found the safety switch he still had to cock the lever, a task that Kyle didn't seem to have a clue about. Before Zeke reached him, Kyle tossed the M4 to the ground with a terrified look on his face and ran away back up the road.

When Zeke returned to Bandana, the man had removed the cloth from his head and was using it to stop the flow of blood pouring from his broken nose. "You want to live or die?" Zeke asked while waving the shotgun toward him.

The man looked up at Zeke. His eyes were watering. "Live," he said.

Zeke stared down at him. After a long pause he said, "You know where we can find a working vehicle?"

The man shook his head.

"That's too bad," Zeke said with a click of one of the shotgun's hammers.

"Ford F-150 down there," the man said in a nasal voice as he pointed down the road with the bloody bandana. "Keys are in it."

"Okay," Zeke said, gesturing for the man to take off after his younger buddy. "If I see either one of you again I'll kill you both."

The man struggled to his feet and trotted away up the dirt road in the same direction Kyle had headed earlier. Zeke glanced at Albright who now had his arm around his son's shoulders, a look of solemn appreciation on his face as he looked at Zeke.

"You think there really is a truck down there?" Stover asked.

Zeke picked up the wallets on the ground. "Let's go find out," he said while handing the wallets back to the men. He glanced at Matt while putting on his M4 and backpack. "You did a good job back there taking care of Billy. Thanks."

Matt shrugged without saying anything.

After strapping on their backpacks, everyone followed Zeke down the steep trail. Around a bend they saw the Ford pickup, an older model with faded blue paint. After examining the interior and seeing the keys in the ignition, Zeke placed the shotgun behind the seat before heading to the rear of the truck and lowering the tailgate. "Up!" he commanded Billy. The dog jumped into the truck bed and was soon followed my Matt. Albright was heading to the passenger side of the cab when Zeke said, "Why don't you ride in back with your son. I'd like to talk to Paul and the doctor if you don't mind."

Albright didn't like it but he climbed into the truck bed as Zeke closed the tailgate and tossed in his backpack. Zeke got behind the wheel, placing the M4 on the floorboard as Margolian sat next to him. Stover took the passenger side spot in the cab. Zeke started the ignition, put the transmission in gear, and drove a short distance up the trail until he found a spot to turn around.

After driving for some distance in their intended direction, the trail widened into a dirt road that could be handled easily by the Ford pickup truck. Zeke drove in silence, keeping his eye out for any of Bandana's friends who might try to ambush them.

Margolian finally broke the silence. "You handled those ruffians well back there," he said in a serious tone. "I've been in similar circumstances before and I have to admit I couldn't have handled the situation any better myself."

Zeke glanced over at Stover sitting on the other side of the renown archeologist. They both shared a quick smile before Zeke returned his eyes to the road and said, "Thanks, Doc."

"You're quite welcome."

With some of the ice broken, Stover decided to initiate a conversation with Margolian. "So Doctor Margolian," he began, "what was the subject of your work, before everything happened?"

Margolian didn't hesitate to answer. "Probably the most important archeological discovery in history."

"Are you serious?"

"Do you know the word *Nephilim?*" Margolian asked.

Stover paused for a moment. "Fallen angels?" he finally said.

"Very good," Margolian said. "The Hebrew word translates as *'rejects'* or *'fallen ones.'* Many believe that the translation in the Greek Septuagint means *'giants,'* but I disagree. I believe it means *'earthborn.'* Anyway, throughout the Bible, the word nephilim seems to be used with those fallen angels *or* their offspring with the earthly women—the ones mentioned in Genesis 6, Numbers 13, and other books of the Bible."

"Giants," Stover said. "Like Goliath."

"Yes," Margolian said. "Goliath of Gath. A descendant of the Nephilim."

Stover thought for a moment before asking, "Are you saying you discovered evidence of giants?"

"If I say yes, will you believe me?"

Zeke butted in with a question of his own. "What does it matter if we believe you or not?"

Margolian hesitated. "You're right," he said. "It doesn't matter. Without the evidence in my possession what I say really doesn't matter."

"What *you* believe does matter," Stover said. "It matters to me." He saw a small smile grow on Margolian's weathered face with that shock of curly white hair on top. The archeologist reminded him of an elderly Harpo Marx.

"That's nice of you to say," Margolian said. "So let me ask you something."

Zeke just drove, glad to stay out of the conversation for the moment, wondering if Margolian was going to say he'd found giant skeletons buried somewhere in the Middle East.

"Have you ever read the Book of Enoch?" Margolian asked Stover.

"No, but I've heard about it," Stover said.

"You've probably heard that the reason it wasn't canonized into the Bible as holy scripture was because it wasn't divinely inspired," Margolian said. "Am I right?"

"Yes."

"But any scholarly research will reveal that the early church fathers accepted it entirely, especially its reference to the *Watchers*—angels who made a pact with one another to go to Earth in human form for the sole purpose of having relations with women, thus performing a great sin against God. Until the third century, the church supported the idea of this other group of fallen angels, the *Nephilim*, the ones Enoch called the *Watchers*. Then, due to the influence of one of the church fathers, the idea seemed to be rejected, or at least downplayed to a great degree."

"I know the story of these fallen angels and their giant offspring are mentioned in the Bible," Stover said. "I just don't remember exactly where at the moment."

"Yes," Margolian said patiently. "As I said before, the Book of Genesis and the Book of Numbers in the Torah. But also through Enoch and other secular sources."

"So," Stover said, "what's this have to do with your discovery?"

"I'm getting there," Margolian said. "Just be patient. Can I have a drink?"

Stover started reaching for the water container at his feet.

"In the words of W. C. Fields," Margolian said. "Water is for bathing. Got anything with more substance to it?"

Zeke smiled and reached for the flask of whiskey in a leg pocket. He handed the flask to Margolian. "Try this."

The archeologist's face lit up. "Yes!" he exclaimed. "That's more like it!" He unscrewed the flask and took a big gulp. He exhaled after swallowing the warm liquor, his face revealing maximum satisfaction. Zeke and Stover shared a quick smile.

"You were saying?" Stover prodded Margolian. "Your discovery?"

"Yes," Margolian said before taking another swig of whiskey. "Enoch."

"Noah's grandfather," Stover said.

"Great-grandfather," Margolian corrected him.

Zeke spoke up. "This Enoch, Noah's great-grandfather. Are we talking about *the* Noah? As in Noah of Noah's ark?"

"Yes," Margolian and Stover both answered at the same time.

"Good," Zeke said. "At least I'm following something here."

"You see," Margolian explained, ignoring Zeke's comment, "these descendants of the fallen angels so corrupted Earth's inhabitants that God decided to destroy all the nephilim and humans on the planet except for Noah and his family."

"That's correct," Stover said.

"Okay, let's move on," Margolian said. "In the Jewish writings known as the Book of Jubilees, a story is told of Kainam, Noah's grandson, who after the Great Flood came upon a writing that *'men of old'* had carved on a rock. The writings contained certain teachings of the Watchers, teachings in accordance with the methods they used to observe the omens of the moon, sun, and all the signs of heaven. Kainam then copied the teachings carved on the rock and held onto them in secret."

Margolian paused to take another gulp of whiskey. Zeke reached over and took back the flask before asking, "Why in secret?"

"Why?" Margolian said in disbelief.

Zeke glanced at Stover and said, "Can you bring me up to speed on this story? You have an *ancient-biblical-knowledge-for-dummies* type of explanation?"

Stover laughed. "Okay," he said. "I'll try. Before the creation of Man, an archangel named Lucifer rebelled against God, causing God to cast him and a third of the angels out of heaven. Sometime later, God created Adam and Eve in the Garden of Eden. Lucifer, now known as Satan, came to Eve as a serpent and tempted her and Adam into sinning against God, hence, the fall of man. Humans would now toil and hunger and know death, something that was not in God's original plan for humankind. As descendants of Adam and Eve began populating the Earth, God sent angels to minister and council to the toiling humans. But certain groups of these angels lusted after earthly women and slept with them, sinning against God in this unholy union. The offspring from this unholy union being the giants we're talking about."

"So there was a *second* group of angels that fell from heaven," Zeke said.

"They were actually sent," Margolian said while gesturing for the flask in Zeke's hand. Zeke handed it to him.

"That's right," Stover said. "But after these angelic beings fornicated with human women, they were booted out of heaven, so yes, they was a second group of angels that fell from heaven. And the offspring of these angels and the women of Earth were . . . different."

Margolian chuckled in agreement before taking a healthy snort of whiskey from the flask. "Yes, you could say that."

"In what ways were they different?" Zeke asked.

"Well, for starters," Stover began, "they were larger physically. Much larger, I would guess. Giants. Like Goliath. The Bible described his height in cubits; roughly about nine and a half feet tall."

Margolian nodded in agreement. "The Book of Numbers describes the dimensions of the bed belonging to Og, King of Bashan, at over fifteen feet in length."

"And I suppose they were superior to humans in many ways," Stover went on. "After all, they were descended from angelic beings from heaven. But apparently they were wicked, evil at heart, one of the negative results of their angelic fathers sinning against God—something I'm sure we don't understand fully. Anyway, these giants influenced the world to such a sinful state that God decided to destroy life and start all over."

"The Flood," Zeke said.

"Yes. So God found one righteous man on Earth, Noah, and instructed him to build the ark."

Margolian butted in. "And Noah believed the Watchers were to blame for the condition of humanity and God's decision to create the flood."

"And this is why Noah's grandson kept the stone carving secret?" Zeke said.

"Yes," Margolian said. "He feared punishment from Noah. The Book of Jubliees states that after the flood, Noah constantly warned his entire clan from having any dealings with the Watchers or their descendants."

Zeke thought about this for a moment before saying, "So obviously, the flood did not destroy the Watchers or their offspring."

"No," Margolian said. "Not all of them."

"Angels are spirit beings," Stover said. "These Watcher's offspring are half-human-being from their mother, but also half-angelic-being from their father."

"The Book of Jubilees states that their half-mortal bodies could be slain," Margolian said, "but their half-angel souls could not and that they wander in the spiritual dimension until the Final Judgement Day."

"Demons," said Zeke, not really believing any of this.

"Exactly," Margolian said. "The demonic world with its demonic spirits are the same as these Watcher spirits and their offspring."

Zeke couldn't resist it anymore. "And both of you believe all this about fallen angels and demons and their giant offspring?"

Stover said nothing. Margolian hesitated for just a moment before saying, "Yes."

"I'm surprised, Doctor Margolian," Zeke said. "I thought you were a man of science and grounded your beliefs according to scientific evidence."

Margolian straightened his posture in the seat. "I am a man of science," he declared. "And my beliefs *are* grounded in scientific evidence."

Zeke kept pressing the archeologist, hoping to make him crack, if for no other reason than to jar his memories and bring him back to reality. "If this rock carving Noah's grandson found had all these teachings of the Watchers carved into it, wouldn't the rock have to be huge? I mean really huge! Unless of course, the Watchers' skills included micro-engraving."

"Ha-ha," Margolian said. "That would be a very clever thought and I would be laughing in earnest if I hadn't had the same thought hundreds of times, probably while you were still pooping in your diaper."

Zeke raised his eyebrows, amused by the comment.

"First of all," Margolian explained, "the rock he referred to could have been extremely large, like the side of a cliff. I personally do not believe this, though. Anyway, whatever its size, Kainam copied the teachings so he could take them with him and study them in secret. Now, we also know this: scholars researching Jewish writings found in various caves of Qumran, known to the world as the *Dead Sea Scrolls*, have revealed that Kainam was the brother of Chesed, father of Ur, the man who founded the famous Chaldean city of Ur in what you may know as ancient Mesopotamia, the cradle of civilization, some like to say. The Chaldeans have amazed the entire world with their legendary wisdom, especially regarding divining future events from the signs of heaven. I admit it was tempting to conclude that this fact alone suggested that this legendary wisdom of the Chaldeans was the result of supernatural knowledge learned from the Watchers and passed down through generations by Kainam, grandson of Noah, but that was not enough to *prove* it to me."

"Then what *proved* it to you?" asked Zeke.

"When I found Kainam's copy," Margolian said nonchalantly. "Carved into seven stone tablets or tiles stacked together."

"You actually found them?" Stover said in amazement.

"Yes. They were found along with many other artifacts."

"How old are they?" asked Zeke.

"Carbon fourteen dating is not accurate beyond five thousand years," Margolian said, "but along with the other artifacts, I'd guess it to be from somewhere earlier than three thousand BCE." He waited for a moment before saying, "Aren't you going to ask me about the other artifacts?"

"A skeleton of a giant," Zeke said quickly.

"That's right," Margolian said. "But other skeletal remains buried near it were just as amazing as the giant skeleton."

"Other remains?" asked Stover.

"One was reptilian in nature, similar to some prehistoric dinosaur fossils I have seen in museums but smaller and more humanoid than the fossils. Other remains were about the size of human children but with extremely large heads. All of them hideous." Margolian's expression fell a few notches before he regained control of his emotions.

"You have to admit, Dr. Margolian," Zeke said, "that this is a lot to take in all at once. Take this giant skeleton for starters. How do you know it didn't belong to a large mammal, like a giant ape, or a Bigfoot or something?"

Margolian chuckled. "I like the Bigfoot part," he said. "I haven't made that comparison before. But concerning the question about it belonging to a large mammal, I think it is a moot point since it was still wearing its bronze armor, including a helmet the size of a sixteen-gallon keg of beer."

Zeke almost laughed. This man was certainly suffering from some form of mental delusions, despite how intelligent and eloquent he spoke.

"How big are we talking?" Stover suddenly asked. "In height?"

"Slightly over eleven feet from head to toe."

Silence filled the cab of the pickup.

"Look," Margolian said. "I wish I could say that I really don't care if you believe my story or not. But the truth is, I do care. But it's like I said before, without the evidence on display for the world to see, it doesn't really matter, does it?"

"Then why do you care if we believe you or not?" asked Zeke.

"Because I need your help," came the answer.

"Help with what?" Zeke asked.

"Help with recovering those artifacts, particularly Kainam's tablets."

"But we are in Texas," Zeke said. "Not Mesopotamia."

"I know," Margolian mumbled to himself.

"Why are the tablets more important than the other artifacts?" Stover asked. "What did they reveal?"

"Dates."

"Dates of what?" asked Stover. "Dates on the Hebrew calendar?"

"No, they were signs of the heavens," Margolian said. "Alignments of stars and planets, constellations, and other astronomical events in the galaxies."

Zeke and Stover glanced at each other but said nothing.

"We didn't proceed far enough to reveal all the dates," Margolian explained. "But we deciphered all the first tablet and most of the rest."

"What were they about?" asked Stover.

"According to the introduction," Margolian said, "the dates marked major events of the fallen ones here on Earth—changes in their strategies, eras where their influence would take great leaps among the human race."

"Have these dates already occurred?" Stover asked.

"Many have," Margolian answered, his tone turning more serious. "But there are more coming in the days ahead."

"How soon?" this time from Zeke.

"In the near future," Margolian said, his expression revealing a bit of confusion with the subject. "I don't remember any exact dates."

"And how do you connect these astronomical events to our calendar?" Zeke asked. "Or to any calendar, for that matter."

"Before Johannes Kepler," Margolian said, "the great mathematician of the seventeenth century, it was virtually impossible. Observers of the night sky could only record the movements in the heavens over accumulated observances through multiple lifetimes, like ancient Egyptians, Mayans, and other cultures did over centuries. Even after Kepler had published his Laws of Planetary Motion, it was a daunting task to calculate these alignments to the calendar by hand, with pen and ink. But now, even a simple laptop can perform this task in fractions of a second."

They drove in silence for several minutes, each contemplating his own thoughts. Margolian finally broke the silence. "Throughout my entire career I never believed in any of this I'm telling you. It was all mythology as far as I was concerned, but mythology from a culture I was very interested in. All that changed after our discovery."

"Our?" Zeke said.

"My team and I," Margolian said. "One of the world's leading paleontologists was a member. Another was an anthropologist renown for her work around the globe. Also one of the world's leading astronomers. About twelve people in all, including the hired locals on site. It wasn't just me like some *Indiana Jones* character. That's not how modern archeology works."

"So where do you think your team is now?" Stover asked.

"Well, that's the sixty-four-thousand dollar question, isn't it?" Margolian said with a sad smile. "How did I get here . . . in Texas of all places? And the most important part: Why?"

"You said you were captured," Zeke said. "Where did your captors take you? Do you think it was somewhere in the Middle East, or here in Texas?"

"Neither," Margolian said in a dark tone of voice.

Zeke knew the archeologist wasn't telling everything he knew, even if he was stark raving mad and had made up the entire story in his head.

They drove silently for another couple of minutes until Margolian said, "Can we pull over for a bit? I need to relieve myself."

Zeke pulled the Ford to a stop and stepped out. "Pee break," he announced. He lowered the tailgate for Billy and the Albrights before walking a short distance to relieve his own bladder. After zipping up he returned to the Ford where Stover stood outside the door. "What do you think?" Stover asked. "You think he's out of his mind?"

"If it weren't for the fact that you know who he is," Zeke said, "the famous archeologist and all, I'd say he had probably escaped from some mental hospital nearby."

Stover didn't respond.

Zeke said, "Do you believe his story?"

Stover looked Zeke squarely in the eyes. After a long moment he said, "I believe that he believes his story is true."

"I guess the real question for me is not about his sanity," Zeke said.

"Then what?"

"The possibility of a race of giants once roaming the Earth," Zeke said. "Giants that descended from fallen angels who caused God to flood the world. All that stuff in the Bible. That's what is hard for me to believe."

"It really doesn't matter if it's hard to believe," Stover said. "If the truth is the truth, it doesn't matter how hard it is to believe."

Before Zeke had time to respond, Albright suddenly returned to the Ford. "I want to thank you, Zeke," he said. "For taking care of us back there."

"Just doing my job," Zeke said. "What I'm paid to do."

Stover moved away to give them some privacy.

"Yes," Albright said. "I guess so. Still want to thank you, though. We could have been killed by those hoodlums."

"It's always possible," Zeke said, amused by the word *hoodlums*.

"What a shame to be killed for a few worthless credit cards."

"Your credit cards are no good?" Zeke asked with a smile.

Albright smiled back. "You know what I mean."

"Don't forget," Zeke said. "I've got quite a bit of cash stashed on my person and belongings."

"Yeah, I know," Albright said. "But I got a feeling anyone would have their hands full trying to take it from you."

"Let's hope so," Zeke said while returning to the cab of the Ford. "You want to ride up front for a while? I'm sure Paul or the Doctor would be more than willing to trade spots with you."

"No, that's okay," Albright said. "I'm actually enjoying spending time with Matt."

They continued on down the dirt road with Stover and Margolian in the cab next to Zeke and the two Albrights in back with Billy, just as before. Zeke thought about the oddities of everything going on these days. *Was this EMP attack—or whatever it was—an attack from America's enemies or by aliens from another dimension who are hunting for Albright and some knowledge he possesses? Now we got a world famous archeologist who thinks he should still be in the Middle East digging up evidence of giants, descendants of fallen angels from heaven that did the naughty with earthly women. There was even more to the story: Reptilian humanoids and little creatures with big heads buried along with the giant still dressed in his gigantic bronze armor. And somehow this world famous archeologist just magically appeared in a rural mountainous area in West Texas and ran into me in the wilderness.* Zeke's head felt like it was going to explode.

An hour later he stopped the Ford again. He dug his maps out of his backpack and estimated their general location, figuring the highway was only four or five miles away. He decided to change their game plan. It seemed fairly obvious that Albright's pursuers—either human or alien—were not nipping at their heels, and if they were they didn't seem to be in a hurry to apprehend them. If Albright was correct in his assumption that the pursuers hadn't figured out his identity yet, it was all the more reason to enact his new plan.

"Listen up," Zeke told the others. "The plan has changed."

Albright and Stover gave him concerned looks. Margolian looked unconcerned.

"We're going to drive toward the highway," he explained while pointing to a spot on the topo map. "Before we get there I'm going to scout the highway, and if it looks clear we're going to take it all the way to Interstate 10." Zeke looked up from the map and met Albright's stare before returning his attention to the map. "If the highway is *not* clear we'll find a crossing somewhere and proceed to this route to cross the Delawares, the same plan as before."

As Zeke folded the map and returned it to his backpack, Stover said, "Won't we be spotted on the highway?"

"I'll check it out first," Zeke assured him.

"And what about fuel?" Albright asked. "The truck is half empty."

"Which also means it's half full," Zeke said with a wan smile.

Albright started to say something but Zeke cut him off, "Look, the faster we move the better. That bandit business back there was definitely bizarre but that's how life is. Always expect the unexpected. We all need to keep that in mind in the future. And as a far as gasoline goes, we'll just have to improvise with the situation as it unfolds."

Albright watched his son playing with Billy a few yards off the road, oblivious to the decisions being made regarding their travel plans. "Sounds good to me, Zeke," he said. "Lead the way."

Stover nodded. "Yes, lead the way, Kemosabe."

"Ah, from the Lone Ranger, I believe," Zeke said.

"Yes," Stover said.

"Kemosabe is an Indian word for trusted scout," Margolian said, suddenly joining the conversation.

"Really?" Zeke asked.

Stover said, "Actually, I think it means horse's rear-end." He chuckled with that staccato laughter of his. "A little inside joke between the television writers, I think."

"Well," Zeke said with a chuckle of his own. "Both definitions seem to apply to me."

Twenty minutes later Zeke pulled the Ford off the road and parked it behind a small grove of juniper. The position was hidden from the road but it enabled them to regain the dirt road if necessary. He turned off the engine. The ridge of mountain before him was the spot he'd been looking for. A gentle breeze blew through the opened windows of the Ford as everyone climbed out. He grabbed his M4 and backpack, then gave his M9 handgun to Albright. "I won't be long. If someone confronts you, use it. If you're not sure, fire a warning shot into the air. I won't be far away. Agreed?"

"Agreed," Albright said.

Zeke took off for the ridge with an unleashed Billy running beside him. They traversed the incline of the ridge, making good time despite all the loose rock. Zeke pushed himself hard, enjoying the physical exertion, his controlled breathing in rhythm with his movements.

He finally reached a good spot to survey the landscape before him. The highway snaked around the foot of the mountain less than two miles away. North, to his left, the highway wound its way beyond the horizon. It looked barren and devoid of any human traffic. To the south was a different story. Much to his surprise, perhaps three of four miles in the distance he saw a roadblock. Through his binoculars he could barely make out several vehicles with maybe a half dozen men wearing olive drab uniforms. The Corn Ranch facility wasn't too far away. *Are the space-vehicle yuppies somehow involved in all the crazy stuff going on?*

Zeke had begun to seriously doubt Albright's belief that they were being chased. Until now. *Why were troops, military or nonmilitary, guarding the highway out here in the middle of nowhere?* If this crisis was truly nationwide, the heavily populated urban centers would be the main focus of attention for the authorities. Resources and personnel would be scarce enough for that task, leaving little attention for the wide expanses of rural areas, especially in this part of West Texas. But there they were. Whoever they were.

Zeke scanned the terrain on the northeast side of the highway. He studied the topo map, alternating between his binoculars and the map until satisfied he had the correct ranch road in sight. He moved to a different location on the ridge to get a better view of the southern section of highway. He searched for sentries on this side of the roadblock, or any electronic monitoring of the section of highway he intended to cross. He saw nothing out of the ordinary. No state-of-the-art military surveillance equipment appeared to be in use at the moment, at least as far as he could tell. Maybe the EMP had caused more damage to the military's sophisticated monitoring gear than he thought, or maybe this roadblock—like the roadblock near the Mangas Bridge—was not part of the United States of America's military establishment at all, covert or otherwise. Either way, he and the others would have to take their chances in crossing the highway onto the dirt ranch road cutting through the wild terrain ahead.

Zeke backtracked down the ridge with Billy out in front. As soon as he was able, Zeke aimed the binoculars toward the grove of trees hiding the Ford pickup truck. Everything looked normal. He hadn't heard the report of the M9 left with Albright. That was good. So he wondered why he felt so uneasy with the situation. Something *felt* wrong. Billy seemed to be experiencing some anxiety, too. The dog's actions were a little more frantic than usual; a trait Zeke had observed many times in the past and had learned not to ignore.

Zeke commanded Billy to halt. While listening for anything out of the ordinary, he squatted and fastened the leash to Billy's harness. That's when he heard it. Zeke and Billy remained motionless beside a rock outcropping halfway down the slope of the ridge. They were well hidden yet still able to see the dull-green '94 Chevrolet pickup truck cruising down the dirt road. Zeke focused the binoculars at the cab of the Chevy and made out a single driver that appeared to be an old farmer or rancher wearing an old-style hunting cap; the type depicted in so many Norman Rockwell paintings Zeke had seen over his lifetime. The Chevy cruised slowly down the dirt road, toward the highway, seemingly unaware of Albright or the Ford pickup hidden just off the road. It continued on, driving past the ridge until out of Zeke's view.

As much as he wanted to check on Albright and the others, Zeke wanted to see what the Chevy did when it reached the highway. He unleashed Billy and quickly scrambled back to his previous vantage point, hoping he'd see which direction the Chevy headed once it reached the highway. If there were any hidden patrols, he would soon find out.

When he reached the position, Zeke scanned the area with the binoculars and saw nothing. The Chevy pickup was nowhere to be seen. He scurried back to his original site, the one that gave the best view of the roadblock miles distant. The scene at the roadblock looked the same as it had earlier. A section of highway was out of view, so he waited to see if the Chevy appeared out of the blind spot while heading toward the roadblock. He waited, and waited some more, allowing enough time for the slow-driving Chevy to come into view. But it did not.

Zeke turned the binoculars back to the dirt road across the highway, hoping to see a dirt cloud or even some fresh tracks made by the Chevy. The distance was too great to make out any tracks but there was definitely no plume or cloud of dry soil made from the wake of a vehicle. *Could I have missed it? Not likely. Unless the Chevy had sped up when out of sight and hauled butt to some location I couldn't see from the ridge.* It seemed that the old truck and its Norman Rockwell driver had just vanished without a trace.

Zeke hauled his own butt double-time down the slope, eager to find Stover and the rest of his little group. When he got to an open area visible from the dirt road, he increased his gait to a run while keeping an eye out for anyone coming down the road. Billy was out in the lead, almost at the grove of trees when Matt came into view. His dad came out next, followed by a smiling Stover with his bald head reflecting the sun's rays. Margolian was sitting on the ground, examining a small rock in his fingertips.

Matt became alarmed when he saw Zeke and Billy running toward them. "What's wrong?"

Zeke slowed his pace as he drew near. "Everyone good?"

"Yeah, I guess," Matt said.

"What's up?" Stover asked.

Zeke took his time to catch his breath. He leaned against his knees and breathed steadily. After taking a sip of water from his nearly empty water bladder, he said, "So the driver didn't spot you?"

Albright or Stover didn't answer. Zeke saw them shoot a look at each other. Stover finally said, "What driver, Zeke?"

"The driver of that green Chevy pickup truck that just drove by a few minutes ago."

Albright and Stover shared another look. This time Albright said, "We didn't see any truck, Zeke."

"You didn't hear it driving down the road?"

Albright and Stover shook their heads.

Zeke turned to the archeologist sitting on the ground.

Margolian returned Zeke's stare with a sly smile. "Didn't see a thing, sir."

"Did you all go somewhere?" Zeke asked no one in particular, becoming a bit frustrated. "Take a little stroll or something?"

Albright picked up on Zeke's frustration. "No, Zeke. We never left this spot."

"Yeah, Mr. Allenby," Matt added. "We stayed here just like you told us."

Zeke examined everyone's eyes. They were telling the truth, which didn't help his understanding of the situation. "But no one saw or heard a vehicle," he said while pointing in the direction of the dirt road less than thirty yards away.

Head shakes from everyone except from Margolian who was still examining the rock in his fingers.

Zeke walked the short distance to the dirt road. He squatted to examine it more closely. To his left, he saw the Ford's tracks left earlier before driving off the road to its hidden position. To his right—where he saw the Chevy pickup driving a short while earlier—were only the timeworn impressions created by various vehicles over the years. But no fresh tire tracks.

Zeke walked a length of the road, unable to except what he was seeing. He returned to the others in the grove. They stood in silence, staring at him with a mix of curiosity and concern in their expressions.

"So . . . you saw a truck?" Stover asked. "Are you sure?"

Zeke didn't respond. He caught Margolian staring at him. "What?" he asked the archeologist in an irritable tone.

Margolian continued staring for a few more moments. "Does it really matter if anyone believes you or not?" he finally said. "You know what you saw, right?"

Touche, Zeke thought to himself, getting Margolian's point. He decided not to answer the question. "Let's just load up and get out of here."

Albright asked, "Is the highway clear?"

Zeke didn't feel like explaining anything. "No, we're continuing off road."

They loaded up, but this time Zeke had Albright and his son ride with him in the cab to give them a break from the bumpy ride in back, and to give him a break from the gloating archeologist. Stover rode in back with Margolian and Billy while Zeke drove the Ford on down the dirt road.

A few minutes later he slowed as they neared the junction of the highway. They were traveling downwind and Zeke didn't want a cloud of dust blowing over the highway when they neared. He drove over the asphalt at a casual speed, veering the Ford slightly to the left until entering the continuation of the dirt road on the other side.

The dirt road meandered across fairly level ground for several miles until reaching more rugged terrain. The Delaware Mountains loomed in the distance. Hopefully, he'd find a route around them by another ranch road where *maybe* they could reach some paved stretch of road heading east. If not, they'd have to get through the mountains; a difficult if not impossible task for the Ford. But if he could find a way around the mountains and get to a ranch road that led to the Interstate, it would save a whole lot of time and trouble. There were still other factors, though: *If* they had enough gas to get there, *if* they could find more gas on the way, *if* there were no more roadblocks once they got there. *A whole lot of ifs.*

When they were less than a mile from the rise of steep terrain facing them, Zeke stopped the Ford and killed the engine. Everyone climbed out and stretched their leg muscles. A cool wind howled around them. Zeke eyed a dark line of clouds behind them in the far western horizon. They still had several hours of daylight left. *At least we'll have fresh water when the rain comes.*

Zeke knew they needed to find camp, but they were too out in the open for his likes. He located a spot through his binoculars, maybe two hundred yards to the north, a draw or small canyon lined with oaks. At the head of the draw was a good choice for camp; level ground above the draw, fairly hidden by the trees, close to the dirt road if they needed to make a hasty escape. When the rain came, he'd have plastic traps ready to fill their water containers.

Zeke got back in the Ford and cranked the ignition. He glanced at the fuel gauge with its needle wavering around the three-eighths mark. He turned to see his little entourage standing near the truck, staring at him with blank looks on their faces. "Follow me," he shouted out the window.

Zeke veered the Ford off the dirt road and headed toward the draw on the rocky, uneven ground surrounding the road. He crept slowly, maneuvering around trees and the biggest of rocks scattered about. He glanced in his mirror and saw everybody walking at a steady pace fifty feet behind. Billy was trotting alongside the Ford, his gait alternating between fast sprints and short pauses to sniff the ground along the way. Zeke pumped the gas pedal as the Ford jerked and bounced over the roughest spots. It wasn't a smooth as he'd hoped. So much for a speedy getaway.

The terrain leveled off a bit and Zeke sped up until reaching the spot he'd chosen. He examined the area for more details before turning the Ford around and backing it underneath a large overhanging oak branch running parallel with the bed of the pickup truck. He killed the engine and stepped out as Billy patrolled the site. The spot was perfect. They'd use the large overhanging oak branch to drape their plastic trash bags, creating a tent-like covering over the truck bed for protection from the rain when it arrived. A dry place to sleep was always better than a wet one.

Zeke was already unloading materials from his backpack when the others arrived. After explaining to them how to overlap the large plastic trash bags to form the tent covering over the truck bed and securing it with duct tape, he went to work on crafting a contraption to collect rainwater. He grabbed an empty one-gallon plastic water jug from behind the seat of the Ford where he'd found it earlier. He cut off the top of the jug and positioned it on the ground near the most exposed part of the Ford in front of the hood and grill. He crafted a makeshift water collection contraption from more plastic trash bags and duct tape. Attaching the plastic to the side mirrors with the tape, he created a V-shape that would channel the rainwater into the jug below.

Matt had been collecting tinder and firewood for a campfire, so when Zeke finished helping Albright, Stover, and Margolian make the plastic tent covering for the truck bed, he walked over to the boy to see how he was doing with the campfire. The western sky was growing darker due to the storm front heading their direction, creating a strange greenish hue to the sky above. Zeke squatted next to Matt as a distant peal of thunder rolled toward them from the west. "How's it coming along, Matt?"

"Good," Matt said while focused on roughing up the nest of juniper bark and dry twigs in his hands.

Zeke watched for another few seconds before rising to his feet. "You're doing a fine job, Matt."

"Thanks," said Matt.

Zeke walked back to the Ford, feeling that something was bothering the boy. He believed he knew why. He remembered the look on Matt's face after the potential robbers surprised them on the dirt road, when the man in the bandana pointed a shotgun toward them. Zeke remembered glancing at the boy and seeing the fear and the tears streaming down his cheeks, natural for that type of situation. *Was the boy feeling ashamed for being afraid?* He knew he needed to talk to Matt about it when the time was right. And now was not the right time with a storm riding down on them and camp not set up.

Zeke helped Albright and Stover tape spots of the plastic trash bag tent to the lip of the truck bed. Stover, Margolian, and the two Albrights would sleep underneath the plastic tent while Zeke would make his bed in the cab, along with his backpack and M4 carbine. Billy would have to spend the night underneath the truck.

The rain started as a drizzle an hour later. They had already wolfed down their MREs next to the campfire that Matt had made with his own hands, and were preparing the sleeping bags in the truck bed when the wind began to pick up. Zeke checked the edges of the plastic tent covering, making sure they were well secured in case the wind increased over the course of the evening.

Albright, Stover, and Margolian decided to call it day. Matt told his dad he would be there in a few minutes. The three adults had no interest in getting wet so they climbed in their respective sleeping bags as the raindrops filtering through the towering oak tree above them dripped onto the plastic covering the truck bed.

Zeke joined Matt at the campfire. The drizzle halted for a while even though distant rumbles of thunder increased in frequency and proximity. The boy stared into the flames while toying with a stick in his hands. Zeke sat down and stared into the flames, waiting for Matt to start a conversation. The boy seemed aloof. Zeke figured the shock from the attempted robbery—along with the traveling conditions over the last several days—was probably setting in right about now. The boy definitely had that faraway look in his eyes; what soldiers called the *thousand-mile-stare*.

Zeke broke the silence. "How ya doin,' Matt?"

"Okay."

Zeke waited for a while before saying, "You did a fine job back there. You're a brave boy."

"Yeah?" Matt said while still staring into the flames.

"Yeah," Zeke said. "I've been in many serious scrapes with soldiers who were not nearly as brave as you." Zeke caught a slight hint of smile trying to form on the boy's face.

"You're just saying that," said Matt.

"I don't *just say* anything," Zeke said in a firm voice. "If I say it, I mean it."

A short pause. Matt finally said, "Well, thanks. But I don't know of anything *brave* I did. The only thing I remember was just being scared."

"And that's exactly what I'm talking about," Zeke said. "Remember what I told you the first day we rode together? The bit about courage?"

The boy thought for a bit. "Yeah, sorta."

"Courage is how you handle yourself when you are scared," Zeke explained, "not because you are *not* afraid, but because you are."

Matt nodded.

"You handled yourself really good back there," Zeke said. "And even though you were frightened you did the right thing by hanging on to Billy. You kept your head and didn't panic and we all got out of the situation alive. That's what I call bravery, son."

Matt's face brightened a bit.

"The reason soldiers are put through so much training is so they will *know* what to do," Zeke said, "and follow their mind instead of their *feelings*. It's like being chased by a bear. You're almost at your cabin where its thick walls and iron door will protect you. You *know* you will get inside long before the bear reaches you, but you still *feel* frightened. Even after you're safe inside, your body might be shaking like a leaf. You *know* you are safe, but you still *feel* scared from the incident. Courageous acts are performed when you don't let your emotions overtake your mind— when you do what you *know* instead of what you *feel*." That make sense, Matt?"

Matt finally turned to make eye contact with Zeke. "Yes, sir," the boy replied. "Thanks, Mr. Allenby."

"Call me Zeke."

"Okay, Zeke," Matt said with a small smile. "But I'll probably still call you Mr. Allenby when Dad's around."

"Okay, no problem," Zeke said, happy the boy was *trying* to come out of his shell.

The boy toyed with the fire, his spirits raised slightly, but he seemed to be falling back into his introspective state.

Zeke chose his words carefully. "I want to tell you something, Matt."

"Okay."

"Look at me," Zeke said, waiting until the boy made eye contact. "I want you to know that I'm going to get you and your dad to Austin. Home, remember?"

Matt nodded, his eyes reflecting some rekindled hope along with the flames of the campfire.

"It not be easy," Zeke continued, "but we'll get there. We may have more adventures along the way but I will get you guys there safe and sound, come hell or high water." Zeke paused to let his words sink in. "You trust me, don't you?"

"Yes, sir," Matt said. "I trust you."

"You know," Zeke added, "with a little luck we could be in Austin within a day or two. But you just remember what I told you. You've already proven that you are brave. And when the time comes, you will know how to use that courage. Copy that?"

The boy nodded. "Copy."

Zeke believed his words of encouragement were getting through to the boy. As an afterthought, Zeke said, "You'd make a fine special forces soldier, Matt."

Matt turned his attention back to the fire. After a short moment of silence he said, "You know, I'm not sure I want to be soldier anymore. Special forces or any other kind."

The situation was becoming clearer to Zeke. "That's okay," he said. "I actually think you're too smart for the job. You don't need to be humping around in the mud dodging bullets, looking for something soft to use to wipe your dirty hiney."

This made the boy laugh. "Is that what you've done?" he asked. "Looked for something soft to wipe your dirty hiney?"

Zeke laughed back. "Yes. Many times."

The boy's laughter died with a large yawn. Night time had arrived during their fireside chat. The sky was dark, the heavy cloud-cover blocking all starlight overhead.

"Why don't you get in your bag and get some sleep," Zeke suggested. "Tomorrow is going to be a long day. You need your rest."

Matt nodded while rising to his feet. "Okay."

Zeke accompanied the boy to the truck bed. He lifted the plastic flap hanging over the tail gate and helped Matt climb in. Stover rustled in his sleeping bag, scooting over slightly to make room for the boy. After Matt was in his sleeping bag, Zeke said goodnight and lowered the plastic over the edge of the tail gate. He went back to the fire and lowered himself into a cross-legged position. The drizzle came again but this time a little harder and steadier than before. He removed the plastic bag wrapped around his M4, poked a hole in the middle, and draped it over his head to form an improvised poncho. He pulled the hood of his sweater through the hole and over his ball cap before bringing the M4 to his lap underneath the plastic. Billy sauntered over to the truck and crawled underneath the bed.

Zeke added more wood to the fire. He heard water dripping into the jug, its gurgling sound mixing with the rain pattering against the plastic draped over his body. The flames in the campfire danced wildly as the wind picked up. Zeke lowered his face to the poncho as puffs of wood smoke blew into his face.

The wind and rain died down a short while later. Zeke had catnapped through most of it. A low growl from Billy woke him up. From the light of the campfire Zeke saw his dog standing near the truck and glaring into the darkness beyond the campsite. Zeke quietly released the safety on the M4 under his plastic poncho while turning his head slowly to the left. Billy growled again. A distant rumble of thunder roared across the terrain, echoing off the rock slopes a few miles in the distance. Zeke narrowed his eyes, still aiming them at the darkness ahead as Billy moved next to him, his chest rumbling with a low growl. Zeke's eyes were not adjusted to the dark due to the light of the campfire so he kept his head still to detect any motion; maybe a shadow moving among other shadows in the surrounding darkness. He heard some noises but the raindrops pattering on the plastic and the crackling of the burning wood in the fire made it difficult to discern the sounds. Billy's growling became more intense.

After several minutes of waiting, Zeke thought he detected some silhouettes fifty meters in front of him, toward the section of terrain he'd driven the Ford over earlier. With his M4 at the ready under the poncho, Zeke whispered several commands to keep Billy calm but alert. Suddenly, several lightning bolts in the sky flashed like a giant strobe light pulsing on and off, illuminating the area for a fraction of a second. The scene captured by the lightning flash was hard to believe.

A moment later the four riders on horseback crept forward into the light of the campfire. Billy's growl was slow and steady, just as it had been before the riders came into view. Zeke didn't move, his eyes staring at the riders and their horses. For a moment he wondered if it was all an apparition because he knew he wasn't dreaming. The riders were dressed in buckskins with long black braids falling to their shoulders. Their dark brown faces were painted with streaks of red and white. Even the horses were painted with some type of pigment, their leather bridles adorned with bird feathers and other Native American decorations. Several of the horses snorted while shuffling in place, their riders keeping tight grips on the leather reigns held in their hands.

After what seemed like an eternity Zeke heard himself say, "May I help you?"

One of the riders replied in a low baritone, "What are you doing here?"

"Sitting," said Zeke.

The rider didn't respond. He took a glimpse toward the truck and said, "Who's with you?"

"Three men and a boy."

The rider nodded and moved his mount a few steps closer to the campfire. Zeke saw that the Native American sitting bareback on his horse was a big man with powerful arms and chest stretching the buckskin covering them. "Whatcha packing under your poncho?" the big man asked.

"M4 carbine with a thirty round clip."

The big man nodded as if he'd known the answer. "You army?"

"Not anymore," Zeke said.

The big Native American cocked his head slightly. "What outfit?"

Zeke took his time to answer. "Seventy-fifth Rangers."

The big man thought before asking, "First Battalion?"

"Third," said Zeke.

"Did you know a Sgt. John Nahche?"

The name surprised Zeke. "Moonie Nahche?" he finally said.

The big Native American grinned, his white teeth shining from the firelight. "Yes. Moonie was my brother."

Zeke released a hand from the M4 and lifted the brim of his ball cap. He dug deep into his memories bank. "Would you be Little Willy Nahche?"

The smile grew on Little Willy's face. "Yes, but you can see I'm not that little anymore." Little Willy patted his gut to make his point before sheathing the 30-30 rifle in his left hand and climbing off the horse. He took a few steps and squatted before Billy, extending the back of his big hand to the dog.

Zeke muttered something to Billy and the dog began wagging his tail and lapping the air with his long tongue. The dog craned his neck and licked the back of Little Willy's hand. The silver cradling the huge hunks of turquoise on his rings glimmered in the firelight.

"Good boy," Little Willy said in a low voice. He looked up at Zeke. "So what's your name?"

Since the rain had halted—and any apparent danger for the moment— Zeke removed the M4 from beneath the plastic poncho and set it on the ground next to his backpack. "I'm Zeke Allenby."

Little Willy tossed a long braid of hair behind his shoulder. A large hawk feather attached to the braid wavered with the movement. "I think you are the one my brother called Ezekiel, like the one in the Bible."

"Yeah, that's me," Zeke said. "But any similarity between me and the guy in the Bible is pure coincidence."

Little Willy smiled with that big grin of his.

Zeke opened his arms, gesturing to his surroundings. "I'd offer you something to drink or eat but I seem to be a little shorthanded at the moment."

Little Willy turned to the other riders sitting patiently on their mounts. "Bring the bag," he said to one of them.

A young Native American, probably in his late-teens, jumped off his horse and brought a sheepskin bag with him to the fire. He gave the bag to Little Willy and returned to remount his horse. Little Willy sat on the ground and started rummaging through the bag. He removed a pint bottle of cheap whiskey. He offered the bottle to Zeke. "Firewater?"

Zeke smiled and took the bottle. They shared it in silence, each taking swigs and handing it back and forth. Stover's snoring from the truck bed got louder. Little Willy and Zeke shared a look before breaking into laughter.

"They're exhausted," Zeke said. "We had a run-in with some wannabe highway robbers a ways back. These guys aren't used to that sort of thing."

Little Willy took another swig from the bottle before screwing the lid back on and replacing the bottle in the sheepskin bag. "Those hippies living on the old Patterson Ranch?"

"If you say so."

"I though I recognized the pickup truck," Little Willy said while gesturing toward the Ford. "When old man Patterson croaked, his place went to his two worthless sons. We have land near their place. We tried to buy it but the eldest son said he wasn't selling to no *stinkin' Injuns.*"

Zeke struggled to remember all the details Moonie had told him about his family. He remembered that Moonie's father owned a large sheep ranch somewhere in Texas, and according to Moonie they were quite well off. *"At least for Apaches,"* Moonie had said with his wide grin—a grin almost identical to Little Willy's grin.

"How much gas you got?" Little Willy asked.

"Less than a quarter tank."

"Any bloodshed with the brothers?" asked Little Willy.

"Not really," Zeke said. "Busted the oldest one's nose, I think."

Little Willy laughed. "Did he still have that old double-barrel that belonged to his father?" he asked.

"Yeah," Zeke said before gesturing to the truck. "It's behind the seat. He had a name for it."

"What was the name?" asked Little Willy.

"Jihad."

"Jihad," Little Willy repeated. "What does that mean?"

"Holy War."

"Holy War," Little Willy said before rummaging through his bag. "Well, if I find any of our sheep on their land, they're going to get a taste of *Apache* Jihad."

Zeke smiled, finally deciding to ask the obvious. "So what's up with the warpaint, Willy? Ya'll going out for an evening ride or raiding a wagon train or something?"

Little Willy removed a cloth bundle from his bag and began unfolding it. "I've been teaching my son and his cousins some of the ancient ways," he said, revealing some dried meat or jerky in the cloth bundle. He sliced off a hunk with a hunting knife sheathed to his side and offered it to Zeke. "Venison."

Zeke placed the hunk in his mouth and sucked on the savory, smoky flavor.

"But earlier today," Little Willy continued, cutting a piece of venison for himself, "some make-believe soldiers out on fifty-four hassled my nephew while he was trying to cross his herd of sheep across the highway. They roughed him up a bit when he fought back and called him some ugly names. We're going to pay them a little surprise visit tonight. Give them an encounter with some 'stinking Injuns' so they have a good story to tell their grandchildren—if they live long enough to have grandchildren."

Zeke saw a flicker of fire in Little Willy's eyes, and it wasn't coming from any reflection of the campfire. "They armed?" asked Zeke.

"Yes, but they'll be too surprised to react. It'll be a hit-and-run operation."

"Are you talking about a roadblock on the highway?" Zeke asked.

"Yeah," Little Willy replied with a knowing look in his eyes. "They seem to be looking for someone in particular."

Zeke didn't play in to it. "National Guard?"

"I don't think so. Maybe employees from some NGO outfit. Hired hands, I'm not sure. But all the crazies and their little militias are coming out of the woodwork these days."

Yeah, I've noticed, Zeke thought but kept it to himself.

Little Willy gestured to the Ford. "You a hired gun for those folks?"

"More of a guide, actually," Zeke said.

"Where are you heading?"

"East."

Little Willy nodded and stayed silent for a long moment. "I don't stick my nose in other men's business," he finally said. "But if I were trying to head east and avoid any militias looking for me, I'd take the right fork in the narrow gap between the big peak and the little flattop just east of here, and follow it through the Delawares until I got to a dirt road that turns north before turning back southeast. It'll eventually dump me onto a road that'll lead me beyond where 110 and 120 meet, well past the last of the roadblocks."

Zeke stared back at Little Willy. "No more roadblocks you say?"

"At least all the way to San Antonio," Little Willy said. "I know that for sure. There's also two gas rationing locations on 110. They only sell ten gallons per automobile twice a week, on Mondays and Thursdays I think. One is near Junction, the other is just outside of San Antonio. Be ready to wait in long lines, though. A cousin of mine said he waited for six hours at the one near San Antonio."

Zeke kept his eyes locked onto Willy's eyes. "That's good information, Willy."

Little Willy nodded before saying, "When did you last see Moonie, Ezekiel?"

"About a minute before he got it," Zeke answered without flinching.

Little Willy raised his chin while staring at Zeke, waiting for him to continue.

"We had some bad intelligence from the regional spooks," Zeke said. "The Taliban had us cornered in some burned-out village ruins. We lost seven that day, including your brother, but if it hadn't been for Moonie opening a way out for us, none of us would've survived. He saved a bunch of Ranger lives that day. And just so you know, Moonie took a few Taliban into the spirit world with him."

"That's the way he was," Little Willy said. "He wanted to die in battle. He always talked about that."

Zeke decided to lighten the mood. "Can I ask you something, Willy?"

"Sure."

"How did Moonie get his nickname? He told us it had something to do with him being born during a full moon."

Little Willy responded with another one of his huge grins. "I'm not sure about that," he said. "But he liked to lead sheriff deputies into high-speed chases out on the highway. He'd lead them onto some dirt road until their vehicles bottomed out in some rut. Legend has it that he would shout at them from a bluff above, and when they shined their flashlights on him, he would drop his drawers and give them a full moon!"

Zeke joined Little Willy in laughter. The smiles stayed on their faces while they chewed the venison. Slowly the smiles faded. Little Willy placed the bundle of venison jerky on the ground near the fire. He then removed the pint whiskey bottle from the sheepskin bag and unscrewed the top. "To Moonie," he said before taking a snort. He handed the bottle to Zeke.

"To Moonie," Zeke said before taking his own swig in toast.

Little Willy stood to his feet, his large frame towering over Zeke and the campfire. His war dress was quite impressive and would probably scare the daylights out of the guards at the roadblock. "Good luck, Ezekiel Allenby."

"Good luck to you, Little Willy Nahche," Zeke replied while standing to his feet.

Little Willy pointed to the water collection contraption at the front of the Ford. "You'll get rain before the sun rises," he said while patting Billy on the head. "Don't forget to fill your canteens."

"I won't," Zeke said. "Thanks, Willy."

Little Willy mounted his horse effortlessly, and as quietly as they had entered, Little Willy's band of Indians rode silently out of camp. As soon as they were gone the rain started to come down. Zeke grabbed the M4, backpack, and bundle of venison jerky, and took it all with him to the cab of the Ford. Billy returned to his spot beneath the truck bed as Zeke stretched out on the Ford's bench seat, using his backpack for a pillow. As raindrops pattered on the roof of the cab, Zeke shut his eyes while making a mental note to wake in about an hour to fill the water bladders. He fell asleep quickly, dreaming of marauding Indians attacking ancient ruins somewhere in Afghanistan.

*　*　*

SIX

The groups numbered in the dozens, most of them huddled around small campfires fueled by deadwood from the forest of pine trees bordering a large clearing. The relief camp was actually ten miles beyond *The Woodlands* north of Houston. The site stood off I45 and had been a gathering place and picnic area for families just a few weeks earlier. Folks were still gathering all right, but there weren't any picnics at the moment.

Ruth didn't know the exact time, but she knew the sun had set nearly an hour ago. She remained wary as Connor and Amy followed her toward several people huddled around a fire burning in a large metal trash barrel. A woman with hair pulled back into a ponytail was eating something from a plastic wrapper. She stopped chewing when she saw Ruth and the kids coming toward her. The light of the flickering flames licking the top of the trash-barrel danced on the woman's weary face. The scene reminded Ruth of an old magazine photograph she saw years ago; a snapshot of homeless people dressed in rags, huddled around barrel fires in some city ghetto.

Ruth and the kids had been walking all day—their second day on foot—with nothing to eat since finishing the fruit cocktail and apple fruit bars the day before. Ruth had refused to eat any of those items until Connor had insisted she have part of the last fruit bar, which she ate reluctantly. Her kids came first.

At least water hadn't been an issue. On the interstate around noon of the first day, a *Good Samaritan* had been handing out bottled waters from the back of a horse-drawn cart. His generous actions had reminded Ruth of how much good was still left in the world.

Ruth approached the ponytailed woman standing near the barrel fire. "Hello," Ruth said while trying not to stare at the candy bar in the woman's hand.

"There's nothing to share," the ponytailed woman said in a brusque tone of voice. Two men stood near the woman, sharing a cigarette and a bottle of cheap whiskey. The men stared at Ruth with expectant looks on their faces.

"I'll buy something," Ruth said. "For my children. They haven't had anything to eat for a long time."

"What are you gonna buy with?" one of the men asked with a cruel grin.

Ruth began digging in the purse strapped over her shoulder. "I have money, not a lot, but it's all I have." She fished out a crumpled dollar bill and some loose change.

"Keep it," the woman said. "That won't buy an old chicken bone around here."

"But my children," Ruth insisted. "They need something to—"

"—Join the club," the woman said, her voice starting to rise. "We're all in the same boat, honey!"

"Maybe you could—"

"—Get lost!" the ponytailed woman shouted before smirking at the surprised expression on Ruth's face. She finished the remainder of the candy bar. "Now beat it before I lose my cool and crack your scull open like a raw egg!"

The two men standing nearby snickered. Ruth saw a glimmer of metal from the hammer the woman held in her other fist. "Okay," Ruth said. "Sorry."

Ruth put her arms around Connor and Amy and walked toward another campfire a few yards away. Several old men in shabby coats turned to her when she neared. She saw they were empty-handed so she moved on. Besides, she didn't like the look one of them gave her.

Ruth scanned the area, examining the people standing near the fires, their tired and angry faces glowing like demons, reminding her of a *Dante's Inferno* illustration she had seen in school a million years ago. *Where are the children? There has to be some families out here among this rabble.*

Ruth needed to sit. Connor and Amy joined her on the rocky ground. They sat in an open area, close enough to the fires to see, but not too close. An early *norther* had blown in around midday and now it was downright cold. The children snuggled close to their mother. Despite her thick parka, little Amy shivered against her mother's side, the cough she'd developed the day before getting worse by the minute. Ruth put her arms around her children and held them close. She tried to keep her eyes open. *So tired.* She had to stay awake. The children's heads leaning against her were getting heavier and heavier. Connor was already starting to snore. Ruth's eyelids became too heavy to keep open any longer. She began falling into a deep world of nothingness, falling deeper and deeper, until the real world around her drifted away . . .

. . . Her eyes opened in a flash. She was in her bed at home. Another crash sounded from the living room, louder than the crash that had awakened her. Men's voices. No, boy's voices. Maybe both. Laughter. Evil laughter. The sounds were moving throughout the dark house. The children! She tried to rise from the bed but she couldn't move a muscle! Amy! Connor! She had to get up! She screamed their names again! No sound came from her throat! She fought to move her body! GET UP! GET UP! . . .

Ruth's eyes opened back to the real world, or what was left of it. The man's stinking breath suffocated her as his whiskered face pressed closer to hers. He had her pinned to the ground. Amy was crying hysterically while Connor pounded in vain on the man's back, shouting for him to get off his mother. Stink Breath struggled to get Ruth's jeans unfastened. She began fighting with all her strength. She wiggled frantically, trying to stop him from pulling off her jeans. She whipped her head up violently, her forehead making hard contact with his drooling mouth. He cursed as blood began trickling from his lower lip. His strength increased with his anger. He yanked angrily on her jeans, pulling them down slightly below her hips.

Connor's flailing fists pounding on the man's back stopped abruptly. A second later the man's weight decreased dramatically as he seemed to fly backwards into the air, finally leaving her body free to move. She caught a glimpse of his face, contorted in surprise as he tumbled backwards to the ground. A tall figure stood near Ruth, staring at the would-be-rapist on the ground. Stink Breath screamed in rage as he jumped to his feet and charged the tall figure. Ruth didn't see what happened next but she heard Stink Breath's war cry change into a wet, choking sound. When she stood to her feet she could see better. The tall figure was clenching Stink Breath's throat, their faces just inches apart. Neither men said a word.

Ruth took a few wobbly steps to her left as she wiggled her jeans up over her hips, the change in angle providing more light onto the scene from the fires nearby. She couldn't see clearly in the darkness but she saw enough to see the look of sheer terror on Stink Breath's face. The tall figure released his grip and Stink Breath ran away like a frightened child, stumbling a few times but never looking back as he disappeared into the darkness.

The tall figure turned toward Ruth. The glow from the fires illuminated the man's radiant face, revealing a kind and gentle expression as his mouth slowly formed a smile.

"You're okay now," he said in a voice both soft and forceful.

Her mouth couldn't find the words but her mind shouted thanks over and over to her savior of the night. She felt her children hugging her legs. "Thank you, mister," Connor said. "Thanks for saving my mom."

The tall man smiled and ruffled Connor's hair. "You did your share, son. You are a very brave boy."

Ruth began brushing dirt from the back of her jeans. She tried to smooth out the tangles in her hair. "Thank you . . . sir," was the only thing she managed to say.

The tall man took a step back, as if to get a better look at Ruth and the kids, but it suddenly occurred to her that he was actually giving them a better look of himself as the firelight illuminated more of his features. Ruth saw his camouflaged pants, their hems tucked into military-style suede boots. A dark tee-shirt revealed a strong chest along with powerful biceps that stretched the tee-shirt's sleeves. She noticed a pair of aviator-style sunglasses hanging from his collar. His dark ball cap lacked any visible logo but she wouldn't have been surprised to see some military design stitched on it. She recognized his type easily. Her brother-in-law, Zeke, was one of these types.

"Now," he said. "Who's hungry?"

Ruth could only make a chuffing sound but the kids piped right up. "We are! We are!" they shouted in unison.

The man pointed toward a campfire fifty yards away at the edge of some pine trees bordering the clearing. "Care to join me for supper?"

"Sure!" the kids shouted.

Ruth found herself following the kids and the mysterious man—the man who had just saved her and her children from a horrible nightmare, maybe even from death. As they walked toward the campfire near the trees a thought suddenly arose in Ruth, coming from a place deep down inside her, that place that all mothers have involving the protection of their children. The thought made her stop in her tracks: *What if this man had only saved them for his own twisted desires?*

The man turned his head toward her while leading them to his campsite. "You and your little ones are safe with me," he said softly. "Trust me. Totally safe."

And something in that voice—not the words themselves, something else much more powerful—assured her this was absolute truth.

When they reached his campsite Ruth said, "Uh, my name is Ruth. May I ask your name?"

"My name is not important," he replied. "You can call me whatever you wish."

Ruth contemplated this for a moment when little Amy suddenly said, "You look like GI Joe. Let's call you Joe."

The man laughed heartedly. "That will be fine. Joe it is."

They sat crosslegged around the campfire as if this was nothing more than a family outing at a church picnic. Ruth half suspected that at any moment now Joe would pull out a bag of marshmallows for them to roast on the fire. Instead, he set a backpack in his lap and started removing items. He reached over to the fire and removed the lid of an aluminum pot sitting above the coals. Steam billowed out of the pot like a white cloud, along with an aroma that made Ruth's mouth water. She hadn't seen or smelled the pot of food a moment earlier. It was as if the pot materialized out of nowhere when he reached for the lid. *I'm so tired I didn't notice,* she thought to herself. She didn't contemplate that for long, though. She was too hungry to think about anything except eating whatever was in that steaming pot with its wonderful aroma.

Joe began ladling contents from the pot into the bowls he'd removed from the backpack. He offered the first bowl to little Amy who started to say something but began coughing instead. The cough sounded wetter than before, what Ruth's mother had called a *Crooping Cough* when Ruth was a little girl.

"Vegetable soup with magical herbs," Joe said with a smile to Amy after the coughing halted, his words sounding like an answer to a question. "It will help your cough go bye-bye."

"Oh," she said before having another brief coughing spell.

Joe waited for the coughing to stop before handing her the bowl. He passed another bowl to Connor, then Ruth. A few seconds later he was passing out metal spoons to each of them. "Go ahead and eat," he said. "Don't wait for me."

"Thank you, but we'll wait," Ruth said, nudging Connor with her elbow, stopping the boy from eating the spoonful of soup already on its way to his mouth. "We would like to say *Grace* before eating, if that's okay with you . . . Joe."

Joe nodded, then filled his own bowl before setting it into his lap and bowing his head. Ruth spoke a short prayer of thanks, followed by the children chorusing *"amen"* a bit faster than usual. The soup was delicious. No, beyond delicious. In fact, words couldn't express how good it tasted to Ruth. And by the way her children slurped it down she knew they felt the same. *Where in the world did he find all the fresh vegetables?* she asked herself. *Does he have a garden hidden somewhere nearby?*

Joe also seemed to relish the tasty soup full of potatoes, carrots, onions, celery, tomatoes, and various herbs that seemed vaguely familiar to Ruth. He ate slowly, methodically, grunting approvingly after every spoonful. A moment later he set his bowl on the ground and filled three paper cups with a liquid from his canteen. He offered each of them the filled cups—water, Ruth assumed—before filling a cup for himself.

"Mmm!" Connor said after taking a big gulp from his cup. "Grape Kool-Aid, my favorite!"

"Mine, too!" Joe said.

Ruth paused her eating, a question forming on her face while eyeing the mysterious stranger who wouldn't give his real name. She thought of how to ask: *Excuse me, I don't mean to pry . . . but where did you get the fresh vegetables?*

Ruth parted her lips to speak but Joe seemed to speak first. "From the garden," she heard him whisper but did not actually see his lips move.

His words caught her off guard. Ruth cleared her throat. "Pardon me?"

Joe finished his Kool-Aid in one swallow as Connor suddenly asked, "Mr. Joe, may I have more soup, please?"

"As much as you want, son," Joe said, grabbing the boy's bowl and ladling more hot soup into it.

Ruth went back to eating her soup while continuing her thoughts: *He must have read my mind by the way I was staring at him. I can be so rude sometimes. Still, I wonder how he knew . . .*

"How's your cough now, Amy?" Joe asked little Amy.

"Much better, sir," Amy replied in her polite little voice. "I think it went bye-bye."

"Good," Joe said before going back to his soup.

Ruth's eyes narrowed as she looked at Amy, noticing that even the little girl's pallor looked much better than just minutes earlier. She was happy for that but something else nagged her—a question she wouldn't keep to herself any longer. "Uh, excuse me, Joe?"

Joe cocked his head in her direction. "Yes?"

"How did you know my daughter's name was Amy?"

His answer came without hesitation. "I heard you call her name."

While Ruth tried to remember calling out for her daughter, Joe said, "Your shouting of her name is what caught my attention." He paused to let his words sink in before adding, "When you were being attacked."

Ruth suddenly remembered the dream: invaders in her home, her trying to scream her children's names but could not. "I remember dreaming about . . . something, and trying to call their names. But I couldn't make a sound . . . in my dream, that is."

"You did, Mom," Connor said suddenly.

"Excuse me?"

"I heard you scream Amy's name," the boy continued. "That's what woke me up."

Ruth took a deep breath, satisfied with the answer to her question. She went back to her bowl of soup. Her stomach was getting full fast. She set the bowl of soup in her lap and watched Joe eat. "Were you in the army, Joe?" she asked in a casual tone.

Joe swallowed a spoonful of soup. "Yes, and I still am in a way."

Ruth smiled. "I understand. My brother-in-law, Zeke, has answered that question many times in the same way."

"Where is your brother-in-law?" Joe asked.

"Good question," she said with a sigh. "He lives near a little town in West Texas. A long way from here."

"You've talked with him recently?"

"No," she said. "He was supposed to visit us before taking an overseas job. He was going to leave his dog with us." She paused before continuing. "Of course, that was before . . . the bomb or whatever it was put everyone in this mess. I waited for a while, hoping he would find his way to us somehow, but I couldn't stay at home any longer with no food or water. It was getting too dangerous, anyway."

Joe nodded in an understanding way while Ruth began staring into the fire with a sad look on her face.

"He'll find us, Mom," Connor said, still woofing down the soup. "Don't worry. I know he will."

"That's the spirit," Joe said. "Keep encouraging those around you and good things will find their way to you."

"I pray that Zeke's okay," Ruth told Joe. "It's the not-knowing part that's so difficult." She started on her soup again. "One thing I do know: if anyone can survive, Zeke can."

"You say he was in the army?" Joe said.

"Yes," she answered. "Army Rangers, then some secret stuff abroad. I say secret because he never talks about it. I don't know, maybe it was something secret he was involved in. You know how the military is about its *special operations*. Anyway, he got out of the business entirely when his wife, my sister, Amber became pregnant." Ruth's expression fell several notches. "Then not long after the baby was born, she and the baby were killed in a horrible tragedy. Zeke stayed with us for a while before going back into the business, taking a contract job overseas. Military stuff. He's continued ever since. Usually gone for months at a time. It's the type of work that takes him to the far reaches of the world from time to time."

As Joe waited for her to continue, Ruth swallowed a spoonful of soup, glad she hadn't mentioned anything about her deadbeat husband, Jerry, taking off with some stripper and leaving her and the kids all alone. "How about you?" she said, trying to leave her sad thoughts behind. "Travel often?"

"Yes," Joe said. "My work has also taken me to the far reaches of the world, but I liked the way you put it: *'from time to time.'*"

"Regular army?" she said. "No, don't tell me. Green Berets?"

Joe only smiled.

"Delta Force?"

Still, just the smile.

"Well," Ruth said, pretending to give up on the guessing game. "I'd say some type of special forces. Right?"

Joe laughed in a friendly way. "Yes, special forces for sure."

Ruth began to laugh. "You're not going to confess to anything, are you?"

Joe continued his laughter. "I have nothing to confess."

After their laughter died they went back to eating their soup. As Ruth and the children filled their stomachs she saw Joe finish his soup and set the empty bowl next to the fire. "Feel free to have as much soup as you want," he said. "Just help yourself."

Ruth watched as he excused himself and stood to his feet. He walked a short distance into the dark woods surrounding the campfire site. Thinking that he was relieving himself somewhere in the trees, Ruth finished her bowl and went for a second helping.

A moment later he returned with a bundle of something in his arms. He set the bundle on the ground ten feet or so from the campfire and started unrolling it. It wasn't long before he began assembling a small tent. Ruth stood quickly to her feet to lend a hand. "Let me help you."

Joe made a few more moves and the small tent folded into shape. "Thanks, but I've got it." He pointed to several rolls left on the ground. "There are two sleeping bags there. Connor can have one, and you and Amy can share the other. That okay?"

"Oh," Ruth said. "You don't have to do this. You've helped us enough."

"Nonsense," he said while unzipping the tent entrance and placing a battery-powered lantern inside. "You and your children are my guests."

Ruth stared at the small tent, wondering where Joe planned to sleep.

"I'll be out here by the fire," he said. "I've got some reading to catch up on."

Ruth began carrying the rolled sleeping bags into the tent where she unrolled them side by side. When she returned to the campfire she saw Joe sitting cross-legged next to the kids. He was doing something with his hands in his lap, but since they were facing the fire with their backs to her, she couldn't see. She moved up next to them and chuckled to herself when she saw him attaching marshmallows to the end of some freshly whittled sticks.

"How about you?" he said to Ruth. "Want to join us for dessert?"

Ruth squatted down next to him. "Sure."

After roasting their marshmallows—almost half a bag—the kids were done. She tucked them into the sleeping bags and both were asleep before she had time to leave the tent. Joe was still sitting next to the fire. When she sat down, he closed the book in his lap. *A Bible? No, too thin. But it sort of looks like a Bible with its gold-leaf pages.*

"I'll be gone early," he told her. "Don't bother with the tent and sleeping bags. I'll be back later to get them."

"But what about those people?" she asked while glancing toward the fires in the near distance, thinking about how far away their world seemed at the moment. *Fifty yards away but they might as well be fifty-billion miles away.* "Won't they try to steal your stuff?"

"Thanks for your concern," he said. "But they won't bother my stuff. Trust me."

Ruth chuckled, thinking anyone would be crazy to try to steal anything from this man. If he could frighten someone by just looking at them, like that thug who tried to rape her, causing him to run away in the dark like a scared rabbit, what else was Joe capable of doing? "Yes," she said. "I think you're right."

Joe turned his face toward her. She stared into his eyes, seeing their light-blue color better at this close distance. Inside that brilliant shade of blue were hundreds, maybe thousands, of thin streaks the color of the sun, all of them flashing like tiny lightning strikes in the universe of his eyeball. The sight took her breath away. When she finally remembered to breath, a warmth came from within her, radiating outward through her skin, causing a million goose-bumps to cover her body.

"Listen carefully," he said in a quiet voice. "Continue north on the highway tomorrow. After about a three hour walk you will cross the bridge over Dagger Creek. Look for a large oak tree standing alone behind the bridge. Beyond it you will find a faint trail wandering over a rise in the terrain. Follow it. Two miles up the trail you will reach a gate. Are you with me so far?"

Ruth seemed lost in those eyes but she had heard every word. "Yes. We'll reach a gate."

"Tell the guard that I sent you," he continued. "You and your children will be safe there. Understand?"

"Yes."

Ruth felt like she had been in a trance. She suddenly felt very tired and sleepy but contented in a way that she hadn't felt in a long time.

"Now," Joe said. "Get some sleep. You have busy days ahead of you."

His last sentence puzzled her but she didn't question him. "Thank you, Joe," she said while putting her hand on his shoulder. She felt a tiny, almost imperceptible recoil in his muscles when she touched him. She casually removed her hand. "How can I ever repay you for all you've done."

"Repayment is unimportant," he said. "Now get some sleep."

Ruth stood to head for the tent. "But where will you sleep? You've given us your tent and sleeping bags."

"Don't worry about me. I told you I have some reading to catch up on, and besides, I don't need much sleep."

She reached the tent entrance and turned one last time. "Will we see you again?"

"Yes, Ruth," he said. "We will see each other again. Trust me."

She did. She had only known this man for probably an hour or so yet she trusted him completely.

Ruth entered the tent to the gentle snores of her sleeping children. She turned off the electric lantern and climbed into the sleeping bag with little Amy, thinking about the strange night. The rational part of her brain wanted explanations for everything but she was not in the mood for anymore thoughts or explanations. She just wanted to sleep. She was exhausted beyond exhaustion. Her last silent words before falling into deep sleep came easily: *Thank you, Lord. Thank you for Joe.* And with that . . . the long day was over.

*   *   *

SEVEN

Zeke awakened only once after Little Willy and his band of Apache warriors had left camp. The rain had been light but steady for at least an hour so he climbed out of the dry pickup truck cab and filled the water bladders from the jug of fresh rainwater. When he returned to the cab, Billy came out of his shelter beneath the truck and looked up at Zeke with sad, pleading eyes. Zeke let his dog curl up on the passenger-side floorboard before they both fell asleep in the cramped but dry cab.

When Zeke awoke, the blue sky overhead was clear of any clouds. The rain had washed the land thoroughly, leaving the fresh fragrance of juniper and sage to fill the air. The soil was a bit muddy but most of the rainfall had washed down the draw below them. Zeke knew the mud would probably become an issue as they headed toward the mountain range but he would deal with that when he had to.

Stover, Margolian and the two Albrights climbed out of the truck bed, the men moving slowly while trying to stretch their sore muscles. Matt wasn't affected. He threw a stick for Billy and played chase as his dad struggled to change clothes.

After eating their MREs they began to break camp; removing the plastic coverings on the Ford and repacking their backpacks. Zeke decided to cut two large tree limbs to carry in the truck bed to use if the rear wheels lost traction in mud along the way. He was disassembling the water collection contraption when something caught his eye a few feet away. Two ten-gallon metal fuel canisters sat side by side with a large hawk feather dangling from one of the handles. The feather whipped gently in the morning breeze. Zeke chuckled to himself as he lifted each canister one at a time, checking for the amount of fuel inside. One was completely full and the other three-quarters full. Stover came walking up while brushing his teeth. "What's that?"

This got Albright's attention. He sauntered over and stared at the gas canisters. "Where'd they come from, Zeke?"

Zeke grabbed the full canister and limped to the Ford. "You wouldn't believe me if I told you." He made brief eye contact with the archeologist. "Right, Doctor Margolian?"

Margolian smiled in a friendly way but said nothing.

Albright and Stover shared a look. As Zeke removed the Ford's gas cap to pour in the fuel, Albright said, "Try us."

Zeke began pouring the gasoline carefully, spilling just a small amount before getting the flow smooth and even. "So would you believe me if I told you," he began, "that last night after all of you went to sleep, a band of Apache warriors dressed in buckskin and wearing warpaint came into camp on horseback?"

Stover scrunched his face, trying to decipher a punch line out of what Zeke was saying. Albright remained pokerfaced. Matt ran up to them with a stick in his hand as Billy chased after him. The boy stared at Zeke filling the gas tank. "Did you just find that?" he asked.

Zeke turned to him while increasing the angle of the gas canister, careful not to tilt it too fast. "Yes, I did."

Billy pranced in front of Matt, wanting him to throw the stick. "Cool," Matt said before running away and tossing the stick so Billy could chase after it.

As Zeke swapped canisters, Albright and Stover continued to stare at him. He returned their looks with a smile while removing the hawk feather from the second canister. He examined the feather in a way where Albright and Stover could get a good look at it. Margolian extended his hand and said, "May I take a look at that?"

Zeke handed him the feather before starting on the second canister. Stover went back to brushing his teeth. Albright grew a small grin as he made eye contact with Zeke. "Good job, Zeke. I knew you were the right man for the job."

Zeke smiled back. "Don't congratulate me yet," he said. "The day is just beginning."

Margolian finished examining the hawk feather and handed back to Zeke. "Interesting," was all he said as he joined the others to break camp.

Everyone finished squaring away their backpacks and loaded them into the truck bed next to the two limbs Zeke had cut. Zeke replaced one of the empty gas canisters on the ground where he'd found it, then loaded the other empty one into the truck bed to use when they found more gasoline. He removed a 5.56mm round from the clip of his M4 and set it on top of the empty canister on the ground.

They broke camp and left, this time with Albright sitting in the cab as Stover, Margolian, Matt, and Billy rode in back. The Ford's tires kicked up a lot of mud in its wake but they didn't get stuck as Zeke drove onto the dirt road toward the Delaware Mountains looming in front of them. He searched for the pass Little Willy had described, looking for a gap where the path forked between a big peak and a little flattop. There seemed to be hundreds of *big peaks* and *little flattops*.

Albright had not said a thing, aware that Zeke was concentrating on the route. He finally said, "So what *really* happened last night, Zeke?"

"I already told you," Zeke replied. "It happened just as I said. We were trespassing on their land and they came to check us out. Turned out that the chief of the band was the brother of an old army buddy of mine. We sat by the fire and had council."

"You didn't share a peace pipe?" Albright asked with a smile.

"No, but we shared a bottle of firewater," Zeke replied while returning the smile. "A bottle of *Old Granddad*, I believe."

This got a chuckle from Albright. "Okay, what else?"

"He told me how to get around the roadblocks."

Albright's jovial mood stiffened a bit. "There's more roadblocks?"

"Yes," Zeke said while spotting the gap ahead where the road forked.

The information had a sobering effect on Albright. He stared ahead through the windshield, wondering if they would ever make it to Austin.

"In regards to the roadblocks," Zeke said, "we owe them thanks for the gas."

"Owe who thanks?" Albright asked. "The roadblock or the Indians?"

"Both."

Albright stared at Zeke, wondering if he should believe him or not. *Had Zeke left camp on foot during the night and stolen the gasoline from one of the roadblocks? Hiking miles in the darkness during a rainstorm, carrying almost twenty gallons of gasoline that he'd managed to steal from armed men at a roadblock?* The story of Apache warriors made much more sense.

The Ford pickup began climbing the dirt road through the mountains.

The surface of the road was slick but Zeke kept the engine steady. The Ford's rear end slid and sashayed on the steeper sections of road but her tires held their traction. They reached one part of the road with a deep depression and got stuck in the mud. The rear tires spun in vain as Zeke revved the engine. Everyone, including Albright, got out and used the tree limbs to apply leverage under the rear tires. Zeke revved the engine and eventually rocked the Ford out of the muddy depression. He tried not to laugh when Albright got back in the cab, his face and body covered with mud splatter.

Albright used an old tee-shirt to wipe the mud from his face, aware of Zeke's amusement. "You should see Paul," he said. "With that bald head of his he looks like the *Creature From The Black Lagoon*."

Two hours went by. Once they reached the far side of the gap Zeke finally stopped the Ford. Everyone hopped out to stretch their legs and follow Zeke to a spot overlooking the vista before them. "Sure is beautiful country," Stover said. "Rugged but beautiful."

"Yes, it is," replied Zeke as he followed the faint impression of dirt road snaking its way through the rough terrain before him. He saw Matt head off the road with a roll of toilet paper in his hand.

"Keep your eyes out for rattlesnakes," his father said.

"Okay," Matt replied.

Billy followed him, causing the boy to shout, "No, Billy! This is private! It's a number two, not a number one!"

The men laughed.

After Matt returned from his morning constitution they all climbed back in the Ford to continue their journey through the Delawares. The stretch of dirt road before them descended rapidly for several miles. Stover got in the cab as the rest rode in the truck bed. Zeke put the Ford in low gear to keep traction on the tires, making sure to control the speed without throwing anyone out the back of the truck bed in case he hit a large rut or small boulder in the road.

Less than an hour later they reached the bottom of the steepest section of terrain. Onward they went, making better time now, putting the miles behind them faster than before. Everything was going well. The dirt road meandered northward until cutting back to the southeast, exactly as Little Willy had described. Stover was taking a nap, his bald head leaning against the passenger-side window. Zeke glanced at the gas gauge hovering just above the half-full mark, wondering how far the Ford would get them before running empty. If their pursuers got to Little Willy and extracted information from him, they would probably believe Zeke and his bunch were planning to take I10 or I20 for their journey east. But Zeke planned to stay off the major highways, using the backroads instead. Most people believed the interstate highway system offered more fuel and food services; a fact in normal times. But these were not normal times. Zeke believed the backroad highways and their small towns gave them a better chance at finding fuel, although most of it would be hidden and protected by self-reliant farmers and ranchers who stored away more supplies than city folk. But with cash—especially lots of it—Zeke planned to buy what they needed. And the only thing they really needed was gasoline.

As the terrain leveled out, Zeke concentrated less on the road and more on sighting a farm or ranch, looking mainly for wood-framed windmills used for pumping water from a well into a holding tank for livestock. Zeke thought about the situation while driving. As far as the evidence went, there was little to prove that they were being chased at all, either by humans or non-humans from another dimension. Zeke felt like laughing. Stover's story about extra-dimensional aliens was insane. *Believing the story was even more insane,* he told himself. Stover seemed to be a rational, intelligent man, but apparently he believed that beings from another dimension were responsible for the mess everyone was in. *Let's look at the facts,* Zeke told himself. *America—or at least parts of it—had been crippled by some type of electromagnetic pulse bomb or something similar. There were roadblocks with armed soldiers, either military or nonmilitary. Little Willy indicated the roadblocks were not Army. I've believed that too every since the experience at the Mangas Bridge roadblock. Little Willy also believed the soldiers were looking for someone, hinting strongly that the someone was me and my companions.*

But despite all this evidence, there was one thing that convinced Zeke they were being chased: The feeling of being hunted. Call it a hunch, or a premonition, or whatever you want to call it, Zeke knew the feeling well. He'd first experienced the feeling in combat during his early days in the army, and he'd learned not to ignore it. He felt it now, the same as he'd felt it from the beginning of this little adventure. Even before his first meeting with Albright and Stover when he came to Gold Tree after finding his cabin trashed. He remembered when he was in town. He felt like he was being watched.

As the drive went on, Zeke glanced more often to the horizon south of him, toward the direction of Apache Mountain and I10 and I20 beyond, still many miles away. Ahead were miles and miles of flat land broken sporadically by bumps of mountains jutting out of the desert floor surrounding them—stereotypical West Texas terrain of big sky and three-hundred-sixty degrees of horizon. If Zeke turned the Ford due east he would eventually reach Horsehead Crossing on the Pecos River, the famous river ford that Comanches used for centuries during their raids on helpless Mexican villages and towns south of the border. But he wouldn't be crossing the Pecos River yet. He planned to take 285 just south of the town of Pecos, hopefully, with a full tank of gas in the Ford pickup truck.

Eventually the Ford reached a ranch road signpost that seemed to stick out of nowhere. The numbers on the sign read twenty-one-something because the metal sign was full of bullet holes which obliterated the last two digits. Zeke sat behind the wheel with the engine idling while studying a county roadmap in his lap.

Stover awakened from his nap. He studied Zeke and the map. "What's up, Kemosabe?"

Zeke was satisfied with his findings on the map. He folded the map and said, "The ride's going to get better. It shouldn't be long before we reach paved highway."

"How's the gas?"

Zeke put the Ford in gear and turned east on the ranch road. "It could be better," he finally said.

"What's the plan?"

"I'm working on it," Zeke replied. He waited for a moment before saying, "You might want to go back to your nap while you got the chance."

Stover raised his eyebrows. "I can see you're really enjoying my company."

"All I mean is," Zeke said, trying to clarify himself, "that we might be on foot soon. And if I were you I'd be taking advantage of every bit of shuteye I could get."

Zeke really liked Paul Stover, which said a lot for the man since he was a lawyer, which was not one of Zeke's favorite types of people. Paul never complained and always saw the bright side of everything. He was optimistic and upbeat despite the trials and tribulations of life. And Zeke believed he was excessively honest—not your typical *modus operandi* for an attorney.

The two lane, asphalt ranch road was definitely smoother than the dirt trails they'd been on but it still had to be an uncomfortable affair on the metal floorboard of the truck bed. He thought of swapping positions with Margolian, Albright, and Matt, letting them ride in the relative comfort of the cab. He wouldn't mind getting a bit of *shuteye* himself but he didn't want to miss an opportunity of finding gasoline. So Zeke kept driving while glancing at the gas gauge more frequently, watching the needle falling relentlessly toward the *E* on the gauge. He started seeing more buildings off the road, most of them looking like oil field storage facilities, some with corrugated roofs covering long sections of pipe stacked underneath. A few country homes could be seen in the distance on both sides of the road but so far no vehicles or living beings driving them. The endless line of telephone wire strung between old-fashioned creosote poles was comforting in a way, even though they weren't carrying any telephone conversations anymore.

A half-hour later Albright suddenly knocked on the window in back of the cab. Stover rustled and turned his face toward the truck bed. Zeke looked in his rearview mirror and saw Albright gesturing for him to stop the Ford. Zeke stopped, not bothering to pull the truck to the edge of the road. He killed the engine to conserve as much fuel as possible, then stepped out of the Ford to see Matt leaning against his father and not looking so well. "What's up?"

"He's sick at his stomach," Albright replied. "Has been for a while."

Zeke believed motion sickness could be the culprit. I've got some Dramamine in my back pack," he said. "Does your abdomen feel all right, Matt? Or are you just nauseous?"

"Nauseous," Matt replied. "I feel like I want to puke."

Zeke leaned over and grabbed his backpack at the foot of the truck bed. He dug into a pocket for the Dramamine. "We'll take a break," he said while removing a ziplock with various medicines inside. "Once you feel better we'll move you up front while your dad drives for a while."

The queazy boy didn't respond. He leaned his head against Albright's arm with a groan.

Zeke noticed that even Billy didn't look so hot. The dog normally jumped to attention when Zeke approached, but now he stayed in a curled position, his eyes droopy and sad looking. Zeke gave a short whistle before saying, "Come on, boy!"

Billy stood slowly to his feet, looking a bit wobbly with his tail hanging lower than normal. The dog finally mustered enough energy to leap out of the truck bed. Within a few seconds he began patrolling the area with his snout to the ground, acting like he never felt better.

"I think everyone needs a break," Zeke said while handing a tablet to Albright. "One will be fine. Make sure he drinks plenty of water with it."

Albright offered the tablet to Matt. "Here you go, son. This will make you feel better."

Matt reluctantly raised his head to swallow the pill and drink some water from his father's water bladder.

Zeke stretched his back and walked to the front of the Ford, examining the stretch of road before him. Margolian walked a short distance away to relieve himself while Stover stood nearby, taking a leak at the edge of the road. "You think we're close to civilization?" he asked Zeke.

"I don't know how civilized anyplace will be these days," Zeke said.

Stover zipped his fly and came closer to Zeke. "If we find a little quick stop or gas station, how are we going to get gas since the pumps are electric?"

"I doubt any gas stations or stores are going to be operating," Zeke said. "But there may be gasoline still in the underground fuel tanks. If I can find some tubing like a length of garden hose or something, I might be able to siphon some fuel from the tanks."

Stover nodded but seemed to be thinking about something. "You know," he finally said, "the closer we get to population, the better the chance we have of finding another vehicle . . . with gas already in its tank."

Zeke had already made this option his priority but so far he hadn't seen any abandoned vehicles on their journey—or any vehicles, for that matter. *Except for the '94 Chevy pickup that no one else saw.* He quickly put the thought out of his head. He decided to play a little with Stover. "Paul? Are you suggesting we steal someone's vehicle?"

Stover played along with a sly smile but remained sincere. "No, I'm suggesting we *borrow* some abandoned vehicle that no one is using at the moment. I will make it my personal responsibility to make amends to the owner or owners of the vehicle at a later date."

"Maybe you should go ahead and draw up a contract," Zeke said.

"That's not a bad idea," Stover said, playing along. "I'll get to work on it when you find the vehicle."

"Deal."

"Deal."

Soon they were back in the Ford, continuing toward their destination of Austin, Texas, still over three-hundred miles away. Zeke and Stover sat in the truck bed with Margolian and Billy. Albright drove with Matt stretched out on the seat in the cab, the Dramamine helping the boy sleep away the nausea.

The sun's position in the sky told Zeke it was near midday. He saw a few homes sitting a half mile or so off the road—little ranch-styles or doublewides looking lonely and vacant. He knew they were closing the distance between themselves and human population, although that might be an exaggeration since the largest town anywhere close to them was Pecos, with barely seven thousand souls in the best of times. Highway 285 flowed southeasterly through the town while I20 cut through it from the southwest to the northeast. Little Willy had said there were no roadblocks beyond the I10-I20 junction all the way to San Antonio, which was on I10, so they should be in the clear regardless of which route they took—*if* Little Willy's information was accurate and *if* the situation hadn't changed since Little Willy gathered his information.

Zeke leaned back and stared at the totally clear sky overhead. There was a fresh crispness in the dry air but not the freezing temperatures that could fall in this territory during the middle of November. He was happy they weren't driving in snow. He turned his body in a position to view the road ahead. Up on their left Zeke saw a small gas station, a one-room building with a two-bay garage and two gas pumps under the awning in front. He knocked on Albright's window and pointed to the station. As they pulled into the station Zeke saw that the windows were boarded up with sheets of plywood.

Albright pulled up next to the pumps and killed the ignition. Zeke hopped out of the truck bed, deciding to leave the M4 behind the seat in the cab. He touched his holstered M9 on his hip—a habit of reassurance when investigating the unknown. The pumps were powerless, of course, and their nozzles were padlocked in place. He checked the garage bay doors which were locked shut with deadbolts. He peered through the small square windows of the bay doors and saw the typical setup: a car lift, a tire mounting apparatus, and several large metal tool boxes in back of the room.

Zeke ventured around the rear of the building with Billy staying close by. The dog did his usual bit of searching for scents while Zeke rummaged through piles of junk and trash behind the building. He disconnected a water hose from an outside faucet and coiled it while searching for more useful items in the piles of junk. He found a rusty tire tool and grabbed it. After searching for several more minutes he walked back to the Ford with the hose coiled over his shoulder and the tire tool in his hand.

Albright was relieving his bladder a short distance away while Stover leaned his back against the Ford's passenger door, his arms folded while staring out toward the nothingness across the road. Zeke set the coiled hose in the truck bed before opening the driver door and placing the tire tool behind the seat next to the M4, careful with his movements to not awaken Matt on the Ford's bench seat. The boy's feet were pressed against the passenger door, his knees slightly bent into a partial fetal position. Zeke walked around to the other side of the Ford and saw that Stover's chin was lowered and his lips were moving as he muttered something under his breath.

A moment later Stover raised his head and turned to Zeke. "Find anything useful?"

"Yes," Zeke said as Albright joined them.

"Any gas cans full of gas?" Stover asked with a smile.

"No, afraid not."

"I don't know how accurate that gas gauge is," Albright said while joining them, "but I think we may be running on fumes."

"Let's just keep driving as far as we can," Zeke said while heading to the driver side of the Ford.

"Yes," Stover agreed. "I got a feeling we'll find what we need up ahead."

Albright, Stover, Margolian, and Billy climbed back into the truck bed. Zeke slid in next to Matt in the cab of the Ford. The boy curled into a tighter position to give Zeke more room. Zeke started the ignition and checked the gas gauge. The needle pointed directly at the *E,* but how much lower it would fall he didn't know.

He put the Ford in gear and drove back onto the road. He passed several more closed businesses with boarded windows. Then less than a mile away he saw a car entering an intersection up ahead. The car turned onto the crossroad and sped away. Zeke knew they were near some little town not far from Pecos and it shouldn't be long before he made contact with someone.

Zeke drove to the intersection, the out-of-order stoplight dangling on its wire above him. He scanned the area quickly and turned left in the same direction the vehicle had turned. He saw a building with a *Piggly Wiggly* sign on top. When he reached the abandoned grocery store he saw no forms of life or any vehicles in the parking lot. The windows and main entrance were boarded shut with more plywood. He continued on, his attention focused on finding the vehicle he saw earlier. He saw a flash of light in the corner of his eye; like a mirror in the distance reflecting sunlight. He knew the general location the flash came from but now he couldn't see it. While searching for the origin of the flash Zeke suddenly saw an old man wearing a ball cap walking away from a small metal building. The old man was heading toward an ancient-looking silver Cadillac, probably from the 1980s.

Zeke drove the Ford toward the Cadillac and parked a short distance away to not alarm the old-timer. The old man was carrying a brown paper bag in his arms. He didn't look surprised or alarmed by the Ford's sudden appearance, he just stared at the pickup as Zeke shut off the ignition.

"Howdy," Zeke said while stepping out from behind the wheel. He walked toward the old man and said, "How's it going?"

The old man looked squarely into Zeke's eyes. "Fair to midland, I reckon."

Zeke extended his hand. "I'm Zeke."

The old man tucked the paper bag under an arm and shook Zeke's hand. "W. J. Patton, but everyone calls me Jack."

Jack Patton's weathered hand looked and felt like old saddle-leather. He wore a western-styled, collared shirt tucked into a pair of creased kakis, a *John Deere* ball cap shading his tanned, wrinkled face.

"You know where we can get some gas?" Zeke asked. "We're running on fumes."

"You folks ain't from around here," Jack said before reaching through the Cadillac's opened window and setting his paper bag in the front seat.

"No, sir," Zeke said.

Jack returned his attention to Zeke. His steely blue eyes showed strength and alertness that belied the rest of his old frame. "Where you headed?"

"East," Zeke said. "We've got a sick boy and I'm trying to get him and his father home."

Jack nodded while eyeing the Ford. "That a ninety-six or a ninety-seven?"

Zeke didn't know the answer for sure but he now knew that Jack Patton was more shrewd than he'd first appeared. If Jack knew the correct year and was acting like he didn't to determine if Zeke had stolen the Ford, Zeke wasn't going to fall into the trap. "Don't know for sure," he answered. "It belongs to the other fellow in back. I'm just taking my turn driving."

"Good trucks," Jack said after a long moment. "Had one years ago."

Zeke nodded patiently.

"You say ya gotta sick boy with ya?" Jack asked.

"Yeah," Zeke said. "Trying to get him home."

Jack stared into Zeke's eyes with a penetrating stare. "Where'd you say home was?"

Zeke almost said, *"didn't say,"* but he wanted to keep it friendly with the sly old man. He didn't want to reveal their true destination, but he didn't want to weave too many lies before he had a chance to talk to Albright and Stover. "San Antonio."

"San Antone," Jack said. "Home of the Alamo, and that Air Force base . . . can't recall the name at the moment."

Zeke was getting tired of the game. "Lackland," he said.

"Huh?"

"Lackland Air Force Base," Zeke said in a louder voice.

"Yeah," Jack said. "That's it."

"So, Jack," Zeke said, "is there any gas around here to be had?"

"After everybody headed out of town toward that relief camp in Midland," Jack explained, "any gas left was *requisitioned* by Sheriff Clayton Ward for official use, if you know what I mean."

Zeke broke eye contact to glance at Jack's old Cadillac sedan. He turned back to meet Jack's stare. "So where do you get your gas, Jack?"

"Had a full tank when all this started," Jack said without hesitation. "Don't drive much except to get an odd 'n end from town ever now and then."

What kind of odd 'n ends? Zeke thought, wondering what was in the paper bag Jack tossed in the Cadillac. He also wondered what was in the metal building behind them. "You know, Jack," Zeke said, "I'd be willing to pay a hefty price for whatever gas I could get my hands on."

"Oh yeah?"

Zeke kept nodding his head. "I'd even be willing to buy another vehicle," he explained. "You know, one that had a full tank when all this started."

Jack's steely blue eyes seemed to smile. "You would?"

"Yeah," Zeke said. "With cash. Hard, cold cash."

Jack's eyes narrowed to a squint. "How much hard, cold cash?"

"Depends on the vehicle."

"Well . . ." Jack began, the old wheels in his mind running without a squeak, "I may know of someone willin' to let go of their car for the right price."

"What about this one?" Zeke asked, pointing to the Cadillac.

"Nah, I couldn't sell her," Jack said. "Had her too long. But the one I got in mind *could* be available. I'd have to make sure the cash was on-hand, though. Wouldn't want to waste their time with an empty offer—not that I'm saying you're just pulling my leg."

Zeke was already pulling out a roll of hundred-dollar bills from a leg pocket, one of several stashes of cash he carried on his body and in his backpack. He pealed off two one-hundred-dollar bills from the fat roll and handed them to Jack. "This is for your finder's fee," he said.

Jack finally smiled. "Okay, you wanna wait here while I go talk to 'em?"

"I'd rather all us go with you," Zeke said while gesturing to the Ford where Albright, Stover, and Margolian stared at them. "That way we can make a deal with your *seller* on the spot and be on our way. Mind taking us with you?"

Jack raised his eyebrows while looking at the Ford and it's human and animal occupants. He glanced at the roll of cash Zeke replaced in the leg pocket. "Whatcha gonna do with the pickup?"

"Leave it here for the moment," Zeke said, planning to leave it there a lot longer than a moment. "I don't think there's enough fuel in it to go anywhere."

"Okay," Jack finally said with a grin. "Grab your folks and we'll take a ride. It's not far from here."

"Great," Zeke said while walking briskly back to the Ford. He noticed Jack following him. Zeke picked up his pace to reach the Ford before Jack got there, but the old man was walking as fast as he was. When Zeke reached the Ford he said, "Hey, everyone! This is Jack Patton." Zeke gave the men in back a wink. "He's going to help us get home to San Antonio."

Jack peered into the cab of the Ford and saw Matt still sleeping. "He unconscious?"

"No, he's just sleeping," Zeke replied.

Jack greeted Albright, Stover, and Margolian in the truck bed. He even greeted Billy with a tip of his ball cap while Zeke awakened Matt. The sleepy boy looked confused for a moment as everyone began loading their gear into the Cadillac's spacious trunk. Zeke managed to remove his M4 from the floorboard and get it into the Cadillac's trunk without Jack noticing. He decided to leave Jihad the shotgun in the Ford's cab behind the seat.

Albright and Matt sat in front with Jack, while Zeke, Stover, Margolian, and Billy crammed in the Cadillac's spacious rear seat. Jack veered the big automobile out of the parking lot and gunned the gas pedal when they hit the road. Zeke and Stover shared a smile as Jack drove the Cadillac like a bank robber running from the cops, not even slowing at the intersection where the dead traffic light dangled in the wind.

"You feeling better, boy?" Jack asked Matt who was leaning against his father's shoulder, trying to keep as much distance as possible between him and the old man speeding down the road. "A little bit," the boy said in a weak voice.

Four or five miles later, Jack jerked the wheel onto a dirt road leading to a ranch-style house badly in need of a paint job. He pulled the Cadillac directly in front of the covered front porch and braked hard. The Cadillac slid to a stop, the dust in its wake blowing over them and into the acres of flat land beyond. "Here we are," Jack croaked in his old but strong voice.

Everyone piled out of the Cadillac and stood by the porch. Jack said, "I'll be right back," and disappeared inside the house after unlocking the front door. Albright came close to Zeke and whispered, "You didn't tell him where we were from, did you?"

Zeke shook his head.

Albright nodded and sat on the porch next to Matt. The boy looked like he felt a little better.

Jack came back to the porch with a ring of keys in his hand. "Come this way," he said, eager to get to a tin-roofed barn not far away.

Margolian said, "You have a phone I can use?"

Jack gave him a peculiar look before stepping closer to Zeke. "He okay?" he asked in a whisper. "You know, in the head?"

Zeke shrugged his shoulders to let Jack think Margolian was *not* okay in the head, which as fas as Zeke knew might be the truth. "You can answer him, though," Zeke whispered back to Jack.

Jack turned toward Margolian. "No, sir!" he said in a loud clear voice. "No phones around here work!"

Margolian gave Zeke a knowing look and sat down on a porch step, going back into his quiet, depressed state.

Zeke followed the old man to the barn where Jack unlocked a padlocked clasp on the large double doors. "He get kicked in the head or something?" Jack asked Zeke.

"Nah," Zeke replied. "He's just been this way for a while. He doesn't even know where he is most of the time."

Jack nodded in understanding. "Yeah, I had an uncle that way many years ago."

Zeke helped to open the doors before Jack went inside and fired up a gas-powered generator around the corner. The genny purred to life and a lightbulb hanging above them twinkled to life. Zeke saw some type of vehicle covered with a dirty tarpaulin. Jack grabbed one end of the tarp and started yanking it off the vehicle underneath, creating a cloud of dust that hovered in the thick air of the barn. Jack tossed the tarp aside, revealing a red Dodge Caravan more than ten years old. "A minivan," Zeke said, more to himself than to Jack.

"Caravan Sport," Jack said. "Two-thousand-one model, but only has about eighty-thousand miles on her."

"That all?" said Zeke.

"Tires are all good," Jack said, starting to sound more and more like a used car salesman. "Tape deck, AC, the works."

Tape deck? Zeke hadn't heard that expression since he was a boy.

"She's got the V6 under her hood," Jack explained. "Not the four cylinder they made on earlier models. I bought it for my youngest daughter. She used it until her worthless husband bought her one of those foreign hybrids, the one they left town in."

"Crank her up," Zeke said, not really interested in Jack's family backstory.

Jack propped open the Caravan's small hood with the metal support piece, then went over to a stack of boxes and other junk filling the barn. He removed a car battery from one of the boxes and carried it to the opened hood. "Had to take her battery out a while back," Jack said while setting the battery in position, "to use in the Caddy. But this one's brand new. Never gotta chance to replace it."

Zeke realized it was probably good the Dodge's electrical system hadn't been wired to a battery during the EMP event. "How much gas she got?"

"As much as you need," came the reply.

After attaching the cables to the battery, Jack opened the driver door. The interior lights came on immediately as he sat behind the wheel and found the right key to put in the ignition. A little bell sound *dinged-dinged* repeatedly. Jack cranked the ignition several times until the Dodge's engine started. "There you go," he said. "Fit as a fiddle."

Zeke peered inside at the gauges in the dash. The battery showed a full charge. The needle in the gas gauge pointed at the half-full mark. The interior looked in good shape, not that it really mattered.

Jack revved the engine a few times before turning off the ignition. "Well?"

Zeke knew the key to bargaining was getting the other party to quote a number first. "How much you want?" he asked.

Jack pursed his lips in thought. "In a normal situation I could get five for her. But considering the situation these days, I'd say somewhere around ten."

Zeke knew that Jack was shrewd and he also knew Jack had the upper hand, anyway you looked at it. "Let's say," Zeke counter-offered, "seventy-five-hundred."

"My youngest daughter drove it," Jack said without responding to Zeke's counteroffer. "And she drove like a granny."

Zeke laughed. "Yeah, well *you* don't drive like a granny."

Jack laughed back. "That's true," he said. "But I don't drive it. Never have. Not enough horsepower for my taste."

Zeke chuckled while shaking his head.

"Eighty-five," said Jack.

Zeke stared back. "And a full tank of gas?"

Jack stuck out his leathery hand to seal the deal. "You got it."

"Deal," Zeke said, shaking Jack's hand.

Jack reached into the glove box. "Got the paperwork right here," he said while removing some folded papers. He handed the car keys to Zeke and said, "Follow me and we'll close our business."

Zeke followed Jack back to the house. Albright and Stover stared at

Zeke with expectant looks on their faces while Margolian sat on the porch staring at his feet. "You guys load the gear into our new ride," Zeke said with a smile. "I'll be there in a second."

Zeke walked up the porch and into the house. The air inside was musty. It reeked of old sweat and fried bacon. Jack went behind a wooden desk cluttered with papers and boxes and dirty coffee mugs. He lighted a kerosene lamp on the desk, adjusted the wick, then dug through a drawer and removed a pair of reading glasses. "That'll be eighty-five-hundred dollars," he said. "Cash."

"Cash," Zeke said while digging out two rolls of bills from different pockets, happy he found the vehicle but still feeling like he got out-haggled by the old man. He'd paid more than thirty grand for beat-up Toyota pickups in Afghanistan, inflation caused by so much American dollars flooding the country, but this felt different. Maybe it wasn't so different. He began thumbing hundred-dollar-bills onto the desk, stacking them in piles of one-thousand each. "Don't you have a genny for the house, Jack?"

"Yeah," Jack said while grabbing each pile and counting it with his bony fingers, not allowing himself to get distracted from his counting.

After counting all the money, Jack scooped it up and placed it all in a *White Owl* cigar box. He put the cigar box in a lower desk drawer and turned his attention to the folded papers. He unfolded the papers and wrote something on them. "I need to see your driver's license."

Zeke hesitated and Jack noticed.

"Look, son," Jack said. "I just need to write the information on the deed. The deed's for you, not me."

Zeke removed his wallet from one of his many pockets. He slid out his driver's license that still had a Houston address on it. He never got around to changing it since he bought the cabin near Gold Tree. He handed it to Jack.

Jack copied Zeke's full name and driver's license number onto the deed. He slid the deed and driver's license across the table to Zeke. "Put your John Hancock right there next to mine."

Zeke took the pen and looked at the paper. The deed to the Dodge Caravan was in Jack's name. Jack had written a short note on top of the deed, indicating the sale price, date of the transaction, and the information from Zeke's driver's license. Zeke scribbled his name on the paper and handed the pen back to Jack, wondering if all this was really necessary.

"Pleasure doing business with ya!" Jack said while reaching inside the paper bag he'd carried inside earlier. He removed a fifth of Jack Daniel's whiskey and tore the plastic wrapping on the neck with an old fingernail. He pulled the cork and took a generous plug of whiskey into his mouth. He relished the flavor for a few seconds before wiping the top with a sleeve and handing it to Zeke.

Zeke took a sip from the bottle and handed it back.

"Always like to end a business transaction with a little snort," Jack said, taking another gulp from the bottle. He offered the bottle back to Zeke.

Zeke shook his head and asked, "How about the gas, Jack?"

"Follow me," Jack said while re-corking the bottle and setting it on his messy desk. He led Zeke back outside to the porch. "Bring her around over here and we'll get you gassed up." Jack said while heading to a path running behind the barn.

Zeke walked to the barn where Stover, Margolian, and the two Albrights were standing next to the opened rear hatch, their gear loaded behind the third seat row. Billy came running up to meet Zeke. He rubbed his dog's head vigorously. "We're in business, boys," he told everyone. He asked Stover in a quiet voice, "You get the M4?"

"Yes," Stover replied in a whisper. "Its underneath the seat behind the bags."

"Good," Zeke said while getting behind the wheel and putting the keys into the ignition. "You guys get in. We're going to pull around and get the tank topped off."

Stover shut the rear hatch and got in the passenger seat. Margolian and the two Albrights climbed inside the Caravan through its sliding side door while Billy hopped back on the third row bench seat.

"What'd you have to give for it?" Albright asked.

"Eighty-five," Zeke answered.

"Eighty-five dollars?" Matt asked in an incredulous voice.

"Eighty-five-hundred," his father answered for Zeke. "That ain't bad, Zeke. And with a full tank, too. Good job."

"Yeah, I guess," Zeke said while backing the minivan out the barn and driving onto the path leading behind the barn. Jack stood there waiting, a gas nozzle in his hand that connected by hose to a large tank mounted on a metal-frame platform. It had to be at least a five-hundred gallon tank. Jack started pumping gas after Zeke popped open the lid covering the gas cap.

Zeke stepped out and said, "I thought you said the Sheriff requisitioned all the gasoline."

"Let's just say that he makes allowances for me."

"How's that?"

"Well, for one thing," Jack explained, "he's married to my oldest daughter and I've been kickin' his skinny butt since he was a snot-nosed kid trying to date her."

This made Zeke laugh. "Okay."

"And secondly," Jack continued, "I'm the one who got him elected Sheriff and the one who *keeps* him getting elected each term."

Zeke nodded and leaned his head inside the minivan. "Where's the empty gas canister?" he asked Stover.

"With the bags," Stover said.

Zeke opened the rear of the minivan and grabbed the empty ten-gallon canister. He carried it over to Jack and set it near him.

Jack ignored it while still filling the minivan. A moment passed before he said, "That'll cost you an extra hundred."

"What?"

"You didn't say nothing about any extra gas cans," Jack said. "Just because I'm old don't mean I'm stupid."

Zeke sighed and placed a folded hundred-dollar bill in Jack's front shirt pocket. "You got any oil, Jack?"

"Got some thirty-weight in the barn," Jack said. "I'll grab it when I'm done.

"How much is that going to set me back?"

"Fifty bucks," said Jack.

"Fifty bucks!" Zeke exclaimed, mostly for fun, but still surprised. "That's highway robbery!"

"I only got a half case left," Jack said in his defense. "I was planning on selling you two quarts out of the goodness of my heart."

"How generous of you," Zeke said. "So how about twenty bucks?"

"That sounds fair," Jack said, getting a surprised look from Zeke. "Twenty bucks a pop. That comes out to forty even."

"You're one of a kind, Jack," Zeke said. He actually admired the old coot. He bet Jack Patton was a force to be reckoned with in his younger days. *Probably still is,* Zeke said to himself.

Jack finished filling the minivan and went to work filling the ten-gallon canister. When Jack finished with the canister Zeke loaded it in the rear before paying him for the two quarts of *Pennzoil* thirty-weight. "Thanks, Jack Patton," Zeke said. "I enjoyed your company."

"Same here," said Jack.

"Wish I could say the same about our business dealings," Zeke added.

Jack chuckled while setting the oil cans next to the gas canister and closing the rear hatch. "When you get to the end of my drive, take a right and you'll run into Kiowa Road."

"Yes, sir."

Jack leaned in a little closer. "Now listen, son," he said in a stern voice. "The Sheriff's got just two patrol cars running, and they ain't doin' much patrolling due to the gas shortage and all, so they pick a few spots to hide, usually near the ramps to the interstates. You stay on Kiowa Road and it'll lead you to ten-west eventually, way south of their hideouts. Believe me, them deputies ain't got nothing better to do these days than hassle out-of-town folk. You hear me, boy?"

"Loud and clear, Jack."

"Okay," Jack said with a wide grin. "You folks take care and have a good trip home."

Zeke got behind the wheel and with one final wave to Jack Patton he drove the Dodge Caravan away from the property onto the dirt road. Everyone's spirits were lifted by the comfortable ride and the prospect of getting to Austin soon. Everyone except for Margolian, who sat quietly, lost somewhere inside his head. Matt seemed to feel better now. From the seat behind Zeke and Stover, the boy joked with his dad and laughed loudly as Albright tickled his ribs. Billy, in the rear on the third row bench seat, stuck his nose against the window while examining the landscape beyond.

After turning onto Kiowa Road, Zeke accustomed himself with the minivan's dash controls. He flipped on the radio and got the static. He pushed the CD button and heard the player's motor engage. A few seconds later, country music began playing through the minivan's speakers. Zeke hadn't heard any music in a while. Even though he wasn't a country music fan, the song made him feel good. Stover began singing along, apparently familiar with the song and its lyrics. Albright and Matt joined in on the chorus: *"This killin' time is killin' me. Drinkin' myself blind, thinkin' I won't see..."*

Zeke started singing along even though he didn't know the lyrics. Stover laughed at his attempt. When the chorus came back around, Zeke jumped back in, singing even louder than before. Margolian began to smile and tried to join in. Stover tried to lead him: "... *that if I cross that line and they bury me, I just might find I'll be killin' time for eternity...*"

They were enjoying themselves so much with the music blaring out the speakers that no one noticed the patrol car tailgating the minivan, its emergency lights flashing. Zeke caught the lights in his rearview mirror and turned the CD's volume down. They all heard the single blast of the siren. "What did we do?" Matt asked.

Zeke didn't answer as he unclipped his M9 holster and handed it to Stover. Stover didn't need instructions. He placed the holstered firearm under his seat, keeping his body movements to a minimum as Zeke pulled the minivan off the road and came to a halt. Zeke rolled down his window, watching the patrol car in his side mirror while waiting for the officer to emerge.

After a long moment of waiting, Zeke saw a tall officer climb out of the patrol car. He wore a Stetson cowboy hat with a badge on his white, button-down, collared shirt. The deputy rested one hand on his holstered pistol as he approached. He stopped near the rear of the minivan and shouted, "Driver! Step out of the vehicle!"

"Oh, boy," Zeke muttered. "It's one of those."

"I said step out of the vehicle!" the deputy shouted again.

Zeke opened the door and stepped out, keeping his arms clear of his sides. "What's the problem, officer?" he asked.

"Put your hands on top of your head!" the deputy ordered.

"Ah, come on—"

"—I said put your hands on top of your head!"

Zeke reluctantly placed his hands on the top of the ball cap covering his head.

"Now move to the rear of the vehicle!"

Zeke followed the orders, knowing it was futile to argue.

"Now turn around," the deputy said in a slightly lower voice, "and lean against the vehicle. Arms and legs spread."

Zeke leaned against the minivan. Billy licked the glass from inside, inches away from Zeke's face. He saw the reflection of the tall deputy approaching him from behind. The deputy began patting him down for weapons. When he got to the sheathed K-Bar knife on Zeke's leg above his boot, Zeke felt him remove the knife slowly from the sheath. "Whatcha do with this?" the deputy asked. "Skin bucks?"

"Sometimes," replied Zeke.

"Who you got in there with ya?" the deputy asked while pulling Zeke's left arm behind his back.

Zeke felt a handcuff tighten on his wrist. "Three men and an eleven-year-old boy," Zeke said while the deputy grabbed his other arm and handcuffed his wrists together. "And my dog."

The deputy had obviously already seen Billy in the rear. He took a few steps back and shouted, "You in the passenger seat! Step out of the vehicle and place your hands on top of your head!"

Stover stepped out with his hands already on his head. He turned and looked expectantly at Zeke and the deputy.

The deputy started to say something when all of a sudden everyone heard a car screeching to a halt behind the patrol car. Zeke turned his head and saw wiry Jack Patton slamming his Cadillac's door shut and marching toward them. "Garth Wooley! What in the world do you think you're doing!"

"They're drivin' Aunt Missy's car, Granddad," Deputy Wooley said in a sheepish voice.

"That's my car, boy!" Jack said. "I just sold it to them. Did ya even take a look at the papers?"

"Well, no . . . I didn't—"

"—Get those cuffs off!" Jack shouted.

After the deputy had unlocked and removed the cuffs, Zeke turned and walked toward Jack while rubbing his wrists. He gave Jack a big smile. "Jack."

"Zeke," Jack said before turning his attention back to his grandson, Deputy Garth Wooley. "Turn off your vehicle, boy. You're wasting gasoline."

Deputy Wooley hung his head and sat behind the wheel of his patrol car before killing the ignition.

"You got them papers we signed?" Jack asked Zeke.

"Yeah," Zeke said. "They're in the glove box."

"Grab 'em, would ya?"

Zeke turned to Paul who still had his hands on his bald head while standing outside the door. Zeke chuckled and shouted, "Hey, Paul! Grab the deed! It's in the glove box!"

Stover nodded and leaned into the opened passenger door to get the papers.

Deputy Wooley stepped back out his patrol car while adjusting the gun belt on his big frame. Stover came trotting over to the men, the folded papers in his hand.

Jack reached for the papers and unfolded them. He handed them to the deputy and said, "Read that. I know you can read a little."

Deputy Wooley read Jack's scribbled handwriting and handed back the papers.

Jack passed them back to Zeke who passed them on to Stover. "Don't you think you should've asked for these before you start making arrests?" Jack asked the deputy.

"I saw strangers driving the car, Granddad," Deputy Wooley protested. "I figured they stole it. I was worried they knocked you over the head or something."

"What?" Jack guffawed. "Have you ever known of anyone knockin' me over the head and livin' to tell about it?"

Deputy Wooley bit back a smile trying to form on his face. "No, sir."

"I'm gone," Jack said while turning and storming back to his big Cadillac. Without turning his head, he shouted, "Good luck on your trip, Zeke!"

Stover headed back to the minivan while Zeke stood there with Deputy Wooley looking awkwardly at him. The deputy turned and reached into the patrol car to grab something. He returned with Zeke's K-Bar knife in his hand. "Here ya go. No hard feelings."

Zeke took the knife. "No hard feelings."

Jack gunned the Cadillac and did a one-eighty turn, shooting gravel toward the patrol car before speeding back down the highway. Zeke and the deputy exchanged small grins.

"I recognized the vehicle," Deputy Wooley said. "I thought you stole it."

"I understand," Zeke said while returning the knife to the sheath beneath his pant leg. "I probably would've thought the same thing."

The big deputy nodded in an approving way. "When you see my granddad again," he said, "maybe you can explain that to him."

"You got it," Zeke said before touching the bill of his ball cap and heading back to the minivan. He climbed back behind the wheel and said, "Well, that was fun."

"The old man obviously has some pull around these parts," Albright said.

"I think I agree with you," Zeke said, watching the patrol car in the side mirror head back the way it came. Zeke put the minivan in gear and floored the accelerator, unable to get the tires to squeal like Jack had done in his Cadillac. He turned the CD player volume back up. A different song was playing. "Put it back on that song, Paul."

Stover changed track selection. The song started again. Zeke yanked the volume way up and began trying to sing along, glancing at Stover's lips to follow the lyrics. When the chorus arrived everyone joined in. Even Margolian seemed happy.

Zeke turned the volume down a bit and said, "How about digging out some MREs. Getting searched and cuffed always makes me hungry."

"You got a lot of experience with that?" Stover asked with a grin.

While Matt climbed in back to get the MREs, Zeke turned the CD volume back up. The words hit home as he listened to Clint Black singing: *"I don't know nothing 'bout tomorrow, I've been lost in yesterday. I've spent all my life just dying for a love that passed away. If there's an end to all my sorrow and it's the only price I'll pay, I'll be a happy man when I go, and I can't wait another day . . ."*

*   *   *

EIGHT

William Lloyd Fowler, Gold Tree's resident vagrant, known and addressed by most locals simply as *Billy,* followed the trail out of the park toward his main residence—an old canvas tent with duct tape patches to keep out the bugs and rain. *And soon the snow,* he thought as he shuffled along the dirt trail. Of course when winter came in full force he'd be spending most of his time at the Methodist church, Gold Tree's only church, which in the past had offered him shelter in trade for some basic building maintenance and other janitorial services. This year would be different, though, with no electricity and other essentials like food, medicine, and fresh water. Billy knew the church would be sheltering many other folks this season. He'd already been hanging around the church more often than usual, hoping Pastor Harding and the staff would still supply him with a cot and three square meals a day once the cold weather came.

Billy left the main trail and headed to his tent hidden in a small clearing nestled in the trees and brush. When he entered the clearing three young men stepped into view. He recognized one of them, Jared, a town bully that Billy had crossed paths with several times in the last year or so. The other two Billy had seen before but didn't know.

"Hey, old man," Jared said while taking a step toward him. He wrinkled his nose. "You been hanging out in a dumpster or something?"

Billy took a step back while keeping his eyes on the other two trying to circle behind him. "Whatcha want, Jared?"

"Whatcha got?"

"I ain't got nothing!" Billy said, trying not to show the fear he felt.

"Really?" Jared said while reaching inside his jacket pocket to pull out a pint bottle of cheap whiskey—Billy's bottle of whiskey that had been stored in the tent.

Billy glanced at his open tent flap and knew they had already found his hiding place where a few meager items were stashed. One of the men, probably in his early twenties, stepped closer with a nasty smirk on his face. Billy noticed the gray hoodie sweater he wore. The *Army Rangers* stencil on the front of the hoodie seemed vaguely familiar but he couldn't remember why at the moment.

Jared unscrewed the top of the whiskey bottle and brought it to his lips, but instead of taking a sip, he turned it upside-down and poured some of the whiskey onto the ground.

"Hey, man!" Billy complained. "Why would you do that for?"

"Because I wanted to," Jared hissed. He took another step toward Billy, still holding the bottle as if he might pour the remaining contents onto the ground. "You seen your friend lately?"

"What friend?" Billy replied, not having a clue of who Jared was talking about.

"The one you were seen talking to in the park."

"I talk to a lot of people in the park," Billy replied honestly. "I don't know who you're talking about."

Jared squinted his eyes, trying to look mean. "He had a *dog* with him," he said. "You petted it. You even gave it some food, you old fool. A bum, digging through trash cans and then you gave it away to some mutt. What an idiot."

The memory started coming back to Billy. He remembered the man and the dog. The dog shared his name. "Oh yeah," he said eagerly. "The dog's name was Billy, the same as mine!"

"How cool!" Jared mocked him. "Now what did you talk to him about?"

"The dog?"

Jared's face turned red as he saw his two cohorts smile. He shot them both a nasty look before turning his attention back on Billy. "THE MAN!" he screamed.

Billy flinched in fear. He struggled to remember the conversation that day in the park. "Let's see, he gave me some good whiskey."

"Of course you'd remember that," Jared mumbled.

"And he was asking about . . ." Billy remembered about the sweater. He shot a quick look at the young man wearing the hoodie. " . . . about a sweater."

"A what?" Jared said in disbelief.

Billy pointed accusingly at the young man's hoodie. "He asked me about a sweater," he repeated. "That one right there!"

Jared glanced at the Army Rangers hoodie and then back to Billy. "And what about it?"

"He asked me if I'd seen anyone wearing it," Billy explained.

"And why would he do that?" Jared asked.

"Because it belonged to him, I guess."

Jared exhaled loudly, making a show of his loss of patience.

"And I wouldn't wanna be in your shoes, sonny boy," Billy said to the young man in the hoodie, "if he sees you wearing it."

The young man smiled, but betrayed a bit of nervousness as he looked to Jared for support.

"And why is that, old man?" Jared asked with a smile.

"Because he looked like the sort you wouldn't wanna mess with," Billy said. "He was armed with a pistol and a big knife under his clothes, the kind those army guys carry, you know, them Delta squads, or whatever they call 'em."

Jared and his two cohorts chuckled together. "Those Delta squads, huh?"

Billy didn't get the joke and he was getting more frightened by the moment.

The sweater says *'Army Rangers'* on it, you dimwit!" Jared scoffed before moving in close and causing Billy to stumble. "Are you trying to make us believe your conversation was just about some old sweater?"

"That's the honest truth," Billy replied, his voice starting to waver. "I swear it!" He suddenly remembered talking to the man with the dog about the day all the electric power died and his sighting of a UFO before it all happened, but he decided not to mention that to Jared.

"You're lying," Jared said while removing a small club from beneath his jacket. He began slapping the club against his palm. "It's funny," he said with a smile. "You know what they call this?"

Billy shook his head in response, feeling his heart starting to beat out of control.

"It's called a *Billy* club," Jared said before laughing loudly. "Get it?"

Billy got it. He tried to back away but Jared had him cornered near a tree. "What I need to know," Jared began while still slapping his palm with the club, "is where this guy was going. This is your last chance."

"I don't know," Billy insisted. "He never said nothin' about where he was going. I swear on my mama's grave!"

Jared made a facial expression suggesting an *oh-well-if-that's-the-way-you-want-it* attitude. He lowered the club beside his own leg, planning on striking Billy's knee first before questioning him again and working on the rest of his body if necessary.

"Enough," a voice suddenly announced.

They all turned to the sound and saw a man standing on the trail. Billy stared at his savior of the moment. The man was dressed in kakis, hunting boots, and a red plaid flannel shirt with an old-fashioned hunting cap on his head. The whole wardrobe looked like it had come straight from the store and never worn before. The man's head looked too long and narrow for the rest of his body. His lips were thick and wide and when he spoke they seemed to stretch beyond normal.

"Leave us now," the man said to Jared and his cohorts.

And to Billy's amazement, they did just that, leaving the campsite without a word.

The man approached Billy with a funny walk, his steps small and awkward as if he had a disability or injury. "You are safe now," the man said, his voice low but clear. "Were you harmed?"

Billy shook his head as he watched the man intently. He couldn't seem to take his eyes off the odd face with those thick lips.

"What did they want from you?" the man asked.

"They wanted to know about some fellow I met in the park a while back," Billy said. "They wanted to know where he went and I told 'em I didn't know, which is the honest to God truth."

"Sometimes the memories are there," the man said while digging in a wicker satchel on his side that Billy hadn't noticed before. "They just have to be found."

Billy watched as the man removed a full bottle of Jack Daniel's whiskey from the satchel, holding it so Billy got a good look at it. The man walked a few paces and set the bottle on a tree stump Billy sometimes used as a stool. "Would you like a drink?" the man asked.

Billy licked his lips. "Oh brother, would I!" he said before heading for the bottle. While removing the seal on the bottle Billy watched the man remove a brand new pack of Marlboro cigarettes from the satchel. After taking a big gulp of whiskey he took the cigarette the man offered. The man lighted the cigarette in Billy's lips with a disposable lighter before asking, "This man in the park, did he mention any relatives he might be visiting? Like a brother? Or a sister?"

Billy sighed in contentment as he exhaled smoke from the cigarette. He took another generous swallow of whiskey before looking toward the man. "No, not that I recall," he said, a part of him wondering why this strange person was asking the same questions Jared had been asking, but another part of him caring only about the whiskey and cigarettes and the assurance that they would keep coming his way.

The man guided Billy to the tree stump. "Why don't you sit here and relax."

Billy shrugged and sat on the stump as the man sauntered around the campsite with that odd walk of his. "I didn't catch your name," Billy said, happily drinking the whiskey and puffing on the cigarette.

The man didn't look at Billy. His attention seemed distracted by something in the woods surrounding them. "You can call me . . . friend."

"Well, Mr. Friend," Billy said after swallowing a big gulp of whiskey, a sly smirk on his face. "I want to thank you for your help back there, not to mention the fine drink and smoke."

The man didn't answer. He walked in his weird gait toward the opposite side of the small campsite. He turned and faced Billy, his thick lips widening into a wicked grin.

Billy stared at the man's mouth. Something seemed to be moving inside but it didn't look like a tongue, at least not a normal human tongue. At this exact time, Billy heard something. Actually, he *felt* something. A low rumbling vibrated the ground around him, making his hair stand on end—not from fright but from some type of electric pulse, as if a giant electromagnet pulled at him from somewhere near his abdomen.

A short distance away, near the eastern edge of the park, J.D. Singletary, a Gold Tree town maintenance engineer stopped raking a pile of leaves, his attention diverted by a single scream coming from the woods behind the park. It sounded like a man's scream. As J.D. stood in silence he listened for any other sounds but heard none. He glanced around the empty park and then back toward the direction the scream came from. He'd only seen two people in the park that afternoon. One was a woman walking her cocker spaniel that pooped everywhere, and the other, the town bum, Billy, heading out of the park toward his makeshift home in the woods.

J.D. leaned his rake against the wheelbarrow he used for the leaves and headed for the trail leading out of the park into the woods. A few moments later he saw Billy's canvas tent peeking through the trees. He approached cautiously while keeping a close watch on the woods surrounding him. He noticed a foul odor as he neared the tent. When he peered inside the tent the smell became worse. The old blankets piled about reeked of booze, old sweat, and other bodily fluids he didn't want to think about. He stepped away from the tent and cupped his hands around his mouth. "Billy!" he shouted. He waited for some type of response. Nothing but silence. Even the birds and squirrels were silent.

J.D. left the campsite and headed back up the trail to the park. He never saw the small wisp of smoke rising from a smoldering cigarette butt on the ground near the tree stump, or the whiskey bottle laying on its side, its spilled contents forming a dark puddle before being absorbed into the dry Texas soil.

* * *

NINE

After leaving Jack Patton and his grandson deputy, Zeke and his crew followed a route of county backroads running parallel with I10. Finding no sources of gasoline and with the sun falling rapidly, Zeke decided to call it a day. They needed to find a decent campsite for the evening. Albright was eager to get to Austin. He wanted to keep driving but Zeke explained that they needed more gas to get there. Even though the ten gallons in the canister hadn't been used yet they would still need more to complete the trip. A realistic search needed to be done during daylight hours and would probably require getting on I10 where gas was being rationed at one of the locations Little Willy mentioned. They needed to stop for the night. Albright reluctantly agreed.

Without saying anything about it, Zeke also knew they had only one round of MREs left. Their water was nearly gone. If he found gasoline, the food and water wasn't that important. With enough gas they could be in Austin within the day. He was going to have to take a chance and get on I10 at some point. If his hunches were right, whoever was chasing them was still a good distance behind. The pursuers only course of action at the moment was the roadblocks. If he could avoid the roadblocks, chances were good that I10 would provide the necessary fuel needed to get to Austin. The first ration location near Junction, if Little Willy was correct, would be the logical choice. Then after refueling he would turn on a northeast heading, avoiding San Antonio and entering Austin via Highway 71. From Junction, Texas this was roughly a four hour drive and currently they were still a good one-hundred-fifty miles from Junction. With the ten gallons in the canister this was no problem but they would still need more gas to get all the way to Austin.

Zeke found a good location for camp beneath a large oak tree fifty yards off the road. The temperature had been dropping the last hour or so with a chilly wind blowing from the northwest, and now it was downright cold. Zeke told everyone they were going to have to weather it out. They could sleep in the minivan but they couldn't run the engine for heat. They needed to conserve fuel. At least they wouldn't have to deal with the wind, he told them. Everyone's body heat would help a bit.

They unloaded their gear from the back of the minivan to make room for Billy then grabbed their sleeping bags to make their beds. Zeke suggested that Matt and his father take one of the bench seats, Margolian would take the other bench seat, then Stover would sleep in the passenger seat up front. Everyone agreed.

While climbing into their sleeping bags for the evening they listened to the cold wind howling outside. Zeke started the engine and turned the minivan's heat control on high while they got situated. Before long, it actually got stuffy inside from the hot air blowing out the vents. Occasionally, a strong gust would rock the Caravan, reminding everyone how lucky they were to have shelter, especially heated, even though the warmth at the moment was just temporary.

When everyone finally got nestled into their sleeping bags it was completely dark outside the minivan's windows. Zeke killed the ignition. The silencing of the engine and heater fan, along with the total darkness surrounding them was dramatic. Zeke said "goodnight" and received a chorus of "goodnights" in reply.

About ten minutes later the wind picked up, causing all types of strange, haunting sounds from outside the minivan. With his head on his father's lap, Matt asked "What's that?" several times, getting responses from Zeke and his father about the whistling effects of wind blowing through tree branches and around objects like the minivan. Stover and Margolian were already sound asleep, snoring gently but steadily.

The driver's seat wouldn't recline all the way but Zeke didn't care. If he could get just three or four hours of sleep he'd be good. He started to doze while listening to the wind howl. Soon he was completely asleep.

*

The tapping sound awakened him. Zeke opened his eyes and sat absolutely still while listening, wondering where the sound came from. *Tap-tap-tap.* There it was again, barely audible but still heard. *Was it on the roof?* He listened hard, hearing nothing but the wind howling outside.

He heard it again. *Tap-tap-tap.* This time he was able to discern where the tapping was coming from. It was directly in front of him, on the minivan's windshield. Although it was pitch black outside, Zeke could still see the dark silhouette of the oak tree and its huge limbs hanging overhead, swaying with the strong gusts of wind. *Tap-tap-tap.* This time it sounded like it was beneath the minivan. *What in the world?* He listened carefully, staring at the same spot on the oak tree silhouette through the windshield, allowing his peripheral vision to notice any subtle movements to his left or to his right. He felt the hair on his arms rising. He instinctively reached for the M9 on his hip. It wasn't there. He remembered giving it to Stover earlier when he got pulled over by the deputy. Stover probably stuffed it under the passenger seat. The *tap-tap-tap* came again, but this time there was no mistaking where it came from. The tapping continued just inches away from his ear on the glass of the window next to his face. It was a gentle, consistent tapping, sounding like it was made by the tip of a claw or long fingernail barely making contact with the glass. Zeke turned to face the window. The face there began to glow a dull fluorescent green with a hideous expression that seemed to be smiling and scowling all at the same time. The thing staring back at him stopped its tapping, its eyes raging with anger. Its lips were thick and oversized, shiny from some type of gore oozing over them. It wore a Native American headband with a black feather attached to one side. It backed away from the window so Zeke could see its entire form glowing the same fluorescent green as the face. The legs were bowed like a lizard, covered slightly by a buckskin loincloth with moccasins on feet that looked too long to be human. It began dancing—its reptilian extremities gyrating to some unheard drum beat. One clawed hand held a feathered rattle, the other a tomahawk with a blade that gleamed from the light of a moon that Zeke couldn't see. It danced toward the window and moved its face closer. The lips began mouthing words Zeke couldn't hear. The thing kept repeating the silent message with a smile that made Zeke's skin crawl. Zeke's lip-reading finally enabled him to decipher the message: *We are coming for you . . . we are coming for you . . . we are coming for you . . .* All of a sudden the Native American-reptile thing jumped backwards nearly ten feet. With a scream that vibrated the minivan, it lunged forward with the tomahawk raised in its claw-like hand. It smashed the window, causing the glass to shatter into a psychedelic cobweb design of broken shards.

Zeke awoke with a loud exhale. *What a nightmare!* he thought while sitting motionless in the darkened minivan, hearing snoring from the seat behind him. It was cold inside the minivan. Tiny pellets of sleet were tapping on the roof, tapping on the windshield, and tapping on the window next to his face. Zeke turned the ignition switch to the first position. The dash lights illuminated the front seats. Stover was wrapped in his sleeping bag, his face the only part of him visible. His mouth was hanging open as he breathed steadily in his deep sleep.

Zeke started the engine. While waiting for it to warm he turned on the headlights. The trunk of the oak tree stood there in the stark light, its branches dancing in the wind as sleet fell at an angle through the headlight beams. He heard someone behind him rustling in their sleeping bag. "Everything okay?" Albright asked in a hushed voice.

"Yeah," Zeke replied. "Just going to run some heat for a little while."

Stover, with his eyes still shut said, "Thank you."

Zeke turned on the heater fan. The air blowing out was still cool but it was getting warmer. He revved the engine to heat it up faster. Billy was rustling around in back. He started to whine. Zeke didn't want to get out of his sleeping bag to let the dog out but his dog needed to go. *When you gotta go, you gotta go.*

Zeke shimmied out of his sleeping bag and opened the door. The cold blast of air brought him fully awake as sleet pellets bounced off his ball cap. He shut the door and hurried to the rear of the minivan to let Billy out. Zeke opened the rear hatch and the interior lights came on again. Billy jumped out. Zeke saw Matt's head rise above the seats. The boy scratched a spot in his tussled hair while turning to look at the opened rear hatch and the cold air entering. He looked at Zeke with squinted eyes before collapsing back on the seat, his head resting on his father's lap.

Zeke closed the hatch and headed back to the driver's seat inside the minivan. *Man, its cold,* he said to himself while sitting behind the wheel and watching Billy wander into a small clearing beyond the oak tree, sniffing the ground for a spot to do his business. In the minivan's headlights, like an actor taking center stage, *Billy The Amazing German Shepherd* maneuvered into that comical position dogs undertake to take a crap, totally unconcerned if anyone is watching or not. *A dogsquat,* one of Zeke's scout leaders used to call it.

Billy finished his business and continued to sniff the ground beneath the swaying canopy of the big oak tree. *Come on, Billy. It's time to get back inside.*

Zeke waited. The air blowing through the vents was warm now. He heard Stover begin to snore. After two more minutes of waiting Zeke stepped back out of the warmth of the minivan into the icy conditions raging outside—conditions that didn't seem to bother Billy one tiny bit as he continued following some scent on the ground.

"Come on, Billy!" Zeke commanded his dog.

Billy seemed concentrated on one particular spot at the base of the old tree. Zeke marched toward him, squinting his eyes from the icy pellets raining down upon them. "Billy!" he shouted, this time getting the dog's attention. "Come!"

Billy came toward him and that's when Zeke saw the scratches on the trunk of the oak tree. *No, not just scratches, but three deep gouges like from the claws of a large predator.* He also noticed that the claw mark on the big oak tree trunk was about six feet up from the ground. *No bears in these parts,* Zeke told himself. *And mountain lions don't mark trees this way.* But the most unsettling factor was the freshness of the scratches. Shreds of bark were still hanging at the bottom of the scratches; the exposed parts of the tree still green and moist. Zeke had a difficulty believing what he was seeing.

He coaxed Billy back to the minivan. The wind howling all around him sounded like distant laughter. When Zeke opened the rear hatch, he dug under the rear bench seat and grabbed his M4 assault rifle before letting Billy hop inside. He closed the hatch and returned to his seat behind the wheel, lowering the M4 to a position next to his right leg. Zeke stared at the tree trunk in the bright glare of the headlights. He could still see the scratch marks, the shredded bark hanging from the fresh cuts, the hideous face in his nightmare, the grotesque lips mouthing the warning. All the images were rushing through his brain as he hit the master lock on the door's electrical panel. He turned off the headlights and killed the ignition. He sat there in the darkness, listening to the *tap-tap-tap* sound of sleet pellets hitting the minivan, his hand on the grip of the M4, finger on the trigger, waiting for sunrise, knowing that sleep was entirely out of the picture.

*　*　*

TEN

There was nothing but brown matter, similar to smoke but more like fog. It swirled in abstract patterns made up of trillions of slimy tendrils the diameter of a human hair, all of it spinning and spiraling like worms swimming in a putrid soup of raw sewage. This was the atmosphere surrounding him.

He looked down at his nakedness, suspended in a spread eagle position, hovering somehow in the swirling brown fog, his arms and legs bound by some unknown force he couldn't see but he could certainly feel. There were others like him nearby. He couldn't always see them through the brown fog but he heard their terrifying screams while they were being *interrogated* by the captors. He caught a glimpse of one of his fellow captives sometime earlier. A filthy, scrawny man with long, unkept hair and scraggly beard was bound and suspended not far away. The captors—those horrible little gray creatures—had been questioning the scrawny man. He couldn't hear the creatures' questions but he heard the scrawny man babbling something about an army sweater. That's all he could hear before the captive began screaming again.

Shortly after that he knew why the scrawny man screamed the way he did. The creatures came to him next, morphing from the brown fog until he was surrounded by them. He wasn't sure if they were speaking or not, but he heard their words clearly in his head: *Where was the soldier going? The one named Ezekiel Allenby.* He resisted any cooperation at first, then they applied some unseen force which not only attacked his body but his mind and spirit as well. The feeling was so horrific that he would have rather been in some medieval dungeon having hot coals pressed to his flesh. When he finally relented, all he could say was that Allenby was heading east. That's all he knew. The creatures finally left to go torment other captives, their screams clearly heard through the brown fog. *If this was not Hell, it was a close copy,* he thought to himself.

Sometime later he *felt* the creatures returning. Like a scene projected onto a smoky mirror, he saw two of the creatures escorting a naked old man into this hellish existence. The old man's shriveled, pasty-white flesh showed signs of sunburn on his forearms, face, and neck; what was sometimes referred to as a carpenter's tan. Despite the old man's weak appearance, he fought relentlessly with his captors, cursing them and refusing to cooperate in any fashion. But soon they applied that unseen force to the old man. His cries of agony reverberated in the brown fog even though there were no walls or other reflective surfaces to be seen. Then the defiant old man finally began to talk. "All he told me was he was goin' to San Antone! That's all he said!"

More screams. More agony. "Okay, okay," the old man said, his voice traveling through the brown fog warped and distorted. "Yes! It said he was from Houston! You know, Houston? Like, 'Houston, we have a problem!' That's all I know!"

He heard the old man start to scream again, but then a dark mass, blacker than black, floated through the brown fog toward the old man and his captors. The dark mass was followed by several reptilian-looking creatures. He clearly heard a voice, an inhuman voice, utter a single syllable word that didn't come from any earthly language. The voice was so low and powerful that it resonated through the fog, causing the swirling tendrils to slither away from the black mass in fear. The little gray creatures immediately lowered themselves onto one scrawny knee with their faces bowing in respect, humbling themselves in the presence of their king or ruler. The black mass floated away into the brown fog. Even though there was no sense of temperature in this existence, he could still sense the absolute lack of heat emanating from the black mass, a cold so frigid that no human could really understand.

After the black mass had left, the gray creatures backed away as the reptilian creatures stepped forward. One of them offered something in its taloned hands to the old man. The thing in its hands slithered like a snake or huge worm. It was green and squishy, about as long and big around as a large cigar. *A giant green slug with no eyes or other features,* was the best he could describe it. The reptilian creature holding the slug began squeezing and kneading it in an obscene way—a bizarre massaging ritual that actually caused it to shrink in the creature's hand. The slug became smaller and smaller until he couldn't see it anymore, but he knew it was still in the creature's grasp by the way it held it.

The creature then moved slowly behind the suspended old man, apparently placing the now tiny slug on the back of the old man's head near his neck. The old man screamed for a long moment before passing out or dying. It was impossible to know for sure.

The reptilian creatures finally left the old man and came toward him. When they got close to him, he shouted, clearly hearing his voice although it sounded strange and distant. "You like tormenting helpless old men? Why don't you release these bonds and give me a chance to bash-in your ugly lizard heads?"

The reptilian creatures didn't respond.

"I'm not afraid to die," he said. "Why don't you just kill me and get it over with."

One of the reptilian creatures in its nonverbal way said: *We would if we could. But it is not allowed.*

Not allowed? He was contemplating this when he saw the reptilian creature in front of him holding the green slug. At this close distance the slug appeared even more hideous than before. Its segmented body throbbed and squirmed in the creature's taloned hands.

He brought his eyes up from the slug and stared into the beady eyes of the creature holding it. He wanted the creature to know that he wasn't afraid, that he would rip their lizard-like bodies to shreds if he could get out of his bonds. The creature holding the slug began moving around behind him. The slug in the creature's hands was now so small that the creature held it between the tips of two talons—like someone would hold a tick or other tiny insect between their fingernails as they removed it from their body.

He sensed the creature directly behind him now. He felt the creature gently lifting the long black hair on the back of his head. A sensation began at the base of his skull just above the neck. The sensation felt like a small electrical shock that grew with such intensity he arched his back in pain and screamed in agony. He felt himself starting to pass out. And with that, Little Willy lost consciousness, fading into a world without manlike lizard creatures and oversized slugs and black masses.

*　　*　　*

ELEVEN

The line of cars started at the entrance of TFRF #497—the Junction, Texas gasoline rationing facility Little Willy had mentioned to Zeke. The line extended nearly a half-mile down the feeder road off Interstate 10. Zeke had partially filled the minivan early that morning, using the remainder of the gasoline in the canister. They arrived in Junction uneventfully late in the morning. According to the signs on the Interstate, the rationing was supposed to begin at two in the afternoon. Zeke figured they were about thirty cars from the front of the line so they had a good chance of getting their share of gasoline before the facility shut down, leaving many disappointed and angry people in the line of cars behind him.

Most people were standing outside of their cars and pickup trucks. Some were conversing with each other in small groups. Others were playing Frisbee with their kids or just sitting in portable lounge chairs next to their automobiles. Zeke saw a few people with portable grills cooking hamburger patties—or what looked like hamburger patties. The cooking meat didn't smell like beef to Zeke. He also noticed that very few pets accompanied the people waiting outside their vehicles. Besides Billy, Zeke saw only one other dog; a small poodle on a leash held by a middle-aged woman a few cars behind the minivan. *Better keep an eye on your dog,* Zeke said to himself.

Leaving Billy with the others in the minivan, Zeke walked toward the facility's entrance, passing all the people standing or sitting outside near their parked cars. A small group of college-aged youths sat on the ground while one of them played a guitar. A dozen cars up the line, an elderly trio, two men and a woman, sat around a portable card table outside their vehicle, playing dominoes and chatting away like this was a picnic. Others were not so happy, griping about the long line and why the government

155

kept them waiting so long and why the fuel was so expensive and why there was such a small amount allotted to everyone. The list went on and on, typical for situations like this even in the best of times.

Zeke walked closer to the front of the line of cars and pickup trucks waiting for the gas. A short distance off the road he saw several men huddled around a wooden table. A homemade sign on the table read:

US GRADE A GROUND BEEF:
1/2 POUND BURGER-15$
OR BY THE POUND-25$
EGGS-20$ Per Dozen.
HOMEMADE BREAD-20$ Per Loaf.
FRESH BOTTLED WATER-20$ Per Liter

Fifty feet behind the men and the table sat an old camping trailer. Zeke saw a woman stepping from the trailer with an armful of wet towels. She hung them on a makeshift clothesline stretched between the trailer and a tall two-by-four hammered into the ground.

Zeke walked toward the table. One of the men was in his early twenties, wearing a ball cap with a white undershirt and jeans. He sat in a wooden chair while whittling on a stick with a pocketknife. Another man sat in a lounge chair with a shotgun sitting across his lap. He wore a black, wide-brimmed cowboy hat that matched his long black hair and beard. Next to him sat an older man with a whiskered face, most likely the head honcho of this little food stand. All three turned to stare at Zeke as he approached.

"What can we help you with?" asked Whiskers.

Zeke studied the sign before asking, "Where'd you get the beef?"

"Huh?"

"Where does the beef come from?" Zeke asked again.

"Well, from cows, of course," Whiskers said with a snicker. The other men at the table chuckled.

Zeke laughed along. "Yeah, cows. That's a good one."

Whiskers' smile faded quickly. "So you wanna buy something or what?"

"Well, I'd like to take a look at your 'US Grade A Ground Beef' before I buy."

Whiskers turned and shouted at the woman hanging out the wet towels. "Kim! Bring a roll of ground beef over here! Make it pronto!"

The woman nodded and ducked back into the trailer.

Zeke gestured at the sign. "So this twenty dollar water," he said. "Is it bottled water from a manufacturer?"

Whiskers gave him a peculiar look. "Huh?"

"You know, *Ozarka, Evian*? Bottled water that *used* to be sold in stores."

"Oh, yeah," Whiskers said. "But it's not Ozarka . . . or the other one you mentioned."

"Okay," Zeke said. "I'll take four liters then."

Whiskers nodded at the young man whittling on a stick. The young man headed toward the trailer.

While waiting for the woman to bring the meat, Zeke glanced at the black-hatted dude with the shotgun. The man returned Zeke's look with a hard stare that almost made Zeke laugh. "Business kind of slow, isn't it?" Zeke said to no one in particular.

"Still early," Whiskers said. "But once we crank up the grill and they smell that cooking meat we'll have a line nearly as long as that one waiting for the gas."

The woman came shuffling out the trailer with a package in her arms. She offered it to Whiskers. Zeke noticed the haggard look on her face. No makeup, stringy mousey hair, and frightened eyes that wouldn't hold your gaze very long. He saw the fresh bruise on her right cheek.

"It's about time," Whiskers said while yanking the package from her arms. He unwrapped the butcher paper to reveal a several-pound roll of ground meat.

Zeke saw the high level of fat and gristle marbling though the ground meat. He touched the part still wrapped in paper and it felt cool. He lowered his head close to the package to smell it. It smelled fresh but a bit gamey. Definitely not beef. Probably venison, if not some other meat Zeke didn't want to think about. "So what type of meat is this?"

Whiskers squinted his squinty eyes. "Can't you read?"

"That's not beef," Zeke said, staring hard into the Whiskers' eyes. "It might be deer or some other critter, but that's not cow meat."

Whiskers pulled the package away. "You're a smart one, ain't ya, boy?"

"Not really," Zeke said while starting to unroll some hundred-dollar bills from his thick money roll.

Whiskers' eyes darted toward the roll of cash. He tried to hide a grin.

"I didn't say I wasn't going to buy any of your meat," Zeke said, keeping several hundred-dollar bills in his hand and replacing the larger roll of cash in his pocket. "I just have a problem with people selling something and saying it's something it's not."

Whiskers sighed before looking around him and saying in a hushed voice, "It's venison, mister. But it's fresh. I butchered it myself."

"Then why don't you just say it's venison?"

"Cause some folks don't like venison," Whiskers said. "They think of Bambi or some other nonsense. They couldn't care less about some poor old steer getting its throat cut, though."

Zeke saw the younger man coming from behind the trailer with the bottled water. He was screwing the cap on one bottle while trying to carry the three other bottles in his arms. He placed all the plastic bottles in a cardboard box found near the door of the trailer before bringing it to the table. "Here you go," the young man said.

Zeke lifted one of bottles from the box and inspected it in the light. He replaced it in the box and said, "You got a barrel of water back there?"

"Don't know what you're talkin' about," Whiskers said.

Zeke stepped around the table and started to walk toward the trailer. "You mind if I take a look at your water source?"

The black-hatted dude with the shotgun stood from his chair and blocked the path to the trailer. He was even bigger than Zeke had thought. "Yeah," the black-hatted dude said. "I mind."

Zeke tried to step around him but the big man shoved him back with the stock and barrel of the shotgun. Zeke's immediate reaction was to grab the shotgun in both hands while placing his right foot behind the black-hatted dude's leg and performing a simple move that would make the man fall flat on his back. If necessary, with the shotgun free from the man's grasp, Zeke could jab him in the solar plexus with the gunstock, ending any fight before it started. But he didn't do any of this.

Zeke stared up at the black-hatted dude, wondering what had stopped him from taking the big man down. All of a sudden something compelled him to look back at the line of cars on the feeder road. He studied the scene for a moment and saw nothing out of the ordinary. A moment later he smiled at the big man and went back to the table to face old Whiskers. A thought formed in his mind from out of nowhere. "That water might be good or it might not be," Zeke told him. "Maybe you got it out of some creek nearby and maybe you boiled it or maybe you didn't. Doesn't matter one way or another because I don't want any of it. I want what you drink. And I'll pay you for it."

"And what are you gonna do if I say no?" Whiskers asked with a smirk.

"Well," Zeke began while glancing at the line of cars, "I guess I'll just walk up and down that line of cars over there and tell all of them you're selling poodle burgers and contaminated water full of parasites that will have them puking for weeks."

Rage filled Whisker's eyes. "That's a dang lie!"

"Maybe," Zeke said. "Maybe not. Won't matter after I'm done with my speech to the crowd, though. You and your little roadside cafe will be out of business, regardless of the truth."

The rage in Whiskers' eyes softened to a look of concern. He stared back for a long moment before saying, "What do you want, mister?"

"Two gallon jugs of the fresh water you and your bunch drink," Zeke said. "And that roll of meat cooked into a half-dozen burgers with a loaf of your bread. I'll pay with cash money."

Whiskers sighed and said, "Is there any other kind?" He glanced between Zeke and the line of cars on the feeder road. "I only got one jug of water I can let go."

"That will do," said Zeke.

Whiskers turned and nodded at the young man in the ball cap who took off back to the trailer. Whiskers grabbed a small pencil from behind his ear and started jotting down numbers on a piece of paper. When he finished adding the numbers, he said, "That's one four-pound roll of meat at twenty-five a pound, one loaf of bread at twenty, and the water I'll give you for fifty. Want any eggs?"

"They come from chickens?" Zeke asked with a smile.

Whiskers smiled back. "I reckon so."

Zeke had already done the math and was planning to give him two-hundred dollars. "Yes. Give me a dozen. Can I get them hard boiled or does that cost extra?"

"Just five bucks extra."

Zeke sighed and said, "Okay. A dozen hardboiled eggs."

"That comes to one-hundred and ninety-five bucks."

Zeke gave him two one-hundred-dollar bills. "Here you go. Keep the change."

Whiskers grinned without comment.

"How long will it take?"

"Thirty minutes or so," Whiskers said. "Just need to get the grill going."

Zeke nodded and headed back to the line of cars. He examined the scene, wondering which direction the fuel trucks would arrive from when the rationing began. He spotted the elderly trio playing dominoes beside the car and decided to stop and talk to them. They looked up at him when he reached their table. "How you folks doing?"

"Fine," one of the old men said.

"How are you doing?" the elderly woman asked.

"Pretty good, ma'am," Zeke said.

"That's good," she said.

"You folks been here before?"

"Several times," said the old man.

"How much gas are you allowed to buy?"

"Used to be ten gallons but I heard they raised it to fifteen for today."

"How many cars get gas before they run out?" asked Zeke.

The old man looked across the table at the other old gentleman, an octogenarian with a large head sitting on a skinny neck. "I don't know. Forty? Fifty maybe? That about right, Bill?"

Bill the octogenarian pursed his lips and thought for a moment. "Yeah. That sounds about right." Bill and the other old man went back to their game of dominoes.

"Where is your car?" the elderly women asked in a friendly voice.

Zeke glanced down the line of cars toward the minivan. "I guess I'm about twenty-five or thirty cars from the front of the line."

"Oh you'll be fine," she said with a warm smile.

Zeke smiled back at her. "That's good to know. Thank you."

"Certainly," she said.

Zeke made a quick study of their vehicle, a twenty-year-old Cadillac in mint condition. "Fifteen gallons probably barely fills this baby."

She smiled and said, "We just keep enough gas in it to get here. My husband siphons most of the gasoline into our generator at home. They won't let you put gas into anything but an automobile tank, you see."

"Really?"

"Fifteen gallons per vehicle," Bill said, still focused on his game. "Used to be ten, though."

"Well, thanks for the information," Zeke said. "I hope ya'll have a great day."

"Same to you," the elderly woman said.

Zeke smiled as he walked away and heard the elderly woman say to the old men at the table, "What a nice young man." That was one of the things Zeke liked most about Texas. Texans in general were much more friendly than most folks across the country. *Even the bad cases,* he thought. *They might kill you for looking at them wrong but at least they're friendly about it.*

Zeke felt good. He believed the rest of the trip to Austin would be easy. He didn't know why he felt this way but he knew it all the same. *Drop them off in Austin then head to Houston to find Ruth, Connor, and little Amy.* Everything was going to be fine.

Several hours later, after eating their venison burgers and boiled eggs, and receiving their government-issued gasoline ration at seven dollars a gallon, the minivan entered I10, heading toward an exit to a highway that cut north toward Austin. While Zeke drove east he never noticed the green '94 Chevy pickup drive from the back of the line of cars and onto the interstate, staying a good distance behind the minivan. As the Chevy passed the rationing facility without getting gas, a tall man wearing military fatigues, ball cap, and aviator sunglasses stood near a tree on the opposite of the interstate, watching the pickup follow the minivan down the long stretch of road.

* * *

TWELVE

Zeke read the computer printout sheet: numbers, statistics, demographics, all representing the millions of lost people trying to survive in America. Houston's stats were even worse than most large cities. Looting, robberies, assaults, rapes, and murders were all off the charts in America's third largest city. The breakdown of society had happened faster than most experts had predicted.

"So what's being done?" Zeke asked, trying not to sound as pessimistic as he felt.

"As much as possible at the moment," Albright answered. "FEMA definitely has their hands full. Organizing a network of thousands of state and local emergency relief agencies under our current state of communications is difficult, to say the least. Also, on the local level, law enforcement seems to be unravelling. Many policemen have deserted their posts to take care of their families, which is not a difficult decision for most cops without any paychecks coming their way. The financial system in this country has collapsed overnight. Hopefully, that's only temporarily but for now the situation looks bleak."

Zeke knew these problems were just the tip of the iceberg. Without law enforcement the law of the jungle took over quickly. *What happens when the jails and prisons are emptied, their inmates running loose on the streets? One thing for sure, when that happens most folks will wish those inmates were still locked in those jails and prisons. Most people couldn't imagine how bad things would get.* Unfortunately, Zeke had little problem imagining the chaos following a disaster of this proportion. His experience in war-torn regions around the world supported his belief that things can *always* get worse, no matter how bad they seem at the time.

Zeke turned his attention away from the printout sheet and glanced at Paul Stover. Stover sat a short distance away, talking on the one satellite phone system working at the moment. Albright's Austin hideaway—which he called *The Bunker*—was located in the basement level of an antique house in the countryside outside the city limits. The entire facility was state-of-the-art, complete with a commercial-grade generator system and food storage that probably rivaled most secure military bunkers. There were four bedrooms with private bathrooms, a kitchen and dining area, and a large recreation room with a pool table, big-screen HDTV with several DVR hard drives, and four pinball machines scattered around the room. But the most impressive part of the basement was the office-communication room full of computers and satellite phone gear. Zeke learned that the entire underground facility was EMP-hardened, a feature that had cost Albright a small fortune.

After arriving the evening before, Albright told Zeke that no one knew about this location except for Stover and Matt, and now Doctor Margolian, which Albright was not happy about. He also told Zeke that his main residence—a large estate on Lake Travis—was twenty miles distant. The house above *The Bunker* looked ordinary. Nobody would suspect a secure, high-tech facility located beneath the old house. The special insulating features of *The Bunker* were not complex but required precise construction. Basically, the entire facility was constructed within a metallic enclosure of fine-mesh copper screening connected directly to earth-ground—a feature which prevented any stray electromagnetic fields from entering the room.

Paul Stover finally ended his conversation on the sat-phone. "They said transmission will start in an hour."

Albright turned to Zeke. "I'll have some information about her house shortly."

"Yeah?" Zeke replied, trying to sound optimistic. Earlier that day Zeke had given Albright Ruth's Houston address when he'd asked for it. He didn't know how Albright could gather intel under the circumstances but he didn't care. He just wanted to know if Ruth and the kids were okay. Zeke stood from his chair. "I'm going to give Billy a nature break. Mind if I take Matt along?"

"No," Albright said. "I think that's a good idea."

"Where's Margolian?" asked Zeke.

"Still sleeping," Albright said, not hiding his disgust for allowing the man to stay at his secret bunker in the country.

Zeke walked through a door leading to the kitchen. The room had a full-size refrigerator and a breakfast table that seated six. Matt was reading a comic book while eating a bowl of cereal at the table. Billy was curled up on the floor next to the boy's feet.

"Hey, Matt," Zeke said. "Sleep well?"

"Yes, sir," Matt said. "I didn't even wake up once through the night."

"Yeah, I know what you mean."

"Want something to eat?" the boy asked.

"No thanks. I ate earlier." Zeke eyed the bowl of cereal. "What do you think about the powdered milk?"

Matt shrugged his shoulders. "It's okay. Better than the powdered eggs, I guess."

"Pretty smart of your dad having a place like this."

"Yeah," Matt said before finishing the last spoonful of cereal. "We've used it once before, just for fun. I never thought we would ever have to use it for real."

Zeke nodded and said, "I'm going to take Billy outside. You want to come?"

"Sure."

They walked up a set of stairs and exited *The Bunker* through a doorway—a false section of wall in the house above—and went outside through the house's backdoor. They strolled into a large grassy area of rolling hills surrounding the house, a small portion of the two-hundred acre property Albright owned. Zeke noticed a pair of birds singing loudly from a Spanish oak nearby. A chilly breeze blew into his face, bringing him distant memories of his childhood. And not too happy ones at that. Zeke never told anyone except for his late wife, Amber, that he had been orphaned since birth, living in and out of orphanages and foster homes until he was old enough to join the military. Since Amber had been gone, it was back to Zeke's secret and his secret alone.

As Billy did his business in the brush, Matt asked, "You're going to be leaving soon, aren't you?"

"Yes, as soon as I can."

The sun felt good on Matt's face. He picked up a stick from the ground, enjoying the fresh outdoor air while choosing his words carefully. "Do you think your sister-in-law and her kids are all right?"

"I hope so."

"Well," the boy said, "if you need any help I'll be glad to go with you."

"Thanks, Matt," Zeke said. "That really means a lot to me but I think you should stay with your dad. He needs you more than you probably know."

"Yeah, I know," Matt said. "Still, if you need me I'll be there for you."

"I appreciate that, Matt," Zeke said, truly touched by the boy's words. He leaned over and removed the leash from Billy's harness. "Why don't you toss that stick and give Billy a little exercise."

Matt threw the stick as far as he could and watched Billy lope after it. Zeke stood there and watched. The simplest things in life seemed to be the most powerful: birds singing from a tree, old feelings and memories brought back by the changing seasons, a boy throwing a stick for a dog. Beneath all these simple moments there seemed to be a simple truth bigger than any thoughts or grandiose plans of man.

A half-hour later they walked back to the house. When they descended the hidden staircase to *The Bunker* and entered the kitchen area, Stover greeted them from the table, eating something from a bowl while studying some papers on the table. "Nice day outside?"

"Yes," Matt replied. "Nice and sunny."

"Very secluded," Zeke added. "I wish the rest of the country was as peaceful as this place."

Matt and Stover were obviously in good spirits, happy the trip was over and they were now living in the relative safety and comfort of *The Bunker*. Zeke wished he felt the same. The welfare of Ruth and the kids weighed heavily on his mind. His instinct to act immediately—*right this minute*—nagged him, but waiting for Albright to verify the situation at Ruth's house was worth waiting for. The information could save Zeke days of useless searching. Besides, any bit of rest would be beneficial for the trip ahead.

Stover continued to eat the whatever-it-was in the bowl while examining the papers on the table.

"You need help with anything?" Zeke asked.

"Yes," Stover said with a smile. "How well do you know AES-256 encryption?"

"Sorry," Zeke said, trying to force a smile. "I think that's out of my league. Good luck though."

"I don't believe in luck."

"No?"

"Or coincidences," Stover added. "Everything happens for a reason."

"And what is the reason behind the current state of affairs?" Zeke asked.

"I didn't say I *know* the reason," Stover said. "I only said there *is* a reason. And I might add that we will never understand *all* of God's reasons, even if the events are prophesied in scripture and the prophecies have been fulfilled."

The question in Zeke's eyes told Stover to continue.

"What if I were to tell you that what is happening today around the globe was foretold more than twenty-six hundred years ago?" Stover explained. "Would you think I'm nuts? Or just a victim of wishful thinking?"

"Maybe. Maybe not," Zeke said. "Are we talking about doomsday, Armageddon, end-of-the-world stuff?"

"Not exactly," Stover answered without hesitation. "I'm talking about events *preceding* the last days. Zeke, how familiar are you with the Old Testament?"

"Considering I don't even own an old or new testament," Zeke said. "Not very familiar."

"Well, I suggest you get a copy and read chapters thirty-eight and thirty-nine of the Book of Ezekiel," Stover said. "Inspired prophecy revealed to the prophet Ezekiel. Your namesake, by the way."

"Actually," Zeke said, "I go by Zeke, not Ezekiel."

"What's it say on your birth certificate?"

"Ezekiel," Zeke said with a sigh.

"Even if the name on your birth certificate was not Ezekiel," Stover said, "it wouldn't matter. The name *Zeke* is derived from *Ezekiel*—the biblical Ezekiel I'm talking about."

"Okay," Zeke relented. "I should know better than to argue with a lawyer."

"Yes, you should," Stover said with a smile.

"Can you just give me the *Bible Prophecy For Dummies* version?"

"Sure," Stover began. "The prophecy tells of an alliance between certain nations *near* the end times, nations that can be identified in the present. The principal nations are Iran and Russia, and their alliance involves a concentrated attack on Israel. But God will intercede and destroy Israel's enemies in a way that the entire world will see."

"Do you believe this is happening now?"

"Not yet," Stover said. "But it may soon. Listen, Zeke, I've studied this prophecy for decades. Back in my early days, this prophecy's possibility seemed as remote as it had been for the last twenty-five hundred years. Iran and Russia? Never has there been any alliance between the two, only tension, especially during the Soviet Union's reign. But this all changed after the Soviet government collapsed and Vladimir Putin took control. Then the Russians began developing Iran's nuclear program with enough materials and scientific knowledge to wreak havoc on the world, particularly Israel. Giving nuclear weapons to a rogue state of Islamic terrorists that want to eliminate Israel and eventually every Jew from the face of the planet? Ever ask yourself *why* the Russians would do this?"

"Oil," Zeke answered after a moment of thought. "Russia has plenty of weapons and technology but they need oil. Iran has plenty of oil but needs weapons and technology."

"Yes," Stover said, "but Iran is not the only place Russia can get oil."

Zeke thought for another moment. "They want control of the Persian Gulf?"

"Yes," Stover said. "Controlling the Gulf is the key to controlling the entire Middle East, and that is definitely too much of a temptation for the Russians to resist. All of this is referred to as the *War Of Gog And Magog* as prophesied in the Book of Ezekiel and it is about the Russian and Islamic armies coming to attack Israel."

"Which Islamic armies?"

"Besides Iran," Stover said. "Syria, Lebanon, Turkey, also many of those Muslim nations that used to be part of the Soviet Union. I find the nations mentioned in the prophecy interesting but not as interesting as the nations *not* mentioned. One in particular is Iraq. Can you think of any reason why Iraq would *not* be a part of this alliance to destroy Israel?"

"It's obvious," Zeke said. "Obvious since 2003, that is."

"That's right," Stover said. "But to me, the most unusual omission from the list of nations involved is the good old United States of America. Why would the most powerful nation in the world not come to the defense of Israel, the nation we have armed and defended since its creation in 1948?"

After a moment of thought, Zeke said, "Because we are unwilling to help? Or maybe *unable* to help."

"Maybe both," Stover said.

Albright suddenly came into the kitchen. "I'm going to take a short nap," he told Stover. "Let me know when the communication arrives."

"Yes, sir," Stover said.

After Albright left the kitchen, Stover said, "Can I show you something, Zeke?"

Zeke followed Stover into the communication room. Stover closed the door and sat in front of a monitor. He opened a file of pictures and text. "I downloaded this late last night."

"The good old WWW is still working?" Zeke asked.

"Most servers located in North America that were *not* EMP protected have been damaged," Stover said, "but the rest of the world seems largely unaffected. America's situation is still front page news of course but apparently nobody knows what really happened although many groups are taking credit for the attack, especially from the world of radical Islam. Anyway, it took a while but I was able to *dig* up—pun fully intended— some info regarding our good friend Dr. Margolian. I think you'll find it interesting."

Zeke studied the page on the monitor. Along with the text he saw several photographs of Margolian on location somewhere in the Middle East. One of the photo's captions said the location was in a remote section of Turkey. The photograph showed Margolian displaying several large arrowheads in his open palms. Other photos showed Margolian with members of his archeological team. In one particular photo an attractive brunette in shorts and hiking boots stood on one side of the curly haired doctor while a tanned man wearing sunglasses stood on his other side. Their names were mentioned in the caption beneath the photo but they meant nothing to Zeke. As he scrolled down the page and read the text he eventually came to the crux of the story which talked about Margolian and his team's unexplained disappearance.

Stover opened another news article in a different window. "All of them say the same thing," he said. "Authorities are clueless to the cause of their disappearance. Some Turkish officials suggest foul play from looters but they have zero evidence for support."

"Incredible," Zeke said. "It's just as he said."

"Yes," Stover agreed, "but there's more. I'm surprised you missed it."

This got Zeke's attention. He studied the news articles, trying to find what he'd missed. He began shaking his head. "I don't understand, Paul."

"The dates," Stover said. "Look at the dates the articles were published, not to mention the date Margolian and his team supposedly disappeared."

Zeke saw the dates. He clicked on all the articles, his deadpan expression revealing his disbelief as he tried to rationalize the situation. He stared at a picture of Margolian on the monitor for a while before saying, "He looks the same now as he did in these photos. Exactly the same. Not a day older. Especially not *ten* years older."

"A decade ago," Stover said. "And where has he been all this time?"

"And not aging in the process," Zeke added. After a long pause he asked, "Have you shown this to him?"

"No," Stover said. "I wanted you to see it first."

"What about Albright?" Zeke said. "Has he seen this?"

Stover shook his head. "No."

Zeke noticed there was something else on Stover's mind. "What's on your mind, Paul?"

Stover returned his attention to the computer monitor. "Wait till you see this," he said. "I've been saving the best for last."

Stover began typing on the computer keyboard. Within a moment a series of numbers and text filled the monitor screen. He highlighted a section of text and numbers with the mouse. "This is the message sequence I told you about after we'd first met. It is a repeated sequence that has been modified to conventional computer software for examination purposes. The original appears nothing like this. You wouldn't recognize anything about it in *that* form." He dragged the highlighted portion to another window on the monitor and tapped on the keyboard. A repeated sequence of a simple five-word sentence replaced the lines of text and numbers: *'We are coming for you . . . We are coming for you . . . We are coming for you . . .'*

"This message was sequenced in thirteen-second intervals about a billion times before we deciphered it," Stover said. "We were working on other sequences before we ran out of time."

Zeke heard Stover's words but he wasn't paying attention to them. He stared at the simple sentence on the monitor screen while trying to control his breathing. The dream of the Native American reptilian thing dancing outside the minivan replayed in his mind, its thick rubbery lips mouthing the words . . . the same words on the monitor screen in front of him. Zeke tried to rationalize the connection between the dream and the message on the computer monitor screen: *The dream was nothing but a dream. This is just a coincidence.*

"You okay, Zeke?" Stover asked.

"Yeah," Zeke lied.

Stover closed the window on the monitor and opened a new one. Hundreds of odd-shaped symbols covered the screen. He clicked the mouse and the symbols began to rotate before clustering together to form some type of pattern that made no sense to Zeke. "I can't demonstrate the actual process of how we deciphered these," Stover explained while advancing through different phases of the collected data. "These are just copies, converted to digital form so we can see them on a conventional system."

A few more clicks on the mouse and the clusters of symbols reduced in size before appearing on precise geographic locations on a map of the world. Stover clicked the mouse again and an animation progress began. Most of the symbols in the clusters began disappearing and reappearing in a way that seemed random. Stover stopped the animation on one particular page. He zoomed in tighter until the nation of Turkey filled the monitor. A date was displayed in the upper right hand corner of the window. "This was a little over ten years ago," he said while zooming in tighter on the map. "Notice the spiral symbol," he said while pointing to one of the many symbols shaped like a spiral.

"Yes, I see it."

"And you see this symbol here?" Stover said while pointing to a symbol of a circle with two smaller concentric circles within it. "Whenever this symbol appears, the spiral symbol appears almost immediately."

"Okay," Zeke said, trying to grasp the meaning but failing. "What do these symbols mean?"

"They represent . . ." Stover searched for the word, ". . . *transmission signatures,* I guess I could say. It's difficult to explain. Quantum computing is a strange new world for us. We assigned these symbols to the *transmission signatures* so we can analyze them."

"So these pages represent timelines when the *transmission signatures* occurred from these locations?"

"Yes," Stover said. "Not a continuous second by second timeline, but still a chronological timeline."

"And this sequence is from ten years ago?"

"Yes."

"How long have you been doing this, Paul?" Zeke asked. "You've been tracking these things that long?"

Stover turned to face Zeke. "We haven't been tracking anything," he explained. "We've only been aware of any of this for just a few months."

Zeke's face showed his confusion.

"You see," Stover tried to explain, "quantum computing deals with issues beyond our logic. Some of these issues involve other dimensions—dimensions where time is . . . different."

"Okay," Zeke said. "I don't even want to know how this stuff works, but from what I understand you can go back in time and retrieve these *transmission signatures?*"

"Yes."

"How far can you go back?" Zeke asked.

Stover shrugged. "Theoretically, as far back as the signatures have been occurring. We went back nearly twelve years, until we ran out of time."

"Can you go in the future?" Zeke asked.

"No," Stover said quickly. "Which doesn't mean it's impossible, it just means *we* are not capable of it yet. But our work in this field suggests that going into the future with this is unlikely." Stover returned his attention to the symbols on the monitor. "Anyway, look at this, Zeke," he said while bringing another window on the monitor of one of the news articles about Margolian. This article included a small map. Stover positioned the two windows on the monitor where they could compare both maps. The point was well made.

"So is Margolian represented by one of these symbols?" Zeke asked.

"No," Stover said. "But you can see that wherever he excavated, *they* were there. Especially when he was at this location, the site of his last excavation."

Zeke compared the maps and saw the name on both: *Doyitahlibad.* "This is where he found the giant skeleton and the other things?"

"It's the last dig he was working," Stover said. "When he and the team disappeared."

"So those who are represented by these symbols, or *transmission signatures* as you call them," Zeke said. "They are responsible for Margolian's disappearance?"

"It looks that way," Stover said. "Don't you agree?"

Zeke gave Stover a look. "Let me ask you a question," he said. "Have you found these symbols anywhere after this time period? After his disappearance?"

Stover nodded before typing in some commands. Various locations on the program's maps appeared in a animated sequence, moving their way through time as they moved up through the years.

Zeke began to notice a familiar pattern. "Can you enlarge the date and year?" he asked.

"Sure," Stover said while typing on the keyboard. "Do you see something?"

Zeke didn't answer as he studied the animation of the symbols appearing in different locations around the world. He finally said, "Can you go to a specific date?"

"If it's in the sequence," Stover replied. "What date?"

"July fifth," Zeke said. "Same year you're on now."

Stover sped up the program. It found the date. July fifth was in the sequence. He paused the animation. The symbols hovered over a location north of London, England. He turned and watched Zeke staring at the monitor.

The wheels in Zeke's mind were definitely turning. "Can you go to August . . . seventeen, I believe."

Stover found the date in the sequence. This time the location was in a nondescript area of Uzbekistan, an area Zeke knew well. "One more," Zeke said. "August twenty-four through twenty-six."

The next three dates in the sequence were August 24, 25, and 26. The location was exactly where Zeke knew it would be in Afghanistan.

Stover stayed silent, waiting for Zeke to continue asking for dates.

"Last one," Zeke said, knowing that this last one would confirm the truth for him. "December thirty-first, end of the year."

Stover sped up the animation. The date was in the sequence.

Zeke had closed his eyes. When he opened them he saw the symbols hovering around the area of Gold Tree, Texas, exactly where he knew they would be. He knew if he went back far enough—even to that fateful date during the Christmas holidays so many years ago—the symbols would be in Houston. But he didn't want to go there.

Stover turned to face Zeke. After a long moment he said, "It's you, isn't it?"

Zeke didn't say anything.

"They've been following you?" Stover said in disbelief. His own wheels began spinning in his mind. "When we first discovered all this Steve thought it was about us, because of the transmissions from Gold Tree. But it's you they're interested in!"

Zeke gave Stover a cold look. "I never said that."

"Zeke, why else would those dates be significant to you?"

"I don't know!" Zeke said in a defensive tone. "Maybe it had to do with someone else I know!"

Stover seemed surprised by Zeke's reaction. "I'm not blaming you, Zeke," he said. "I'm just saying, wow, isn't this amazing? The connection between this and Margolian, and then our paths crossing in a precise spot of the world at the exact same moment. That's pretty amazing! Don't you think?"

"Yeah, amazing," Zeke said in an emotionless voice. All of this didn't excite his curiosity. It was actually making him angry. Very angry. He felt violated. Being followed and possibly manipulated for years had him fuming with rage. He knew he'd been followed over the last week, that feeling had been clear, but over years? He felt like breaking something with his hands.

"I think I should go get Margolian," Stover said eagerly. "I'm anxious to hear the rest of his story after showing him this."

"You really think that's a good idea?" Zeke said in an angry voice.

Stover was surprised by Zeke's behavior. "You don't think—"

"—No, I think it's a crappy idea! The guy is confused to the point of a mental breakdown—a condition I'm starting to feel myself—and you're just going to show him that a decade of his life has disappeared, along with his team mates, but everything's going to be just hunky-dory?"

Stover swallowed hard. "Sorry, Zeke. I didn't mean to upset you."

Zeke took a deep breath, somehow managing to calm himself a bit. "Look, Paul," he said. "Nothing personal. This is just a lot for me to absorb at the moment."

Stover nodded in understanding. "Sorry, I should have been more sensitive," he said. "This has been perplexing me for so long that I just got excited, that's all."

A thought entered Zeke's head: *What if Albright and Stover had been tracking my movements, putting this data, these so-called transmission signatures into their little concocted computer program.* He reflected on this for a long moment before asking himself the obvious question. *But why?*

"You okay, Zeke?" Stover asked again.

"Why did you show this to me, Paul?"

"I wanted to see if you saw any patterns," Stover said. "Which I know you did."

Zeke stood from his chair and headed for the door. "I'll be heading out as soon as Steve learns something about Ruth and the kids."

Stover stood and watched Zeke head to the door. "Zeke, I'm sorry. I didn't—"

"—Good luck with the doctor," Zeke cut him off. "I'm sure he'll be surprised when he learns he's ten years older than he thinks he is."

"Actually," Stover began, trying to end this meeting on a positive note, "he's ten years *younger* than he thinks he is." Stover punctuated this with a smile.

"You are right," Zeke said without returning a smile. "I guess it's all about how you look at things, Paul."

Zeke left the room.

Paul Stover sat heavily in his chair while staring at the monitor. He sighed before going back to the dates in the animation sequence Zeke had asked about. The London date. The Uzbek date. The Afghan date. Even the Gold Tree date. He began writing on a notepad, recording the data for future evaluation. He felt a bit guilty about not revealing these new discoveries to his boss, Steve Albright, but something nagged him about that, something Albright had said to him a long time ago, something that had no meaning to Stover at the time. He couldn't remember what it was Albright had said, but he knew it was significant to the situation now regarding Zeke, Margolian, and the transmission signatures. He strained his brain to remember but nothing was coming. Not wanting to frustrate himself, he returned to his work and hoped it would all come back to him.

Stover finally finished taking his notes. He needed to talk to Margolian. Maybe he would learn more from the famous archeologist after showing him the data on the computer. Then he would share it all with Steve Albright. *Maybe.*

*

Two hours later Stover entered the kitchen. Albright and Zeke were facing each other. They turned when he entered. "Steve gave me some information regarding Ruth and the kids." Zeke said to Stover.

"That's great," Stover replied. "Are they okay?"

"Well," Albright answered for Zeke, "it looks like the entire neighborhood has been evacuated. Two of the investigators entered her home and found a note on the refrigerator door. A note to Zeke informing him that they were heading to a relief camp north of the city."

Stover didn't seem surprised. "So you'll be leaving right away, Zeke?"

"Yes," Zeke said, still wondering how in the world Albright had managed to gather all of this intelligence, including getting *investigators* to search Ruth's house.

"I wish I knew more," Albright said. "But at least it's a start."

"Yes," Zeke said. "Thank you again. Thank you both."

"Thank *you*," Stover said. "For getting us here in one piece."

"Amen to that," Albright said. "I'll go get the rest of your money."

"That's not necessary," Zeke said. "I still have plenty of the money you gave me. How about we take care of the remainder after I get Ruth and her children?"

"Deal," Albright said with a smile. "Why don't you drive the minivan around to the metal building behind the house. We'll top off the gas tank there."

It didn't surprise Zeke that there was fuel located somewhere on the property since Albright had apparently thought of everything in the construction of his high-tech hideaway in the hills near Austin.

After topping off the minivan's gas tank from Albright's large fuel reserve in the metal building behind the house, Zeke said goodbye to Albright and Stover, saving Matt for last. He got a big hug from the boy and when he saw Matt's tears, Zeke had to dab at his own eyes. "You take care of these adults, Matt Albright," Zeke said with a tired smile.

"Yes, sir," Matt replied, trying to smile back. "I'll do that."

"Wish the doctor good luck for me," Zeke told Stover. "I hope he figures it all out. I hope all of you do."

Matt gave Billy a big hug before Zeke loaded the dog into the minivan and drove away, feeling like it might be the last time he saw any of them. Zeke brushed away the feeling as he drove eastward—toward Houston and Ruth and her two children and what the future would unfold for all of them.

*   *   *

THIRTEEN

Margolian finally awoke the evening after Zeke left. When Albright and Matt went to bed, Stover took the archeologist to the communication room and showed him everything he showed Zeke. Margolian took it all in stride. He told Stover that many memories had returned to him after waking from his long slumber. He also told Stover that his captivity felt like it had lasted for days, maybe even weeks, but definitely not years. And *ten* years at that. He didn't seem very bothered, though. The fact that he couldn't account for a decade of his life seemed trivial compared to something else. He was now concerned about one thing and one thing only: He *had* to talk to Zeke.

"Why," Stover had asked.

"I have to tell him something," Margolian insisted. "I wish you would have awakened me before he left."

Stover reassured Margolian that he would help him find Zeke, but first the doctor had to fill him in on what was going on. Margolian agreed. He didn't get too graphic with the details but he told Stover the basics. When Margolian finished his story, Stover didn't know what to think. He knew Margolian had just recited to him a tale of alien abduction—although with some different twists—but part of him believed the famous, *missing* archeologist. "So they wanted to know what you told the *soldier?*" Stover asked.

"Yes," Margolian repeated. "Which was impossible since I didn't even know him at the time. His name meant nothing to me. After probing my mind or soul or whatever they did, they must have decided that I was telling the truth so they let me go. Now I know who they were interested in. I remember now that Ezekiel Allenby was the name they used."

Even though it all seemed so insane, things were starting to make sense to Stover. "So it sounds like their timeline was messed up, if that makes any sense."

"It makes sense to me now," Margolian said. "They got to me too early. *Before* I had even met him."

Ten years too early, Stover thought. He decided to keep the conversation moving. "So you think Zeke might get abducted?"

"No," Margolian said, getting a surprised look from Stover. "He *will* get abducted. And you or I cannot prevent this from happening."

Why didn't they already abduct Zeke? Stover thought to himself. *What was preventing them from nabbing him at any time?* "What do you need to tell him?"

"The timeframe," Margolian said.

"What timeframe?"

"I think it unwise to tell you," Margolian replied. "For your own sake."

Stover thought for a moment before asking, "You mean the data from Kainam's stone tablets?"

"Yes, but I need to tell him the *exact* timeframe."

"Why do you need to give him this . . . timeframe?"

"I don't know why," Margolian replied. "I just know I have to."

"That's it?"

"No, there's more."

"What?"

"At some part of my ordeal," Margolian explained, "I anticipated another session of torment and I began weeping like a small child. Then an ancient memory from my childhood came from nowhere, when I was a boy in Sunday School, when I still believed in a God that loved me. It was a song—" Margolian became very emotional and began to weep intensely.

Stover tried to console him with a hand on his shoulder. He truly felt pity for the doctor's experience in captivity.

Margolian regained enough control to continue. "It was a song I sang as a young boy in Sunday School." Margolian began singing in a tremulous voice. *"Jesus loves me, this I know, for the Bible tells me so . . ."* He broke off again in tears.

Stover tried to console him. "It's okay," he said. "Go on, please. So this song had something to do with them releasing you?"

"Not the song itself," Margolian said after composing himself. "You see, when the song came to me seemingly out of nowhere I began singing it aloud. One of the little *Grays* who usually handled the interrogations came waddling angrily towards me. I knew why, but being an atheist I didn't know any scripture to quote so I just began saying anything that came to mind that had the word *God* in it." Margolian chuckled a bit. "I began singing *God Bless America*, reciting the *Pledge of Allegiance*, anything I could think of that had the word *God* in it. But when I went back to the Sunday School song I discovered what really drove them mad."

"What was that?" asked Stover.

"The name of Jesus," Margolian confessed. "The Son of God. That drove them to panic as they released the unseen bonds holding me. They left in a hurry. That's when this . . . angel came to me and led me out of there. But not before he told me that I must give the soldier the timeframe. The next thing I know I'm running. Then I see Zeke and his dog. But I didn't remember what the angel told me to do. I finally remembered when I awoke today."

Stover stared into Margolian's eyes, wanting and *not* wanting to believe the story.

"I don't perceive Zeke as a religious man," Margolian said. "I don't know if he will think of invoking the name of Jesus when he's captured."

"The same could have been said about you," Stover said. "That song did not come to you from *nowhere*. It definitely came from somewhere very specific."

"Yes, you are right," Margolian said. "But it may not come to him. That's why I must warn him."

"I understand."

"Will you help me?"

Stover wondered how he would explain this to Albright. He knew his boss already thought Margolian was nuts and would most likely balk at the idea of accompanying the nutty archeologist on a mission to find Zeke, to tell him the *timeframe* of an upcoming event planned by fallen angels and to warn him about how to become free from alien abductors— *Grays*, as Margolian called them. Stover knew the only way he could pull this off was to sneak away without Albright knowing, something he wasn't keen on doing. He finally smiled at Margolian. "What will you do after all this is over?"

"Go looking for my team members," Margolian said, "wherever that leads me. Then I will tell my story to the world."

"That will be quite a story," Stover said before lowering his head and praying for guidance. Whatever insight he received from God would be the answer. Several minutes later he opened his eyes. "We will leave tonight."

*   *   *

FOURTEEN

Zeke and Billy walked into the crowd of people loitering around the relief camp off Interstate 45 north of Houston. The camp was located in a large clearing surrounded by tall pine trees. Signs in the clearing stated that the next supply drop-off would begin at one in the afternoon. The people meandering in the clearing looked like refugees—gaunt and dirty with desperate eyes that betrayed their fear and anger. Makeshift dwellings of cardboard and pine boughs were scattered about beneath the pine trees bordering the clearing. Dozens of campfires left trails of smoke wafting through the trees to the blue sky above.

Zeke searched for Ruth and the kids in the clearing while people eyed him and Billy suspiciously. Zeke couldn't see any children in the clearing so he made his way to the crude dwellings beneath the trees. Most of the deadwood had already been burned so people were burning fresh limbs cut from the trees. He approached a small group of men, women, and children sitting around a small campfire. "Has anyone seen a woman and her two kids?" he asked. "In her thirties, nine-year-old boy, and a little girl about four?"

"Sure," a woman at the campfire said. "I've seen lots of them." A teenaged boy sitting next to her snickered.

A short, stocky man wearing a straw cowboy hat approached the campfire with a small load of firewood in his arms. "I might of saw 'em," he said.

"Where?"

"Right over there," the man said while pointing his chin to a spot in the clearing.

"When?"

"I don't know," the man in the cowboy hat said. "A while ago, I suppose.

It was a couple, though. A man and a woman with two kids. The reason I remember is because the man had a fight earlier."

The situation didn't sound right. "What did the woman and the kids look like?"

"Well, it was dark," the man in the cowboy hat said. "But from what I could see, the kids looked 'bout like you described 'em. A boy and a girl. I do recall that the little girl was wearing a winter coat."

This got Zeke's attention. "A parka?"

"Huh?"

"The winter coat," Zeke said. "What color was it?"

"Oh, I don't know. Light colored . . . green I think."

"It wasn't green," a woman in a wool ski cap said while walking toward them. "It was blue. Baby-blue to be exact."

Zeke knew Amy had a baby-blue parka because he had given it to her the previous Christmas. "Are they still here?"

The woman moved even closer. "You got anything to drink, man?"

Zeke had left his backpack and M4 locked in the minivan parked on the interstate feeder road. "Sorry. I'd give you something if I had anything. Now, where did you see them last?"

The woman pointed back toward the interstate. "I saw them leaving three or four days ago," she said before turning toward the man in the cowboy hat. "And she and the kids were alone. Weren't no man with them."

The man in the cowboy hat just shrugged. "I'm just sayin' what I saw."

The woman turned back to Zeke. "You got anything to eat? Candy bar, anything?"

Zeke shook his head. "Did you see which way they went on the highway?"

"No," the woman said curtly. She appeared frustrated that her help was going unrewarded. She stepped closer to Zeke, keeping one eye on the German Shepherd sitting calmly on his haunches. "Can't you get me something to eat or drink?"

"Sorry," said Zeke. "I have nothing on me."

The woman cursed under her breath. "Then I ain't telling you nothing else."

The man in the cowboy hat spoke in her direction. "That's because you don't know nothin' else."

The woman shot him an angry look while walking away back through the trees.

"What did the man look like?" Zeke asked the man in the cowboy hat. "The man you saw with the woman and the kids . . . the one that got in the fight?"

"Too dark to tell. He was tall, though. Wearing a ball cap I believe."

Zeke decided to move on. "Thanks for your help."

The man in the cowboy hat smiled. "Hope you find 'em."

"Thanks." Zeke led Billy away from the campfire. They searched the entire site for nearly an hour until Zeke was convinced that Ruth and the kids were not there. But he was sure they *had* been there. And not just because of the woman's description of a little girl wearing a baby-blue parka, but because he could sense it.

Zeke and Billy left the site, heading to the feeder road where he'd left the minivan. He knew something was wrong before he even got close to the vehicle. As he got closer he saw that the hood wasn't latched shut properly. When he reached the minivan he tried to open the driver's door. It was still locked although he could see where someone had tried to pry it open with a large screwdriver or something similar. He saw his backpack still in the passenger seat along with some bottled water he'd brought from Albright's hideaway. He pressed the *unlock* button on the minivan's remote and nothing happened. He knew why. He manually unlocked the door with the key and grabbed his backpack with the bottled water. He reached into the floorboard behind the seat and removed the M4 hidden under a sheet. After strapping on the M4 and backpack, he shut the door and walked to the hood. It had been pried open with the same tool tried on the door, although if someone knew what they were doing they could have easily opened the hood latch by finding the release with the tool. He lifted the hood and saw the spot where the battery used to be. He lowered the hood and looked down at Billy. "Well, it looks like we're on foot again," he said to his dog. "My two feet and your four."

Billy just looked up at him with that happy expression he always wore, his tail wagging eagerly.

Zeke and Billy began walking. Interstate 45 and its feeder road were silent and desolate. He and Billy seemed to be the only living things around for miles as they marched north. Zeke wondered where in the world Ruth and the kids were heading—if it was truly Ruth that the people at the relief camp saw. *And what about Cowboy Hat's story? Had*

Ruth teamed up with someone? Was her ex-husband with her? No way. He'd bailed on his wife and children a long time ago. Besides, her ex-husband was short and Cowboy Hat said the man was tall.

As they walked along the deserted interstate, Zeke thought about everything that had happened over the last several weeks. Then he tried *not* to think about it—especially the part about the message Stover showed him and the dream of the Native American reptilian thing.

Several hours later Zeke and Billy walked across a bridged section of the interstate. A sign at the beginning of the bridge read: *'Dagger Creek.'*

They continued on down the lonesome highway, taking no special notice of the old oak tree standing on the far side of the bridge and the pathway behind it leading into the woods beyond.

* * *

FIFTEEN

A cool wind gained strength as it blew through the trees. Despite the low temperature, there was a hint in the air that Spring was near. Any day now the last remnants of snow and ice from the long winter would be gone. Zeke swept a strand of dirty, unkept hair from his weathered face. He appeared in a daze as he fed a small campfire dry twigs and branches found near his spruce lean-to shelter. The fire did little to warm his body but it gave him some type of companionship. Questions were coming more frequently than just a few days ago. At first, the questions were basic: *Who am I? Where am I?* Then he asked questions regarding what had happened to him and how long he'd been like this. But he couldn't answer these questions. The cold wind blew through the shelter. Smoke from the moist campfire invaded his nostrils and made his eyes water. A sad realization came with a vengeance:

Billy's gone.

The thought made his heart skip a beat, bringing on a despair he seemed to know from long ago but couldn't recall at the moment. *What happened to him?* Jumbled scenes swam in his brain—eating trout near a creek, hiking through the mountains with some men and a boy, an old bum feeding Billy cheese crackers—but the memories joined randomly without the organization needed to assemble a timeline. But Zeke did remember that he once had a dog and the dog's name was Billy and he loved Billy very much. And now Billy was gone.

Zeke sat close to the fire for hours, desperately trying to piece his memories together. His frustration reached a crescendo with a scream which broke him from his trancelike state. It took a moment for him to realize the scream was his own.

Zeke removed a hunk of venison jerky from a pocket of his overcoat and sliced off a piece with his survival knife. He placed the slice thoughtfully in his mouth. *You were a soldier,* a voice in his head announced. Some foggy images rushed through his mind but did little to help. He snuffed out the fire with his boot, grabbed a rusty deer rifle he got from somewhere, and strapped on his worn-out, tattered backpack before struggling to his feet with some difficulty. He swayed on his feet for a few seconds until the dizziness subsided. After regaining his balance he began walking.

He walked for several hours while the non-stop-question-answer session in his brain continued relentlessly:

What am I doing?
Hunting for something.
Yes, you're hunting for shelter.
I'm always hunting for shelter but also for something else.
Like what?
I don't know.
How can you not know?
I'm hunting for something just like I was hunting for something before.
No, not for something but for someone.
Who?
I don't know.

Zeke saw a thin line of smoke in the distance. He hiked toward it and soon found a wooden A-frame house sitting alone among the trees, a metal chimney poking out one side of the steep roof.

He reached the A-frame's front porch and approached the door. He knocked on it and waited, then again, this time with a verbal greeting. "Hello! Anybody home?"

No answer. He grabbed the handle and turned it. The door opened to a warm room full of ambient sunlight streaming through glass panels mounted in both ceilings.

"Hello! Anyone here?"

Still no answer. He examined the room and its contents. Several artist easels stood by a small kitchen table covered with oil paints and brushes. Both easels had bed sheets draped over their canvases, concealing the artist's work. Across the room a sofa and recliner faced a burning woodstove. A steaming mug of aromatic tea sat upon the coffee table near the sofa.

"Hello," he announced again while entering and heading to the back of the A-frame. He stepped inside a bedroom and glanced toward a closet door. "I'm not here to hurt anyone," he said in a voice that sounded foreign to himself. He opened the closet door, saw hanging clothes, then inspected the tiny adjoining bathroom. He turned a faucet handle in the sink. No water, as he'd expected, but the bathtub looked like it had been used recently. *They must have a well or they're packing water from a creek nearby.*

As he went back into the main room he realized that whoever lived here had fled when seeing him approach the house. He stepped over to one of the covered easels and removed the sheet. He stared at the artist's rendition of a nature setting: a small clearing bordered by a thick forest of pine, similar to the landscape surrounding the A-frame. The oils painted onto the canvass appeared dry, probably finished a long time ago. He stepped back from the painting, taking in the entirety of the scene before noticing a cone of light focused on a human figure painted into the shadow of some towering trees in the foreground. The figure was hunched over, hiding behind some bushes, peering toward the source of the light. Zeke followed the beam of light and saw its source hovering above. The object was almost translucent against the tree line in the background, but it was definitely a craft of some sort, cylindrical, not saucer-shaped but not unlike many artist renderings of supposed alien spacecraft. The more he pondered the scene on the canvass the more the back of his head ached.

Zeke covered the canvass with the sheet and walked over to the woodstove before dropping the backpack and overcoat on the floor. He leaned the deer rifle against the back of the sofa and grabbed the steaming mug of tea from the coffee table. He brought the mug to his lips and sipped the contents, a strange blend of herbs that tasted exotic and wonderful. After finishing the tea he sat on the sofa, marveling at the softness of the cushions. He grabbed the rifle and positioned it beside him as he raised his legs and stretched out on the sofa. With a sigh he closed his eyes and within seconds he was sound asleep.

Zeke opened his eyes to flickering shadows dancing on the wall. It was nighttime. A second later he realized the shadows came from flames behind him. He sat up quickly and saw a roaring fire beyond the woodstove's opened door. Still disoriented, not knowing who or where he was, he spotted the easels near the kitchen table and remembered the A-frame he'd entered earlier. He reached for his rifle. It was gone. Thinking it might have slid behind the cushions of the sofa, he stuck his hand down the crack and felt crumbs and other trash. "It's not there," a calm female voice said from the darkness. "You don't need it, do you?"

Zeke followed the direction of the voice and saw a woman sitting at the kitchen table, her features hidden in shadow from one of the easels. "Not at the moment," he replied. "But I'll need it when I leave. For food."

"You're going to eat it?" she said before standing from the table. She walked toward the front door and leaned his rifle against the wall. The light from the roaring fire in the woodstove enabled him to see her better. She looked to be in her thirties, dark hair, wearing jeans and a blue-checkered flannel shirt. She approached him and offered him a mug. He brought it to his face, smelling the same aromatic tea he had earlier. "Thanks," he said before taking a sip.

"I knew you'd like it," she said while going back into the kitchen area and grabbing something from a shelf, "since you drank the cup I'd made for myself earlier."

"Sorry," he said. "I saw it sitting there and it smelled so good."

She returned and sat in the chair opposite the sofa and began lighting a fat candle on the coffee table with a wooden match. "You in the habit of breaking into people's homes and helping yourself to whatever you like?" There was no rancor in her voice, only a playful ribbing.

"Well, these days," he began, "if no one is there, yes."

The candlelight now illuminated her facial features. She was quite striking. Zeke knew he must look hideous so he brought the mug up and had another sip, trying to hide as much of his face as possible.

"Well, at least your honest," she said, rising to her feet and lighting several more candles on a shelf nearby.

After lighting all the candles, she returned to the chair and leaned over him with one of the candles in her hand. She seemed to be examining his face as he tried to hide his features with the mug. She gently reached for the mug, took it from his hand, and set it on the coffee table. Angling the candle for better light she studied his face for another moment. "Uh-huh," she finally said, satisfied with her examination of his face. She set the candle back on the coffee table and leaned back in the chair with her own mug of tea cupped in her hands.

"What do you mean, uh-huh?" Zeke said. When she didn't respond he added, "I'm not him."

"Him?" she asked.

"Yes," he said firmly. "Whoever you think I am, I'm not."

"How do you know who I think you are?"

Zeke let it go and continued sipping his tea.

"So what's your story?" she asked after a short pause. "What brought you to my neck of the woods?"

Zeke hesitated before trying to answer. "I'm not sure."

She waited for him to continue while sipping from her mug.

"What I mean is," Zeke explained, feeling awkward and foolish, "I don't remember much of anything these days."

"Recent events or long ago events?" she asked.

"Both. Mainly recent. Some memories are trying to come forward but they're all mixed up."

"Remember your name?"

Zeke hadn't even thought about his name and was surprised when he heard his voice say, "Zeke." He thought a little more. "Zeke Allenby."

"Well, Zeke Allenby," she said, extending her hand across the coffee table. "I'm Sabrina LaFleur."

Zeke shook her hand gently, self-conscious of his grimy palm.

Sabrina leaned back in her chair. "Don't worry, it took me a while to remember."

"Remember what?"

"Anything."

Zeke thought for a long moment before asking, "You lost your memory, too?"

"Yes," Sabrina said while rising from her chair. Using an oven mitt, she grabbed a steaming bucket from the top of the woodstove and carried it to the back of the A-frame.

Zeke leaned forward on the sofa to watch her enter the candlelit bathroom and pour the hot contents into the tub.

She came back and set the empty bucket on the floor. "There's a tub of hot water in the bathroom," she said. "I think you know where it is. There's some fresh clothes in there, too. I think they'll fit you just fine."

Zeke was lost for words as he stood and walked to the bathroom. Four or five burning candles illuminated the tiny room. He closed the door and looked in the mirror above the sink, staring at the stranger looking back at him. A rough looking character for sure, but vaguely familiar, as anyone's own face should be. Unless they lost their memory, that is.

He began to peel off the layers of filthy clothing from his body. Only now, with the sweet scent of the candles all around him did he realize how badly he smelled. The scent wasn't even human. More like an animal. He wondered how Sabrina could even sit in the same room with him. As he lowered himself into the tub of steaming water, he let out a sigh, wishing this feeling would never end. Several long minutes later he saw the bar of soap and wash rag on the edge of the tub. He began scrubbing vigorously, removing the layers of dirt and grime from his body while occasionally dipping his head below the waterline.

The bath water was nearly cool by the time he'd finished. He stepped out and dried off with the towel she'd set near the clothes. The jeans were a little big but they were clean. *Did these belong to a husband or boyfriend?* he asked himself. *If so, where was this man now?* Zeke figured he'd find out soon enough. Right now he was too tired to care. He looked at his pile of rags on the floor and decided they needed to be burned out of existence. After slipping into a pullover sweater, he looked in the mirror and tried to comb his long hair with his fingers. His hair was just too tangled so he smoothed it back with his fingers as much as possible. He winced with pain as his fingers touched a sore spot on the back of his head just above the neckline. He wished he had a razor to get rid of the scruffy beard covering his face, but at least he didn't smell like an ogre anymore.

Zeke grabbed the pile of filthy clothes from the floor and left the bathroom. He saw Sabrina sitting at the kitchen table while writing in a book, perhaps a diary or journal. She closed the book when he appeared. "Feel better?" she asked.

"Yes, thank you."

Sabrina headed toward the woodstove and began ladling something from two steaming metal pots on the stovetop into a dinner bowl. "Hungry?"

Zeke had been so used to being hungry he seldom thought about it. "Yes, I am."

"I hope you like rice and beans," she said while bringing the bowl to the kitchen table. "Menu is kinda limited these days."

"You have somewhere I can put these rags?" he said, still holding the bundle of dirty clothes in his arms.

She pointed to a large cardboard box near the door. "I put your overcoat in there earlier. I think it was alive."

Zeke dumped the pile into the box and sat at the table. The smell of the steaming rice and beans in the bowl was intoxicating. Nothing had ever smelled better. He ran his hand over his hair to smooth it back before starting on the food.

"I'll give you a shave and a haircut tomorrow," she said. "If you like."

Zeke closed his eyes, as if in prayer, wondering why she was doing all this for him, a complete stranger. He opened his eyes and smiled at her. "Thank you."

"You're welcome."

After finishing two bowls of the rice and beans, Zeke insisted on cleaning his bowl, using water from a large barrel near the sink. When he finished, he found Sabrina making a bed for him on the sofa with some sheets and a blanket. She fluffed a pillow near one end of the sofa. "I hope you sleep well," she said.

Zeke stood awkwardly near the sofa, wanting to find the right words to thank her. He felt foolish, like a little boy who had lost his way from home. He started to say something but she interrupted. "Get some sleep. We'll talk tomorrow."

After blowing out all the candles she gave him one last smile before leaving for her own bedroom. "Goodnight, Zeke Allenby."

"Goodnight," he said while lowering himself onto the sofa. He watched the flames through the woodstove's opened door, his eyes getting heavy. Sleep came easily with the crackling of the wood and the shadows dancing around the room.

Things are going to be better than before, he thought while falling in deep sleep.

*

"I hope you like it short, because I won't be able to get some of these tangles out."

"I prefer it short," Zeke said as he sat in a wooden chair on the A-frame's porch, a sheet draped around his body.

"Okay."

"Those look like professional shears," Zeke said as Sabrina cut large hunks of his messy hair and let them fall to the ground. "Were you a hair stylist or something?"

"Me?" Sabrina said. "No way, but I knew some *hair benders* once upon a time."

"Hair benders," Zeke said with a smile. "I've never heard that expression."

Zeke felt like a new man. He'd slept soundly and had awoke to the smell of eggs frying on the woodstove. He couldn't remember the last time he smelled something so wonderful. After eating a hearty breakfast he asked Sabrina where she got the eggs. She laughed and gave him a curious look. "From chickens, silly," she'd said before leading him out to the porch for the shave and haircut. Her joke reminded him of something from long ago but he couldn't remember any details.

As she cut his long hair, letting the locks fall to the ground, he winced a few times when Sabrina let the shears get too close to the sore spot on the back of his head. "What is that?" Zeke asked.

"Some type of cut or something," she said. "It looks like it's almost healed, though."

"Well, it doesn't feel that way," Zeke replied.

"Sorry," she said. "I'll be careful cutting around it."

Zeke enjoyed the shave most of all. He couldn't remember getting a shave with a straight razor from anyone before, especially from a woman, and such an attractive woman as Sabrina. Her dark hair was pulled back into a ponytail, exposing her creamy complexion and bright green eyes as she delicately removed his long whiskers with the sharp blade.

When she had finished with the shave and haircut she offered Zeke a hand-mirror to inspect the results. "Wow," he said. "Looks like a different man than the one in the mirror last night."

"Not bad," she said, removing the sheet from his body and shaking hair from it.

"You mean the haircut?" he said with a grin. "Or me?"

Sabrina smiled, and after a short pause she said, "Both."

"I bet you say that to all the bums that crash your pad," he said.

"Actually," she began, "you are the first bum to crash my pad."

"I'm not sure I like being called a bum."

Sabrina shrugged her shoulders. "It was your choice of words."

"Well, if I was a bum, this would be my favorite place to crash."

"Thank you."

Zeke stood and walked around the small porch, examining the wooded surroundings while Sabrina began gathering the razor, scissors, and the rest of the grooming implements from a small table. "This is going to sound crazy," he finally said. "But where are we?"

Sabrina continued to gather her stuff. "North of Paris."

Zeke blinked. "We're in France?"

"Oui, cannot you tell by the way I speak?" she said in a decent French accent.

Zeke smiled patiently, waiting for her to continue.

"Oklahoma is that way," she said while pointing north. "Just across the river. And where is your home, Zeke Allenby?"

Zeke took a moment to answer. "Texas."

"Well, that's a big help."

"A long way from here," he said, struggling to remember. "Way out west."

Sabrina noticed the embarrassed look on his face. "Don't worry," she said. "It will eventually come back to you."

Zeke stared at her for a while. "Last night," he finally said, "you told me you'd lost your memory."

"That's right," she said, walking toward the door to take her haircutting tools back inside the A-frame.

"How did you lose it?"

Sabrina turned and grinned. "I don't remember."

As she went inside Zeke decided not to press the issue. She would tell him when she was ready.

Sabrina reappeared on the porch with two mugs of herb tea in her hands.

Zeke took one of the mugs. "I thought I might take my rifle out later and see if I can bag a doe or something," he said. "To supplement those rice and beans. You aren't a vegetarian, are you?"

"No, I'm not a vegetarian," she answered, "but . . ."

"But what?"

"Well, you can shoot something if you like," she said, "or we could pick out some meat at a little market not far from here. I need to pick up some other supplies while we're at it."

Zeke wasn't sure if she was joking or not.

"I was thinking about spaghetti and a homemade sauce I make from my little garden out back," she said. "Maybe some French bread to go with it."

"French bread," was all he could say.

"Martin, at the store, sometimes has a bottle or two of cheap wine hidden below the counter," she continued. "Maybe we'll get lucky?"

"Lucky."

Sabrina noticed his strange behavior, then misinterpreted the meaning. "I meant *lucky* with getting the wine. That's all."

Zeke, lost in thought, didn't catch any of it. "Okay, lets go to the store."

She gave him a curious look. "Okay."

Zeke remained silent as they climbed inside Sabrina's little Saturn two-door hidden behind the A-frame. He didn't show any reaction to the cars they passed on the highway, or to the little town and its food market when they arrived.

"Welcome to the thriving metropolis of Blossom Lea," Sabrina said while parking.

After buying the groceries—including a bottle of red merlot from Martin who definitely had eyes for Sabrina—they stopped at a small clothing store in town and picked up a few new items for Zeke to wear, including a pair of cheap leather loafers to replace his filthy hiking boots.

An hour later they were back in the Saturn, heading to Sabrina's A-frame home in the woods. Zeke hadn't spoken in a while and Sabrina said, "Are you okay?"

Zeke turned his head to face her. "You know, I'm amazed how quickly everything has been restored. I seem to remember that things were much worse not long ago."

Sabrina knew his memories were starting to come back to him. "What do you mean?" she asked, intentionally trying to exercise his memory functions.

Zeke frowned while rubbing the back of his head. "Something happened," he finally said. "A loss of power. A shortage of food and water. Chaos."

"That's right," she said. "Some type of magnetic pulse shut things down. Maybe from a giant solar flare. Nobody knows for sure."

"Well, you have food and fuel and power—which brings up another question I'll get to in a minute—and most experts believed it would take at least a year, or years, to *start* rebuilding the infrastructure."

"It did take a while to get things somewhat back in order," she explained, "but it's not back to the way things were before. Supplies are limited. There's only a few gas stations in the area but it's a lot better than it was immediately after eleven-nine."

"Eleven-nine?" Zeke asked. "You mean nine-eleven?"

"No," Sabrina said. "I mean eleven-nine. You know, November the ninth? The day everything changed?"

"What month is this?" he asked.

"March."

Zeke broke eye contact. Something in Sabrina's voice rang a distant bell. The way her voice sounded reminded him of something . . . *Amber*. The memory of his late wife, Amber and their infant son rushed forward like a tsunami, overwhelming him with surprise and grief. He shut his eyes and began rocking in the passenger seat.

"You okay?" Sabrina said with a bit of alarm in her voice. "What's wrong?"

Zeke didn't hear her. He was back in his past, reliving that moment of shock and horror when he learned his young family had been taken from him—yanked out of existence by a brutal and senseless act.

"Zeke," she said in a calm voice. "It's okay. Part of your memory is returning."

"Let me out!" Zeke shouted while reaching for the door handle. "Pull over!"

Sabrina swerved the Saturn off the highway and parked on the shoulder. Zeke jumped out and marched toward a small tree a short distance away. Sabrina followed him for a few paces before stopping and watching him from the distance. She watched as he leaned against the tree for support. His stomach seemed to be convulsing.

As the traumatic memory returned in full, Zeke inhaled and exhaled steadily, coming to terms with this part of his past. He didn't realize it yet but other memories had also returned, the result of making this single connection to his distant past.

Zeke stood against the tree for nearly fifteen minutes. When Sabrina finally turned off the Saturn's ignition, the silence got his attention. He turned, took another moment to compose himself, then returned to the Saturn.

"I didn't mean to alarm you," he said after sitting back in the car.

"You didn't alarm me," she said as she started the Saturn's ignition. "Well, maybe a little bit," she added while pulling back onto the highway. "Actually, I can still feel the adrenaline rushing through my veins."

"I wouldn't mind having some alcohol rush through my veins right about now," Zeke said, a weary smile on his face.

Sabrina glanced at her wrist, as if a watch was there. "Is it past noon?"

"No," he said with a chuckle, glancing at his own wrist and noticing his watch was missing. He couldn't remember the last time he'd even cared about the time of day.

"Oh well," she said. "I don't know who made up that dumb rule, anyway."

"Alcoholics, probably."

Sabrina smiled and patted him on the knee before pulling back onto the highway. Before she could pull her hand away Zeke set his own hand on top of hers and squeezed it gently, enjoying the feeling of touching and being touched by a woman—a feeling he hadn't felt for ages.

* * *

SIXTEEN

"Just like it was before," Steve Albright said, shuffling through the trash on the floor with the toe of his shoe. "He hasn't been back, son."

"What do you think happened to him?" Matt asked.

Albright shook his head. "I don't know. We've been through all this before, Matt."

"I know," Matt said. "But I still care."

"I care, too."

Matt wasn't sure if his dad really cared. To Matt, the only thing his dad seemed to care about was his company, ADS . . . and the move to Europe coming up.

Steve and Matt Albright left Zeke's abandoned cabin and walked toward a brand new Mercedes sedan parked outside. "Maybe they're living somewhere else," Matt said. "In a different town or a different state." He glanced at Zeke's Jeep Cherokee up on cinderblocks not far from the cabin, the wheels gone, stolen by thieves sometime after his dad had the vehicle and their Land Rover brought back from where they had left them, before they continued on foot through the rugged wilderness with Zeke as their guide.

"It's possible," Albright told his son, although he really believed otherwise.

"Do we really have to move to Europe?"

"I thought you were excited about going?" Albright said. "London, Rome, Paris . . . we're going to have a blast."

Yeah, a blast, Matt said to himself, knowing his dad would be busy all the time and he would be stuck with some tutor, which for the most part would be just an overpaid babysitter.

Albright and his son drove in silence down the dirt road back toward

Gold Tree. When they reached the junction of the main highway leading to town, Matt broke the silence. "Do you think he's still alive?"

Albright didn't respond right away. A moment later he said, "I think if anyone has a chance of surviving, it's Zeke Allenby."

"Then why didn't he return to Austin like he said he would?"

Albright didn't answer the question. They had been through all this before. "We've done everything we can to find him, Matt," he finally said. "There's nothing else we can do."

They remained silent as they drove on the quiet highway, passing only a few vehicles along the way. Several minutes later Matt asked, "Do you think God has a plan for everyone?"

The question caught Albright off guard. "Uh . . . I guess so."

Matt remembered asking Paul Stover the same question a long time ago:

"Yes," Paul had said. "He has a plan for everyone."

"Even if they don't believe in God?"

"Yes, even if they don't believe."

"What do you mean?"

"Sometimes people lose their way," Stover had explained. "Sometimes, something really bad happens in their life and they become angry. A lot of times they direct that anger toward God by outwardly denying his existence. That doesn't mean they don't believe, it only means they are angry and blaming God for their problems."

"Paul?"

"Yes."

"Why does God allow all the bad stuff in the world to happen. You know, why doesn't he just make it all stop?"

"Because God gave us free will, Matt," Stover had said. "God gave us the freedom to choose. We can choose to do the right thing or choose to do the wrong thing. Many bad choices are made which accounts for many of the bad things happening in the world. But the point is this: We were given the freedom to make choices, whether good or bad. If God created us to make good choices all the time, automatically, wouldn't we all be just a bunch of robots?"

"Yes, I guess so."

"By the way, how's your game design going, Matt?"

"It's going pretty good."

"Are your characters behaving better?"

"No."

"Why don't you just program them to behave?"

"Where would the fun be in that?"

"Well, maybe that's why God gave mankind free will."

"Yeah, maybe so."

Matt recalled the rest of the conversation:

"Are you afraid to die, Paul?"

"No," Stover had said. *"I might be afraid of* how *I will die, but not death itself."*

"Why is that?"

"Because my eternal life is guaranteed through Jesus Christ."

Matt remembered *wanting* to believe that.

"Most people believe that death is a bad thing, right?" Stover had continued.

"Isn't it?"

"Eternal death, yes. Worldly death, no. Many people think that when you die it is the end of everything, so therefore death is bad. But God promises that eternal life with him is more wonderful than we can imagine. However, eternal life without him is worse than we can imagine. You following me?"

"Yes, sir."

Matt smiled at the memory of the conversation with Paul Stover—the last conversation he had with his dad's lawyer and business partner. He missed Paul. Deep inside he knew his dad missed him, too. The two men had become good friends a long time ago and had become even closer after Matt's mom passed away. Matt knew that many people had vanished since 11-9 but Paul Stover's disappearance didn't make sense to anyone. His dad believed it had something to do with that Dr. Margolian, *'the nutty archeologist'* as Albright called him. Paul and the doctor had left together from Austin, the same day Zeke had left to go hunt for his sister-in-law near Houston.

When the Mercedes reached Gold Tree's town square, Matt stared out the window and watched the townsfolk doing their daily routines: buying groceries, visiting the Post Office, strolling the sidewalks, all the normal things in the life of a small town. To a stranger everything probably appeared normal, as if 11-9 had never even happened. But Matt knew things were different now and would never be the same. Despite the obvious shortages and rationing there was something else, something he couldn't point a finger at—something in everybody's thoughts and beliefs and reactions to things. He never discussed it with anyone, including his dad, because he didn't know how to explain it. At first, everyone had suspected that America had been attacked with some type of *pulse bomb*. But as time went on, most of those experts including his dad weren't so sure anymore. His dad said there was some evidence of a giant solar flare being the cause but no one was certain. Matt believed most people didn't care anymore. Most adults and kids seemed content as long as they had plenty of food and drink and all their little electronic toys. They didn't want to know about any weird lights in the skies.

As Matt's dad turned the Mercedes up the driveway to their luxurious Gold Tree cabin, Matt stared out the window while thinking about his own ideas of what had happened, not only to Paul Stover, but everything since 11-9. He knew what his dad thought. He knew what Paul Stover had thought. And he knew what he thought. He didn't know how all the theories came together but he knew his secret was part of it, maybe a *big* part of it. Every since the night when he washed the plates beside that little creek, and the two times since, he knew his secret was somehow part of all the strange things happening in the world . . . or at least the world he could see.

*   *   *

SEVENTEEN

Zeke Allenby and Sabrina LaFleur finished their plates of spaghetti along with most of the French bread. Now they sipped their wine across the table from one another. The afternoon sun was still high in the sky. Streams of sunlight beamed through the Plexiglas ceiling panels, illuminating most of the A-frame's interior.

"So your husband," Zeke said. "He left a long time ago?"

"We weren't married," she said. "We were just living together. What my mother would have called *living in sin*. But yes, he left about four years ago."

"Out here all alone," Zeke said, "no electricity, no running water. Don't you get tired of the pioneer way of life?"

Sabrina laughed. "Well, I actually miss the running water. But the well pump died years ago and I haven't bothered to fix it. I guess I'm just a *pioneer* woman at heart. A pioneer woman with a Saturn two-door."

They both laughed and sipped on their wine. A moment later Zeke went back to the subject discussed earlier during dinner. "So once some of your memories came back, do you know how long you were gone?"

"There's still about a year of my life missing," Sabrina said. "Leading up to the moment I found myself wandering in the woods not knowing who I was."

"A year?" he said in disbelief.

"Yes," she replied. "All told, I've been dealing with this for more than two years."

"Good grief," Zeke said with a shake of his head. "And after going through all that, then you have 11-9 dumped onto you. You've had a rough time."

Sabrina responded with a sad smile but no words.

Zeke started falling into some painful thought again. All through dinner his mood had changed by the minute. One moment he'd be sitting upright, confident, full of energy, eager to converse about anything. The next moment he'd lose eye contact and slump in his chair—like he was beginning to do now. He rubbed the sore spot on the back of his head and suddenly blurted out that he had to find his sister-in-law and her two children.

"Where are they?" Sabrina asked.

"They lived in Houston but I think they were evacuated to some relief camp north of the city." Zeke thought for a moment before saying, "That's the last place I remember visiting before . . . whatever happened. I left the camp on foot, heading up Interstate 45." He paused again. "I've still got to find them."

"Don't worry," Sabrina said while touching his shoulder. "I'll help you."

Zeke began staring into his wine glass, peering into some dark corner of his past, trying to process the memories returning to his consciousness.

Sabrina tried to steer the conversation to where it needed to go. "So you were saying, after you left the relief camp, looking for your sister-in-law and her kids, you headed up the highway on foot. Right?"

Zeke broke from his near trancelike state. "Huh? Yes, on foot. Me and Billy."

"Your dog."

"Yes, my dog."

"What happened next?" she asked, hoping to hold his attention as long as possible. "Where did you go?"

Zeke returned his attention to his wine glass. He seemed to be really struggling to remember. "I . . ." he began and stopped. Visions flashed in his mind's eye, images of scenes in unfamiliar places with people he didn't recognize, none of it following any obvious timeline, as if some lunatic film editor had chopped up a roll of movie film and taped it back together in random order. The images disappeared as quickly as they arrived, like tiny electrical charges flashing brilliantly before sizzling away, leaving nothing but crackling static in their place. "I don't know," he finally said. "I see things but I can't put them in order."

"Just give it time," Sabrina said. "It'll come back to you. It just takes time."

"Time," he said. "Time seems to be a major problem these days."

Sabrina stood from her chair and stepped toward her easels nearby. She slid one of them next to her chair so it faced Zeke across the table.

Zeke glanced at the easel with the sheet still covering its canvas, feeling like an executive about to be pitched a new product.

Sabrina lifted the sheet from the easel, revealing the painting Zeke had seen earlier. "I know you already saw this," she said, her tone a bit darker than usual. "But I want you to look closer this time."

Zeke studied the scene in the painting. He saw the same wooded setting, the same hovering craft, the same figure of a man hiding behind some bushes illuminated by a cone of light beaming down from the spacecraft.

"I told you how I woke up in the woods," she said in a low voice. "How I couldn't remember a thing. How I stumbled through the woods for days before finding my way back here to my home. But I didn't know it was my home at the time. Eventually, being back here helped some of my lost memories return."

"Are you telling me that this painting is from one of those memories?"

"Not just one of those memories," she said. "The *last* memory I had before I lost my memory, if that makes sense."

Zeke turned his attention away from the canvas and looked her squarely in the eyes. "You actually saw a UFO? Like this one in the painting?"

Sabrina didn't respond to his question. She turned to look at her painting. "Like I said earlier," she explained, "when the memories started coming back there is still a missing gap. My missing gap is whatever happened after the scene in this depiction. You following me?"

"Sort of."

You see," she went on, "I walked down to the creek to fill the water bucket. It was close to dusk. I got turned around in the dark and couldn't find my way back home. I was lost. Then I started hearing sounds. Scuffling sounds in the trees, like people or animals running, chasing something. The sounds seemed to be coming toward me. I got scared and started to run. I ran for a long time. A while later I tripped and fell and was so tired I couldn't get up. I decided to stay where I was, hidden behind a large tree. A moment later I saw some lights in the sky. They moved slowly above the trees. Then I saw a man crouching behind some bushes a hundred yards or so away. I think a dog was with him."

Zeke turned back to the scene on the canvas and saw the figure crouching behind the bushes. He saw an animal in the painting near the edge of the canvas. It wasn't a great rendering but he could make out its shape. It looked more like a cat than a dog.

"Eventually, I noticed that the lights were joined to form a single object," she continued. "A flying object. And suddenly, a beam of light descended the object like a giant searchlight looking for a fugitive. The man hiding behind the bushes stared up into the light. The next thing I knew I was wandering alone in the woods, not knowing who I was or where I was."

Zeke studied the painting for another moment before turning to her. "You think something could have triggered this memory, making you *think* you saw all this?"

"I don't *think* I saw it," she replied in a stern voice. "I *saw* it."

"So what happened to the man?"

"I don't know."

"Was he beamed up into the craft?" Zeke asked.

"I don't know," she said. "I didn't see what happened. Or I don't remember seeing it." She pointed at her painting. "This *exact* scene is the last thing I remember before *whatever* happened next. Like I said, the next thing I remembered was wandering around the woods later. Now I know it was *much* later."

"Sabrina, do you believe you were abducted by this . . . UFO?"

Sabrina didn't answer but she stared intensely into his eyes as if she was trying to communicate with him telepathically.

Zeke had to be careful how he continued. He didn't want to hurt her feelings or make her sound like a crazed woman who saw flying saucers abducting people in the woods. "What about this man?" he asked casually, trying to veer the subject away from the UFO thing. "Did you ever find out who he was or anything about him?"

Sabrina kept her eyes locked on his. "No," she said. "Not until now."

Zeke wanted to laugh but he controlled the urge. "Sabrina, you think the man was me?"

Sabrina kept her eyes locked on his. "It *was* you."

Zeke didn't know where to begin. "Sabrina, that's impossible. Don't you think I'd remember—" he stopped, realizing what he was saying. Feeling a bit trapped he started to become agitated. "This is crazy!"

"It's okay," she said. "I know what you're feeling. I felt the same way when it started coming back to me."

"Nothing is coming back to me!" he shouted. "This is all in *your* brain, not mine!"

Sabrina flinched at his shouting but she remained firm. "No. It's the truth."

Zeke tried to control his emotions and organize his thoughts. He lowered the tone of his voice. "Okay," he began. "First of all, I don't believe in UFOs and even if I did there are too many problems with your story."

"Like what?"

"Like the timeline," he said. "You said yourself that it took almost a year to get these memories back."

"That's right," she said, her voice a bit shaky.

"Well, that's a big problem," he said calmly. "So how long ago do you think all this happened?"

"A little over two years ago."

"Okay," he said, feeling confident he could convince her he was *not* the man in her story. "You said this is March, right?"

"Yes," she said. "March twenty-first to be exact."

"March twenty-first," he repeated while doing the math. "Sabrina, two years ago I was fulfilling an NGO contract overseas. I wasn't even in the United States. I was in a country you probably never heard of, providing protection for an Uzbek warlord I *know* you've never heard of."

Sabrina said nothing but she listened attentively.

Zeke didn't want to hurt her feelings. "I'm so sorry you had to go through this ordeal, Sabrina," he said. "I thought my situation was bad because I've lost track of a few months of my life. But that's nothing compared to your situation."

Sabrina waited to make sure he was finished before saying, "What makes you think it was only a few months?"

Her question caused him to hesitate. "Well," he finally said, "you said today is March twenty-first, right?"

"Right."

"So the last day I remember," he said while thinking it through, "was somewhere around ten days or so after 11-9 when I left the relief camp north of Houston, looking for Ruth and the kids. So November to March. That's four months, right?"

Sabrina reached across the table and placed her hand on top of his. "Zeke," she said. "November ninth, four months ago, was the second anniversary of 11-9."

Time seemed to stand still. He searched her expression for any sign of a joke. He realized she wasn't joking. "That's impossible," he said, not knowing what else to say.

"It's the truth," came the reply. "11-9 was almost two and a half years ago."

Zeke stared back at her, trying to control his frustration. Here was a woman he'd known barely one day telling him that two years of his life was missing because aliens beamed him aboard their spacecraft. What had happened? Had they performed medical experiments on him the entire time? Took samples of his bodily fluids? Just enjoyed his company and wanted to keep him around for a while? Anyone would believe she was insane!

Thoughts began racing in his head:

Anger built up deep inside him. *She's nuts! Totally off her rocker!*

He argued with himself. *Okay, so if she's not insane, why is she doing this to me?*

The anger turned to self pity. *Maybe I'm the one who is insane.*

Somehow, his logic fought through the madness he felt at the moment. A two and a half year period of lost memory explained why the little town they visited earlier seemed back to normal. *Because it took years not months for the United States of America to get back on track after a collapse of its infrastructure.*

Sabrina gently squeezed his hand while moving her face closer to his. "Don't you think it's just a little bit of a coincidence that we both lost a significant period of our lives at nearly the exact same time? That we both awakened here, in the same geographical location, with our memories gone bye-bye?"

Zeke slumped in his chair as Sabrina went on and on. She leaned back and pointed forcefully toward the canvas on the easel. "The man in this painting is you!" she exclaimed. "I saw you! The same eyes! The same physique! The same movement when you turn your head to look at something! I saw your face! The same face I'm seeing now!"

Zeke stared back at her, hoping this was all a nightmare, hoping he'd wake up any moment and let out a sigh of relief.

"When I saw someone approaching the house yesterday," she said, her voice calm, "I hid around back and waited. Then I saw it was you." Sabrina stood from her chair and dragged the other covered easel to the table. "I painted this several months ago."

Zeke looked between her and the covered easel—the other hidden work of art he saw when he first arrived but didn't unveil at the time.

Sabrina hesitated for a moment before saying, "I'm still recalling lost memories. No, not memories exactly, but images, images that don't make any sense, but I know they come from the same place memories come from."

Zeke sat motionless, waiting for the canvas unveiling, waiting like an accused criminal as the jury prepared to read the verdict. The back of his head began to throb with pain.

"Tell me what you see, Zeke." Sabrina yanked the sheet away from the easel to reveal the artwork on the canvas.

At first Zeke was confused. All he saw was swirls of green paint. The swirling brush marks formed an imprecise winding spiral but any other characteristics were difficult to discern. The texture of the paint was thick and coarse, possibly giving the impression of reptile scales or something similar, but nothing else in the image was obvious to the average viewer. But then Zeke saw something else. He saw an image of himself dominating the foreground, looking the same as he had the night before when staring at his reflection in Sabrina's bathroom mirror. The Zeke in the painting stood near someone extending their arms toward him, the rest of their body not revealed on the canvas. His skin began to crawl as he stared at the strange geometric shape of an oblong room, the walls crawling with a sickly green matter that seemed to be alive. And then, in the distant background of the painting were two reptilian-humanoid shapes moving relentlessly toward the foreground. They seemed alive on the canvas, moving relentlessly forward. The creatures suddenly stopped their movements, their hideous facial expressions full of malice while glaring at the Zeke staring into the painting. A second later they seemed to be drawing him into the canvas, pulling him from someplace near his navel. He tried to scream but he couldn't.

Sabrina noticed him starting to wobble in his chair, looking like he might be losing consciousness. "Zeke!" she shouted.

Zeke's eyes started rolling in their sockets.

"Zeke!" she shouted again while shaking his shoulders. "Hey, Zeke! Zeke! Snap out of it!"

Zeke finally came back into the real world. He shook his head violently before looking over at Sabrina who was covering the easel with the sheet.

She knelt in front of him. "Zeke," she said in a concerned voice. "What happened? What did you see?"

He stared at her with a blank expression, his head still wobbling on his shoulders. A wave of despair started in his chest and worked its way up to his face. He began sobbing uncontrollably, his entire body shaking the wooden chair he sat in.

Sabrina tried to soothe him. "It's okay now, Zeke. Everything's okay now. Can you tell me what you saw?"

After a long moment Zeke calmed a bit.

"Tell me," she insisted. "You need to get it off your chest, Zeke. In order to move forward into a healthy life, you need to tell me."

Zeke controlled his breathing, but when he tried to speak, his emotions started taking over again. After a few attempts he was finally able to get it out. "I-I saw them," he said with tears still falling from his cheeks. "They were there!"

"Who was there, Zeke?" Sabrina asked.

Zeke's eyes clenched shut but he was able to spit it out. "My wife and son! They were there!" He lost control and leaned over into his hands to weep. "They were there!"

"Were they captives, too?" asked Sabrina, a surprised tone in her voice.

Zeke removed his hands from his face and turned to her. "No," he said. "They have been dead for nearly a decade."

"Oh," Sabrina said while putting her arms around him and trying to console him. She stared off into the distance while thinking about what he just told her. They remained in this position for nearly a half-hour with Sabrina stroking his shoulders. As if on some unseen cue they both stood from their chairs. A pair of songbirds were perched on a limb outside the kitchen window, both of them singing their hearts out.

Sabrina grabbed Zeke's hand and led him outside where they sat down on the top porch step. They listened to the pleasant sounds of the outdoors, including the singing birds on the limb near the kitchen window. After a while of just sitting and holding hands Sabrina finally broke the silence. "Do you remember anything in particular during you're captivity?"

"What do you mean?"

"Like other captives there with you?"

Zeke thought for a long moment. "Maybe another man," he finally said.

"What about me?" she asked. "Do you remember seeing me there?"

"No," he said flatly. "Were you there?"

"I'm not sure," she replied. "My memories are still jumbled but I think it's possible that I was there." Sabrina squeezed his hand gently. "Zeke? Do you know *why* they abducted you?" A pause before adding, "Or us?"

Zeke shook his head slowly. "Something to do with a war," he said. "And I don't know how I even know that."

"I think you're right," Sabrina said. "It is about a war. But I think there is more. Lots more."

Zeke turned to face her, surprised by her confident statements. "You remember something?"

"Yes," she said. "I was there. And now I remember what they told me. They said a war was coming. A war that could destroy the planet."

"Go on."

"They told me how they were the ones who originally seeded the planet," she explained. "And they were here to protect the planet from being destroyed."

"They told you all that?"

"They also said they were making arrangements to reseed the planet if necessary," she continued. "They blame the proliferators of war for this."

"Politicians?"

"Yes," she said. "And soldiers who perform the dirty deeds."

That would explain their hostility toward me, Zeke thought to himself. He wanted to change the subject.

They sat in silence for a while.

"I need to find Ruth and the kids," Zeke said, breaking the silence.

"Do you have her phone number?"

Zeke shook his head, ashamed. "I can't remember it."

"Well, we can look her up on the Internet," Sabrina suggested "We can use a phone and computer in town. I know several people who will help us."

"Thank you," Zeke said sincerely. "Thank you so much."

Zeke and Sabrina stared into each other's eyes for a long moment. He caught himself moving his lips toward hers.

She seemed disappointed when he stopped. "What, Zeke?"

He took a deep breath and said, "I have too many things to do."

Sabrina waited several seconds before asking, "Where do we begin?"

Three words came from his lips. "Two years ago."

* * *

EIGHTEEN

The twelve-foot tall wooden fence that once protected the Lost Valley Compound was gone now, but the twenty acres of hidden valley with a dozen or so rustic log cabins remained. The main building with a copper cross topping its bell tower still stood, but the grounds were now part of the Lost Valley Christian Church, built after the chaos of 11-9 as the nation came back to some of the peace it once had. A few years ago the log cabins and their stone chimneys had trailed wisps of wood smoke into the air where the prevailing winds dispersed them into the clear Texas sky. Dozens of people had moved throughout the protected compound during those days, performing daily chores and visiting in small groups, everyone enjoying the protection from the harsh winter and the world outside the tall fence. But the country had changed since then. Now the sign on the highway marked the unpaved road leading past the old oak tree to the church's gravel parking lot.

In the administrative section of the church Ruth Sennot worked at a desk. Two framed portraits of Connor and Amy sat on the desktop next to a smaller frame with a snapshot of her brother-in-law, Zeke Allenby, apparently one of the many people lost in the aftermath of 11-9.

Ruth's administrative work for the church dealt mainly with homeless folks given temporary housing in the log cabins built during the dark days of post-11-9. But back then practically everyone was homeless, including Ruth and her children. Since then, as the nation struggled back on its feet, the homeless were the usual transients and mentally impaired. The church still offered shelter in its little log cabins scattered around the area.

One of these homeless people—a man that arrived over six months ago in practically a catatonic state—had made a miraculous recovery from whatever illness or ordeal that afflicted him. Ruth knew the prayers of all those at the church had been responsible for his recovery so she took a moment to give thanks before returning to the man's file in the church's computer. Mr. Stover was leaving today to head back into the real world.

As Ruth typed on her keyboard to update the file, she heard someone clear their throat from the doorway to her office. She looked up and saw Paul Stover standing in the doorway with a large cardboard box in his arms. "Excuse me, Miss Sennot," he said. "May I come in?"

Ruth smiled and said, "Yes, come in!"

Stover approached her, trying to find a spot on her desk to set the box. Ruth stood and began rearranging the objects on her desk to make room. "What in the world do you have?" she asked while scooting the framed photographs to one side.

Stover set the box on the floor next to her desk. He touched the back of his bald head and rubbed it gently before saying, "A little gift for you." He reached inside the box and removed an object made of twigs and branches glued together to form an elaborate birdhouse. When he'd first arrived at the church compound, Ruth and some other women tried to get him out of bed. He never responded to them, continuing to stay in bed all day without saying a word. A few weeks later one of the church's helpers came running into Ruth's office to tell her that the man in cabin seven was standing at his window and feeding some robins scraps of bread from his breakfast plate. Paul came out of his trancelike state gradually by feeding his new winged friends every morning from his own plate of food. Eventually, he built the birdhouse for them using nothing but sticks found near his cabin and a bottle of white glue Ruth had given him during one of her daily visits.

"Oh, Mr. Stover!" Ruth exclaimed. "For me?"

"And my little friends who live outside."

"That's so sweet!" she said, dabbing away a tear forming in her eye.

While Stover carefully set the birdhouse on the cleared spot of her desk he saw the framed photographs pushed to the side. The pleasant expression on his face dropped suddenly as he stared at Zeke's photograph.

Ruth saw the change in his face. "What's wrong? Are you okay, Mr. Stover?"

After a short pause he said, "Miss Sennot, is your name Ruth?"

"Yes," she said, surprised by the question.

Stover stared at the framed photos. "Are those your children?"

"Yes," Ruth replied, becoming more alarmed now. "Why do you ask?"

"Because I know the man in that photo," he said in an even voice. "His name is Zeke Allenby and I was with him after 11-9."

Ruth tried to hold her composure. "You knew him?"

"Yes," Stover said, rubbing the scar on the back of his head. He barely remembered trying to remove something beneath his scalp with a dull table knife shortly after arriving at the compound. "We met in Gold Tree. He was going to Houston to look for you and your children."

Ruth had to sit down in her chair. She kept her eyes locked on to Stover's. "Is he alive, Mr. Stover?"

"He was when I last saw him."

"When was that?" she asked patiently, wanting to grab Stover's shoulders to shake him to get all the answers as fast as she could.

"A couple of weeks after 11-9," Stover lied, unwilling to tell her when he *last* saw Zeke.

Disappointment settled on Ruth's face. "I see."

"I take it he never found you," Stover said.

Ruth shook her head. "I know he made it to Austin," she said, "but after that it's still a mystery."

"How do you know he made it to Austin?" asked Stover.

"I got a call sometime back from a man that said he'd hired Zeke to escort him and some others to Austin. He said Zeke left there to go looking for us."

Stover cleared his throat and asked, "Was the man that called you named Albright?"

Ruth nodded while remembering. "I think so. I believe his first name was Steve."

"Did you tell him I was here?"

"No," she said, perplexed by the question. "I didn't even know you two knew each other."

"Good."

"I don't understand," Ruth said. "What does his call have to do with you?"

"I was one of the *others* Zeke escorted from Gold Tree to Austin."

Ruth tried to remember the conversation with the man named Albright. She finally asked, "Do you think this Steve person had something to do with Zeke's disappearance?"

Stover didn't answer. He didn't need to go there at the moment. "How did Steve know you were here?"

"I don't remember him saying," she said. "And I don't think I even asked." She thought for a short moment. "Beth, from the pastor's office, accompanied me to Gold Tree when I went to look for Zeke. Maybe that's how he found me."

"You went to Gold Tree?"

"Yes. We didn't know how to find Zeke's cabin so we asked several people in town. We eventually went to the Sheriff's Office and they helped us locate the cabin. It was abandoned, of course. In shambles, actually."

"Was your trip to Gold Tree before or after you got the call from Steve Albright?"

"Before," Ruth answered. "A few weeks, I think."

Stover took a seat in a chair next to the desk and proceeded to tell her about how he and his former boss, Steve Albright, had met her brother-in-law, Zeke Allenby. He told her about their trip through the mountains in West Texas and how Zeke had expertly guided them to Austin since Gold Tree had been sealed off by army troops "for some reason or another." He closed the story when Zeke and his dog, Billy, departed from Austin in the Dodge Caravan minivan, heading for the relief camp north of Houston. He didn't mention the next time he saw Zeke though. He knew he would never tell anyone. Ever. Even when he thought about telling someone he realized how insane it sounded and vowed to keep the memory to himself.

Ruth listened to every word Stover told her. The same question she'd had for years was still unanswered. "So where is he now?"

"I don't know," Stover said while thinking about the one part of his nightmarish ordeal he had the most trouble rationalizing. *Why did I get rescued but not Zeke?*

"Can I ask you a personal question, Mr. Stover?" Ruth asked, interrupting Stover's thoughts.

"Yes?"

"What happened to you?"

Stover gave her a quizzical look. "What do you mean?"

"When you arrived here," she said, "you were practically a vegetable. What happened to you?"

Stover didn't like it but he had to be dishonest. "I don't know."

"They told me you cut the back of your head after arriving here," she said. "They didn't let you have any sharp objects after that. Do you remember that?"

Stover remembered but he wasn't going to discuss it. "I can't remember much of anything."

Ruth gave him a sympathetic look.

"I do recall someone bringing me here, though," Stover said, remembering the one who eventually came to the hellish place and escorted him away. *Why didn't he save Zeke, too?*

"That was Joe," she said in a matter-of-fact way.

"Joe?"

"Well, that's what I call him," Ruth explained. "My daughter gave him that name. He wouldn't tell us his *real* name."

"So you know him?" asked Stover.

"Sort of," she said. "He rescued me and my children. He's the one who sent us here. I haven't seen him since he brought you here, though."

Stover marveled at the link between Zeke, Ruth, and himself—all connected to each other by this Joe. *A mighty angel of the Lord Most High named Joe,* Stover marveled to himself. The thought almost made him chuckle. "Listen, Ruth," he said. "I want you to know that I will do everything in my power to find Zeke. I give you my word."

"Do you believe he is alive?" she asked, not bothering with concealing her emotions.

"Yes," he said, believing that Zeke had somehow survived the ordeal they experienced. "And I think I can find him with your help."

"Of course!" she said, ready to jump out of her skin. "But how can I help?"

"I need to speak to . . . *Joe,*" Stover said, having difficulty calling the angel by that name. "As soon as possible."

"How can he help?"

"I can't explain at the moment," Stover said. "But trust me, he can help."

Ruth stared into Stover's eyes while saying, "Okay, I believe you. If anybody can help it would be Joe." She bit on her lower lip while thinking. "I'm trying to think of who would know how to reach him."

"What about the pastor?"

"Yes," Ruth said. "If anyone knows, Pastor Davis will."

"Talking with him is imperative in finding Zeke."

Ruth blinked several times. "Okay," she said. "I'll do everything I can, Mr. Stover."

"Call me Paul."

"Okay, Paul," she said. "How will I contact you?"

Stover dug a piece of paper from his shirt pocket and set it on her desk. "This is the motel where I'll be staying. Call me when you hear something."

"I will."

Stover reached out and gently touched the birdhouse. A sad expression consumed his face. "Tell my little friends goodbye for me, too."

Ruth watched Paul Stover walk out of her office. She sat motionless for a few moments, wondering how all this could be just a coincidence, then realizing she didn't believe in coincidences. *Everything was somehow part of God's plan.* She snapped back to the situation at hand and grabbed the phone on her desk. While she waited for someone in the pastor's office to answer she ran the plans through her head, not knowing exactly how she would reach Joe but knowing that she would, no matter how difficult it became or how long it took. Zeke was coming back into her life. She didn't know how she knew this . . . but she did.

*   *   *

NINETEEN

The telephone rang once before getting picked up by his father in the master bedroom of the hotel suite. Matt continued working on his software, his attention focused completely on the large flatscreen monitor before him. He worked on the part of the software platform dealing with bringing previously used AI characters back into his *Creating Civilization* software game—the game Zeke had told him that one day might make him millions. Matt didn't care so much about the millions. He needed something else. Something he wasn't getting from the people around him these days.

The phone rang again. His dad was busy today. They were planning to see some sites over the weekend; a side trip to Pompeii followed by a five-day trip to Greece. But things came up and Steve Albright had meetings in the hotel for the next few days. Antonio, Matt's tutor while in Rome, was coming over today and after they finished his algebra assignment, Antonio promised to take him to a movie, a movie in English.

The phone started ringing again but this time his father didn't pick up. Matt answered, "Hello?"

Just gentle static on the other end.

"Hello?" Matt said again, thinking he could hear someone breathing on the other end. He waited for a response but got none. "Don't you have anything better to do on a Saturday morning?"

On the other end, Paul Stover hung up the phone.

Matt hung up the phone and returned to his work on the computer.

Steve Albright came into the room a moment later, a robe wrapped around his ample frame and a towel around his neck. "Who was that, Matt?"

"I don't know. Some crank caller."

"What did they say?"

"They didn't say anything."

"Then what did they do?"

"They just sat there, breathing."

Albright frowned and left the room, toweling his wet hair as he walked. "I'll call the front desk about that."

Matt focused on his software. He wished his father cared about him like he used to but those days were long gone. Ever since Paul Stover's disappearance, his father had been distant and grumpy. He drank a lot more now, too. For many nights Matt had pretended to be asleep when his father came home drunk, ready to rag on him about why he wasn't doing this or why he wasn't doing that. It wasn't because business was bad. His father had expanded his interests into owning several large technology companies and ADS was actually busier and more prosperous than ever, making his father a very wealthy man. But all this success didn't translate into any type of joy or happiness at home. Matt felt like he'd become a major disappointment to his father because he hadn't made straight A's at school or lettered in any sports back in the States. His father also thought that Matt's game creation *Creating Civilization* was a complete waste of time, even though Matt had designed the game from conception to writing the code with no help at all from his father or anybody. Matt often wondered how different everything would have been if his mother hadn't died, or if Paul Stover hadn't disappeared out of his life.

While working on the part of the software enabling him to bring dead characters back into the game, Matt wished he could do the same in real life. Push a button and his mom would be back in his life. Push another and Zeke would be back. Push another and Paul Stover would be right back here beside him at the computer, offering advice on not only the game design but life in general. Matt often prayed late at night for God to push those buttons . . .

* * *

TWENTY

The lights in the night sky twinkled brightly. The gentle wind blew in his face as he continued his long trek home. During the first part of his journey, after escaping from the men and their loud sticks, he traveled a distance before getting ambushed by a pack of wild dogs. Although severely injured, he managed to fight off his attackers, inflicting some serious wounds of his own before being rescued by the old man. The old man took him in his home, fed him, tended his wounds, and provided a soft bed for sleep and rest. Day after day the old man continued to take care of him, treating him kindly with good food and genuine love.

Then one day when he felt strong again, and the time felt right, he left the old man to continue his journey. Along the way, packs of men were avoided. He traveled under the stars and found shelter for rest during the hours of sunlight. Every night he saw moving lights in the sky. One of the lights seemed to guide him. Although he didn't need help with the direction, the light encouraged him in a way he didn't understand. Many hills were climbed. Many waters were crossed. He was closer now but still had many moonlit nights to travel before reaching his destination. The same light appeared each night the skies were clear enough to see. The light's path across the sky remained the same but its duration changed, slowing its own movement as he and the light came closer to their goal. Thirst and hunger was his constant companion but he moved onward. When the wind was too cold, shelter was provided. When hunger became too great, food was provided. When thirst became too great, water was provided. Now, as his senses detected familiar landscapes with their myriad of scents, Billy the German Shepherd moved with greater urgency, eager to reach his destination, where he knew he would find his Master waiting for him.

*   *   *

TWENTY ONE

The Saturn cruised down the two-lane highway with a full tank of gas and a plastic ten gallon container in the trunk for reserve, a safety precaution still practiced by most travelers making long-distance automobile trips, according to Sabrina. They had stopped briefly at the same little market they visited the day before. Her friend, Martin, let them use his phone and computer in the back office but they were unsuccessful at finding any information on the whereabouts of Ruth Sennot in Houston or any of the other localities they checked on north of the city. They spent nearly an hour before deciding to leave. Zeke decided Austin would be their first stop. He hoped he could remember how to reach Albright's safe house in the country.

While Zeke drove, Sabrina sat in the passenger seat with a map opened on her lap. "We'll reach I35 in Dallas," she said. "We'll take it all the way to Austin."

Zeke didn't appear to be listening to her. He kept messing with the *scan* button on the Saturn's AM/FM radio as it stopped on an AM station for a few seconds before moving up the frequency range and stopping at the next station. Most of the time he got nothing but static with some faint music in the background. The radio stopped on a talk show. " . . . as our school systems still treat these theories as fact," the man on the radio said, "despite modern evidence in DNA research, molecular biology, and other hard sciences."

"Hello! Earth to Zeke Allenby!" Sabrina announced.

Zeke glanced her direction before returning his eyes to the road. "What?"

"Did you hear what I said?"

"Yes, I heard you," he answered before switching off the radio. "Earth to Zeke Allenby."

"Before that."

"I35 in Dallas," he said. "Got it."

"Yeah, right," she said. "Whatever."

Sabrina had been playing a little game every since they left her A-frame, a game where she would end their conversations with *"whatever"* every chance she could. The game started during some discussion they were having earlier in the trip, and Zeke, being a bit grumpy in the early morning hour, proceeded to lecture her about how he disliked the phrase. "It suggests weakness and apathy," he said before going on and on about it. Sabrina listened to his entire little sermon. When it was over she paused a beat before saying, *"whatever."* Zeke began laughing, amazed at how comfortable he was with this woman, a woman he'd only known for a couple of days. He wondered if she felt the same.

As he drove the Saturn down the highway, Zeke tried to keep his mind off Sabrina's artwork. He decided he would keep his thoughts in the present. He thought about how normal everything appeared. Sure, there were less cars and trucks on the road than before 11-9, and more boarded-up convenience stores and businesses than before, but most things seemed back to normal. But he knew things were *not* back to normal and they never would be again. Ever. He wondered if there were more memories still repressed in Sabrina's subconscious or if they had all returned, like her memories of the *aliens* telling her they were returning to *save the planet,* something he had difficulty believing. At any rate, he didn't want to go there right now. "You getting hungry?" he asked her.

"Starving," she said before reaching behind the seat and grabbing a paper sack full of snacks they bought at Martin's store. She reached into the sack and began inspecting the various items. "We got Premium Beef Jerky, Cheese Crackers, and something that resembles Twinkies and Ding Dongs from long ago."

"Sounds like a recipe for a heart attack," Zeke said. "You trying to get rid of me or something?"

"Oh, here's my favorite," she said while pulling out a small plastic bag. "Porky's Pork Rinds."

Zeke took the bag and opened it. "I hadn't these since I was a kid."

Sabrina removed the last items from the sack. "Two bottles of water and one apple and one banana." She began peeling the banana.

Zeke ate a pork rind, making loud crunching sounds as he chewed it. He began making a face and offered the bag to Sabrina. "Here, I'll trade you."

"For the banana?" she said while taking a huge bite of the banana.

"Not now," he said. "Okay, let me try the crackers then."

"Are you sure? Don't you want the fake Twinkies or Ding Dongs?"

"No thanks," he said, giving her the bag of pork rinds and taking the package of cheese crackers. "And I don't even know what a Ding Dong is . . . or want to know."

After finishing her banana Sabrina started on the pork rinds. "Not bad," she said while crunching loudly and reading the ingredient label on back of the bag. "Saturated fat, not bad. Trans fat, not bad. Cholesterol, not bad. Sodium, bad."

Zeke smiled, knowing her performance was for his benefit. "I'm shocked, Sabrina," he said. "I took you for one those organic Tofu munchers."

Sabrina ignored him while eating the pork rinds and reading the bag. "And artificial flavoring, my favorite!" She placed the half-eaten bag of pork rinds back into the paper sack and removed one of the bottled waters. After drinking several gulps of water she said, "I used to be one of those organic . . . what did you call them?"

"Tofu munchers," he said.

"Right. Tofu munchers. But that was before 11-9. I remember a few times I was so hungry I could have eaten a dead horse."

"They aren't that bad," Zeke said. "As long as they're cooked."

"Kinda like the pork rinds," she said.

"Not really."

Sabrina screwed the lid back on her bottled water. She began reaching behind the seat for something else. "I remember an aunt of mine, Aunt Doris, who liked to read gossip magazines where she got all these crazy ideas about things. My mother told me that one day at church, Aunt Doris asked the preacher if you could still get to heaven if you ate pork."

Zeke waited for her to continue. When she didn't he said, "And?"

"The preacher said sure, you can get to heaven if you eat pork. In fact, you'll get there a lot faster."

Zeke kept a straight face. "You need a drum roll for that one."

"That was a true story," she said while finally finding the item she'd been looking for and setting it in her lap. "As far as you know."

Zeke took several glances at the jug of clear liquid in her lap. While trying to keep his eyes on the road he began reading the large label out loud as she found a plastic cup behind her seat. "'Ninety-nine point eight percent Aloe Vera juice. Made with organically grown cold processed Aloe.' You got to be kidding. You're actually going to drink that stuff?"

Sabrina poured some of the liquid into the cup. "Here, have some."

"No thanks."

"Come on," Sabrina insisted. "I cleaned up the outside of your body, now it's time to clean up the inside."

"I like my insides the way they are."

"You mean full of parasites, worms, and who knows what else," she said. "I can only imagine what you were eating before I found you."

"Believe me, you don't want to know," Zeke said. He had learned how to eat all types of things in survival situations while in the military, not including what he had to eat the last couple of years. Truth was, he could eat almost anything and the squeamish act he'd been playing with Sabrina was for fun.

"Drink it," she said. "It's good for you."

Zeke took the cup and downed the Aloe liquid in one large gulp. He made a terrible face as if he was going to be sick. "That's awful!"

Sabrina couldn't hold back a chuckle. "What a big baby."

Zeke offered Sabrina the empty cup, keeping his eyes on a narrow bend of highway winding through a forest of trees. He glanced at her at the same time she began taking the cup from his hand. When his attention came back to the bend in the road he saw the stopped vehicle in their lane, a tall man standing beside the opened driver's door staring back at them with a placid look on his face. Something else was on the road in front of the vehicle. All of this flashed in front of Zeke's eyes within a second.

Zeke stomped on the brakes and yanked the Saturn's steering wheel hard to the right. The little Saturn swerved before fishtailing toward the shoulder of the highway. The Saturn barely missed colliding with the vehicle in the road but it wasn't so lucky with an oak tree in a small clearing off the road. When the Saturn smashed the tree, the little car came to a sudden and violent stop. Zeke's shoulder-belt did its job, keeping him from smashing his face on the steering wheel. He was glad the airbag hadn't engaged. He sat there a moment, hearing nothing but the hissing of the engine's radiator and the man in the road shouting something. Zeke turned and saw Sabrina trying to release her shoulder-belt, her sweater and jeans soaked in liquid. "Are you all right?" he asked her.

"Yes, I think so. How about you?"

"I'm good."

224

They both got out of the Saturn as the man reached them. "You okay?" he shouted. "Are you hurt?"

"No, we're fine," Zeke said.

"Thank God," the man said. "Everything happened so fast."

Zeke looked up at the man, probably in his early forties, powerful build, tall, maybe six-five or six-six with cropped blonde hair. The man could be a lineman for the Cowboys or some other football team in the NFL. Zeke glanced toward the white, mid-sized sedan stopped in the road. He saw a deer lying in the road a few feet in front of the sedan's bumper. He started walking toward it. "We need to clear the road before there's another accident," he told the big man as they walked toward the car.

Zeke glanced down the highway, making sure another vehicle wasn't coming before approaching the dead deer. When he reached the front of the sedan Zeke noticed little damage on its front end, just a small dent on the bumper which could've been there before the accident. The deer, a young doe, didn't seem to be breathing. Zeke and the man started reaching for the hind legs to drag the carcass off the road. Zeke already had a hand gripping one of the animal's rear legs when it jerked violently and jumped upright. "Whoa!" Zeke shouted while he and the man moved out of the way, the doe's resurrection startling them both. The doe bolted across the highway and disappeared into the thick trees beyond, continuing its journey that had been interrupted just minutes earlier. "Well, you don't see that everyday!" the man said. "I thought he was dead for sure."

"She," Zeke corrected him. "It might be a good idea to move your car off the road before something else happens."

"Yes, you're right," the big man said, lumbering toward the sedan and climbing behind the wheel. He put the sedan in gear and drove it off the road as Zeke and Sabrina walked back to the wrecked Saturn.

Zeke inspected the Saturn's smashed front end. Steam rose from the folded hood, suggesting a damaged radiator at the very least. He pointed to Sabrina's sweater where the aloe juice had spilled all over her. "At least I won't have to drink any more of that plant juice," he said with a smile.

"Oh I can buy more," she replied with a tired smile.

"You sure you're okay?" he asked her.

"Fine."

"Cheer up," he said. "We'll get your car fixed and be on our way in no time."

"I have enough money for gas and food, Zeke," she replied. "But not enough for any car repair."

"What about insurance?"

Sabrina shook her head.

"We'll be fine," he said. "I told you before. I have money in the bank. I just have to remember what bank." Zeke smiled at her. "When we get to my place we'll be set."

Sabrina smiled and said, "Whatever."

The big man returned. "It all happened so fast," he said in a voice that matched his size. "I slowed down when I saw it running toward the highway. I didn't think I hit it that hard. I just stepped out of the car to examine it when I saw you coming."

"That makes sense," Zeke said. "Apparently she was just stunned."

The man offered his hand. "I'm Andrew Coleman."

Zeke shook Andrew's big, meaty paw of a hand. "Zeke Allenby," he said. "This is Sabrina LaFleur."

Sabrina nodded at the man, not masking her disappointment with the Saturn's condition.

"I'll be glad to give you folks a ride," Andrew said. "Where are you heading?"

"To Austin," replied Zeke. "Then on to West Texas."

"I see," Andrew said. "I wasn't planning on going that far."

Sabrina didn't say anything but she couldn't hide the frustration on her face.

Andrew thought a moment before saying, "I have a friend that can probably help with the repair. If you'd like, I can give you a ride into town and we can call him. We can have lunch while we wait. My treat."

Zeke looked at Sabrina for her response. Sabrina responded with a look that seemed to say: *what choice do we have?* "Sure," she finally said. "Lunch. Sounds good."

Zeke and Sabrina grabbed their belongings from the backseat of the Saturn before following Andrew to his white sedan, a Buick, Zeke now noticed. After putting their bags in the Buick's trunk, Sabrina got in the front seat while Zeke climbed in the back seat. He noticed the noxious odor of a flower-scented air freshener in the car. Although old and worn, and a bit cramped for Andrew's size, the car's interior was neat and organized—a hint of the user's personality according to Zeke.

Fifteen minutes later they turned off the main highway onto a narrow, winding road. A small town appeared in their view within minutes. "Welcome to White Clouds, Texas," Andrew announced in his big booming voice. As Zeke studied the little town's layout from the back seat, Andrew suddenly turned into the parking lot of the *Hilltop Church*. He parked the Buick near a rear entrance of the building. "Here we are," he said. "We can make the calls here."

"You work at the church?" Zeke asked him.

Sabrina turned toward the backseat and gave Zeke a look that said: *Duh!*

"Yes," Andrew said before stepping out of the Buick.

Sabrina's sweater was now sticky from the spilled aloe juice and she wanted to change tops. After grabbing her bag from the trunk, Zeke and Sabrina followed Andrew through a back door of the church into a series of small offices. In one of the offices they found a middle-aged woman working behind a desk. "Heather," Andrew said. "This is Sabrina and Zeke."

Heather smiled as Zeke and Sabrina exchanged greetings with her.

"Heather, would you call Ricky Boles?" Andrew asked. "Let me know when you get him on the line. Will you, please?"

"Yes, Pastor Coleman," Heather replied, going to an old Rolodex and flipping through the cards.

Zeke and Sabrina exchanged another glance before following Pastor Andrew Coleman to his office. "Have a seat," he said. "Make yourselves comfortable."

"Uh, do you have somewhere I can change?" Sabrina asked.

"Absolutely," Andrew replied. "Down the hall, second door on your right."

After Sabrina left the room, Zeke sat in a chair facing the desk while Andrew dug through his top desk drawer for something.

"Sorry," Andrew said. "I don't mean to be rude but I've misplaced something."

"You're not being rude," Zeke said. "Do what you need to do."

"Ah-ha!" Andrew said a moment later, a checkbook now in his hand.

"How long have you been here, Pastor Coleman?" Zeke asked.

"Seven years at this church," Andrew replied, "and please, call me Andrew."

"I saw the name of the church out front," Zeke said, "but didn't catch the denomination."

"That's because we're non-denominational," Andrew said. "We're just a simple Bible-based church with a small but loyal congregation."

Heather's voice suddenly came from the intercom of his desk phone. "Ricky Boles is on line one."

"Thanks," Andrew said. He grabbed the phone's receiver to take the call. "Good morning, Ricky. Listen, I was involved in an accident an hour or so ago . . . no, no, I'm fine but there was some damage to the other folk's car."

Sabrina returned from changing clothes and examined the various pictures and knickknacks in the office while Andrew talked on the phone.

Heather came into the room. "Would you two like some coffee?" she asked in a hushed voice. "I just made a fresh pot."

Zeke and Sabrina accepted the offer and followed Heather into a small room with a refrigerator, microwave, and coffee maker. A kitchen table with several chairs stood opposite the appliances.

Heather poured coffee into several cups and brought them to the table. "There's sugar and sugar substitute on the table," Heather said. "I have some cream in the fridge if you like."

"That's okay," Sabrina said. "I like mine black."

"Me, too," said Zeke.

Heather smiled before heading back to her office. "Let me know if you need anything."

While Zeke and Sabrina sipped their coffee they could still hear Andrew's booming voice from his office down the hall. Zeke examined the few religious prints hanging on the walls: a child sitting in Jesus's lap while other children gathered around; Jesus praying near a rock; Jesus ascending into the sky, surrounded by a cloud. This last depiction struck a chord with Zeke. Something about the shape of the cloud seemed familiar to him. He could almost sense its motion.

Andrew suddenly entered the room. "Good news, folks," he said in his powerful voice. "Ricky is stopping by to pick up your car keys then he'll head out to get your car and tow it back to his shop. How about we go to lunch at the local diner. My treat. Ricky said he'll contact us later to give you an estimate."

After leaving the Saturn ignition keys with Heather, they left the church in Andrew's Buick and drove a short distance to the *White Clouds Diner*. The smell of coffee and baked pastries hit them when they entered the diner. After sitting in a booth in back a waitress scurried toward them. Her expression brightened when she saw Pastor Coleman sitting in the booth. "Good day, Pastor Coleman!" she said, glancing at Zeke and Sabrina with the same smile.

"Hi, Tammy!" Andrew said, his voice filling the diner.

Tammy handed out the menus. "The lunch special today is country steak and gravy with your choice of two vegetables," Tammy said in her Texas drawl. "What can I get ya'll to drink?"

Zeke and Andrew turned their attention to Sabrina. "Just water for me," Sabrina said.

"Iced tea," said Zeke.

"Same for me," Andrew said.

"I'll be back in a sec with your drinks and some rolls and butter," Tammy said.

Zeke and Sabrina studied the menu but Andrew did not. When Tammy came back with the drinks and rolls, ready to take their order, Sabrina ordered a chicken salad sandwich and Zeke went with the Pastor's choice of the lunch special.

As the minutes passed by, the *White Clouds Diner* began filling with the lunch crowd. Throughout the lunch, people from adjoining tables stopped by frequently to pay their respects to Pastor Coleman. He was quite the public figure it seemed and although the people stopping by their booth were always polite they only glanced at Zeke and Sabrina with curious expressions. Andrew introduced them at first but eventually let it go to shorten the conversations so they could eat their lunch.

"I guess you're never really off work," Sabrina said. "Kind of like a doctor."

"Yes," Andrew said. "In a way I am a doctor. A doctor of the spirit."

"What do you do for relaxation?" Zeke asked. "Any hobbies?"

"Well," Andrew began. "Between preparing my Sunday sermons, visiting sick folks in the hospital, performing weddings and funerals, counseling married couples on the verge of divorce, there's not much time for any hobbies. I like to shoot hoops with the youth group at church, though. Sometimes a little volleyball."

A young man in mechanic clothes entered the diner and began searching the tables with his eyes. He spotted their booth and walked toward them.

"Hey, Ricky!" Andrew said. "This is Sabrina and Zeke, the owners of the car."

Ricky nodded at both of them. He had a mop of dyed, jet-black hair with a stud earring in one earlobe.

"You already got the car?" Zeke asked.

"No, sir," Ricky replied, turning his attention back toward Andrew. "I've been leasing out my wrecker to Charlie Dormeyer. I talked to him a little while ago and soon as he's finished with another job he's gonna pick it up."

"These folks have a long trip ahead of them," Andrew said. "I'd like to get it fixed as soon as possible."

"I'll do my best," Ricky said. "But I won't know nothing until I look at it and order the parts."

Andrew pulled out his checkbook from a pocket. "Do you need a deposit to get it going, Ricky?"

"No, sir," Ricky said with a smile. "Your word is good enough for me."

As Ricky left the booth Zeke told Andrew, "You don't need to pay for anything."

"I want to pay," Andrew said. "If I would've moved off the road none of this would've happened."

"That's generous of you," Zeke said, "but you've helped us enough." He felt Sabrina nudge her knee against his under the table.

Andrew smiled patiently but Zeke knew this man wasn't the type that changed his mind easily.

"Excuse me one moment," Andrew said before raising his large frame from the booth and walking toward the rear of the diner.

Zeke and Sabrina watched Andrew greet people as he made his way to the diner's restrooms.

"Why don't you let him pay for the damage?" Sabrina whispered. "He's offering, you know."

"Because it wasn't his fault," Zeke whispered back. "It could've happened to anybody. It was just an accident."

Sabrina sighed and looked away.

Zeke watched Andrew continue to greet and talk to people as he neared the restrooms. "Popular guy," he said. "He seems to know everyone here."

"Well," Sabrina said. "He definitely doesn't get much peace, that's for sure."

Zeke shrugged and said, "I don't know. He seems to be really happy doing what he does. I'd say he was a man at *peace* with who and what he is."

Sabrina frowned. "I never said he wasn't a man at peace with himself."

Zeke started to respond when an elderly woman using a walker dropped her purse onto the floor as she and her husband left a table nearby. Zeke moved quickly from the booth and retrieved the purse for her.

"Thank you, young man," the woman said as Zeke handed the purse to the husband.

"Your welcome, ma'am," Zeke replied.

When Zeke sat back in the booth Sabrina said, "You were in the Boy Scouts, weren't you?"

"Yes, I was."

"Ah," she said. "I knew it."

"What's wrong with being in the Boy Scouts?"

"Nothing," she said while trying to hide a smile.

Andrew returned to the booth from the restroom. "After lunch I can drop you two off at my house where you can relax while waiting to hear about your car. You might not get the car fixed today so I'd love to have you as my guests."

"Thanks," Sabrina said, "but we can find a motel for the evening."

"You don't need to do that," Andrew said. "You guys save your money. It's the least I can do, really."

"We wouldn't want to impose on you," Sabrina said. "You've been more than helpful and—"

"—Nonsense," Andrew interrupted. "I've had an empty house ever since my wife passed away. I would like you both to be my guests."

Tammy the waitress approached the table. "Can I get you folks some dessert?"

Everybody declined. Andrew handed Tammy some folded bills. "This should take care of everything."

"Thank you, Pastor Coleman," Tammy said before grabbing some of the dirty plates from the table. "Ya'll have a great day!"

They left the diner and climbed back in Andrew's Buick. They drove back the way they came, past the church, and onto a road with rows of brick homes lining the way. Andrew turned into the driveway of one of the homes and parked. "Here we are," he said while climbing out the car. The single-story, red-brick house stood behind a neat lawn with a towering oak in the middle.

They climbed out of the Buick. Sabrina asked, "Aren't most parsonages near their church?"

Andrew chuckled. "Yes, but this is a small congregation with a small budget. That was part of the deal when I arrived. You gotta get your own pad if you want to preach here was basically what they said."

Zeke was impressed by Pastor Coleman's candidness as the big man smiled and grabbed the bags from the trunk. Zeke really like this powerful but gentle giant.

When they entered through the front door Zeke saw a tidy formal dining room to his right. Opposite this room a parlor-style setup with sofa and chairs, stylish but practical. Zeke and Sabrina followed Andrew past these rooms and into a hallway where several bedrooms stood on either side. "Take your pick," Andrew said. "I have a housekeeper that comes in once a week so the sheets and towels are fresh."

"I'll take this one," Sabrina said, picking the first room they came to. She leaned close to Zeke and whispered in his ear, "Maybe you can pay me a visit later tonight."

Zeke was shocked at her forwardness. "Okay . . ." he whispered hesitantly. Sabrina had always been friendly towards him but not like this. He might have been eager to take her up on her proposition if they weren't in the home of a pastor. It didn't seem right under the circumstances. He dropped her suitcase in the room before taking an old duffel bag she had lent him into the bedroom across the hall.

Zeke and Sabrina took a few minutes to freshen up in the bathrooms of their *separate* bedrooms. A short while later they met Andrew in the kitchen while he finished a telephone conversation. After ending the phone call Andrew said, "I've got to run. I should be back around six." He removed a key on his keyring and set it on the kitchen table. "If you leave the house please lock up and hide the key under the rear door mat."

"We'll probably take a walk," Sabrina said. "To see the sights."

Andrew laughed. "I'm afraid you won't see many sights in White Clouds. But there is a nice little park not far from here." He suddenly remembered something. "Oh, I just remembered. Follow me."

Zeke and Sabrina followed him out the back door to the garage at the end of the driveway. He manually lifted the garage door. They saw a lawn mower, some gardening tools hanging from a wall, and a half-dozen or so cardboard boxes stacked neatly in one corner. Andrew walked to a pair of bicycles leaning against the boxes. He grabbed the first one and examined it. "Tires look good," he said. "There's an air pump around here somewhere if you need to pump them up a bit."

"Thank you," Sabrina said. "A bike ride sounds good."

Zeke noticed the old bikes were a his-and-hers matching set. He remembered having a similar set many years ago in his previous life.

"I haven't used them since Marla passed away," Andrew said. "I'm glad someone will get some use out of them. Well, I've gotta run. Enjoy yourselves."

"Thanks, Andrew," Zeke said. He watched the big man climb into the Buick and back out of the driveway. Andrew's mentioning of his late wife had taken Zeke back to memories of his own wife, Amber, and his son, Josh, the son that never got the chance to see life beyond the few months he lived. *He would've been in elementary school by now,* Zeke told himself. The thought had invaded him suddenly. He had to force himself back into the present. "So lets take a ride," he said to Sabrina.

"I'm ready when you are."

A few minutes later they were on the bikes, riding through the neighborhood with no destination in mind. The sun warmed their skin despite the cool breeze in the air. They eventually found the small park Andrew mentioned. They took a break from the bike ride and sat against the trunk of a large tree. The park was empty except for a young woman and her toddler playing in a small playground nearby.

Sabrina slid a small backpack from her shoulders and removed two bottled waters. "It's certainly peaceful here," she said while handing Zeke one of the bottles.

Zeke took a drink of water.

"If they can't fix the car," she said, "maybe we should think about taking a bus. I've got enough money for a couple of tickets. What do you think?"

"Uh-huh," Zeke said absentmindedly.

"Zeke," she said. "Did you hear what I said?"

Zeke nodded while staring off in the distance.

"I don't want to be stuck in some stranger's house," she said, mainly to get his attention. "Do you think they will be able to fix the car soon?"

"Uh-huh."

Sabrina exhaled loudly and leaned back against the tree. She resisted the urge to say *whatever.*

Zeke saw a man dressed in peculiar clothing walking across the park toward the woman and the toddler in the playground.

Sabrina tried again. "Maybe we should check out the bus station when we get back," she said. "What do you think?"

Zeke didn't answer as he watched the man approach the woman and toddler. The child played with a stuffed animal while the man talked with the woman.

"You think that's a good idea?" Sabrina insisted.

Zeke saw the woman shaking her head at the man.

"Zeke?"

The woman kept her eye on the man while she gathered her child in her arms.

"Zeke?" Sabrina said louder.

"Yeah?" he finally replied, still watching the scene in the playground.

Sabrina glanced toward the scene. She saw the man, woman, and child. The woman grabbed the child from the ground and walked away, leaving the man alone in the playground.

Zeke rubbed the back of his head while staring at the oddly dressed man. The man wore an old-fashioned seersucker suit with a felt fedora hat. He suddenly made eye contact with Zeke. He started walking toward him in small, careful steps, as if he had trouble moving his legs.

Zeke stood when the man neared. The man's face was definitely odd-looking.

"How are you both today?" the man said as he shuffled toward them.

"We're okay," Zeke replied, studying the man's elongated face and oversized mouth. "How about you?"

"Oh, I have had better days," the man said. "My car won't start and I can't find the problem."

"Oh, yeah?" Zeke said.

"Do you know anything about combustion engines?" the man asked. "I am afraid my knowledge on the subject is limited."

The man's strange, formal speech amused Zeke. "I know a little," Zeke said. "Let's go take a look."

Zeke followed the man to a graveled parking area nearby where an old Chevy pickup sat. The man's post-World War II city duds didn't match up with the old pickup truck, usually owned by farmers or ranchers. Zeke opened the driver's door and sat behind the wheel. The man stood a few feet away while Sabrina remained near the tree, drinking her bottled water. Zeke turned the ignition switch several times, unable to start the engine. He reached under the steering column to release the hood latch. "Man, this is an antique," he said while releasing the latch and backing out of the cab. "How long have you had it?"

The man only shrugged with the same goofy smile.

Zeke checked the battery first, noticing plenty of corrosion on the terminals. He turned toward the man. "You got any tools?"

The man shook his head. "No."

Zeke felt instinctively that the man had some ulterior motive in all this but he wasn't concerned. The man was no real threat to him. Zeke turned back to the engine. Seeing no obvious reasons for the engine problem other than the corroded battery terminals, Zeke turned toward the man. "I need a screwdriver or a set of pliers."

The man turned suddenly toward the trees bordering the park. His movement was sudden and swift, unlike his movements earlier. A worried look covered his face. A second later his expression changed. Now he looked angry.

Zeke glanced at the trees. He didn't see or hear anything unusual. "Something wrong?"

The man didn't reply. He kept taking quick glances in all directions. Suddenly, he muttered something under his breath and rushed past Zeke toward the pickup. He slammed the hood shut and hoisted himself inside the cab behind the wheel. Zeke watched in amazement as the man started the engine on the first try, jammed the transmission in gear, and sped out of the parking area while the spinning tires peppered the area with flying gravel.

Sabrina joined Zeke as the pickup sped away. "What was that all about?"

"That was very weird."

"What happened?" asked Sabrina. "Did you fix his truck?"

Zeke examined the park's perimeter more closely. He still couldn't see or hear anything out of the ordinary. He started back toward their bicycles as Sabrina followed. "Something spooked him," he said. "But I don't know what."

"What do you mean?" asked Sabrina.

"Nothing," Zeke said, seeing no reason to explain since she didn't appear to be alarmed by any of it. "Didn't he appear a little strange to you?"

"Yeah, I guess," Sabrina said. "Probably just mentally impaired."

Zeke didn't say it but he didn't believe the man was mentally impaired at all, physically perhaps, but mentally the man seemed very lucid.

While they climbed on their bicycles and rode back to the road, Zeke felt compelled to look back over his shoulder toward the trees bordering the park. He still didn't see anything out of the ordinary but his actions made Sabrina nervous. She frowned as she pedaled her bike, not talking as much as usual.

As soon as the bikes hit the pavement of the road, Andrew's Buick came to a stop not ten feet away from them. They stopped their bikes as the big pastor got out of his car and walked toward them. "I thought I might find you here," he said, his voice even but alarmed.

"What's up?" asked Zeke.

Andrew took a deep breath before speaking. "When I got to my office," he began, "Ricky had left several messages for me to call him back. He told me the wrecker driver he sent to get your car couldn't find it. Ricky said he eventually drove out there himself, to the exact spot I described to him. He said the car wasn't there."

"You sure he went to the right location?" Zeke asked.

"Yes," Andrew answered. "He said he found the tree you smacked into. He could see bits of paint on it. Even saw the tire skids on the road."

"Someone stole my car?" Sabrina asked.

"Or it got towed," Andrew said. "The Sheriff's waiting to hear back from us. He needs the plate number, then he can run it through the state and county records to see if anyone hauled it off."

"Unbelievable," Zeke muttered to himself, his mind still processing the strange encounter with the weirdo in the park.

"This is our lucky day," Sabrina said under her breath.

They loaded the bikes haphazardly in the trunk, tying the lid down with a set of bungee cords Andrew had before climbing back into the Buick. "We can call him from the house," Andrew said while driving away from the park. "Sometimes I wish I still had a cell phone but after 11-9 I never reinstated mine. I don't even know where I put it. In a drawer somewhere I suppose. Most of the time I'm glad I don't have one."

"I'd like to drive out where we left the car," Zeke said. "I want to see for myself."

"Okay," Andrew said. "After we call the Sheriff I'll take us out there."

A short drive later the Buick pulled into Andrew's driveway with the trunk lid banging against the bicycles in back.

"I'll unload the bikes while you guys make the call," Zeke said as they all climbed out of the car. While Sabrina and Andrew went inside the house, Zeke unloaded the bikes and stored them back into the garage. He doubted the car got towed so quickly. That's why he wanted to examine the site himself. If the Saturn wasn't towed it was stolen. Hot-wired, since they didn't leave the keys in the car, unless Ricky was part of some auto-theft ring. *Hey, stranger things have happened . . . especially lately.*

After Sabrina and Andrew returned from the house they all climbed into the Buick to drive to the highway where they left the Saturn.

"Did you get a hold of the Sheriff?" Zeke asked Sabrina.

"No," she said, obviously exasperated. "We got his voicemail. Can you believe that?"

"Yes, I can."

When they reached the spot where the Saturn had collided with the tree, Andrew, at Zeke's suggestion, parked the Buick on the shoulder of the road a short distance away. Zeke noticed the skid marks as he approached the site, mentally recreating the scene when the Saturn began to fishtail before hitting the tree. The sandy soil still showed signs of the Saturn's tires sweeping through the dirt before it came to its sudden stop with the tree, but there were no other visible tire tracks. None. Which meant the Saturn wasn't driven away. Or towed. Apparently, it just hovered from the ground and took off. Either that, or a crane lifted it vertically from the ground—which seemed just as likely as the hover theory. He examined the soil more carefully, noticing plenty of footprints but mostly their own.

"Well, it's definitely gone," Sabrina said. "Unbelievable."

Zeke knew Sabrina and Andrew hadn't noticed the tire tracks—or the lack of them—and probably wouldn't. He knew how crazy it was going to sound although nothing sounded very crazy to him anymore. He decided to keep it to himself for the moment and let the cops investigate and give their own explanation. Let them sound like the loonies.

Zeke asked Andrew, "How well do you know this Ricky fellow and his wrecker driver friend?"

The question took Andrew by surprise. "I've known Ricky since he was a youngster. He and his family are members of the church. Well, his family, at least. I haven't seen him in a while . . . until today."

"How about the wrecker driver?"

"Don't know him," Andrew said.

Zeke studied the site a bit more before saying, "There's nothing else here to see."

They walked back to the Buick and climbed back inside. Andrew asked, "You think Ricky and his friend had something to do with this?"

"I don't know," Zeke answered. "You think it's possible?"

"I suppose anything is possible," Andrew sighed. "But I still find it hard to believe."

"I'm just asking," Zeke said. "I'm not throwing accusations his way. I'm just curious. I figured since you're an acquaintance of his and the pastor of his family's church, you might know something about him, that's all."

"I understand," Andrew said. "Far as I know he's never been in any serious trouble."

Sabrina looked back at Zeke from the passenger seat. They exchanged looks for a brief moment. Zeke wasn't sure if the look meant: *I was thinking the same thing*, or, *why are you casting suspicion on this Ricky character?*

"I'm sure the Sheriff will know," said Andrew. "I'll ask him when I talk to him."

Zeke didn't respond. He'd lost faith a long time ago in law enforcement telling anybody anything they wanted to know. As far as he knew, this Sheriff could even be involved in the Saturn's disappearance.

They drove in silence on the way back to Andrew's home. When they got there Andrew checked his voicemail on the box in the kitchen while Sabrina went to her bedroom. She seemed very angry. Zeke sat at the kitchen table, feeling antsy and unsettled. His right knee bobbed up and down rapidly as Andrew began returning missed calls.

Zeke finally stood from the table and exited the kitchen's back door. He walked across a small lawn fenced in by chain-link fence. Beyond the fence stood a narrow dirt and gravel road—an alley lined with portable storage shacks on both sides, each one standing near the gates of each fenced property. He heard vehicle tires crunching gravel while cruising down the alley. A sedan with a young couple in the front seat came into view while driving slowly down the alley until vanishing from sight.

Zeke meandered around the backyard for a few more minutes, hoping to ease the restlessness he felt. The back of his head was starting to throb with pain. He started back for the house. He was near the rear door when he heard another vehicle crunching gravel in the alley. He turned to glance over his shoulder and barely caught the tail-end of a pickup

truck bed vanishing behind the storage shacks. The fleeting glimpse of
the pickup truck was enough for Zeke to make the connection. He ran
back across the lawn and hopped the fence, hoping to make it to the alley
before the old Chevy vanished. He heard the engine rev louder as he got
to the alley and saw it turn the corner to the road, the engine roaring as
the pickup accelerated away.

When Zeke returned to Andrew's backyard the big pastor met him
halfway. "What's going on, Zeke?"

"I wanted to catch the driver of that pickup."

"What for?" Andrew asked with plenty of curiosity in his eyes.

Zeke decided to tell him about the incident involving the strange
character and the old Chevy pickup truck in the park. After listening
to the story Andrew asked, "You think it has something to do with the
disappearance of Sabrina's car?"

Zeke knew instinctively that the two events were linked but he didn't
know how exactly. "Who knows," he said. "Maybe."

Zeke and Andrew walked back into the house. Zeke headed to the
bedrooms to find Sabrina. Sabrina met him in the hallway. "What do you
think about calling a bus line?"

"I think we can do that in the morning," Zeke said. "I think we should
hang here tonight in case we learn something about your car. Doesn't that
make sense?"

Sabrina nodded but she didn't look enthusiastic about the idea.

They both went back into the kitchen where Andrew was checking
his voicemail again.

"Since it doesn't look like we'll be leaving today," Sabrina said, "how
about I prepare dinner tonight?"

"I think that's a wonderful idea," Andrew said while sharing a look
with Zeke. "Anyone would agree to that if they ever tasted my cooking."

"I'll take your word on that," Zeke said.

"If you make a list of what you need from the grocery," Andrew said,
"I'll stop at the store before heading home. I have to visit the hospital but I
should be back before six. There's a music player in the living room. I also
have a collection of books in my home office. Feel free to browse through
them if you want."

"Thanks," Zeke and Sabrina said at the same time.

Sabrina made the list and gave it to Andrew before he left the house.

Not long after Andrew had left, Zeke went to his guest bedroom and flopped down onto the bed. Within a minute he fell asleep. He entered REM quickly, his rapid eye movements and gentle groans responding to the dream he experienced. At one point in his dream he felt someone stroking his chest, a warm body cuddled up close to him, but when he awoke he was alone. He stared at the ceiling for a moment, trying to remember where he was. When the realization came, he raised himself and sat on the edge of the bed. With a wide yawn he stood to his feet and walked to the bathroom to relieve himself.

After splashing cool water on his face he walked out into the hallway leading to the kitchen. The kitchen was empty. He looked out the kitchen window toward the rear lawn. Sabrina wasn't there either. He walked back down the hallway to her bedroom. The door stood partially open. He peered inside and saw her on the bed, curled up in a fetal position. He heard her steady breathing and closed the door gently.

He went back into the kitchen and glanced at the clock on the microwave. It read a few minutes past five. He walked into the family room and saw a sectional sofa along with several recliners and a coffee table between them. On the far wall next to an old flatscreen television monitor stood a cabinet with an audio amplifier and an ancient DVD/CD player. The shelf below the equipment had stacks of music CD jewel boxes. He sorted through the first row of CDs before heading to the coffee table and grabbing a universal remote control. He switched on the TV. The monitor came to life. He watched the soundless images, realizing he hadn't seen television in years. Before 11-9 he rarely watched TV at all. Now as he watched an advertisement for *ALL* laundry detergent he knew certain things hadn't changed very much. He switched off the TV and left the family room.

He found Andrew's home office at the end of the hallway next to the pastor's bedroom. He studied the bookshelf with its dozens of hardbacks, paperbacks, and binders with printed labels. Most were Christian books but one in particular caught Zeke's attention. He grabbed it from the shelf and read the cover: 'UFOs And The Bible.' He thumbed through the book, reading some of the captions in the illustrated section before taking the book with him to the kitchen. After grabbing a bottle of sparkling water from the fridge he sat at the breakfast table and sipped on the water while perusing the book.

A half hour later he heard Sabrina's bedroom door open and her footsteps coming down the hallway. "Feel better?" he asked as she entered the kitchen.

"Yes, I do." She began rummaging in the pantry and returned with a bag of coffee beans. As Zeke studied his book she asked, "Want some coffee?"

"Sure," he replied while continuing to read about strange objects in the sky reported throughout the scriptures of the Bible. The author cited many references from the Old Testament ranging from columns of spinning clouds to descriptions of strange and complicated mechanical vehicles carrying angelic beings.

A short while later Sabrina poured two cups of coffee from the pot and brought them to the table. "Whatcha reading?" she asked while taking a seat across the table.

Zeke held up the book so she could read the title.

"Oh," she said, her voice revealing an uneasiness with the book's subject. She took a sip of coffee and examined her surroundings in the kitchen.

"You don't approve?" he asked.

"I don't know," she answered. "What does it say?"

"That the sighting of UFOs is reported throughout the Bible."

"Okay."

Zeke went back to the book.

Sabrina sat there, staring at him while drinking her coffee.

Zeke felt her gaze. "What?"

"You okay?"

"Yes, why wouldn't I be?"

"I don't know. Just checking."

Zeke tried to finish the chapter he'd been reading.

A few minutes later Sabrina asked, "Have you remembered anything else about our abduction?"

Zeke raised his eyes to hers. "No."

"Have you tried?"

Zeke took a sip of coffee before responding. "No. And I really don't want to relive any of it at the moment."

Sabrina waited before saying, "I just thought you wanted to find answers, even if that meant reliving some painful memories."

"Okay," he said, a tone of finality in his voice. "Can we change the subject now?"

Sabrina didn't answer. She sipped her coffee and stared toward the alley behind the lawn.

They both heard the sound of a car pulling into Andrew's driveway. The engine stopped and a car door slammed shut. A couple of minutes later Andrew walked inside the kitchen with some grocery bags in his arms. "Hello there!" he said in his big, booming voice.

"Hi, Andrew," Zeke said. "Would you care to join us?"

Andrew lowered his large frame into a chair at the table. "Did you two have a good afternoon?"

"Yes," said Zeke. "We slept through most of it, though."

"Ah," Andrew said with a smile. "I remember the days when I got to take naps."

"How was your hospital visit?" Sabrina asked.

"Difficult," he replied, "as these type of visits often are. Fern Nedermyer is nearly ninety years old and dying of cervical cancer. She's devout in her faith and handling her suffering well but her children and their children are another story. That's the way it usually is. My counseling is as much for them as it is for her."

"I don't think I could handle that," Sabrina said. "I don't know how you do it."

"Well," Andrew said. "It's part of my job description."

They chitchatted for a few more minutes before rising from the kitchen table. Andrew lumbered back to his bedroom while Sabrina sorted through the grocery bags.

Zeke grabbed the 'UFOs And The Bible' book and went to one of the recliners in the family room. He read several chapters filled with biblical references of strange objects in the sky.

The next thing he knew Sabrina was calling his name. "Hey, Zeke. Dinner is on the table." He had fallen asleep, again. He set the book on the coffee table and raised himself from the recliner. "Okay, be right there." *I can't believe I fell asleep again,* he told himself. *Two naps in a row? I'll never be able to get to sleep tonight.* He freshened up quickly, splashing water on his face from the bathroom sink and running a pocket comb through his hair.

Andrew and Zeke sat at the breakfast table as Sabrina brought a bowl of steaming vegetables to the table. Andrew gave the dinner prayer—including a request for the return of Sabrina's car—before they helped themselves to the baked lemon-chicken, steamed yellow squash, and large garden salad she'd prepared for dinner. Andrew was most appreciative of Sabrina's cooking, interjecting compliments throughout their conversation at the table.

After dinner they all took part in cleaning the table and kitchen, silently hoping they would hear something from the Sheriff's office about the whereabouts of the Saturn. But the phone never rang.

Andrew retired to his end of the house early and a short while later Sabrina headed to her bedroom. Zeke knew that after two naps in the same afternoon he wasn't going to be sleeping anytime soon. He went back to the family room and returned to the 'UFOs And The Bible' book. He read steadily, losing track of time. When he paused to get a glass of water from the kitchen he noticed the microwave clock's digital readout: *11:34 pm.* He'd been reading for hours without stopping, unusual for him. He rarely read at all but now he couldn't seem to stop. Sections in the book connecting angelic appearances in the Bible to the modern concept of UFOs didn't seem convincing but other descriptions of *'flying wheels'* and *'chariots of fire'* made Zeke wonder.

A short while later he heard footsteps coming down the hallway toward the kitchen. Andrew rounded the corner to the family room, barefoot, wearing flannel pajama bottoms and a tank top, revealing his muscular arms with a faded tattoo on one bicep. "Can't sleep?" the big pastor asked.

"No," replied Zeke.

"Me, either," Andrew said. "Reading anything interesting?"

Zeke held up the book so the pastor could see the title.

"Oh, yeah," Andrew said. "I think I've read that before."

Zeke smiled. "Probably so. I borrowed it from your bookshelf."

"Yes, that's why it looked familiar," Andrew said with a chuckle as he set a bottled water on the coffee table and lowered himself slowly on the sofa.

"Since you've read it," Zeke said, "what's your opinion?"

"About UFOs?"

"Yes . . . and their references in the Bible."

"As pastor of a small church in a small community," Andrew explained, "I might not preach about it much but yes I believe UFOs are mentioned in the Bible."

"Do you think these UFOs are connected to angels or another race of alien beings?"

"Possibly both."

"So if the angels are the good guys," Zeke continued, "what about the aliens?"

Andrew thought about this for a long moment before saying, "Maybe it's the same as humans. Some choose light, some choose darkness. Actually, this applies to angels, too."

"What do you mean?"

"You have to remember that Satan was once an angel named Lucifer," Andrew said. "A very powerful angel who rebelled against God. A third of the angels in heaven rebelled with him and all were booted out for eternity."

"So angels and aliens," Zeke said. "Good and bad. Just like people."

"Yes, but not because they were created good or bad," Andrew said. "Good actions and bad actions are *choices*. I believe many beings exist in the universe, and like us and the angels, some of these beings may have *chosen* the side of darkness."

Zeke's recollections of his abduction and the feelings associated with the experience left no room for doubt that his captors were *definitely* full of malice for the human race. *Whoever they were, they were bad. Worse than anyone can imagine.*

Andrew interrupted Zeke's thoughts. "How about you? Do you believe in all this?"

"I don't know," Zeke said, "about their connections to the Bible, I mean."

"But you do believe in UFOs?"

Zeke wasn't sure he wanted to answer but he did. "Yes."

Andrew nodded respectfully. "Have you've always believed in them, or has this come about just recently?"

Zeke thought about the best way to handle that question. "For most of my life I never believed in anything like UFOs," he finally said. "I put them in the same category as ghosts and goblins, figments of the imagination, fantasies people came up with to explain things they don't understand. But now I'm not so sure."

"What changed your mind?"

"Experience," Zeke replied.

"Can I ask you a personal question, Zeke?"

"Yes."

"Do you believe in God?"

Over all the years of his life, Zeke couldn't remember anyone asking him the question directly. He shrugged.

"That's not much of an answer."

"I guess it depends on how you define the word *God*," Zeke said.

"How do you define it?"

"Well," Zeke began, "I don't believe he's an old man with white hair and a beard, pointing his finger at the Earth and causing earthquakes and volcanic eruptions."

Andrew smiled. "Okay, so if not that, what?"

"I think if he does exist," Zeke said, "he's something we can't comprehend."

"We can't comprehend everything about God," Andrew said. "But there are plenty of things we *can* comprehend."

"Like what?"

"Like love," Andrew answered without hesitation. "Take birth for an example. It's something we take for granted until we see it with our own eyes. But think about the *love* we feel when that child is ours. Where do you think that *love* comes from?"

Zeke remembered the birth of his son, Josh: *holding Amber's hand as the doctor helped the little guy from her womb, tears rolling down Zeke's face, Josh's first cry, the sound of his little voice echoing in the hospital room.* Zeke tried to bury the memory.

"Skeptics," Andrew continued, "often say that the feeling we call *love* is either an invention of our mind, something we create to feel better about our mysterious existence, or a process of evolution where it's just a mechanism, like an instinct, for the parent to ensure the development of the offspring. But if you have experienced that love you know that's ridiculous. *Prove it,* they say. Can anyone prove their love exists?"

"No."

"No, they cannot," Andrew said. "Although their actions *do* prove their love, it's not proof in the scientific sense. It's sort of like the wind. You can feel it but you can't see it—you can only see the effect it has on things."

"Interesting comparison."

"Here's something else God allows us to comprehend," Andrew said. "Old Testament prophecies of the Messiah, written centuries before Jesus came into this world. Skeptics have argued that those scriptures were written after-the-fact by the early Church but the evidence shows something completely different. There is more than ample evidence in the form of thousands of Old Testament manuscripts in multiple languages, all of them easily dated to centuries before Christ. Archeological discoveries in the caves of Qumran, know to most as the Dead Sea Scrolls, has only corroborated this evidence. And here's perhaps God's universal method of allowing us to comprehend him: math and science."

"I thought science discredited most religious beliefs."

"The fathers of modern science and mathematics may have been at odds with the Church, who claimed authority over matters it couldn't understand," Andrew explained. "But those same scientists and mathematicians were never at odds with the scriptures of the Bible. In fact, until the European Enlightenment and the following neo-Darwinian presuppositions of the nineteenth century, science and God went hand in hand."

Zeke frowned. "You're going to have to explain that."

Andrew's mouth curved into a kind smile. "You ever heard of Johannes Kepler?"

Zeke shook his head although the name rang a bell. A very distant bell.

"How about Galileo?"

"Of course."

"It was once quoted that Galileo and Kepler were the two giants on whose shoulders Sir Isaac Newton stood," Andrew explained. "Kepler was one of the greatest mathematical minds of all history. By 1620 he'd published 'The Three Laws Of Planetary Motion,' the laws that not only allowed space exploration centuries later but is still used today by *all* astronomers and anyone else studying the universe. To be brief, Kepler's laws explained mathematically that the planets' orbits are elliptical, not circular. With his mathematical equations, the exact positions of the stars and planets can be calculated for any day in history, as viewed from any place on the surface of the Earth. Being a Christian, Kepler soon set his equations on the mystery of the Star of Bethlehem, the star announcing Christ's birth, as told in the New Testament book of Matthew."

As Andrew paused to sip his water, Zeke asked, "So . . . did he solve the mystery?"

Andrew shook his head. "Not in his lifetime but I believe others did much later with the assistance of computers." Andrew took another sip of water. "You see, in Kepler's day it took a lot of pen and ink and manpower to do the calculations for any one day in history. Unless they knew the day to look for they were shooting in the dark, but this is easy for even the most basic laptop computer using Kepler's equations. Simple astronomical software can go backwards and forwards in time to *any* date, and even animate it in seconds. I was astonished the first time I saw the astronomical evidence for Christ's birth in the years 3/2 BC, and also for the crucifixion date of April 3, 33 AD. Sir Isaac Newton's papers revealed his belief of the 33 AD date for the crucifixion as well, although I don't know how he determined this." Andrew paused for another swig of water. "My point is this, Zeke: many of the founding fathers of modern science and mathematics were Christians, using their scientific discoveries to answer personal questions regarding God and his creation. In fact, their faith was their motivation."

"And Newton was one of these Christians?" asked Zeke.

"Absolutely," Andrew said. "Most people associate Sir Isaac Newton with his theory of gravitation. Besides being considered the father of Physics, his discoveries in modern optics and other little things like that, little was known about his real passion, what he referred to as the reason for all his work in math and science." Andrew paused. "You bored yet?"

"No," Zeke said. "Please continue."

"Newton became obsessed with Bible prophecy early on," Andrew continued. "Using the books of Daniel and Revelation he worked for years on deciphering numeric codes that he believed revealed key dates in history that would eventually reveal the year of Christ's Second Coming. He titled this work: *'The History Of Things To Come'* and kept it secret since much of this would have been considered heretical by the Anglican Church, punishable by death. Before his death in the 1720s Newton placed all this work in a chest and arranged for it to be kept by a friend. The chest and its papers stayed hidden at his friend's estate in England for over two hundred years. In the 1930s the chest was auctioned at Sotheby's. Finally, in the early 1950s it was bequeathed to the newly formed State of Israel where it still remains today in their national archives. It became available for scholarly research a short time later but the bulk of its content wasn't well known until the early part of the twenty-first century."

"Did he reveal the date of the Second Coming?" asked Zeke.

"Yes," Andrew answered. "2060."

"Seriously?"

"Yes, but I think it's important to put Newton's motivation into context," Andrew explained. "Newton was appalled by all the false predictions of Christ's return by so-called *Christian prophets*. He believed it put Christianity in a bad light when the supposed day of the end of the world came and went so he wanted to reveal the truth to quell other false predictions. Many people may accuse him of being another doomsayer like the ones that disgusted him during his lifetime, but his date of the Second Coming was erroneous for his generation since it was so far into the future. He stood nothing to gain from a date so distant, compared to those who have contemporary dates so they can build a following of believers for personal gain."

"Do you believe in this 2060 date of the return of Christ?"

Andrew said, "Newton's 1,260 and 1,290 year figures derived from the book of Daniel had to be applied to certain key historical events. Newton came up with different dates during his lifelong research, including 2037, but 2060 was the most viable in his opinion. His point was this: regardless of the correct year, *all* the possibilities were in the twenty-first century, far into the future for his day. In Mark 13:32, Jesus said, *'No one knows about that day or hour, not even the angels in heaven, nor the Son, but only the Father.'* So I believe no one knows the day or the hour except for God. Could that day and hour that no one knows happen in 2060? Yes, it could. But any one of us could be breathing our last breaths this very moment. We should be living every moment as if the end was coming today, spreading the good news of Jesus's redemption like we're running out of time . . . which we are, of course."

Zeke smiled but said nothing.

"I apologize I got so carried away," Andrew said. "All I wanted to say was modern science and the Bible do not contradict each other. Scientific discoveries advance and change throughout the ages but the Bible has remained steadfast, never claiming to be a scientific textbook but the Word of God with emphasis on God's relationship with man. The world-in-general has many misconceptions about the Bible. I believe every man and woman needs to find the truth themselves. Don't let popular belief with all its misconceptions and presuppositions guide you away from the truth. Many skeptics will try to mislead you. I know, because I used to be one."

"*You* were skeptical of the Bible?" asked Zeke.

Andrew finished his water in one large gulp. "More than a skeptic," he finally said. "An enemy. A devout atheist out to destroy the church and all its Bible-toting idiots."

Zeke sat silent, surprised by Andrew's confession.

"To me," Andrew continued, "religion was the culprit responsible for all the wars and mayhem in the world."

After a long pause Zeke asked, "So what changed you?"

Andrew smiled. "Before I answer that," he said, "let me say that I had very definite opinions about the world and its workings and none of it had anything to do with a Creator or any type of intelligent design whatsoever. Practically all of my beliefs—or I should say disbeliefs—were based on presuppositions held by most people in the world. Bible prophecy? Just a bunch of intolerant old men who wrote everything after the fact to make it look genuine. Biblical historical record? There's no historical evidence to support the Bible. Science? Evolution proves the random origin of life. Born-again Christians? Losers who need to believe in something to qualify their miserable lives. The list went on and on. Then one day, while waiting at the doctor's office, I browsed through a magazine and started reading an article about recent discoveries in DNA research. The part that caught my attention was the mathematical improbabilities associated with the neo-Darwinian theory of Random Mutation and Chirality due to discoveries in molecular biology unknown in Darwin's day. The improbability numbers of the theories were so large it was hard to comprehend. The odds, in base-ten form, are one in 10^{75} which is one in a million trillion trillion trillion trillion or something close to that. There are roughly 10^{65} atoms in our galaxy, to give you a comparison. Anyway, I started investigating popular beliefs of many different subjects that I had always *supposed* were correct and without question. I ended up making a list with Science, Evolution, Archeology, History, and other subjects to focus my research on. I took one subject at a time and wrote it as the headline on a large marker board. I drew a line down the center creating two sections. One section was titled *'Evidence For,'* and the other *'Evidence Against.'* After repeating this process for each subject I created an summary of my findings. Needless to say, the *'Evidence For'* columns were substantially larger than the *'Evidence Against'* columns. But my findings were still not *proof* of any larger truth. I still had to *choose* to believe.

Zeke wondered about choosing to believe. *Can you really choose to believe?* Zeke had always thought you either believed or you did not believe. He'd never thought about choice being involved in belief, but as he thought about it now he realized all belief was based on choice.

"I remember driving somewhere and a preacher was preaching on the radio," Andrew reminisced. "He said all I had to do was ask Jesus to come into my life, to accept him as my personal savior, and I would inherit eternal life in the Kingdom of God. But I had to *choose* to believe. God isn't asking for *blind* faith. 1 Thessalonians 5:21 says, *'Test everything. Hold onto the good.'* I tested the Bible's validity myself which eventually allowed me to make the right choice. That choice changed my life for good—not to mention granting me eternal life."

Zeke stared back at Andrew. He didn't know what to say but he felt the ironclad resolution of the man's faith.

Andrew chuckled while apparently recalling another distant memory. "I once had a colorful bumper sticker shaped like a rainbow on my old Volvo sedan, the same car I later accepted Jesus in. The sticker read: *'Imagine A World Without Religion.'* One day a man came up to me in a parking lot as I walked to my car. In a thick Russian accent he said, 'I dunt have to ee-magine it. I lived it, you mor-roon!'"

Both men laughed. "That's the worst Russian accent I've ever heard," Zeke finally said. "It sounded more Spanish than Russian!"

"Yeah," Andrew replied with a smile. "Accents never were my strong point." He yawned. "Now, if you don't mind I'm gonna try to get some sleep, Zeke."

"Me, too," Zeke said while rising to his feet. "Thanks, Andrew."

"For what?" Andrew asked.

Zeke began to say something then stopped. "I don't know but thanks anyway."

While heading toward the hallway Zeke stopped and said, "Actually, I do know."

Andrew stopped and waited.

"I guess there's still hope for someone like me," Zeke said. "You think?"

"There's still hope for everyone," Andrew said. "But you have to make the right choice." Andrew paused before adding, "Ask for Jesus to come to you like I did. He knows what's in your heart but tell him how you *want* to believe. That's a good start before you *choose* to accept Him as your personal savior. This is what I did and it worked for me. Be patient and it will work for you, too. Just don't take too long. We never know when we will take our last breath."

And with that, both men went to their bedrooms to end the day.

Zeke got into his bed and fell asleep quickly despite all the naps he'd taken throughout the day. He slept so soundly that he never heard his door crack open or the sound of Sabrina's bare feet approaching his bed.

* * *

TWENTY TWO

Paul Stover tossed and turned in his motel bed. Sleep finally came in intervals but the restlessness haunted him throughout the night. Ruth had not contacted him as he had hoped. He'd called the front desk of the tiny motel several times to make sure his calls were being routed to his motel room. The grumpy man working the front desk didn't hide his irritation with Stover's repeated inquiries about getting his phone calls.

Stover awoke sometime in the middle of the night. He switched on the lamp beside the bed and examined the motel room. He felt certain that someone had been in the room. He got out of bed and walked to the bathroom, noticing the goosebumps on his forearms. The tingling sensation made him uneasy. He stared at the drawn shower curtain, wondering why he felt like someone was lurking behind it. He summoned his courage and slid back the shower curtain in one swift move. The empty shower with its stained, off-white bathtub was a relief. He absentmindedly rubbed the back of his head. He frowned while searching for the scar above the neck near the base of his skull—the scar that never seemed to heal completely. But now it was gone. The skin was smooth where the scar had been.

Stover quickly maneuvered himself to use the full-length mirror on the back of the bathroom door along with the mirror above the sink. The scar was completely gone. He stared at the reflection of the back of his head, rubbing the spot and marveling at the smoothness of the skin where it had been so long. He remembered taking a butter knife from the plate of food the Lost Valley Church had given him back when he'd first arrived there. How he tried to cut out the thing that lived beneath his skin. How he'd been unsuccessful. But now the scar was gone—gone as if it had never been there at all.

Stover made his way back to the bed, trying to rationalize the disappearance of the scar, elated that it was gone but perplexed by its sudden absence. As soon as he was under the covers the phone rang. He lifted the receiver to his ear.

"Leave now, Paul," the male voice said in a soft but firm tone.

"Who is this?" Stover asked, feeling now that all of this was nothing but a dream.

"Get up," the voice said. "Dress quickly."

"Where am I going?"

"Head to the service road and turn right," the voice said. "Walk to the truck stop. There's a blue and white bus waiting there. Get on the bus and take a seat in the back. Don't get off until it reaches its destination."

"Wait a minute," Stover protested. "Who are you and why—"

"—Leave now and get on the bus," the voice insisted. "You must hurry. They are coming for you again."

Stover knew who they were. A shiver went through his body like a wave of electromagnetic energy.

"Someone will meet you when the bus reaches its destination," the voice said. "Now hurry. There's not much time. They won't be able to track you now but you must hurry and get out of there before they arrive."

Stover was already reaching for his pants on the foot of the bed when he heard the phone line go dead. He dressed hurriedly, grabbing his few toiletries from the sink counter and tossing them into a small bag along with the rest of his meager belongings: two changes of clothes and a Bible that the Lost Valley Church had given him during his stay.

Within a minute Stover was ready. With the bag hanging over his shoulder he peered around the edge of the curtain near the door. He saw the eastern sky beyond the window and knew sunrise would be soon. A few cars were parked in the motel parking lot but he couldn't see anything suspicious. He left the room quietly and walked briskly across the parking lot to the highway feeder road just ahead. There was little traffic except for the occasional vehicle rushing by on the main highway. "They are coming for you again," the voice had told him. Those words repeated in his head, causing him to increase his pace as he walked along the edge of the service road. A few minutes later he saw the large neon sign a short distance ahead: Flying J. Truck Stop.

Stover walked into the Flying J's large parking lot, noticing dozens of eighteen-wheelers parked on one side, their drivers either in the store or sleeping in their cabin sleepers. A dozen or more trucks were in the lanes for the diesel pumps, their drivers filling their tanks and performing various chores on their large vehicles. He saw people milling around the entrance to the store and restaurant. He watched an elderly couple walking toward a second group of fuel pumps with a blue and white bus parked in the lane. He cut across the lot toward the bus, wondering what was going to happen when he walked onto the bus. People in the bus would surely notice him as he came aboard. What would he tell them? *Uh, an angel told me to get on this bus because a group of supernatural beings—demons, actually—were trying to recapture me to take me back and torture me some more for information I don't have.*

Despite the terror he felt, the story made him laugh. If the people on the bus called the police he decided he would tell them this story. The cops would surely haul him off to a psych-ward for evaluation, maybe preventing *they* from capturing him, at least for the moment. *They*—the only name he had for the hellish creatures from God-knows-where.

Stover approached the bus as the elderly couple climbed slowly up the steps beyond the opened door. He fell into line behind them and entered the bus. The driver's seat was empty. The dark bus interior had accent lighting along the walkway and a few passengers had their reading lights on, their concentration focused on the book or magazine in their laps. Most of the people in the first few rows of seats seemed to be sleeping. Others were engaged in quiet conversation, talking in low whispers to not wake the passengers sleeping nearby. They all were elderly folks in their seventies and eighties on some group trip, maybe from a church or retirement home. Stover hadn't noticed a name on the bus exterior because his attention had been centered on entering with the elderly couple to avoid being noticed by the other passengers.

After the elderly couple had taken their seats, Stover continued down the walkway toward the rear of the bus. He took a window seat in the last row and waited. A few minutes later he saw more people climbing the steps of the bus. The group chattered a bit as they took their seats while the driver shut the door and sat behind the wheel. Apparently, the driver was confident that all the passengers were onboard. Stover had worried that the driver would perform a head-count before leaving and notice an extra passenger—a *bald* passenger much younger than the other passengers. But the driver simply drove out of the *Flying J* lot and continued to the highway underpass nearby. The bus went through the underpass and turned left, heading to the highway entrance ramp. Stover stared out his window at the motel as they passed by. It was too dark and far away to see any details but he definitely saw a dark van parked near his motel room. Two dark figures stood near the door, their silhouettes motionless. Ten-seconds later the motel was out of sight. Stover sat back in his seat and closed his eyes. For a moment he fantasized about all of this being part of the same weird dream where in reality he was still asleep in the motel room. It was difficult to tell the difference between what was real and what was not these days. But deep inside he was very happy being on the bus instead of being back in the motel room where the two dark shadows lurked just outside the door. On the bus he felt safe and secure. Gone with the scar was any doubt about what he was supposed to do. Although he didn't know how exactly, he knew he was being guided and all he had to do was obey. He knew this was all part of something so huge it was hard to comprehend. And he was part of it. He had actually been *chosen* to be part of it.

And with that last thought and the steady purring of the bus's diesel engine, Paul Stover ceased to worry about anything as he closed his eyes and fell fast asleep.

*   *   *

TWENTY THREE

Zeke woke up and looked at the digital clock beside the bed: *11:34 am*. He was surprised by the late morning hour. *My sleep patterns are getting wackier by the moment.*

While showering he recalled bits of a dream he had during the night—a dream that started in an erotic nature but ended up like a nightmare. He washed away the memories of the dream along with the sweat on his body. After dressing and entering the kitchen he saw Andrew with a suitcase near his feet. "Morning," Zeke said. "Going somewhere?"

Andrew stared back. "Yes," he said. "I'm taking you to your destination."

"You don't have to do that," Zeke said. "We can take a bus."

Andrew shook his head. "No, I have to take you myself."

The resolute look in Andrew's eyes told Zeke there was more to the story than just Andrew performing a good deed. "What's up, Andrew?"

Andrew walked over to the coffee pot and refilled his cup. "Want some coffee?"

"Sure," Zeke said. "Is Sabrina still sleeping?"

"I suppose so," Andrew answered. "I haven't seen her this morning."

After pouring the coffee, Andrew brought both cups to the kitchen table. "Have a seat," he told Zeke. "I need to confide in you."

Zeke took a seat at the table and cradled his cup of coffee with both hands.

Andrew lowered his large frame into a chair and said, "Last night after our conversation I had a dream." He paused and took a sip of coffee. "Actually, I don't think it was a dream at all. I think I was *visited*."

"Visited?" Zeke asked. "Visited by who?"

Andrew stared back at Zeke, his expression a mix of bewilderment and reluctance. "I believe it was an angel."

Zeke didn't know what to say. He almost reminded Andrew about their conversation on the subject of angels and aliens before they went to bed but he knew Andrew was well aware of all that.

A small grin formed on Andrew's face. "You think I'm nuts?"

"No," Zeke said sincerely. "I don't think your nuts." He'd been through too much to disbelieve anything these days but he still suspected Andrew had experienced a dream and not a visitation from an angel.

"Well, let me tell you about the visit," Andrew said, "before you make up your mind about my sanity."

"Okay," Zeke said. He swallowed a sip of coffee. "Tell me."

"My visitor told me how you were abducted by an abominable race of beings he called . . . *the nephilim.*"

Zeke nearly dropped the coffee cup held to his mouth. He listened while staring into the big pastor's eyes, not making a move while processing what he was hearing. *Did Sabrina tell him about the abduction? Or was this influenced by the conversation last night which somehow triggered a psychic ability Andrew didn't know he had?* And Zeke wondered about something else: *Where have I heard that word nephilim?*

"He told me how the beings followed you while you escorted two men and a boy across the state," Andrew continued. "And that one of these men was abducted, too."

Zeke stared back at Andrew, barely able to believe what he was hearing.

"He told me how he'd been watching over you the entire time," Andrew said. "And that he'd created the situation for our paths to cross."

Zeke's mind worked rapidly, his thoughts accompanying images of the stunned deer on the road in front of Andrew's car. He thought of Sabrina's Saturn disappearing without a trace as if it had been beamed away.

"He told me about your late wife and son," Andrew continued. "And how—" Andrew stopped talking when he saw Zeke shaking so violently that hot coffee began splashing from the rim of his cup.

The memory rushed Zeke with a tidal wave of emotion. He stood from his chair and dropped the coffee cup onto the table, it's steaming dark liquid flowing toward the table's edge. His eyes started to roll and Andrew moved quickly to catch him.

Zeke opened his eyes sometime later from the sofa in the living room. He saw Andrew looming over him with a glass of water in his hand.

"Here," Andrew said. "Take a drink."

Zeke grabbed the glass with a shaky hand, wondering where he was and what had happened. He took a sip and handed the glass back to Andrew. The recollection came alive instantly, like a movie in full force when a television is turned on: *There he was, naked and humiliated, bound by some unseen force while hovering in a thick, putrid, brownish haze. The haze dissipated a bit in front of him while two figures approached. When he saw their faces he cried out in longing and agony. "AMBER!" he screamed. The boy standing next to Amber stared at Zeke with a sad look on his face. Although he was not an infant but a boy of ten or eleven years of age, Zeke knew it was Josh, the son he never got to see grow beyond infancy. "Why did you abandon us?" the boy asked. "Why didn't you come for us sooner? Why didn't you save us, Daddy?"*

Zeke heard himself screaming. It took him a moment to realize the scream came from now while on the sofa. He saw Sabrina and Andrew leaning over him. Sabrina stroked his head. "It's okay," she said, trying to calm him. "Everything's okay now."

Zeke stared at her for a moment before closing his eyes. The memory of Amber and Josh confronting him during his captivity tried to return but Zeke couldn't deal with it. He closed the door of his memory vault with a loud slam and raised himself to an upright position on the sofa.

"What happened?" Sabrina asked, her face full of concern.

"I'm not sure," Zeke said. "But I'm better now."

Sabrina looked between Zeke and Andrew, her face full of questions.

Andrew said, "It's my fault. I shouldn't have said anything."

Zeke began rubbing the back of his head. "Nothing was your fault."

"Say anything about what?" Sabrina asked. "At fault for what?"

Andrew gave Zeke a look.

"Just give us a few minutes in private, Sabrina," Zeke told her. "Will you, please?"

Sabrina gave both of them a suspicious look before leaving the room.

Zeke told Andrew in a low voice, "I still don't remember everything, especially the hows and whys, but I can't go back there right now. It's just too much."

Andrew nodded. "I hear you."

"But you need to tell me where we're supposed to go," Zeke said, still rubbing the back of his head. "And *why* wouldn't hurt, either."

"He didn't tell me why," Andrew answered. "But I'm supposed to get you to Gold Tree, Texas. I've already studied my map and I know where to go."

"I'd planned on stopping in Austin on the way," Zeke said.

"I know but that's not necessary. We're to go straight to Gold Tree."

"Okay." Zeke started to say something else but stopped suddenly while still rubbing the back of his head.

Andrew noticed the puzzled look on Zeke's face. "What's wrong?"

Zeke began feeling frantically for the pulsating scar on the back of his head. He stood from the sofa and started digging under his hairline with his fingertips. "Andrew, take a look and tell me what you see."

Andrew stepped over and searched the back of Zeke's head. "I see nothing."

Zeke continued searching while shouting, "Sabrina! Come here!"

Sabrina came running into the room, another alarmed look on her face. "What!"

"Look here," Zeke said, feeling the back of his head. "You see the scar?"

"It's gone," she said while searching his scalp. She paused for just a moment before feeling the back of her own head. "Mine's gone, too."

Zeke stepped behind her and parted her soft, dark-brown hair, never knowing that she too had a scar like his. He turned toward Andrew. "We both had these scars on the backs of our heads. Although I don't know if *scars* is the right word. They were more like old wounds that never seemed to heal. Sometimes mine throbbed with pain for no apparent reason."

Andrew started to say something but decided against it.

"Andrew's going to drive us to Gold Tree," Zeke told Sabrina.

"I don't understand, Zeke," she said with furled eyebrows. "I thought we were going to Austin?"

"Go get your bag, Sabrina."

Sabrina glanced between Zeke and Andrew. She stormed out the room.

Andrew lowered his voice and said, "He told me that your *binds* were removed and that things would become more clear to you now. I suppose those sores you're talking about were the *binds* he referred to. He told me that they wouldn't be able to track you as they had before."

Zeke gave Andrew an inquisitive look. "That's good."

"You had a wife and son," Andrew said. "They died tragically, didn't they?"

"Yes," Zeke said, his voice lacking any emotion.

Andrew thought about the entire revelation from the angel and how he couldn't reveal it all to Zeke at the moment. *'The truth will be revealed on the journey,"* the angel had said. *"He will then know for himself."*

Andrew placed his big paw of a hand on Zeke's shoulder. In a low voice he said, "You will see your family again, Zeke."

Zeke raised his head to meet Andrew's stare. "Promise?" he heard himself say, his voice sounding like the voice of a lost little boy.

"Yes," Andrew replied. "But more important, you have the promise of the Lord Almighty himself."

*　　*　　*

TWENTY FOUR

Paul Stover opened his eyes as the chatter on the bus became more lively. He looked out his window and noticed the sun was high in the sky, which meant he'd slept soundly for at least five hours. The bus slowed and turned into a Wal-Mart parking lot. Stover saw groups of young adults and children standing by cars in the parking lot, apparently waiting to pick up their parents or grandparents from the bus. That's when Stover saw the commotion near one of the parked cars. Some of the bus passengers saw it, too. Their lively chatter halted as they crowded to the window on the left side of the bus and stared at someone collapsed near the trunk of the car. People outside were already crowding around the individual.

"That's Vicky Parker!" one of the elderly women on the bus cried out. The bus came to a complete stop and most of the passengers hurried to the bus door to exit. Stover grabbed his bag and joined the file of passengers anxiously leaving the bus. He stepped out into the cool, clear morning and kept walking through the parking lot toward the front entrance of the Wal-Mart. He turned his head and saw most of the elderly bus passengers crowding around the collapsed woman. He heard a man shout, "Someone call 911!"

As Stover reached the store entrance, some shoppers coming out of the store began noticing the commotion in the parking lot. "What's happening?" asked a hefty woman toting a toddler in her overflowing shopping cart.

"Someone's collapsed," Stover said. "Do you have a cell phone?"

"Yes," the woman said.

"Can you call 911?"

The woman was already punching the numbers into her cell phone.

Stover walked inside the Wal-Mart. He didn't need to buy anything but he needed to use the toilet. *Someone is supposed to meet me,* he told himself. *That's what the voice on the phone said.* But all Stover cared about at the moment was using the toilet. He increased his pace, and once inside the restroom he hurried to the first available stall.

Stover was quite sure the restroom was empty when he'd entered but a few moments later he heard a toilet flush from one of the end stalls. His heart began to race at the thought of who might be in the restroom with him. He calmed a bit when he heard the person walk to the sink and start washing their hands. A moment later he heard them walk out the door, once again leaving him alone in the restroom.

Stover finished his business in the stall, flushed the toilet, and went to the row of sinks to wash his hands and face. After drying his face with a paper towel, he nearly jumped when he saw a man's reflection behind him in the mirror. The man walked toward the sinks. He made brief eye contact with Stover before washing his hands. Stover noticed the man's uniform: blue pants and blue work shirt with some company logo stitched above the right breast pocket. The man said, "Your clothes are hanging in the last stall. After you change I'll lead you to the truck."

Stover almost played dumb, thinking of telling the man he didn't know what he was talking about, but instead he walked back to the last stall and saw a blue uniform identical to the man's uniform hanging behind the door. The logo stitched above the right breast pocket read *Pete's Plumbing* with the name *Paul* stitched in the same font above the left breast pocket.

Stover changed into the uniform and rolled his old clothes into a bundle before dumping them in the restroom trash container. He followed the man through the Wal-Mart to the 'Employees Only' swinging metal doors in the rear of the building. Workers barely gave them a glance as they walked through the store's large storage section toward the loading docks outside. They went down some steps and continued toward a *Pete's Plumbing* van parked a short distance away. The entire episode seemed so surrealistic that Stover couldn't think of anything to say. He climbed into the passenger seat as the man got behind the wheel and drove away via the service road behind the store. The service road eventually reached the Interstate 20 feeder next to the huge parking lot in front of the Wal-Mart. Stover craned his neck and saw an EMS ambulance with lights flashing near the bus in the parking lot. He leaned back in his seat as the man drove the van onto the feeder toward the I20 entrance ramp.

"She'll be okay," the man said. "She'll finally get that checkup she's been putting off."

Stover didn't reply. He just stared out the windshield as the plumbing van entered the freeway.

Back in the Wal-Mart parking lot, the crowd of onlookers began to disperse as the EMTs placed Vicky Parker onto a stretcher and rolled her toward the ambulance. A gangly man wearing biker leathers paced awkwardly toward the back of the ambulance to get a look at the person on the stretcher. One of the EMTs, a large Hispanic man, said, "Please step back, sir."

The gangly biker ignored the EMT and saw the woman on the stretcher. He turned away and walked awkwardly back toward his Harley motorcycle parked nearby. He turned his head toward the far end of the parking lot and shook his head. A pickup truck in that vicinity immediately started coasting away, continuing to patrol the huge parking lot as the gangly biker mounted the Harley and kickstarted it's motor alive.

The Harley and its rider raced toward the store's service entrance to explore the rear of the building. He parked the Harley ten yards away from the exact spot where the *Pete's Plumbing* van had been just moments earlier. He lurched over to the spot and squatted. He rubbed his fingers on the asphalt and brought them to his mouth. He grimaced and spat with a curse. The pickup truck he'd signaled earlier cruised into view a short distance away. The pickup truck driver and the biker stared at each other for a long moment, neither of them making any gestures or expressions on their strange, elongated faces.

* * *

TWENTY FIVE

Sabrina LaFleur hung up the pay phone outside the convenience store and walked back to the restaurant next door. She entered the restaurant through the kitchen and walked straight into the ladies restroom. After applying some eyeliner and touching up her hair she went back to the table where Zeke and Andrew sat in silence, waiting for their dinner to arrive. They had already checked into a motel and at the motel clerk's suggestion they walked to the *Good Times* restaurant down the road from the motel. The mood at their table represented nothing even close to *good times,* though. Gone was any jovial banter or friendly ribbing from Zeke. He now seemed cold and distant to her. Even Andrew treated her differently than before, which really didn't bother her very much. Having to sleep in separate bedrooms at the *pastor's* house had already disrupted her plans. Sabrina was ready to be rid of Andrew Coleman.

When their plates of food arrived they ate their dinner in silence. A half-hour later a commotion broke out in the restaurant. A woman stood from her table and began howling with despair. A man with her at the table was trying to console the grieving woman. With tears in his own eyes he held her by the shoulders to keep her from falling.

Andrew stood from his plate of food and approached the table. At one point the wailing woman threw her cell phone across the room. The entire restaurant became silent as they watched the grief stricken woman. Zeke saw Andrew begin talking to them at the table.

A few moments later Andrew returned to Zeke and Sabrina at their table. He didn't sit in his chair. He leaned over the table and in a quiet voice said, "She just learned that her teenaged daughter was killed in a car accident."

Sabrina gasped. "Oh no! How terrible!"

Zeke could only stare up at the big pastor with a blank expression. He couldn't seem to form any words in his mouth.

"When I offered my help," Andrew explained, "and told them I was a pastor they asked if I would accompany them home for some spiritual counseling—something they will need plenty of, I can assure you that."

Zeke nodded but remained wordless.

"I'll get a ride back to the motel later," Andrew added.

"Okay," Sabrina said. "Good luck, Andrew."

"Yeah," Zeke said. "Good luck to you."

"Later," Andrew said before returning to the grieving man and woman at the table. A moment later Andrew and the man helped the woman out the restaurant and into a car. As soon as they were out the door everyone in the restaurant began chattering about the incident.

Sabrina noticed that Zeke's dark mood had darkened even more. "That poor woman," she said. "I can't imagine how she feels."

"No, you can't," Zeke said under his breath.

Sabrina stared at him for a long moment before asking, "Are you going to tell me what's on your mind?"

"Nothing is on my mind."

Sabrina thought about last night. She had entered Zeke's bedroom after he and Andrew had gone to bed. Things had started off good but then Zeke freaked out and tossed her off the bed. It had taken her a moment to realize that he was still asleep—his romantic behavior in the beginning just part of a dream.

Sabrina wouldn't bring this up to Zeke. It was too humiliating for her. *I've bedded better catches than him,* she told herself. *With very little effort.*

"Maybe I can help you," she said in a patient voice. "But you need to confide in me, Zeke."

"There's nothing to confide," he replied.

"What did Andrew tell you this morning?" she asked, starting to lose some of her patience. "You've been different ever since."

"I have?"

"Zeke," she said. "You collapsed this morning, remember?"

Zeke didn't want to relive the memory of Amber and Josh. "Well, I was just shocked about the sore on the back of my head disappearing."

"You noticed that *after* you collapsed, Zeke."

"I did?"

Sabrina wasn't buying his little act. She kept on although she *knew* what had caused him to collapse. She heard some of it from the hall when Zeke and Andrew were talking in the kitchen but she needed him to bring in up in order to go to the next phase. "Zeke, I know something horrible happened to you. Something a long time ago. Is it about your wife and son, the ones you told me about back at my cabin?"

Zeke continued to stare at her, still not wanting to revisit the memory.

"Is that what happened this morning?" she asked. "Did you . . . see them again?"

Zeke still didn't say anything. He did not want to go there now.

"Is that what happened?" she said, her tone becoming more forceful. "If you don't trust me, Zeke, maybe I should just leave."

Zeke shook his head.

"I can get a bus ticket back home," she said, starting to scoot her chair back from the table. "And you can go on by yourself if that's the way you want it."

"No," Zeke finally said. "I don't want that."

Sabrina relaxed in her chair while waiting for him to continue.

"You've done nothing but help me ever since I've met you," he said. "You've even lost your car because of me."

"Not because of you," Sabrina said. "But because of the big dope that stopped his car in the middle of the highway."

"If it hadn't been for you," Zeke went on, "I'd still be wandering in the wilderness, lost in time."

Sabrina set her hand on top of his.

He parted his lips to speak, halted for a moment, then said, "I told you I had a wife and son. They're dead now."

"Yes," she replied. "I remember you telling me that."

"I lost them in a car accident years ago," he said.

A sympathetic expression covered Sabrina's face. "I'm so sorry."

"Actually, it was more than just an accident," he said. "I still consider it murder. They were kidnapped and the kidnapper lost control of the car during the police chase."

Sabrina concentrated on forming tears. She stared at him as her eyes began to well up with moisture.

"My son was just an infant," Zeke explained. "But I saw both of them while I was in captivity."

"How is that possible?"

"I don't know," he said in a shaky voice. "But when I was there in that place, Amber and my son came to me."

Sabrina waited a few seconds before asking, "You mean their *ghosts* came to you?"

Zeke exhaled loudly before saying, "I guess."

"Well, that's good, isn't it?"

"What do you mean?"

"I mean it's good that their *spirits* still exist," she said. "That means you will be with them again one day."

Zeke thought about that for a moment before saying, "I'm not sure they'll want to be with me."

"Of course they will," she said. "Their deaths weren't your fault."

Why didn't you save us, Daddy?

The *Daddy* part was the most distressing piece of the memory. Zeke clenched his fists and lowered his head.

"You can't blame yourself, Zeke," Sabrina said, making eye contact with an attractive blonde woman sitting at the bar of the restaurant. "It wasn't your fault."

Zeke raised his head. "Then why do they blame me?"

Sabrina waited a moment before saying, "Come on. Let's have a drink at the bar."

Zeke followed her to the bar where they found two open stools. They started to sit down when the blonde said, "Sabrina? Is that you?"

"Caroline?" Sabrina said, her voice full of surprise. "Caroline Fuller?"

They both embraced in a friendly hug. "What are you doing here, Caroline?" Sabrina exclaimed.

"I just came to spend a few days with a friend of mine," Caroline told her. "We're meeting here for a drink before going to her place for a small gathering she's hosting. What a coincidence, Sabrina!"

"I know!" Sabrina replied before introducing Caroline to Zeke. The gorgeous blonde gave Zeke a seductive look, holding his hand a little longer than necessary.

They'd been sitting at the bar about ten minutes—Sabrina and Caroline drinking white wine, Zeke with a scotch on the rocks—when a large woman wearing a long, flower-printed gown appeared at the bar. "Sabrina," Caroline said. "This is Abigail Windsong."

The large woman had cropped, jet-black hair. Her fleshy arms and fingers were covered in bracelets and rings. "Call me Abby," she said to Sabrina.

Abby sat down and begin conversing with Caroline and Sabrina. Within seconds the three women were chattering away, totally ignoring Zeke, which was fine with him. He felt content drinking his scotch and watching a basketball game on the TV hanging above the bar.

The women's conversation quickly turned to the episode regarding the grieving mother earlier. Although he wasn't trying to pay attention to their conversation, Zeke couldn't help from hearing that this Abby woman was a spirit medium or something like that. When Abby left to go to the restroom he overheard Caroline telling Sabrina, "She is amazing, Sabrina. She contacted a late aunt of mine that I was very close to as a child."

"You actually saw your aunt?" Sabrina said. "And spoke to her?"

"Through Abby," Caroline explained. "That's how it works. That's why she's called a spiritual *medium*."

"How do you know it was your aunt she was speaking to?" Sabrina asked.

"Because she knew things that only my aunt would know," Caroline said. "Things that no one else knew except me and her."

Zeke felt Sabrina turn to him but he didn't respond. He knew where all this was heading and he didn't want to go there. He kept his eyes on the TV.

Abby returned and the three woman started discussing Abby's profession. Zeke needed to take a leak. He left his barstool and went to the restroom. When he returned, Sabrina made eye contact with him. He knew why. "What?" he said.

"Abby's a spirit medium," Sabrina said in a whisper while leaning close to him.

"I know," Zeke said. "I heard."

Sabrina implored him with her eyes. "Maybe she can help?"

"You've already told her, haven't you?" Zeke said.

"All I told her was that you lost some loved ones years ago," Sabrina explained. "Nothing more."

Zeke was not thrilled with the idea. He ordered another scotch from the bartender and returned his attention to the basketball game.

"Won't you at least talk to her?" Sabrina insisted. "What do you have to lose?"

Just my sanity, Zeke thought to himself.

Sabrina was persistent. "Zeke? This could really help you."

"Okay," he finally relented. "I'll talk to her."

Sabrina left her barstool and said something to Abby. The large woman came and sat down next to Zeke. He turned to her with an awkward grin on his face. He was starting to feel the effect of the scotch and he was liking it. "Hello," he said.

"Hello," Abby replied with a knowing grin on her round face.

"So you speak to the dead?" Zeke asked out of the blue.

"Yes," Abby said confidently. "And you don't believe that, do you?"

Zeke thought for a moment while sipping on his scotch. "Let's just say," he began, "that I don't believe in anything I can't see, hear, or feel."

Abby just smiled at him. "May I have your hands?"

"For keeps?" he joked.

"Just for a few moments," Abby said with an earnest smile.

Zeke saw something genuine in the big woman, something he liked and appreciated. He placed both his hands in hers.

Abby held his hands for just a few seconds before an enlightened look lit up her face. "You are filled with . . ." she trailed off, " . . . with something special."

"I bet you say that to all your prospective clients," he said. "Before they get the bill, that is."

Abby didn't become angry at his remark. She kept his hands in her soft, warm palms and closed her eyes. "I give no one a bill," she said in a calm, quiet voice.

"How do you make a living then?"

"I was born wealthy," came the reply.

Zeke felt comfortable with her. There seemed to be a glow about her face.

Abby lowered her voice and said, "I see a woman and an infant. A boy. He is appearing older now. Maybe ten or so. The woman has curly brown hair with a gold cross necklace around her neck."

Zeke lost his smile. He realized Sabrina had told this Abby person more than he thought she had. *But I didn't tell Sabrina any of those details, did I?*

"No one tells me anything beforehand," Abby said as if she'd read his mind. "That's part of my practice. I won't allow it."

Zeke said nothing. He was confused. He was becoming angrier and angrier at the situation. He was about to jerk his hands away and give them all a piece of his mind when Abby said, "Her name is Annie. No, she's showing me a color. Amber. Yes, Amber. Is that her name?"

"Yes," Zeke mumbled, not remembering if he told Sabrina his late wife's name.

"Let me ask her a question," Abby said. "A question that only she would know the answer to."

Zeke didn't want to do this but suddenly a thought came to mind. "Okay," he heard his voice saying. "What was I wearing when I asked her to marry me?"

Abby cocked her head for a moment before saying, "That ugly gray sweater of yours with the hood. The one that says *Army Rangers* on the front."

Zeke swallowed hard. "That's impossible," he said.

"She says you always said *nothing is impossible*. She also says she has more to tell you."

Zeke tried to hold on to his emotions. It was true. He used to always tell Amber that nothing was impossible. He had forgotten that until now. "Okay, go ahead."

"I can't," Abby said while opening her eyes and looking into his. "It's too hard in this environment. But I'm holding a session tonight at my place. You're welcome to join us if you like. I would like to follow up on this. There's something special about . . . your situation."

Part of him didn't want to go but he decided to follow through with Abby's offer. "Sorry for any sarcastic remarks I made earlier."

Abby ignored his apology and stood from the barstool. "Okay, it's all set," she announced to Sabrina and Caroline. "You guys are coming over to my place."

They finished their drinks and stood from the bar. Zeke leaned over to the bartender and said, "If you see a big guy come looking for us will you tell him we met some friends and we will see him later?" Zeke reached for the bar tab and his wallet at the same time before realizing he didn't have a wallet, or any cash, for that matter. Abby grabbed the bar tab and handed it and a gold-colored credit card to the bartender. "I'm buying tonight," she said while winking at Zeke and the bartender. "Put their food on this, too."

As Zeke followed the women out the door of the restaurant, a solitary customer at a table in the corner looked up from his plate and watched them leave. His name was Timothy. He was young, maybe twenty-three or twenty-four, wearing a *Dallas Cowboys* ball cap pulled low over his brow. Timothy stood and put a ten dollar bill on the table. He was tall and very thin, wearing a long tee-shirt and baggy jeans that looked like they might fall off his skinny hips at any moment. He left the *Good Times* restaurant and climbed into a beat-up Toyota. He watched in his rearview mirror and watched the three women and man drive away in separate cars. He started the Toyota and began following them, wondering where they were going. He only knew who two of the women were. The third one he had never seen before. Regardless of who she was he knew he had to rescue the man. The poor guy had no idea what he was getting involved in, unlike Timothy, who had found out the hard way.

*   *   *

TWENTY SIX

The *Pete's Plumbing* van drove onto a dirt road that meandered through a desert terrain Stover wasn't familiar with. The driver had not said a word since leaving the WalMart outside of Dallas sometime earlier. Stover had slept most of the way, waking up only a short time ago. He felt rested and refreshed. Then he starting noticing the terrain outside his window. They appeared to be driving on a remote two-lane road somewhere in the desert. The closest desert from the WalMart would be somewhere in southwestern Texas, a good ten to twelve hour drive at best. *I couldn't have slept that long.*

An old, yellow school bus stood parked off the dirt road ahead of them. The van's driver stopped next to the bus and said, "He will take you from here."

It seemed so crazy to Stover but he thanked the driver and climbed out the van. The air was definitely dry and very warm but this place felt different from any other desert location Stover had been in his life. *Where am I?* he asked himself. *And how long did I sleep?*

He walked straight to the school bus and walked up the steps. A man with a face as worn as old leather sat behind the wheel. The man was dressed in white clothes with a cotton skullcap common in much of Islam. His big smile revealed several missing teeth along with some gold replacements. The man said nothing and started the bus's ignition. He pointed to the rear of the bus, gesturing for Stover to take a seat.

Stover walked down the aisle of the empty bus until he saw a bundle of clothes folded neatly on one of the bench seats. The bus started down the dirt road and Stover saw the plumbing van turn to head back the way it came. He caught a brief glimpse of the logo on the side of the van, only it didn't read *Pete's Plumbing* but something written in some Arabic language. Stover was starting to wonder if he was in Texas at all, or even in the United States, for that matter. *That's impossible. Or is it?*

The bundle of folded clothes in the rear of the bus turned out to be simple dungarees and a white cotton shirt. A pair of new leather hiking boots were on the floorboard. He changed out of the *Pete's Plumbing* uniform into the clothes, marveling at how well they fit.

The bus lumbered down the rutted dirt road for an hour before reaching a group of ancient-looking stone structures formed into a semicircle out in the middle of nowhere. "Where are we?" Paul called out to the driver, not really expecting the driver to answer.

The driver said nothing as he brought the bus to a stop. With a wide grin on his weathered face he opened the door and gestured for Stover to exit.

Stover smiled back at the driver while exiting the bus. He walked toward the stone structures, turning when he heard the bus driving away down the dirt road. "Well, here I am," he said under his breath. "Wherever that is . . ."

At that moment a group of barefoot children with dark complexions began running out of one of the stone structures. They were all laughing and chattering in a foreign language Stover didn't speak but still recognized. The children encircled him, tugging on his shirt and jeans in a playful way, trying to lead him to the largest of the structures at the end of the semicircle. He laughed along with them, not understanding their words but understanding their gestures as they walked toward the large stone structure.

When he entered, the children giggled and ran away, leaving him inside a large room barely illuminated by a few narrow windows cut into the thick stone walls. After his eyes had time to adjust, Stover finally saw a person standing across the room near the rear wall. The person took a few steps toward him before stopping. Stover stared in disbelief when he finally recognized the person Ruth Sennot called Joe. The mighty angel of the Lord who rescued him stood before him.

Stover dropped to his knees and lowered his head. "Thank you," he said, not knowing what to call him but not willing to call him Joe. "Thank you so much."

"Stand up," Joe said in a commanding voice. "Do not worship me. We worship the same Master."

Paul stood immediately. This entire exchange sounded familiar but he couldn't place it at the moment. "Sorry," he said. "I just wanted to thank you for all your help."

"I help not because of any affection I have for you or your kind," Joe said. "But because I am commanded by the Father to do so."

Stover nodded, still finding it difficult to look the angel in the eyes. The eyes. He remembered the fear those eyes invoked on the hellish creatures imprisoning him and Zeke not so long ago.

"Sit here," Joe said, pointing to a simple wooden chair in the middle of the room.

Stover sat in the chair and folded his hands in his lap as Joe grabbed another chair to sit in. He faced Stover. "Pray to *him*," Joe said. "Give all your thanks to *him*."

Stover lowered his head and began to pray in silence.

When he finished Joe said, "Look at me, Paul."

Stover raised his head to give his full attention to Joe.

"This is what's at stake," Joe said. "This is what you must do. What *he* wants you to do. Listen to me carefully."

While Joe imparted this knowledge to Stover, a caravan of vehicles came to a halt on the dirt road outside the stone structures. The vehicles had official markings on their doors. The doors opened and uniformed men stepped out. They stared maliciously at the large stone structure and the towering figures standing in front of it. To anyone unaware, the towering figures appeared to be tall statues but the men in uniforms knew *exactly* what type of heavenly angels were standing guard. The men in uniforms began shouting taunts in a language seldom heard on Earth. The towering angels guarding the site seemed unconcerned but when the men in uniforms began approaching, the attitude of the angels changed. They turned their gaze onto the men in uniforms, stopping them in their tracks, causing them to cower back to their official vehicles like scared rats.

Within seconds the caravan of official vehicles turned around and headed back down the dirt road, the dust plumes from their tires obscuring their Syrian license plates.

*   *   *

TWENTY SEVEN

Timothy sat in his Toyota while staring at the large Victorian house across the street, the house where the man and the three women entered earlier. More people had arrived since he'd been watching, making the total somewhere around a dozen. Timothy suspected what was going to happen but he wanted to be positive. If he was right he would warn the man about this recruitment method—a method used for gaining new members by many satanic cults and covens throughout the world.

It was a very dark night due to the low cloud cover overhead. A streetlight fifty yards down the street and the defused lamplight behind the shades of the lower windows in the Victorian home provided the only illumination in the area.

Timothy stepped out of his car and began to cross the street. He stopped in his tracks. On the sidewalk near the path leading to the Victorian's front porch were two motionless figures. It was impossible to make out any details of the figures. He might have written them off as a pair of young trees or some other natural formations bordering the path to the Victorian home but the hair standing on his arms and on the back of his neck told him otherwise. He could sense the figures staring at him. If he could see their faces—and he was glad he could not—he knew they would be smiling at him.

Timothy got back into his car and sat there while wondering what to do. There was a lot more to this than he'd expected. Something unique was happening—something he'd never seen before. He needed his Uncle John on this one. Uncle John would know what to do.

Timothy removed his cell phone from his pant pocket and flipped it open. The light from the phone illuminated his face below the bill of his ball cap. He was scrolling through his stored numbers when he detected something outside the windshield—a movement of a shadow, something so subtle he could've easily missed it. He flipped the cell phone shut immediately while trying to discern the movement again. It was too dark. He was still seeing spots in his vision from the cell phone's light. His heart rate increased dramatically. He set the cell phone in his lap and turned the key to start the ignition. Nothing. No dash lights. No cranking of the engine. Nothing. The Toyota's battery was dead. A battery he'd replaced less than a month ago. His first instinct was to lock the doors. He hit the *auto-lock* button and nothing happened. He fumbled for the manual lock on the driver's door at the same time that he heard the latch on the passenger door click. *Someone was trying to open the door!* He reached for its manual lock in a panic, elated when he discovered it was already locked. He felt the Toyota move ever so slightly. It felt like a strong wind gently rocking the car but the air outside was still. *No wind.* Timothy struggled to control his fear. He tried the ignition again. "Yes!" he exclaimed as the dash lights illuminated a second before the engine cranked up. He crammed the stick into first gear and sped away. The Toyota would have *burned rubber* if the Toyota had been capable of burning rubber.

When Timothy was back on the main road he called his Uncle John from his cell phone. John wasn't really his uncle but he was as close to Timothy as one. Actually closer. John was practically a father to Timothy. Uncle John had rescued Timothy from a cult called *Metallic Baal,* a group of young Satanists that didn't allow its members to leave, like many cults. According to John, *Metallic Baal* were amateurs, somewhere between teenagers who turned over gravestones and advanced Satanists like the group John had once belonged to. John had been High Priest of his branch of *The Elite* for more than a decade. This group of Satanists didn't associate itself publicly with any demonic names or iconography. Most of its members were doctors, lawyers, judges, politicians, even members of various clergies. When John gave his life to Christ and left *The Elite* they tried to assassinate him numerous times—both his character and his physical body. Ever since his conversion to Christ, John had dedicated his life to exposing these groups and hampering their plans. This included their recruitment of the *elect,* as *The Elite* liked to label them. Timothy had been one of these *elect* recruited by *Metallic Baal.*

After Timothy had explained the entire story of the evening to Uncle John over the cell phone, John told him to return to the *Good Times* restaurant and stay there until he got there. Under no circumstances was Timothy to leave before he got there.

Timothy agreed and drove back to the restaurant. He returned to the same table he'd sat at earlier. He ordered a Dr. Pepper and some French fries while waiting. He wasn't afraid anymore. Although he knew he was never truly alone anymore, he still felt a lot better that Uncle John was coming to the rescue.

*

The gathering at Abby Windsong's home was friendly enough but a bit too reserved to be called a party. There were nonalcoholic drinks and finger sandwiches in the kitchen but no booze that Zeke could see. Abby noticed his searching. She came close and whispered, "No alcohol before or during a session," she said. "Cocktails will be available afterwords for those interested."

"Count me in as one of *those interested*," Zeke said. He was nervous. He wasn't afraid but he felt an uneasiness being involved with something like a *séance*.

"Okay everybody," Abby announced in a clear voice. "Follow me into the dining room and we can begin."

Everybody meandered toward the dining room. Most of the people had arrived as couples or trios. They were all well-dressed and well-spoken. *Well-to-do* was another description that came to Zeke's mind. He felt conspicuously underdressed and underpaid. They were all very friendly, though. As Caroline walked him around the room and introduced him, she seemed to be rubbing her body against his in a seductive fashion. Zeke noticed that Sabrina had run into more acquaintances among the people attending Abby's séance. The whole thing was making him uncomfortable. He was ready for all this to be over.

After everyone was seated at a large antique dining table with burning candles in the center, Abby sat at the head and addressed everyone. "Once we begin, please refrain from any conversation at the table. Concentrate on clearing all negative thoughts from your mind as we hold hands and prepare to contact the other side."

Everyone joined hands as the artificial light in the room was dimmed by a small Asian woman, Abby's housekeeper. Zeke sat between Sabrina and Caroline. They each held one of his hands as the candlelight flickered in the dining room.

Abby began speaking a recitation similar to a prayer, beckoning the cooperation of the spirits. "We have several individuals with us tonight," she said. "Souls that wish to contact their dear departed loved ones. Help us spirit guides to bridge our two worlds together so these departed souls can communicate with their loved ones still on this earthly plane."

The room was completely silent. Zeke seemed too aware of his breathing which sounded heavy and wheezy to him. Several minutes went by before Abby said, "One has come forward." A short pause. "A mother. She wears polyester slacks and an apron that has prints of puppies and kittens all over it."

A young red-haired woman sitting across from Zeke gasped. "Oh, My God!" she whispered loudly. She began to sob. "That's my mom!"

"I'm hearing Mandy?" Abby continued. "Or Mimsy—"

"—Mimi!" the redhead interjected.

"Yes," Abby said. "Mimi."

The redhead was clearly weeping now.

"Mimi says don't cry and be happy," Abby reported. "She says she is very happy and you should be too. Things are so wonderful here. We all are eagerly awaiting your arrival."

Abby paused before continuing. "I see a small dog. Princess? Is that the name of the dog?"

The redhead stopped her sobbing.

"Precious," Abby said. "Is that her name?"

The redhead started crying again while nodding her head.

"Yes," Abby said. "Mimi says Precious is waiting for you. She says Precious can't wait to jump in your lap and gave you a lick on the chin."

The redhead laughed between sobs. "Precious was my fox terrier," she told the man sitting next to her, her husband or date for the evening.

Zeke sat there, trying not to fidget in his chair. He was becoming self-conscious of his sweaty palms in the hands of Sabrina and Caroline. *I wish I had a drink.*

Abby went on relaying messages between the redhead and her dead mother for at least five more minutes. Zeke was becoming more antsy by the second. He almost wished he was one of these dead spirits so he could fly away and not have to sit at this table any longer. He was truly dreading the moment Abby would attempt to contact his dead wife and son.

*

Timothy and Uncle John sat at the corner table in the *Good Times* restaurant. John Campise was in his forties, about six feet tall, powerful chest, with black hair slicked back on his head. Although raised Catholic in his Italian-American family in New York City, he strayed from the faith at an early age and continued on a path that eventually led him to worshipping Satan himself. John wore a silver necklace with a simple cross around his neck. His clean-shaven, chiseled chin supported a huge smile of white teeth that charmed most who met him.

Timothy ran through his story again and answered specific questions John asked. Timothy was explaining the layout of the Victorian house when Andrew came walking into the restaurant. "That's him," Timothy told John. "The pastor who went to council the people."

Andrew searched the room for Zeke and Sabrina. He saw two men sitting at a table in the corner of the restaurant. The older of the two beckoned him with a wave. After introducing himself, John began explaining what was going on at the big Victorian house and how Andrew had been intentionally diverted away.

"You mean she didn't lose her daughter in a car accident?" Andrew asked. "They were faking?"

"Did you go with them to identify the bodies?" John asked. "Did you talk to anyone besides them? Like the police, doctors, coroner, anybody?"

"No," Andrew replied, the truth finally settling in. "Come to think of it, it was just them—the grieving mother and her male friend who said very little."

"They're part of the same group," John said. "I'm glad it was faked, though. I've seen cases where real murders are committed for nothing more than a diversion to get someone on their hook like your friend. What's his name?"

"Zeke," Andrew answered.

"Zeke," John repeated. "Don't worry, Pastor. I know how to handle the situation."

"And how is that?"

"Look," John said. "I used to be on the other side, setting up the same type of scenarios for the purpose of recruiting new members like your friend, Zeke, into my group. There's nothing new going on here. It's just one part of the spiritual warfare going on around us all the time."

Andrew had questions about what they were going to do but John told him he would explain the basics on the way to the house.

The three of them left the restaurant and climbed into John's late model BMW. "Her name is Abigail Windsong," John explained once they were in his car. "She's a former Tarot card reader turned spiritual medium. She's unaware—like most of these *new agers* dabbling in the occult. She has no idea *who* she's really dealing with. But the other two women, they're a different story."

"Do you know the one named Sabrina?" Andrew asked.

"Yes," John replied without hesitation. "Sabrina LaFleur. She runs a witches' coven connected with my old group, *The Elite*. She's an old hat at this."

*

"He says just keep doing what you are doing," Abby said. "And keep telling the world that *love* is all that matters."

A man at the table seemed pleased. He was a friend of the departed soul Abby was now in contact with. "All you need is love," the man said in a British accent. "Yes, tell him I will."

Zeke and the rest of the folks at the table had been playing a guessing game ever since Abby first made contact with this spirit. She acted surprised at seeing this particular spirit. She revealed that he had been someone very famous when alive. A musician. From Liverpool. She or the Brit wouldn't use his name but it seemed obvious that it was one of the deceased Beatles. Zeke didn't know which one, though. Or care, for that matter. The whole thing seemed phony. He thought of asking why they wouldn't reveal the famous spirit's name. *Was someone going to ask for an autograph or something?* But Zeke kept his mouth shut, hoping this would all be over soon.

After concluding the communication with one of the Fab Four, Abby looked like she might be done for the evening, which was actually okay with Zeke, but then she seemed to fall into a trance again. Her facial expressions became animated. "She is here," Abby said. "The one I spoke to earlier, Amber, is here. And there is a boy with her. Does the husband wish to talk to them?"

Zeke didn't respond. He felt Sabrina squeeze his hand. "Yes," he finally said.

"We talked about the gray sweater earlier," Abby said. "This is the same spirit."

Zeke began to breathe faster. He felt a bead of sweat running down his temple.

"Would you like to ask her a question?" Abby asked.

"Okay," Zeke heard his voice say. "Are you happy where you're at?"

"She says yes, very happy," Abby said. "She can't wait till you can come and join them."

"Well," Zeke said with some hesitation, "I've done many bad things. I don't know if I'll be allowed to go where they are."

A smile grew on Abby's face. "She says don't be silly. Everyone comes here regardless of what they have done. Our souls are immortal."

Zeke struggled to find the words to the main question on his mind. "When you and Josh came to me before, why did you both blame me for what happened?"

A few folks at the table exchanged glances. This was not the run-of-the-mill questions usually heard at séances.

Abby cocked her head. It took a while before she said, "She says that was just a dream of yours. A bad dream, she says."

"If it was just a dream," Zeke said, "how would you know about it?"

Abby started to say something when she paused suddenly. Her expression became alarmed. She turned her head toward the front door in the foyer, a short distance from the dining room. She turned her attention back to the table. A second later her eyes grew wide as a look of sheer terror covered her face. Her bloodcurdling scream was so loud that some of the other women at the table screamed also.

Abby jumped to her feet and fell backwards, still screaming as she went to the floor, apparently losing consciousness seconds later. Several people from the table ran to her aid. There was so much surprise and commotion in the room that no one noticed Abby's Asian housekeeper opening the front door to let John Campise and Andrew Coleman enter. The two men approached the dining room table and watched the drama centered around Abby on the floor.

Abby began to regain consciousness. Several of the guests helped her to her feet. She began screaming at Zeke. "What have you done? Who are you?" She turned her rage toward Caroline. "How could you? Why have you tricked me like this." Her voice was hysterical. "Get out of my house now! GET OUT! ALL OF YOU! GET OUT!"

"Well, we got here just in time," John Campise said to Andrew. "Just call us the party crashers."

Zeke and Sabrina turned to look behind them. Zeke saw Andrew standing behind him with another man. "Andrew?" he said. "What are you doing here?"

"That was going to be my question," Andrew said.

Sabrina glanced at Andrew but her gaze fell firmly on John. She looked surprised and angry all at the same time. "I should've known it had something to do with you," she said with plenty of venom in her voice.

Zeke looked confused. He looked to Andrew for clarification. Andrew had a sad smile on his face.

"Sabrina, the good witch," John said. "Good for creating misery, that is. Looks like you've moved up in the world. Don't tell me. You're involved with aliens from another planet, aliens that seeded this planet eons ago and we are their descendants, inferior little humans but descendants nevertheless." John turned his attention to Zeke. "The lies never end."

"You two know each other?" Zeke asked while staring at her. "What's he talking about, Sabrina?"

Sabrina looked at Zeke for a moment before rolling her eyes and shoving her way around him. "What difference does it make!"

Zeke watched Sabrina storm out of the room. And just like that she was out of his life, at least for the moment.

"Come on," Andrew said while putting a big arm around Zeke's shoulder. "Let's get out of here."

Abby, still under the care of the guests supporting her massive frame, suddenly noticed John Campise. "You," she called out to John. "Did you have something to do with this?"

John approached her. "What happened, Abby?"

Abby asked the people crowded around her for some privacy. When they left she said, "I saw them, John."

"Saw who?" asked John.

"The ones you told me about when I first met you."

"You mean demons?"

Abby hesitated before nodding her head rapidly. "Yes."

"I warned you," John said. "But you wouldn't believe me."

"They were so normal," she explained. "Then they began to change. Something distracted them and they turned into . . . monsters!"

"That would have been *me* that distracted them," John said. "And by the way, that's how they *really* look."

Abby stared back at him with loads of concern in her eyes. "It just can't be . . ."

"When are you going to wise up, Abby?"

Abby lowered her eyes. "Are you going to quote some scriptures to me now?"

"No, but I'll give you some verses to read on your own," he said. "You have a Bible?"

"I'll get one," she said. "First thing in the morning."

"Okay," John said while removing a pen and notepad from his pocket. He began writing as he spoke. "Leviticus 19:31 says it very plainly. Also chapter 20 verse 6 and verse 27. That's just for starters." He tore the piece of paper from the notepad and handed it and a business card to Abby. "When you are ready give me a call. I can explain it from the enemy's perspective as well since that's where I learned it originally."

Abby took the card. "Thank you, John," she said with a smile. "I'll call you. Now get out of here. You're scaring away my guests."

John laughed and blew her a kiss. "We might make a team yet, Abby!"

John returned to Zeke and Andrew. "My name is John Campise and I'm here to help you," he said to Zeke. "I imagine you have a few questions about what's going on. Once we're out of here I'll tell you what I know."

They walked to John's BMW parked across the dark street where Timothy sat behind the wheel with the engine idling. Timothy was glad the dark figures guarding the path had skedaddled when John and Andrew had marched boldly to the house.

Zeke and Andrew climbed in back as John sat in the passenger seat. "Zeke? This is Timothy. Timothy? This is Zeke."

"Hey," both Zeke and Timothy said at the same time.

"Tell me, Zeke," John said. "Did Sabrina come to you with a story about UFOs?"

"Yes," Zeke said, thinking about her artwork on the canvasses. "She did."

"Yeah," John said. "That's their latest kick. Aliens from other planets warning us that we're destroying the planet but they're here to help us protect it."

"Yes," Zeke said. "That's exactly what she said."

"Along with contacting the dead," John continued, "this is the enemy's newest gag."

"You lost me on that one," Zeke said. "Besides breaking up séances, what else do you do, John?"

"I'm a good cook," John said. "Also, if you lose your car keys I can start your car without them."

"I wonder where you learned that?" Zeke said with a smirk.

"Yeah," John replied. "I wonder?"

Zeke was still confused by what had just occurred at Abby's house, but he felt comfortable in the company of this John Campise character. Although he'd been duped by Sabrina, Zeke felt relieved it was over. Suspicions of her true intent had begun to grow in the last day or so, though he still didn't understand what those intentions were.

"You guys are gonna be guests at my place," John said in his booming New York accent. "I'll explain everything that happened back there when we get there. I'll also make you guys a nice late-night meal, Italiano style! *Capisce?*"

"Do we have a choice?" Zeke asked with a weak smile.

"Not unless you wish to sleep wit de fishes," John said in a mock Mafioso accent.

"Are you supposed to be an Italian mobster or something?" asked Zeke.

John laughed. "No, not hardly." He paused for a moment before saying, "But you know, maybe I am. Only my boss is the *true* Godfather..."

*   *   *

TWENTY EIGHT

Paul Stover punched the phone number into the satellite phone. The eight-hour time difference would place Ruth at her desk in the middle of the afternoon. He stood outside the tent as a warm wind blew, the stars above absolutely extraordinary with the zero light pollution of the area. To his north, Mount Hermon stood silhouetted in the night. To his south, the town of Nimrod, all of it located in the Golan Heights, the small finger of territory in Syria that had been occupied by Israel since the Six-Day War in 1967. The phone on the other end began to ring. Once. Twice. At the start of the third ring he heard, "Lost Valley Church."

"Ruth?"

A slight delay, then, "Yes, this is Ruth. How can I help you?"

"It's Paul. Paul Stover."

"Paul!" she exclaimed. "Where have you been? I've been worried about you!"

"I'm fine, Ruth."

"I'm sorry," she said. "I tried calling you at the number you gave me but they said you had checked out already."

"It's okay, Ruth. Listen—"

"—I put the word out," she kept going, "but I still haven't—"

"—I found Joe, Ruth," Paul interrupted. "Or I should say, he found me."

"That's wonderful! What did he say? Did you learn anything about Zeke?"

"You need to meet me in Gold Tree tomorrow evening."

"Gold Tree?" she said. "Tomorrow? That's a long drive, Paul."

"I know it is, Ruth. But it's important."

"Just tell me one thing. Is Zeke going to be there?"

"He will be there," came the answer.

Ruth was reeling. Zeke was alive. She tried to hold back the tears as

287

Stover babbled about something else. She finally said, "I'm sorry, Paul. What did you say?"

"Beth needs to come with you and the children," Stover repeated himself. "Can you arrange that?"

"Of course," Ruth said. "But why does Beth need to come with us?"

"Listen to me, Ruth," Stover continued. "You must trust me. This comes from Joe. You trust *him*, don't you?"

"Yes," she said without hesitation.

"Good. Then listen. You and Beth and your children cannot tell anyone where you are going."

"I don't want—"

"—I'm not asking you to lie, Ruth," he said. "Tell your pastor that it's a family issue. Tell him you will explain later. Understand?"

Ruth didn't reply.

"It's for his own safety, Ruth," Stover explained. "Do not tell him or anybody else at the church. You'll understand everything soon but for now you must do what I say. Can you do this or not? I need your answer now."

For his own safety? she thought to herself. *Was Paul okay in the head? Was all this cloak and dagger stuff something he's conjured up in his mind? A mind that still wasn't totally healed?*

Ruth hesitated for a couple more seconds before saying, "Yes, I can do it."

"Good. I'll see you tomorrow, late afternoon, early evening."

"I'm really confused, Paul," she said. "What's going to happen when we get there? Is Zeke really going to be there?"

"Yes, I promise."

Ruth wanted to believe.

"Just be patient," Stover said. "You'll understand everything soon enough."

"But my children—"

"—They will be fine."

"Okay," she finally said. "We'll be there, Paul. We are *trusting* you."

"Great," he said. "God bless you."

"Same to you," Ruth replied, not wanting the conversation to end but not knowing what else to say. "Goodbye, Paul."

Paul Stover ended the call and walked back inside the tent. He handed the satellite phone to the company commander's assistant. "Thank you so much."

"You're welcome, sir," the Israeli army officer said.

Paul left the tent and walked back into the night. To find Joe. Or actually to have Joe find him. That's how it always worked with Joe. You didn't find him. He found you.

Ruth sat at her desk back at the Lost Valley Church in Texas, staring off into the distance through her office window. *What if Paul is making all this up? Why would he do that? I don't know, maybe he's just not all there in the head. What choice do I have? He said Zeke will be there!*

Ruth snapped out of her thoughts. "Zeke is alive," she said out loud. She wanted to shout it into the streets but she needed to get organized in order to leave early tomorrow. Besides, she would be careful not to get too excited in case Zeke didn't show up. She didn't know how she would deal with the disappointment if that happened.

Ruth stood from her desk and walked down a small corridor toward some offices in the back of the building. She stepped into an office and waited for Beth to end a phone conversation. Beth was a pretty brunette with a gorgeous smile. Ruth hoped Beth would eventually find the right man to settle down with and raise a family.

Beth ended the call and looked up at Ruth with a big smile. "What's up, Hon?"

"I need to ask you a big favor."

"Sure, name it."

"I need you to take a trip with me," Ruth said. "Out of town."

"No problem," Beth said. "Where are we going?"

Ruth smiled tentatively. "Uh, I can't tell you."

"Really?" Beth said, excited by the unexpected adventure. "I like it!"

"Aren't you going to keep pestering me about the details?"

Beth's smile grew even larger. "No! Just tell me when we are leaving!"

"Tomorrow," Ruth said. "Very early!"

"Great!" Beth said with a grin while turning her attention back to a computer monitor on her desk. "You can tell me all about him later."

"There's no him," Ruth said. "I mean . . . not like that!"

"Yeah, right."

"See you a bit later," Ruth said, not liking what Beth was thinking. She walked to Pastor Davis's office, thinking of what she needed to do in order to leave town early in the morning. The other thoughts took over: *Zeke is alive! I'm going to see him tomorrow! He will be back in our lives! Thank you, Lord! Thank you so much!*

*   *   *

TWENTY NINE

"That's one of the ways they do it," John Campise said while standing over the stove in the kitchen of his condo and scrambling eggs in a frying pan. "In order for you to buy their lies they have to get you to believe that there's life after death."

Zeke and Andrew sat on barstools at the kitchen's island countertop while Timothy sat in the adjoining living area, watching some music videos on John's big-screen television.

"I understand," Andrew said.

"Well, I don't," Zeke said, addressing the statement to both John and Andrew. "You guys are Christians and you don't believe in life after death? What about heaven and hell and all that?"

"They're talking about something different, Zeke," Andrew said. "They're talking about a place where *everyone* goes after they die— everyone except for really bad people like Hitler who *they* decide fit into that category. They bait people with the lie that *everyone* will inherit this heaven-like existence after they die. And the deceased loved one is proof. They say: 'See? My deceased loved one didn't have God in their life and everything is just fine for them in the afterlife. They weren't Christian. All that religious stuff is unnecessary.' This way, those alive can continue doing what they are doing with no concern for God. In other words, the loved one they communicated with at a séance was not someone who gave their life to God, and all seemed well with them in the afterlife, so why should anyone be concerned? Obviously, no one needs Christ. Or God. Or anything. Just keep doing what you are doing as long as you don't kill people or do whatever *you* believe is really bad."

"That's right," John said. "But the problem is, the dead loved one the medium communicates with is *not* your dead loved one at all."

"Then who are they?" asked Zeke.

"Who do you think?" John replied while adding some diced tomatoes to the eggs.

"I think *you* will say it's a demonic spirit," Zeke said. "A spirit from a fallen angel. One of the nephilim."

"Nephilim!" John exclaimed. "I'm impressed, Zeke!"

"Am I right?" Zeke continued. "That *is* what you were going to say, right?"

"Yes," John answered. "But without the fancy *nephilim* word. I was just going to say a demon. And about that subject I know plenty."

"How's that?" asked Zeke.

"I led a satanic cult for nearly a decade," John said in a matter-of-fact tone. "We had the modest name of *The Elite*. I was the head honcho. The big kahuna. My official title was High Priest, though."

Zeke wasn't surprised by much anymore.

"And me and my little group were very familiar with what we called *counseling spirits*," John continued. "We summoned these spirits for guidance. Most demonic spirits have specialties. For example, one particular group of demonic spirits are excellent impersonators. They take great pride in their abilities to imitate any human that once lived on our planet, and I don't mean just in appearance or voice but in knowing intimate details—details that only the deceased and maybe those close to them knew."

This explained a few things for Zeke. *The spirit claiming to be Amber was not Amber at all but one of these demonic spirits that were experts at imitation.*

"Here's how my mentor explained it," John said while preparing four plates with the scrambled egg dish. "There was an important meeting of Satanists in Paris in the early eighteenth century. These Satanists were leaders in their fields, important members of the community, influential people in business and politics. According to my mentor, who learned it from his mentor, who learned it from his mentor, Satan wished to create a different strategy for the new age beginning to dawn in Europe at that time. My mentor said that Satan had been studying the Bible, especially the parts dealing with end time prophecy, Daniel 12 in particular. Hey Timothy! Your food's ready!"

Timothy hurried into the kitchen and grabbed the plate before returning to the sofa and the music videos. Zeke and Andrew made room on the countertop for the plates. They watched John sit in a barstool across from them. He lowered his head for a quick prayer before taking a bite of food. He then opened a leather folder in front of him and rotated it so they could see. Zeke and Andrew saw the layout on a page in the folder:

Satan's General Council of 1720
<u>Christian Idolatry</u>
1. Deny Existence.
2. Necromancy.
3. Hypnotism.
4. Scientific Manipulation.

"Here's what Satan declared," John explained. "*Number one*: To deny the existence of himself and his fallen angels. Before the eighteenth century in Europe everyone believed in the existence of the devil and witchcraft and so on. But for the last three hundred years across Europe and the other advanced nations, Satan invokes images of someone dressed in red leotards with a van dyke beard, horns, tail, and holding a pitchfork. Halloween. Kiddie stuff. They succeeded. Score one for the devil and his minions.

"*Number Two: Necromancy*—the conjuring of spirits, communication with the dead, the very thing we dealt with tonight, all of it detested and forbidden by God as far back as the Book of Genesis, the first book of the Bible. And as you saw, it wasn't your dead loved ones you communicated with, but with demonic spirits. 1 Samuel 28 in the Bible tells the story where King Saul went to the Witch of Endor to consult with a deceased Samuel. Read it and I think you'll get the picture of how all this works.

"*Number Three: Hypnotism.* The plan was to take hypnotism out of the world of mysticism and bring it into the new discipline called *Science*. My mentor explained that Satan himself chose an Austrian physicist named Franz Mesmer for this task. Franz Mesmer came up with the theory of *Animal Magnetism*, which basically explained that certain people have magnetic powers over others, powers that could be exercised through hypnotism. This theory became so widely accepted among scientists across Europe that many doctors were using hypnotism for anesthetic purposes by the early nineteenth century. The term '*mesmerize*' comes from Mesmer's name. In today's world, a popular type of *hypnotism* is found in music, especially where a constant beat goes on and on with chant-like vocals, much of the lyrical content about fighting authority, selling and doing drugs, having sex with anyone you want, and trampling anyone or anything that gets in your way. This type of message is negative but what most people don't realize is that this type of hypnotism works on a deeper level in the subconscious, not just on the surface.

"*Number Four: Scientific Manipulation.* Faith and science were seldom at odds with each other. Church and science, yes, but not faith and science. Many of the world's greatest scientists were men of faith. But along came the *Enlightenment* and later Darwin's *Theory of Evolution* which is so full of holes it's amazing that so many accept it as fact without any question. Anyway, people began discounting God's Word to follow these lies, exactly as Satan had planned."

"Is clinical hypnotism part of all this?" Andrew asked. "Like regressive hypnosis?"

"Yes," John said. "Regressive hypnosis is widely accepted in many academic circles today. For example: A person undergoing regressive hypnosis even administered by a professional will regress into their subconscious, and with help from certain demonic spirits they will recall everything from past lives to alien abductions—which can support the false belief of reincarnation and visitations of extraterrestrials from outer space."

"So you don't believe in aliens and UFOs?" Zeke asked between bites.

"Yes," John said. "I *do* believe in them. I just don't believe they are what people claim they are . . . another race of beings from a distant planet that seeded our own planet and are here to protect it."

"Then who are they?" asked Zeke.

"They are the same spirits we've been talking about," John answered without hesitation. "Part of the same plan of deception decreed in France in the early eighteenth century that had actually begun after the original fall of Lucifer and his angels eons ago."

"What about reincarnation," Andrew asked. "I know people who have been convinced it's true because of knowledge or language of other lives risen from their memory through regressive hypnosis."

"Same spirits that impersonate the dead," John said. "I've witnessed this many times and I have laid many traps this way."

"How's that?" asked Andrew.

"Well, on one occasion one of the members of my group was having problems with a certain Jewish doctor in our community," John explained.

"The member of my group promoted the idea of reincarnation through regressive hypnosis. He had a clinic and was making a fortune regressing people into past lives. People ate this up. Now they could tell others at parties and elsewhere how they were Napoleon or General Custer in their past life. Anyway, this Jewish individual, a respected MD and outspoken critic of this form of therapy, began an attack against our friend and his practice. We conjured a counseling spirit who enabled assistance from another demonic spirit. What happened was this: the MD had a three-year-old son. The spirit possessed the little tyke and had him goose-stepping and speaking fluent German as he marched in front of his father in the living room. The demonic spirits found special amusement in their choice of imitation, a Nazi, since the MD's parents had been survivors of the Holocaust. Needless to say, the Jewish MD became so impressed by his son's apparent past life that he not only stopped his attack on our friend but became an active proponent of this type of therapy and reincarnation in general. This type of demonic activity will increase in the end times. That is why Jesus warned us so many times to *not* be deceived."

Everyone ate their food in silence for several minutes, the only sound coming from the music videos on the television in the adjoining room. Zeke finished his plate and stared at a wall while he digested not only his food but all the explanations John gave him regarding this realm of the demonic, a realm that most people don't believe even exists. *They wouldn't deny it if they ever came face to face with it,* Zeke said to himself. *Had I been face to face with it?* He was still having difficulty believing it, still trapped between his disbelief of the supernatural and the reality of his experiences. Zeke finally asked "So Sabrina planned the whole thing at Abby's tonight?"

"Absolutely," said John. "With help from her friend the blonde."

"What about the woman in the restaurant?" Zeke continued. "The one who lost her daughter in the car wreck?"

"She's also a member of Sabrina's coven," John stated. "Part of the deception to get you away from big Andrew here."

"So her daughter wasn't really killed?" asked Zeke.

"No," John said. "She doesn't even have children. But be thankful. I've seen situations where real innocents were killed for such diversions."

"Why did they do this?" asked Zeke.

"My guess is," John said, finishing his last bite, "for them to destroy any belief in God you may have, something necessary in order to use you."

"Use me for what?"

John could only shrug. "Don't know but I can ensure you it wouldn't be for your general welfare or spiritual health."

"And the UFO thing," Zeke said. "How did you know?"

"Lucky guess," John answered. "Extraterrestrials arriving on Earth is a popular ploy these days. I don't know why but it is."

Zeke tried to stifle a yawn.

"When you guys are ready to call it a night let me know," John said. "I've got two guest bedrooms with extremely awesome mattresses. You'll sleep like babies."

Zeke stood from his barstool. "I think I'll take you up on that," he said. "I'm very sleepy for some reason."

After John showed him to one of the guest bedrooms, Zeke got into the bed and stretched out. The mattress was wonderful. He didn't think about yesterday or tomorrow. He was content for the moment—a strange feeling due to the recent turn of events with Sabrina and the séance. He knew big things were coming his way. He could feel it. He didn't know what exactly but he knew it just the same. He closed his eyes and fell asleep within seconds.

Back in the kitchen Andrew leaned over the countertop and began telling John about the angel's visitation—or least the parts the angel had allowed him to tell. John gave his full attention to the big pastor, realizing that this was *much* bigger than some satanic cult recruitment procedure. He didn't know exactly how big but he knew he had to be a part of it . . . that he was *meant* to be a part of it.

* * *

THIRTY

D r. Robert Margolian sat inside his canvas tent while typing on a laptop computer. He turned toward the tent's entrance after sensing someone standing there. Paul Stover stared back, his expression passive and neutral. Margolian parted his lips to say something but no words came out.

"You better shut your mouth, Doctor," Stover said, "before you start attracting flies or some other type of exotic insect."

"Paul?" was all Margolian could say.

"Yes," Stover said. "Can I come in, Robert?"

Margolian hesitated for just a second. "Yes, of course!" He stood from the portable table before him and offered Stover a chair. "How did you get here? I mean, how did you find me?"

Stover sat in the chair and glanced around the tent's interior before settling his eyes on Margolian. "Do you really want to know?"

Margolian stared back for a moment. "No, not really."

Stover nodded and began eyeing the books and papers scattered on the portable table. "How's work going, Robert?"

"Paul," Margolian began, "I'm so sorry. I never meant for—"

"—There's no need to apologize," Stover interrupted. "It wasn't your fault."

"But if I would have known I would never have dragged you into it."

"It was *meant* for me to be there," Stover said. "By the *highest* authority."

"But why did they take you without me?"

"Because they already had you. They didn't need you again, or so they thought. They screwed up their timing . . . again."

Some relief showed in Margolian's eyes.

"Listen to me, Robert," Stover said. "Do you remember what you told me before we left Austin . . . about the timeframe?"

Margolian didn't have to struggle to remember. "Yes."

"That is why I'm here," Stover said. "I need the timeframe."

Things were staring to make sense to Margolian. He turned his attention toward the laptop and opened a file. "You know, when I first mentioned this to you and Zeke I think I alluded that the timeframe was recorded dates, like that on a calendar. That wasn't exactly true."

"What do you mean?"

"I mean that the carvings from the tablets were not dates," Margolian explained. "Not in the conventional sense. The carvings predate any calendar known today."

"Okay, then what were they?"

"Astronomical events," Margolian said. "Signs from the heavens, remember?"

"Yes," Stover answered while peering at the laptop's screen.

"A specific alignment of certain celestial bodies usually occurs over a period of days if not longer." Margolian had an astronomy program opened on his laptop. "Most alignments repeat themselves in cycles, some of them very long according to our lifespans. This one has occurred only once in the last fifty-two-thousand years."

"I don't need the specifics," Stover said. He seemed to be in a hurry now. "I just need the timeframe. Whatever it is."

Margolian removed a pen and notepad from a pocket. He jotted down something on a piece of paper and tore it off from the pad. He handed the paper to Stover.

Stover looked at it. "I thought it would be more specific," he said. "Fall-winter? That's it?"

"And don't forget the most important part," Margolian said. "The year."

Stover stared at the paper. "It's further away than I thought," he told Margolian. "I presumed it would be sooner."

Margolian just shrugged. "That's when it is."

Stover nodded and folded the paper into a pocket.

"You think that's wise?" Margolian said. "What if they find it?"

"They've already had me, remember?" Stover said. "Besides, I'm not traveling alone."

Margolian just nodded, not really wanting to know anything about Stover's traveling companions.

"Your life back to normal, Doctor?" asked Stover.

"It will never be back to normal," Margolian said. "But I'm back at work which is a good thing."

"How did you get back here in this part of the world?"

"Well, it was not easy. It took about a year to get through all the paperwork in the U.S. alone. At least the media tired of the story quickly."

Stover stood from his chair. "Maybe when I get the time I can come back," he said with a sad smile, knowing this would never happen. "And you can show me around this ancient part of the world."

Margolian stood also. "Yes, I would like that very much, Paul."

"You take care, Robert," Stover said while walking toward the tent's exit. He stood at the opening and turned to Margolian. "What do you think is going to happen during the timeframe on this piece of paper, Robert?"

Margolian lowered his voice. "I think it is when the nephilim are coming back," he said. "Coming back in a big way."

"As extraterrestrials?"

"*Posing* as extraterrestrials," Margolian corrected him.

Stover nodded and said, "I've been thinking the same thing."

Margolian remembered something else. He went to a bag under the table and retrieved a small leather journal before handing it to Stover. "Here, take this."

"What is it?"

"Maybe interesting reading for the toilet," Margolian said. "Or maybe prophecy for the future."

Stover smiled and took the journal, flipping through some pages covered in ink handwriting, apparently notes Margolian had been taking for some unknown time.

"Over the past couple of years while wading through all the bureaucratic red tape to get my identity back," Margolian said, "I became more aware of the political and social situations developing in America and the rest of the globe. During that time I developed a theory possibly explaining the reason for their return."

"Thanks," Stover said. "I'm looking forward to reading it."

The two men stared at each other for a moment, both of them feeling a bit awkward at the farewell. Margolian finally asked, "How come you never married, Paul?"

"Haven't found the right woman yet," Stover answered. "How about you?"

"I've never had the time to find one, I guess."

"Maybe you should make the time," said Stover.

"Yes, maybe I should."

Stover reached out and shook Margolian's hand. "Bye, Robert."

"Goodbye, Paul."

And with that, Stover left the tent. Margolian watched him walk off into the remote Turkish landscape, not following any visible road or path. He saw Stover reading the journal as if he was taking a stroll in the park while reading a paperback, heading to some location only angels knew.

* * *

THIRTY ONE

After retrieving their bags from the motel, Zeke and Andrew rode with John Campise toward Gold Tree, Texas in John's BMW. Sunrise was still an hour or more away. "So your okay leaving your car at the motel?" John asked Andrew who sat in the passenger seat, his long legs cramped as they were in most car interiors.

"Yes," Andrew replied. "I left the keys for Sabrina at the front desk."

"You did?" asked John.

"Of course," Andrew said. "She has to get home, doesn't she? I guess I still feel responsible for the loss of her car."

"Where did she tell you she lived?" John asked while entering the I20 west freeway entrance ramp.

"She didn't tell me," Andrew said. He turned to face Zeke in the backseat.

Zeke stared out the window but he sensed Andrew looking at him. "Not far from some little town called Blossom-something," Zeke answered.

"Blossom Lea?" John asked. "Near Paris?"

Zeke remembered the Paris joke Sabrina made after they'd first met. "Yes."

"Was it a little A-frame shack?" John continued.

"Yes," Zeke said, not really surprised that John knew this.

"Yeah, I know the place," John said. "It's not hers. It belongs to a guy named Reginald Fosterling, a longtime member of *The Elite*. We used the place on occasion for ritual stuff too vile for me to visit even in memory."

Zeke thought about this before asking, "So how did she—or they—know I'd be wandering around nearby in the woods with a severe case of amnesia?"

301

After a moment of silence John looked at Zeke in the rearview mirror and said, "I have no idea because I'm still in the dark with your story. Want to fill me in?"

Andrew looked back at Zeke with raised eyebrows. "Feel like it?"

Zeke didn't feel like it but he knew he would never feel like it. He *did* feel like he owed it to both men, though. "Okay," he said. "You asked for it."

Zeke began his story two and half years ago, when he and Billy left early from their camping trip and headed to his cabin near Gold Tree. Zeke had thought there would be many missing memories but he was surprised how many of those memories came back from the telling of the story. Nearly an hour passed by the time he finished. "So there you are," he said with a hint of sarcasm in his voice. "How'd you like my little tale of intrigue?"

"I liked it," John said, "except for the part about your abduction and the worm-thing they used on you. That was sick. I think—"

"—So you believe it?" Zeke butted in. "You don't think I'm crazy?"

"No, I don't think you are crazy," John replied with a testy tone. "Now do you want to hear what else I think or not?"

"Sure."

"I'd say that the Enemy and his army really wants to prevent you from doing something important," John said. "And the Lord and his army is making sure they are not successful."

"Prevent me from doing what?" Zeke asked. "If God wants me to do something so badly why doesn't he just tell me?"

"Because it usually doesn't work that way," John said. "But it sounds to me like everything is going exactly as planned. It might be impossible for you to see now but one day you'll look back on this and the reason will be clear. Right, Andrew?"

"Yes," Andrew said. "Faith is the key."

"And patience," John added.

Zeke began staring out the window again. "You know," he said after a long pause, "if they want to stop me from doing something why don't they just kill me?"

"Probably because they aren't allowed to," John said.

"Allowed to?" Zeke said with a crazed laugh. "Are you kidding me?"

"Look," John replied. "You can scoff all you want but I know what I'm talking about. The demonic realm is very legalistic. In many situations they are not allowed to take life. Read the story of Job in the Bible and you will see one such example. They can make you suffer as much as they want, though. Or I should say as much as we want."

"We want?" asked Zeke, trying to be patient.

"I should've said as much as we *allow*," John said.

"And how do we allow them to make us suffer?" Zeke continued.

"By sin," this time from Andrew.

"That's right," John said. "We give them the legal right to torment us because of what we have in common with them. And what we have in common with them is sin. I don't want to get too far off the subject right now but if you read the story of Jesus casting out the demons named Legion in Matthew 8:29, Mark 5:7, and Luke 8:28, you will learn that the demons stated they had nothing in common with Jesus. Yet with their ability to influence our thoughts, which usually affects our actions, they proved they had plenty in common with us. That common thing is sin. Now you might be dealing with specific demonic forces with a specific agenda different from the everyday type but they still operate within certain rules. The demonic world is very militaristic, including its hierarchy of rank . . . with Satan at the top."

Zeke didn't say anything as he continued to stare out the window. Even though he wasn't showing it, at some level he was starting to accept John's explanation of this spiritual world of beings existing side by side with our own. He'd had enough of the subject for the moment, though. To change the subject he said, "You know, I just thought of something."

"What?" asked John.

"What do all three of *us* have in common with each other?" asked Zeke.

"That we are three extremely good-looking dudes with brilliant minds and wonderful personalities?" John offered.

"Yes," Zeke said with a smile, "but besides that?"

John shrugged. "I give up. What?"

"None of us have a woman in our life," Zeke said. "As a matter of fact, every man I've been associated with during this entire odyssey has been either single, divorced, or widowed. Just like myself. Don't you find that odd?"

"Boy," John said. "And I thought you were going to say something funny. You're really becoming a Debbie-Downer, aren't you?"

"I didn't say it was a bad thing," Zeke continued. "I just said it was odd."

Andrew spoke up. "I don't know if it's all that odd, Zeke," he said, "with divorce rates as high as they are these days."

"I just find it weird," Zeke went on. "And then I run into this hottie-in-the-woods that turns out to be a witch . . . literally. You know, I was starting to grow pretty fond of her. And then all this."

"I know you are feeling hurt at the moment," John said. "But just remember that it was never real with her. She's a walking-talking lie, out for her own benefit regardless of who it hurts."

Zeke knew that was true. It was also true that he was feeling a little sorry for himself at the moment, something he didn't like one bit. "When I guided the people to Austin," he said, moving away from the subject of Sabrina, "I never thought about it at the time. The man who hired me: a widower. His assistant: never married. Then Andrew here: widowed. And you, John Campise?"

"Divorced," came John's answer. "Her doing, not mine. She didn't want to be married to a Christian."

"So don't you guys think that's a little odd?" Zeke asked. "That all the men I've encountered over the last few years are living without a female in their lives?"

No one said anything for a long moment. Finally Andrew said, "I've found in my life that sometimes when things come to you that way it's really a message."

"What's the message?" asked Zeke.

"It's for you," Andrew replied with a shrug. "Not me."

Zeke was about to say something when John said, "Yeah, you may have a point, Andrew."

"What do you mean?" Zeke asked.

"You were complaining a while ago about God not telling you what he wants you to do," John explained. "Maybe that realization of yours about the lack of women in everyone's lives—including your own—has something to do with what he wants you to do. That's the way it usually is. We're whining about God not answering us when he's been trying to show us all along."

Zeke thought about that for a moment. He got the point but he didn't see how it applied to his situation. And he didn't want anymore frustration at the moment. He tried to make light of the situation. "I get it!" he said in a mock-excited voice. "He wants me to spend more time with happily married men to get rid of losers like you guys!"

John laughed and turned to Andrew. "Will you discipline him for me?"

Andrew reached behind and grabbed Zeke above his knee and began squeezing with his powerful hand.

"Whoa, big guy!" Zeke shouted and laughed while squirming in the backseat, trying to escape Andrew's powerful grip. "Okay, I take it back!"

Andrew let go and gave Zeke a smile while shaking a giant fist at him.

"That's good, guys," John said. "Keep those spirits high. Life's too short to feel weak and beaten. Remember that Paul and Peter wrote much of the New Testament while imprisoned in chains and yet they still let the good news shine on through them!"

Zeke was about to ask a question about the *good news* when John's cell phone rang. "Yo, Timothy!" John answered.

Zeke and Andrew remained quiet in the car.

"You're kidding?" John said into the phone. Then, "So she just stood there outside the door?" John turned to Zeke and Andrew and mouthed the word *"Sabrina"* while listening to Timothy on the other end. Finally John said, "Ah, she's just trying to scare you. Don't pay any attention to that. You're a grown man walking with the Lord. There is nothing they can do and they know it. They just don't know if *you* know it or not. Understand?" More listening, then, "Okay, call me if you need me."

John ended the call and said to Zeke, "You're little hottie paid a visit to my pad a while ago. She scared the daylights out of Timothy who's watching the place for me while I'm gone."

"What did she do?" asked Zeke.

"Screamed through the door," John said. "Thought I was in there. Said that I was over my head this time and if I didn't turn you over to her bad things were going to happen to me."

"Turn me over to her?" Zeke scoffed. "Like her prisoner or something?"

"I guess," John said with a chuckle. "She sounds totally desperate. I wonder who she got involved with this time and what her own consequences are by blowing the deal with you?"

Zeke was speechless. The whole thing with Sabrina still shocked him.

"Did she threaten Timothy?" asked Andrew.

"I don't think she even knew he was there," John said. "Timothy's easily spooked, that's all. He went through quite an ordeal in his youth but it's time for him to grow up and find the strength he now has in Christ. He'll be fine. Sabrina and her coven are just a bunch of self-centered cowards like most members of satanic cults. Most people miss that. Satan's message to humanity isn't so much a spiritual one with animal sacrifices and pentagrams like Hollywood portrays it. The message is actually much more worldly in nature: *Do what you want! Don't let anybody stand in your way! Go out there and get what's rightfully yours! The world is for the taking! Life is short! Get it while you can! If it feels good, do it! He who dies with the most toys wins!*"

"Excuse me while I play the devil's advocate," Zeke said. "But isn't that what it takes to be assertive? To be a go-getter? Someone who succeeds in life?"

"That's exactly what it says," John said. "*Go out there and get it yourself. You don't need God. Life's too short to waste it trying to please some creator that probably doesn't even exist. Make good grades so you get a good job and make lots of money. That's the key to happiness—making lots of money!* That's what is taught these days, with little or no mention of God who gave us this life, let alone honoring Him and giving him thanks for everything we have. You see, all those things like doing good in school and getting a decent job are good in themselves, and that's how Satan deceives us. We put those things above God. That's the brilliance of the devil's trick."

It made sense to Zeke but it seemed strange how all of this had slipped by him in life up to this point. *What's happening to me?*

"So did you like my sermon?" John said in a loud, facetious voice. "Want some more?"

Zeke chuckled to himself. "I'm okay for the moment."

John said, "You didn't know what you were getting yourself into when you decided to take a road trip with *two* preachers, did you?"

"No, I didn't," Zeke said. "But that's how I've been my entire life—jumping into situations regardless of the negatives."

John squinted at Zeke in the rearview mirror before turning to Andrew. "I think that was an insult, Pastor. Your move."

Andrew smiled and reached back for Zeke but this time Zeke was ready. He grabbed Andrew's big arm and twisted it into a leverage hold he learned in ranger training many years earlier. The shock and surprise registered quickly on Andrew's face. The big pastor could only grunt in pain.

John glanced at the scene while trying to keep his eyes on the road, amused by the turn of events in the car. "Zeke! You're an animal!"

Zeke chuckled and released Andrew's arm, letting both John and Andrew know that he'd been playing along with Andrew earlier. It was all in good fun but Zeke wanted them to know he was still an experienced combat soldier, a force to be reckoned with, not some whiny dude in the backseat feeling sorry for himself. Respect. That's all he'd ever asked from anyone. Not adulation, just respect for being a fellow human—a fellow human living out this mystery called life . . .

*   *   *

THIRTY TWO

The Hyundai four-door slowed as it approached the dirt road off to the right of the highway. "This is it," Ruth said. "I'm positive."

"Are you sure?" said Beth. "It looks different for some reason."

"Not to me." Ruth turned her car onto the dirt road.

"When are we gonna be there, Mommy?" Amy asked from the backseat. "I need to go to the bathroom."

Amy's older brother, Connor, sat next to her. He wore a pair of earbuds and hummed along to music from his MP3 player, oblivious to the conversations of the three females in the car.

"You just went a little while ago," Ruth told Amy.

"But I gotta go again," Amy pleaded.

"We'll be at the cabin in a few minutes so sit back and relax." *If the cabin is still there,* Ruth thought.

Beth's flawless face looked radiant in the late morning sun streaming through the windshield. She stared at Ruth from the passenger seat. "You excited?"

Ruth shot a quick glance toward Beth before returning her eyes to the dirt road. "Excited and anxious all at the same time," Ruth said. Then, in a quiet voice, "Beth, what if he's not there?"

"Quit worrying so much," Beth said. "It will all work out."

"What if Paul Stover made all this up? What if he's delusional?"

"What does that mean, Mommy?" Amy asked from the backseat. "Duh-looge . . ."

"Delusional," Ruth said. "It means . . . sick . . . in the brain."

"Oh."

"Relax, Ruth," Beth said with a big smile. "Just think positive."

"You're right, Beth. Just think positive."

The last section of dirt road wound hard to the left and Ruth saw it.

Vegetation had grown wild, obscuring most of the lower parts of the cabin but there it was, looking even more abandoned than it had when Beth and her had visited over a year ago. Ruth's heart sank. "He's not here," she said, her voice revealing the disappointment she felt.

"Chill out, Ruth," Beth said. "We're early. Be patient."

Ruth parked the Hyundai. She stared out the windshield at the Jeep Cherokee parked a short distance from the cabin, its wheels and tires long gone. The rest of the vehicle sat upon cinderblocks partially hidden by tall weeds and grass, exactly as it had on their previous visit.

Ruth and Beth exited the Hyundai, stretching their backs and examining the area. Amy climbed out of the backseat first, then Connor, his attention still distracted by the music playing in his earbuds. Ruth looked distrustfully at the cabin before noticing her daughter shifting from one foot to the other. "Go over there behind those bushes," Ruth told her. "You can relieve yourself there."

"But Mom!" Amy complained. "What about bugs and snakes?"

Ruth rolled her eyes and turned to Connor. "Connor, take your little—" She realized her son couldn't hear her because of the earbuds. She marched over to him and pulled them out. "Connor!"

"Yes?" Connor said in a surprised voice.

"Take your little sister over there near the bushes so she can pee."

"Why do I have—"

"—Just do it!" Ruth said impatiently.

Connor frowned and took Amy by the hand to lead her to some bushes nearby.

Ruth followed Beth who was already heading to the cabin door. They opened the door and looked inside. The place looked the same as it had on their earlier visit, only worse, with more animal droppings and cobwebs covering the floor and cabinets. "Well, it doesn't look like anyone's been here," Ruth said in a told-you-so type of voice. "We were probably the last humans to visit here."

"That's what it looks like," Beth said. "I just hope there's no critters living in here at the moment."

"What kind of critters?"

"Any kind."

Ruth followed Beth into the filthy cabin. They examined the interior, crinkling their noses at the musty smell of mildew and animal feces. Ruth's mind began to work. She glanced at her wristwatch and saw it was just a little after ten in the morning. They had planned to leave Ruth's home before sunrise that morning, getting them to Gold Tree late in the afternoon or early evening, but neither Beth nor Ruth could sleep the night before. They decided to leave that night, letting the children sleep in the backseat while they took turns driving. They arrived in Gold Tree way earlier than planned.

"Let's head into town and buy some cleaning supplies," Ruth said. "Maybe we can get this place livable for humans."

Beth knew this would be a good thing because it would keep Ruth's mind occupied instead of her just sitting around waiting and worrying. "Okay, let's do it," Beth said while going to the kitchen sink and turning on the faucet, not even getting a hint of hissing air from it. "We better remember to get some jugs of water."

"That's a great idea, Beth," Ruth said eagerly. "Let's make a list."

After loading everyone back into the Hyundai, they drove back down the dirt road toward Gold Tree. While Ruth drove, Beth pulled out a pencil and some paper from her purse to make a list of supplies for the cabin. Ruth's optimism made Beth happy. Truth was, Beth didn't know if Zeke was coming or not. She hoped he would because she cared about Ruth. But the only thing she knew about Zeke was what Ruth had told her, most of it about him trying to deal with the loss of his wife, Ruth's sister, and their infant son in a tragic car accident years ago.

After buying the cleaning supplies and a limited amount of groceries—mainly bread and sliced turkey for the kids—they drove the Hyundai back to the cabin. The women worked steadily, sweeping and mopping and wiping while the kids helped by beating the sofa cushions outside, creating huge clouds of dust that made them sneeze and laugh.

The hours went by quickly. Ruth and Beth took a break to make sandwiches for lunch. They ate on paper plates at the small dining table with the door and windows opened to help air out the cabin. Halfway into the lunch they all heard the car door slam shut. Connor and Amy immediately ran to the door while Ruth continued sitting at the table. She wasn't letting her hopes rise out of control. Not yet, at least.

Beth stood from the table and joined the kids at the door. They saw two men climb out of a black BMW. The man that got out from behind the wheel wore sunglasses with dark hair slicked back on his head. The other man had short, light-colored hair and was huge—at least six-foot-six or taller. The men hadn't noticed Beth and the kids standing at the door of the cabin.

Ruth joined them and looked at the men standing outside of the black car. She felt a moment of alarm until the rear door opened and another man stepped out. Ruth's knees nearly buckled when she saw him. The kids shouted Zeke's name at the same time and ran toward him. Ruth watched her brother-in-law lower to the ground to receive the hugs of his niece and nephew. She whispered "Zeke" as tears streamed down her face. Beth stepped aside to let Ruth pass as Zeke looked toward the door. Ruth took a few tentative steps toward him before changing her pace into a run. She joined Zeke and her children for the group hug that followed. Zeke was still in shock. He never imagined Ruth and her children greeting him at the cabin he hadn't seen in over two years. "Ruth, how did you know I was coming?"

Ruth didn't seem to hear the question. She was totally lost in her emotions. Zeke finally stood with the children hanging onto one side while Ruth clung to the other. He introduced Andrew and John to her and the children. It was a joyous moment for all. A moment anticipated for years. Beth watched it all from the cabin doorway with an approving expression written all over her face. She dabbed at a tear in her eye.

"There's sandwiches inside," Ruth said. "If anyone's hungry."

"I'm always hungry," John said with his trademark wide grin.

Zeke could only laugh. The whole scene appeared so surreal he thought he might be still asleep in the car, all this just a dream. A very wonderful dream.

As the group approached the cabin, Zeke saw the pretty woman standing at the door. They both made eye contact for a brief moment. Beth's smile nearly stopped Zeke in his tracks. He heard Ruth introduce the woman to John and Andrew but he didn't hear her name or the words they exchanged with each other. He was too distracted by the brunette's beauty and heart-stopping smile. When Zeke reached the door, Ruth introduced him to Beth. They shook hands, their eyes remaining locked onto each other's a bit longer than normal. Ruth noticed and was both surprised and pleased by it.

Zeke entered his old cabin, feeling like he was still in a dream. He saw they had been cleaning the place but his mind centered on something else; some distant memory trying to emerge. Ruth broke him out of it. "Zeke, how about a turkey sandwich?"

"Sure," he said, examining the cabin's main room as if it were a museum—a museum of memories from a life long gone. *Actually, fairly empty memories.*

The chatter in the room reached a crescendo after lunch was finished. Zeke walked outside to clear his thoughts. Ruth soon followed. She had too many questions to put off any longer. Zeke had a question or two himself. "Ruth, how did you know I would be here?"

"A man named Paul," she said. "Paul Stover."

Zeke blinked. *How was it possible?* "You know Paul Stover?"

Ruth explained how Paul ended up at the Lost Valley Church compound, his condition at the time, his visit to her office when he saw the photos of Zeke on her desk, and finally his phone call yesterday.

"You mean he's coming here?" Zeke asked in disbelief. "Today?"

"That's what he said," Ruth replied. "And he knew you would be here."

"How? I haven't seen him for years." That's when Zeke remembered that Paul Stover had also been in captivity with him; captivity by those hellish creatures, whoever they were. He also remembered Paul's rescue before his own rescue by . . . *an angel?*

Ruth needed to ask the question on her mind for so long. "Zeke, what happened to you? Where have you been?"

Zeke didn't know how to answer the entire question so he told her a short version of the trip to Austin, then heading to the relief camp to look for her and the children. "Some people at the camp thought they might have seen you and the kids," Zeke said. "One of them thought a man was with you. He mentioned something about a fight between the man and another man."

"That was Joe," she said.

"Joe?"

"He rescued us that night," Ruth explained. "A man tried to . . . have his way with me but Joe stopped him. Joe is the one who brought us to the safety of the Lost Valley Compound which became the church where I now work."

Zeke had a feeling he knew who she was talking about although he didn't know him by that name—or any name for that matter. "What did he look like, Ruth?"

Ruth gave him a brief physical description of the man she called Joe: the military garb, the demeanor, and especially the eyes. "He saved us, Zeke."

Zeke now knew for sure. The angel who rescued him and Stover had also rescued Ruth and the children. This angel then visited Andrew to bring them all here together today. Something burst into Zeke's mind like a bolt of lightning. "Shortly after 11-9," Zeke said, "I talked to a vagrant sitting on a bench in Gold Tree's little city park. The vagrant gave Billy some cheese crackers to eat."

Ruth almost gasped. She'd totally forgotten about Zeke's beloved German Shepherd. She now wondered what had happened to the dog.

"While I talked to the vagrant," Zeke continued, "I saw another man leaning against a tree across the park. For some reason I knew he was watching me. He'd been watching me, or I should say *watching over me* for a long time. He was the same one that rescued you, Ruth." Zeke looked into Ruth's eyes with a penetrating stare. "And he is no man, Ruth. He's an angel. Literally, an angel from heaven."

Ruth could hardly believe that her brother-in-law, Zeke, not the most religious man on Earth, was telling her about an angel from heaven rescuing them.

"You believe me, don't you?" he asked.

"Yes, Zeke," she said. "I believe you. And I've believed the same thing about *Joe* ever since I first met him."

"His name is really Joe?" Zeke asked.

"No," she said with a grin. "He was very evasive about his name. Then Amy said he looked like a GI Joe. That's how he got the name."

"That makes sense," Zeke added.

"Zeke," Ruth said. "What happened to Billy?"

Zeke shook his head somberly. "I don't know. That's one part of my memory still lost, the part after I left the relief camp looking for you. I only got the rest of my memory back a week or so ago." He wouldn't get into the part about his abduction yet. It was too early. They had just gotten back together. They should be celebrating.

Beth stuck her head out of the cabin. "Ruth? Sorry to bother you, but where are the paper towels we bought?"

"I think they're still in the trunk," Ruth shouted back before starting for her car.

"No," Beth insisted. "I'll get them while you two visit."

Ruth waved her off as she headed to the Hyundai for the paper towels.

Zeke walked toward the doorway. "Thanks for coming," he said to Beth, turning on his biggest smile and feeling foolish for it.

"No problem," Beth replied. "I wanted to. I'm just thrilled that you two have found each other. I know it means a lot to her and the kids."

Zeke nodded, trying to think of something else to say. "It looks like you guys have been busy trying to clean this rat-trap," he said. "You didn't have to do that."

Beth shrugged with her thousand-watt smile starting to grow on her face. "She was really worried you wouldn't show up. Me, too. It kept us busy until you got here."

Ruth arrived with the big package of paper towel rolls in her arms. The women proceeded to clean the table where everyone had eaten lunch. Connor saw Zeke at the door and ran to him. "Sure good to see you again, Uncle Zeke."

Zeke put his arm around the boy and led him outside. "It's good to see you, too," he said. "Let's go take a look at my wounded Jeep."

They walked to the Jeep sitting up on the cinderblocks.

"What happened to the wheels, Uncle Zeke?"

"They were stolen," Zeke said, managing to open the hood to inspect the motor. The battery was gone as he'd expected but the rest looked intact. "I'm not even sure how it got back here. I left it in the mountains a couple of years ago."

"You think it will still run?"

"Yeah, after a lot of work," he said. "And a lot of cash." Zeke approached the boy and invited him to sit on the ground with him. "I know you and Amy and your mom had a pretty rough time after 11-9."

"I don't know," the boy said shyly. "I guess a little."

"How old are you now?"

"I'll be twelve in August."

Zeke thought of Albright's boy, Matt. They were close to the same age. He wanted to tell Connor how hard he tried to get Houston after 11-9. He wanted to tell the boy how sorry he was that he wasn't able to find them, but he felt it was probably water-under-the-bridge by now, maybe had been for sometime. Maybe the time would arise in the future when he would tell him. "You want to help me fix it up?" Zeke asked.

"You mean the Jeep?" asked Connor, his face lighting up quickly.

"Yeah."

"Yes, sir! When?"

"Well, I got a few things to take care of first," Zeke explained, "but if I can get the parts today we could get started right away."

"Awesome!"

They stood and went inside the cabin. Ruth was talking to John and

Andrew while Amy helped Beth clean the kitchen table. Zeke approached Ruth and the men. They turned to him. "How you doing, Bro?" John asked.

"Great," Zeke said. "You think we could take a drive into town in a little while?"

"Absolutely," John said. "Me and Andrew here was just talking about finding a cheap motel before we leave tomorrow."

"Shouldn't be a problem," Zeke said. "The only motels here are cheap as far as I can remember."

"Is there a Laundromat in town?" Ruth asked. "We can clean the towels and bedsheets if there are."

"You don't have to do that, Ruth," Zeke said.

"I do if you want us to stay here," she replied with a grin.

Zeke hadn't planned on anyone staying at the cabin. He didn't even know if the place would still be standing until he saw it. "How about we go into town and check things out," Zeke said to John, "and then we'll call you in a couple of hours, Ruth. Do you have a cell phone?"

"Yes," Ruth said.

John opened his phone to tap in Ruth's number.

Zeke moved closer to Andrew. "Would you mind staying here, Andrew?" he said in a low voice. "I'd feel a lot better if they weren't left alone."

"Sure, Zeke. I don't mind at all."

"Thanks," Zeke said before turning to John. "Give me a minute. I need to find something."

Zeke went into the bedroom. He examined the sparse furnishings for a moment before heading to the chest-of-drawers against the wall. He opened the top drawer and rummaged through some papers and other trash. It seems that the looters took almost everything of value in the drawer which didn't amount to much. He went to another drawer that served as an unorganized file cabinet of records and other papers. In the pile of shuffled papers he found what he was looking for: a refill of checks for the checkbook he couldn't find. He put them in his pocket before heading back into the main room. He grabbed a box of matches off a table he'd seen earlier and went to the kitchen area. No one paid any attention to him as he entered the pantry and opened the false wall in back. He lighted a match and looked at all the items in his secret storage room. He reached on top of the gun-safe and grabbed his passport, knowing it would be there because he'd always kept it there. He opened it to make sure it was still valid. It was.

After leaving his secret room and pantry, Zeke approached John who was now chatting away with Ruth and Beth. Both women laughed loudly at one of his jokes.

"You ready?" Zeke asked him.

"Ready when you are," John said in an eager voice before excusing himself from the women.

As they started for the door, Zeke saw Connor looking at him with an expectant look on his face. "You want to come with us?" he asked the boy.

Connor grew a big smile. "Yes, sir!"

Zeke turned to Ruth for her permission. She'd already heard and said, "That's fine with me."

Zeke, John, and Connor left the cabin and climbed into the BMW. "Cool car!" Connor said after entering the backseat.

"Thanks!" John said. "It's Connor, right?"

"Yes, sir."

"Hey, manners!" John said. "I like that, Connor!"

"Thanks, sir."

They drove down the dirt road and headed into town. The first thing they did was stop at a small bank where Zeke went inside to cash a check. The young teller didn't recognize Zeke and wouldn't complete the transaction although Zeke had an account there along with a passport for identification. The teller went to her supervisor who helped Zeke get the money and a statement with his account information. He was pleased to find out he still had over twenty-seven thousand dollars in his account.

After cashing out five thousand dollars in hundreds and twenties, they next stopped at the *Little Cactus Inn,* the same motel Zeke stayed at when he first came to Gold Tree years ago. He booked three rooms with double queen beds with the option to extend the stay if necessary. The motel clerk assured him that the motel wasn't in an oversold situation and that would be fine. Zeke paid in advance with cash and returned to the BMW. "Everyone's got rooms for the evening," Zeke said. "Longer if you want them."

"Thanks," John said. "Where to now?"

"There used to be an auto parts store not far down the main drag," Zeke said. "If it's still there I'll buy a battery and a new set of wheels and tires for the Jeep."

"You got it."

As they drove down the drag, Zeke looked for the auto parts store but he couldn't find it. They saw another auto parts store and decided to try it when he noticed a road off the main drag not far away. He remembered where it led. It was the road leading to Steve Albright's mansion-sized cabin. The idea to drive to it came suddenly. "Hey, John. Take a right on that road up there, will you?"

"Sure."

They turned up the road and followed it until they reached Albright's large home.

"Wow," John commented. "Nice spread. You know the folks that live here?"

"I did at one time," Zeke said, noticing a realtor's *For Sale* sign in the front lawn. "Give me a minute. I need to check something out."

"No problem."

Zeke got out of the BMW and walked toward the home's large front entrance supported by huge cedar logs. Everything appeared exactly as he remembered it. The exterior looked well-kept but he sensed the interior was vacant. He was surprised when he saw someone on one end of the large porch, sitting on the wood planks while huddled over a book, apparently reading and not noticing Zeke at all.

Zeke approached the porch. After going up the steps Zeke saw that it was a man. A baldheaded man. The man looked up from the book and said, "What took you so long?"

It took Zeke just a moment for it to register. "Paul?" he finally said. "Is it really you?"

Paul Stover smiled and stood to his feet, a Bible in his left hand. "How many other slick-tops named Paul do you know?"

"Not many!" Zeke said before reaching out and embracing him.

"Surprised?" Stover said after the hug.

"Yes, but I shouldn't be," Zeke said. "Ruth told me you would be here. In Gold Tree, I mean. Not here at this house. We were looking for an auto parts store when I saw the road leading up here. I remembered where it led. We drove up on a fluke."

Paul nodded with that smile Zeke remembered. "There are no flukes."

"That's right," Zeke said with a laugh. After a short pause he asked, "Where is Albright? You seen him recently? How about Matt?"

Stover's mood seemed to darken a bit. "I haven't seen him since you saw him last," he said. "But I learned he and Matt left the country a while ago."

Zeke sensed something wrong. "Why do you think he did that, Paul?"

"To escape from his conscious," Stover said. "If he still has one."

Zeke stared at Stover for a long moment. "What did he do, Paul?"

"Well, for one thing, he sold out his best friend to those monsters," Stover said. "He sold you out, too."

Zeke let it sink in before asking, "He was working with them?"

"Not directly. Through government channels I believe. Doesn't matter, though. He knew we would most likely never be seen again."

"Why would he do that, Paul?"

"Because he gave in to his greed," Stover said. "There were dozens of government contracts we tried to get for years but couldn't. Then in the months and weeks before 11-9 those contracts came easily, making ADS extremely successful and Steve Albright a multibillionaire."

Zeke tried to sort what he was hearing. "Paul, are you saying he was somehow responsible for 11-9?"

"He was definitely in collusion with certain government officials who were responsible."

"You think our own government orchestrated an EMP explosion?"

"Yes," Stover said. "Although I can't prove it, I know without any doubt that it was an inside job."

"But why?" Zeke asked. "Why would they do that?"

"To get control," Stover said. "People are easier to control when they are afraid. You see, during 11-9's aftermath people were concerned about just surviving; getting food and water, having shelter, the basics of life. They weren't able to pay attention to the changes going on inside our government, changes that are being discovered only now, a bit too late I'm afraid."

"What kind of changes?"

"Security clearances mainly," Stover said, "and the legislation to enable those clearances. All the changes will eventually enable our ugly lizard friends and their little gray companions to take part in running not only our nation but the entire world."

Zeke asked the question he'd been wanting to ask, the question that could only be answered by someone who had been there. "Were they real,

Paul?" He tried to rephrase the question. "I know they were real, but what I mean is, something about their appearance seemed phony. Like they were wearing costumes or something."

"Or disguises," Stover offered. "I know exactly what you mean. Here's what I think: They are real entities, but their reptilian and little gray man appearances are for our benefit. But why I don't know."

"That's exactly the feeling I had at the time," Zeke agreed. "And I still feel the same way now."

"Their appearance really doesn't matter, though," Stover said. "They are definitely real forces with definite evil intentions."

"What do they want?" Zeke asked. "To take over the world?"

"Their Master already has control of the world."

"Satan?"

"Yes," Stover said, "but he doesn't have control over the *true* people of God. The *aliens* sudden entrance into the picture will cause what they call *The Great Apostasy*, causing many Christians to fall from their faith because these supposed extraterrestrial alien visitors will tell everyone that *they* created life on Earth, a lie from the pit of hell. You see, they're really just spirits of the nephilim, the fallen angels and their abominable offspring, readying themselves for battle with God in the end times. But people will eat up the bit about them being aliens from another galaxy or whatever—aliens who seeded our planet and have come back to save it from destruction."

"Paul," Zeke said. "How do you know all this?"

"He told me."

"Who?"

"You know who," Stover said. "The one Ruth calls Joe. The one who rescued me. He's taught me many things. That's why he rescued me, Zeke."

"He rescued me, too."

"So I see."

"Most of what he taught me was to be passed on to you," Stover said.

"Why me, Paul? Why does he want me to know anything?"

"Because you are a key element in the strategy against the nephilim."

"How can that be?" Zeke said, his voice rising in frustration. "I'm nobody! I'm just an aging foot soldier who hasn't accomplished anything! I'm worthless!"

"Not according to God."

"I can't even keep a woman!" Zeke ranted, trying to ignore what Stover was telling him. "I'm a loser!"

Stover waited for Zeke to calm down.

John and Connor suddenly appeared at the porch. John examined the situation to make sure everything was okay. "You good, Zeke?" he said, looking squarely at Stover.

"Yes," Zeke said. "John, this is Paul Stover. Paul, John Campise."

John and Stover nodded at each other.

Connor said, "You're the one who called my mom and told us to come here."

"That's right," Stover said. "And you must be Connor."

"Yes, sir."

"Nice to meet you, Connor."

"Same here," the boy said.

"Would you wait for me in the car just a little longer?" Zeke asked John. "You mind?"

"Not at all," John said. "Come on, Connor. Let's give them a moment to talk."

Zeke watched John and the boy walk back to the BMW. He turned to Stover and asked, "What am I supposed to do, Paul?"

"Make a decision," Stover replied.

"A decision about what?"

"To come to Christ or not," Stover said plainly. "To except him as your personal savior or to reject him. It's up to you."

Zeke stared back into Stover's eyes.

"But it has to be your choice," Stover continued. "A genuine choice from your heart. If you choose to reject him, this burden involving the nephilim will be removed from you. You can go back to your life the way it was before."

Zeke felt a heat rising from his chest to his throat.

"But you need to know something, Zeke," Stover said. "This may be the last chance. If a voice inside you is urging you at this very moment, please don't ignore it. It may never come to you again."

The heat rising from Zeke's chest into his throat was now engulfing his face. He felt tears starting to stream down his cheeks. He felt helpless to stop them. "How, Paul?"

"Come to him in faith," Stover said. "The faith of a little child. Just say: Jesus, thank you for shedding your blood for me on the cross."

Zeke dropped to his knees on the wood planks of the porch. He closed his eyes and repeated Stover's words as he heard them.

"Forgive me of my sins and make me into a new creation," Stover continued.

"Forgive me of my sins and . . ."

John and Connor stood outside the BMW. "What are they doing?" Connor asked. "Is Uncle Zeke all right?"

"He is now," John said as he stared at the scene on the porch. "He is now."

*   *   *

THIRTY THREE

The morning sun streamed through the trees onto Zeke's little cabin and his nearly repaired Jeep nearby. He and Connor had already mounted new wheels and tires using an old rusty jack found in some tall weeds behind the cabin to lower the vehicle off the cinderblocks. They'd put a new battery in earlier that morning, their third day of being in Gold Tree. John and Andrew had left in the BMW early yesterday after a wonderful celebration at a local restaurant the night before. The celebration at the restaurant was for everyone coming into one another's lives, but especially for Zeke's acceptance of Christ—a miracle that Zeke could barely express into words. Little did he know that two other miracles were just around the corner.

The first miracle—although he hadn't realized it yet—had already started at the celebration in the restaurant. The restaurant, *Uno Amigo*, a Mexican-food diner with after hours musical entertainment and dancing in the form of a juke box and a dance floor had been nearly empty until Zeke and his entourage arrived. Ruth had noticed Zeke and Beth making eyes at each other throughout dinner so after they'd finished eating Ruth encouraged him to ask Beth for a dance during a slow ballad playing on the juke box. During the dance they kissed lightly. It happened so fast. The last thing Zeke expected to happen on the day he became a Christian was to fall in love with a woman. But he believed he had. And from the way Beth looked back at him he believed she had fallen in love, too.

The second miracle was coming any moment now. Zeke and Connor took a break from working on his Jeep. There seemed to be some type of problem in the electrical wiring and Connor got bored and went into the cabin while Zeke continued working. He tired of it himself a few minutes later, deciding he might have to get a mechanic to come out and fix it. While sitting on the ground and drinking a lukewarm soda, he thought he detected movement through the trees in the direction of the dirt road climbing to his cabin. When he noticed the movement again he stood to his feet to get a better look. Slowly it came into view. A dog. Moving slow. It looked a bit worn and exhausted as it lumbered up the road toward him.

"Billy?" Zeke said to himself before dropping the soda can to the ground. The haggard-looking German Shepherd began wagging his tail as he came closer. A slow wag but steady nevertheless.

Zeke ran to him and dropped to his knees, taking Billy into his arms and weeping harder than he ever had in his life. The dog whined and licked the tears from Zeke's face. The moment seemed to last forever. It could have been minutes or hours, Zeke couldn't tell. Or care. All he knew now was how it felt to be truly blessed. He really did feel like a new creation of God.

While weeping with joy and hugging his long lost dog, Zeke shouted toward the blue sky above him in a loud, clear voice. "Thank you, Father! Thank you, thank you, thank you!"

*　　*　　*

THIRTY FOUR

Zeke made the decision to accompany Beth, Ruth, and the kids back to their home north of Houston. The kids had already missed enough school and Ruth and Beth needed to get back to work. He and Paul Stover rode together in the Jeep after finally getting the electrical fixed by a mechanic in town.

During the trip, Stover made Zeke memorize what he called the *timeframe*—the season and year of the nephilim's supposed return. "During this timeframe," Stover explained, "is when all the world leaders are going to be breaking the big news to everyone: the news about Earth's newest friends arriving from a distant planet or galaxy. At first there will be great fear. Then there will be celebration as we learn they came to save the planet. Most humans will totally believe it without question."

"Did Joe tell you this?" Zeke asked.

"He took me to see Robert Margolian in Turkey," Stover replied. "The season and year came from copies of the nephilim's stone carvings made by Noah's grandson, Kainam—the ones Margolian found in his excavation. Joe took me there specifically to get it from Margolian."

"You saw Margolian?" Zeke marveled. "In Turkey?"

"Yes."

After a long pause, Zeke said, "You don't happen to know what I'm supposed to do with this . . . timeframe, do you?"

"When the time comes you will know," Stover assured him, wondering about the last task on his list and when it would happen. "It will probably be revealed to you in a dream."

"It's all so far away," Zeke said. "I wonder if I'll still be alive by then?"

Stover shrugged his shoulders, knowing it would not make a difference if Zeke was still alive or not—something Stover kept to himself.

Halfway into the trip both vehicles stopped for gas. After gassing up their vehicles, Beth rode with Zeke while Paul rode with Ruth and the kids. Zeke figured that Ruth and Paul had orchestrated the swap so he and Beth could have some time together—which was perfectly fine with him. Zeke and Beth were totally comfortable with each other in conversation and equally comfortable not saying a word as the miles went by.

Somewhere into the trip they began holding hands. Zeke had never been happier in his life. He was honestly excited about his new life and what kind of path God would take him. He couldn't possibly imagine that this was just the beginning of a newfound joy which was going to grow even larger in his future. He felt complete now. He knew he would never be alone again, regardless of what the Lord had in store for him.

*　*　*

EPILOGUE
Thirty Five Years Later

The offices of *ZAEA* were spartan but expansive, taking up most of the seventh floor of a twelve-story glass atrium building on the West Loop, a prestigious business and shopping area not far from downtown Houston. The centerpiece of this fast-growing evangelical association known as the *ZAEA* was none other than its namesake: Ezekiel Allenby, Jr., known to most of America as simply Zeke Allenby, the most famous evangelist in the country. At thirty-three years of age Allenby was quickly becoming the *Billy Graham* of the twenty-first century. In fact, the *Zeke Allenby Evangelistic Association* had built itself based on Graham's business and ethical model, and had tripled in growth in each of its five years of existence, something that staggered the minds of everyone, including Allenby himself.

As he sat behind his desk and stared at the West Houston skyline beyond his seventh floor window, Allenby thought about how much he missed his father who had passed away barely a month ago. He also thought of his mother who died four years earlier. He wished she could've seen how much the ministry had grown since then. He lowered his head in prayer, thanking God for giving him such wonderful parents who raised him with so much love and taught him the Word of God.

Allenby raised his head and stared at the holographic display projected above his desk—the display that listed his schedule. *The schedule*. So tightly compacted were the myriad of events he planned to fulfill throughout the year that it was enough to make most people fatigued just thinking about it. The travel schedule alone was exhausting.

The main events of the *ZAEA* were *The Zeke Allenby Awakenings*, the cornerstones of the ministry. Reaching thousands of people for days and weeks at a time at various venues across the United States and Canada, the *Awakening's* program was patterned after the *Billy Graham Crusades* of the last century but with modernized worship music and more casual dress by all involved. But the message was the same. Bold and direct with a sense of humility. And Allenby delivered it with such sincerity and humility that he won over many who heard him preach and most who got to know him on a personal basis.

Booked around these *Awakenings* were scores of personal appearances on radio and television, along with speaking engagements at churches and universities and business conventions throughout the country. Allenby was a busy man. And yet his plans were to grow even busier if that was actually possible. He hoped to eventually hold *Awakenings* throughout the world, especially in Third World countries where the message was being suppressed by various leaders in those regions. Even though satellite television was available practically everywhere around the globe these days, he knew that the message carried in person was just as powerful. Thousands and thousands of people attending these *Awakenings* felt that Zeke was speaking to them personally. This special characteristic of message delivery had been shared by most of the great speakers in history, including his role model, Billy Graham. And Zeke Allenby had plenty of it.

Through the association's meticulous record-keeping of converts who *came forward* and filled out cards after accepting Christ at the *Awakenings*, an unusually high percentage of former Muslims was discovered at the very beginning of his ministry. For some reason Allenby drew more converts from Islam than any other evangelist past or present. He knew his gift would be best exercised in Muslim countries, mainly in the Middle East, but also throughout Europe where Islam had grown so rapidly over the last half-century. So the hope to take the *Awakenings* everywhere on the planet burned in him continuously, and was at the core of the ministry's prayers. They needed international connections and finances, and he was sure God would provide them when the time was right.

Zeke Allenby looked at his post-screened mailbox on the holographic display and scrolled through his messages. One of the messages caught his eye. It was from his personal secretary, McKenzie, stating that a package awaited him in the outer office. *'Possibly a manuscript'* the note read, *'from a law office in Chicago.'*

He closed the display and left his office. He saw that McKenzie was away from her desk at the moment but the white package sat beside her chair. He looked at the return address label on the package, saw the name of a law firm he didn't recognize, and for a moment wondered if it was a legal brief for a lawsuit being filed against him for one reason or another. Sometimes it felt like the whole world was out to get him, not just the secular world but from the world of so-called *believers* and fellow Christians who despised everything about him from his voice to the way he wore his hair—not to mention the way he preached the Gospel.

Allenby took the package back to his office and checked his schedule on the display again. He'd be in his office all morning working on the last book in a series he'd written over the last several years entitled *'Apologetics'*—all of them bestsellers to date. At lunchtime, he and Nathan, the association's CFO, had a meeting with some potential contributors at a posh restaurant near the Galleria.

Allenby opened the package and saw a large envelope inside with a single page letter clipped to it. He unclipped the letter and looked at the envelope. The name *'Zeke Allenby, Jr.'* was written on the cover in black marker. He turned his attention back to the letter. As he read, he realized this was not about any lawsuit but about a package from his deceased father, Zeke, Sr. The author of the letter, an attorney, explained that arrangements with the firm had been made years ago to hold the package until Zeke Sr.'s death where it would then be turned over to Zeke, Jr.

Allenby set the letter on his desk and opened the old envelope with his name written in black marker. Inside was a two-inch stack of papers that looked like a manuscript. The page on top revealed that it had been written by his father. He turned to the first page and began reading. He became engrossed in the story, oblivious to the time on the antique grandfather clock ticking away on the far wall of his office.

Two hours later McKenzie's voice came through invisible speakers in the room, reminding him of his leave-time for lunch with Nathan and the investors.

"I won't be able to make the lunch, McKenzie," he told her. "Tell Nathan he'll have to handle it on his own. Something very important has come up. I know I have those TV spots to do later today. What time does the taping start?"

"Four-thirty," she said. "But you need to leave by three-thirty to get there in time for make-up."

"Okay," Allenby said. "Come and get me at three-thirty but make sure to clear everything until then."

"Okay . . ." McKenzie said with plenty of question in her voice.

"Thanks, McKenzie."

Allenby went back to the manuscript, marveling at the unbelievable events unfolding in the story, especially the parts about his father's abduction by what appeared to be alien beings, and later his relationship with a woman named Sabrina, a real-life member of a witches' coven. If this hadn't been written by his father he would've never believed it, thinking it was just some fanciful work of fiction. But he knew his father's voice and even though he was reading words on paper he recognized his father's tone and phrasing which came through loud and clear. And one thing everyone who knew his father believed without a shadow of a doubt: The man didn't know how to lie. Period.

Allenby had blown right through the lunch hour without stopping. He glanced at the grandfather clock knowing he still had plenty of time to finish before leaving for the TV taping. He was nearing the end of the manuscript, at the part when his father first met his mother. His father had just been reunited with his beloved dog, Billy, and they had left the cabin in Gold Tree to move near Aunt Ruth's place north of Houston. Not long afterwards his father married Beth Tyler and they moved into a cozy three-bedroom home not far from the Lost Valley Church—the same house and church Allenby grew up in.

But an event was told here that he'd never heard before from either of his parents. Apparently, it happened shortly after his mother and father were married but before he was born. Allenby read his father's words:

'Paul Stover was visiting that Sunday after church. It was a gorgeous summer day, cooler and less humid than normal. We were in the backyard, preparing to grill some steaks. Ruth and Beth were inside the kitchen, cutting vegetables or something when we heard a commotion inside the kitchen through the screen door. Paul was closest to the door so he ran in first. By the time I came in behind him he was already lunging for the woman with the gun pointing at your mother, the assassin's intended target. The gun went off but Paul blocked it, preventing your mother from being shot, taking the bullet himself directly in the chest. I screamed for Ruth to get your mother out of the house and helped shove them both out the screen door behind me. I stared at Paul lying there and I shouted out for someone, anyone, to call 911. I tried to talk Sabrina into dropping the gun, telling her it was over, knowing that every second that went by could be Paul's last. He was bleeding heavily on the kitchen floor. Sabrina smiled at me and raised the gun. I thought I was finished but she brought the barrel to her mouth and pulled the trigger, ending her own life with a bullet to the brain. I rushed to Paul's side. He was still conscious, but barely. "Hang in there, buddy," I encouraged him. Paul was fading fast but he managed to say, "My task is finished, Zeke. You and Beth will have a baby boy. The boy is the reason, Zeke. Remember the timeframe? Give him the timeframe when he's grown." And with that, my friend, Paul Stover, took his last breath.'

Allenby looked up from the manuscript. *I'm the reason? For what?*

He turned to the last page and saw a handwritten letter from his father. The date on the letter read May 7, 2037. *That was,* Allenby did the math, *thirteen years ago.* He began to read the letter:

> To my Beloved Son,
>
> Words can't describe how much I love you and your Mother so I won't try here, but what I want you to know is this: the crazy story you've just read is completely true. Long before you were born, even before I had met your Mother, this Mighty Angel, the one we called Joe, had been working in our lives for one particular reason . . . you. I didn't understand it at the time of course, but it was revealed to me much later when the time was right, just like now I'm revealing it to you for the first time, because the time is right.
>
> Here goes: God knew from the beginning of time that he would make you a powerful disciple and teacher of the Gospel of Jesus Christ. He knew that he would use you in the great spiritual war coming in the last days. Groups of fallen angels, the nephilim, demonic spirits, or whatever you wish to call them, will appear in great numbers on Earth not long before Christ's return. But they will appear in the form of aliens from a distant galaxy, fulfilling the century old belief of UFOs held by millions of humans around the world. Their arrival will be huge. All media outlets around the world will cover nothing else but this story. At first there will be

great fear throughout the human race, but soon the aliens themselves will reveal the purpose of their arrival in the form of a huge lie: to save the planet from destruction by wars, pollution, climate change, and so on. They want to be our friends! Ha! Their real purpose of course is to lead astray as many souls as possible from the love and gift of Jesus Christ. This is their main purpose, orchestrated by none other than their master, the Accuser himself.

From the beginning of the nephilim's arrival, many people will start to look up to them as if they were Gods. The nephilim love this. They will feed the masses what the masses want to hear, supporting concepts like Humanism, Universalism, and Evolution to pull away from God as many souls as possible by encouraging the disbelief of His existence.

Your purpose, Son, is to not only draw as many souls as possible to God through his Son, Jesus Christ, but to reveal the nephilim's plan to the entire world. They have been planning this for thousands of years, and for reasons unknown to us, they must do this within a certain timeframe. This is the reason they came after me and many others, something I couldn't understand at the time. Although I will never understand how they knew, they knew that if they stopped souls like you from coming into existence they would have little resistance to their scheme in the last days. So know this, you are not the only one burdened by this responsibility. There will be others from around the world trying to prevent the nephilim from deceiving humanity, but many will still be deceived. Many followers of Christ will also be deceived and will fall away from their faith. In referring to the end times, Jesus warned us to not be deceived. I believe Jesus was speaking of many things that would happen before the end, but I believe the nephilim's lie is a big part of it.

There is a special weapon for you in exposing the nephilim and their plot to corrupt humanity. The weapon is the "timeframe" of their arrival: Fall 2053 AD on our calendar. I have found it interesting that if you start the date of the seven year Tribulation in 2053, you end up with the 2060 date that Sir Isaac Newton believed would be the year of Christ's Return, calculated by Newton centuries ago from codes he claimed to decipher in the books of Daniel and Revelation of the Bible.

At any rate, when you begin warning the world in the years and months before the nephilim's arrival, many will scoff at you, but many will also believe, and many more will see the truth when the nephilim arrive during the timeframe. It is not unlike preaching the Gospel in ordinary times, Son. Some will believe, some will not. It's their choice. It's your job to deliver the message. It's the listener's job to choose.

Until we reunite in Heaven, God bless you—

Zeke Allenby, Sr.

Allenby broke down in tears. The emotions were strong concerning this final message from his father. He let his emotion's run their course. A moment later he dried his eyes with a tissue and returned his attention to his father's letter.

"Fall 2053 AD," Allenby said to himself in a whisper. *Only three years from now. Not much time really.* A voice inside him in the form of a thought tried to rationalize the situation. *Was Dad going through a period of mental instability when he wrote this? Not only the letter but the story, too?*

Allenby rebuked the voice in his mind. *My father was the most sane, honest man I have ever known,* he told himself. He thought about evidence supporting his father's story. From as far back as early childhood, everything he'd read and seen regarding UFOs in countless magazines and books and television specials seemed to fit together with what was happening in the world today. The reports of benevolent aliens visiting Earth from reputable sources had increased exponentially in the last ten years or so. It was hard to watch the news or read an article in any magazine or newspaper that didn't at least mention something about increasing UFO sightings from around the world. One thing he definitely knew for sure: his father was sound of mind and more lucid than most people until the day he died of a sudden heart attack.

Allenby called McKenzie with a touch of a button built into his desk.

"Yes, sir?" her voiced sounded in his office.

"Can you get me a phone number for the law firm that sent me this package?" Allenby asked.

"Of course," she said. Less than a minute later she called back with the number.

Allenby placed the call to the law firm. After the receptionist at the law firm answered, Allenby said, "Matthew Albright, please. This is Zeke Allenby."

A moment later a man's voice came on the line. "Mr. Allenby," he said in an even tone. "What a pleasant surprise. My condolences to you and your family for your loss."

"Thank you," Allenby said. "I appreciate you taking this call. I know you must be very busy, Mr. Albright."

"Not too busy for you," Matt said. After a short pause he said, "I suppose the reason you are calling has something to do with the package we sent you. Is everything satisfactory with it?"

"Yes," Allenby said. "I was just wondering if you know who dealt with my father when he made arrangements for this package to be sent to me. I'd like to ask him a few questions if possible. Do you know who it might have been?"

There was a moment of hesitation on the other end before Matt said, "Actually, it was me who made the arrangements."

"Oh," Allenby said. "That simplifies things a bit."

"You see," Matt said. "I knew your father when I was young. I didn't know him for very long but the time I spent with him was very special, something I'll never forget."

"How did you know him?"

"He escorted my father and myself and another man across Texas during the 11-9 catastrophe in 2015," Matt said. "I was eleven at the time."

Lightbulbs began flashing in Allenby's mind. *This was the kid! The kid in the story!*

"After getting us safely to Austin," Matt continued, "your father went to look for his sister-in-law in Houston."

"Aunt Ruth," Allenby said more to himself than to the lawyer.

"Yes," Matt said. "Ruth. Anyway, we never heard from him again. My father and I went looking for him in Gold Tree sometime later but we never found him. I didn't see him again until he showed up at my office over a decade ago. That's when we made the arrangements for the package to be sent to you when he died. I was surprised that he even remembered me after all those years. He must have done a fair amount of research just to find me, and I still don't know why he wanted *me* to handle it. He said it was because he trusted me. Funny, we only knew each other for a couple of days, with me still being a kid and all yet he still trusted me for some reason."

"He must have thought a lot of you," Allenby said.

"Well," Matt said. "I definitely thought a lot of him."

Allenby asked the first question he had on his mind. "Mr. Albright, do you know about the contents of the package you sent me?"

"I do not," said Matt. "I only know that it was a sealed envelope loaded with some type of document or documents with your name written on the envelope's exterior."

"When my father made these arrangements," Allenby said, "did he tell you anything about what happened after you had last seen him? When you were a kid?"

After a moment of thought Matt said, "I believe I said something to him about looking for him and wondering what happened to him but he didn't respond and I didn't press the issue."

Allenby was careful how he asked the next question. "Mr. Albright—"

"—Please call me Matt."

"Matt . . . are you familiar with my ministry?"

"Yes," Matt replied. "And I don't think there's anyone in this country who hasn't heard your name or seen your face."

"Is it possible for me to come meet with you in Chicago?" Allenby asked. "I would like to share something with you that I think you will find very interesting . . . especially since it appears you were part of it."

"You've definitely made me curious," Matt said. "Okay, when would you like to meet?"

"As soon as possible."

"I'm in court the day after tomorrow," Matt said while apparently checking his schedule. "We could meet—"

"—What about tomorrow?" Allenby suggested.

Matt chuckled. "Well . . ." he said while still checking his schedule, "I'm actually free tomorrow afternoon after two."

"Great!" Allenby said. "I'll pick you up at your office and maybe you can suggest someplace we can have coffee and a private discussion."

"Okay, Mr. Allenby," Matt said with a friendly laugh. "I'll set it all up."

"Call me Zeke."

"Okay, Zeke. See you tomorrow."

"Oh," Allenby said, suddenly remembering something. "If I send you a data file of the contents of the package, can you read it tonight?"

"How long is it?"

"I don't know," Allenby said. "Twenty-thousand words or so, I guess."

"That doesn't give me much time," Matt said, "but I'll do my best."

"Fair enough."

"See you then."

"Okay, thanks again." Allenby ended the call and grabbed his suit jacket from a rack by the door. He left his office and saw McKenzie rising from her chair.

McKenzie had a small build with extremely curly brown hair. The large lenses in her eyeglasses gave her an owlish look. "Perfect timing," she said while grabbing her briefcase and leading him and a young African-American male intern named Wingate to the elevators outside the offices.

Allenby liked to involve his staff as much as possible with his schedule, believing it was an invaluable lesson in the workings of the ministry. It also helped enforce one of the first rules the *ZAEA* had created in its formation: that Zeke Allenby would never be alone with a woman other than his wife, Gail, whether it be in a hotel room or office or restaurant or elevator or anywhere. Allenby learned the practice from Billy Graham's example. It had prevented that type of scandal from *ever* occurring in Graham's sixty years of ministry—something other ministries would have been wise to follow over the decades since. Of course, these days a man accused of some impropriety while being alone with another man was fairly commonplace—something that in Graham's day would have been almost too outrageous for the media to cover. If a person or persons wanted to accuse him of something, they could. There's nothing anybody could do about that. Although the press loved to see supposed *Men of God* brought down in shame, Allenby believed that ultimately the truth would prevail in such circumstances. He put all that firmly in God's hands.

"Book two flights to Chicago early tomorrow morning, Wingate," Allenby said while tying a necktie around his neck. "One for me and one for you. Business class if they're available. And book a car and driver to pick us up at the airport. No limo or anything too fancy. A plain sedan will do."

Wingate began typing notes into his cell phone. "Yes, sir."

Allenby looked at McKenzie. "Can you assist him if he needs help?"

"Of course," McKenzie said.

"I think I can handle it, sir," Wingate said. "Actually, I know I can."

Allenby smiled at Wingate before turning to McKenzie and saying, "Would you please call Gail and tell her I won't be able to make the meeting at Lindsay's school tomorrow. Tell her I will explain at dinner tonight."

"Got it," McKenzie said.

"Oh," Allenby said, suddenly remembering the manuscript. "When you get back I want you and you only to make a scanned data copy of the manuscript on my desk, the one that came in the package this morning from that law firm in Chicago. Send the data file ASAP to the firm . . . no, on second thought, send it to the lawyer's personal email. It's on his letter with the manuscript. Make sure it's labeled *confidential*."

"I'll take care of it when I get back," McKenzie assured him.

As the elevator door opened and they stepped inside, the burden of preaching end-time prophecy fully registered with Allenby. Especially this prophecy with its UFO and alien connection. He knew he had to overcome any stumbling blocks of his own before he could begin. He was eager to talk to this lawyer, Matthew Albright, and pick his brain on a few details regarding certain parts of the story in the manuscript.

Allenby thought about all of this as they rode the elevator down to the building's parking level. Of course, the bigger message behind all of this was Christ's return. Allenby's father said this alien invasion would occur sometime in the Fall, 2053, *'. . . not long before Christ's return.'* Allenby believed that no one knew the *exact* time of Christ's return because Jesus himself said in Matthew 24: 36: *'No one knows about that day or hour, not even the angels of heaven, nor the Son, but only the Father.'* Allenby suddenly thought about the following verse: Matthew 24: 37: *'As it was in the days of Noah, so will it be at the coming of the Son of Man.'*

Allenby remembered the part in his father's manuscript about the archeologist discovering copies of the nephilim's stone carvings made by Noah's grandson. The connection between Matthew 24: 37 and the nephilim's deceptive invasion three years from now didn't escape Allenby. Another thought came to mind and caused his skin to tingle: *We could be the generation that sees Christ's return!*

*

Matt Albright left his office and entered the firm's large reception area where the young and charismatic evangelist, Zeke Allenby, waited to greet him. Allenby was as handsome as he appeared on TV, but in person, Matt could see the resemblance to Zeke, Sr. much better now. It was something in the way Allenby stood or tilted his head as he spoke. It was hard to pinpoint exactly.

"Zeke Allenby," Matt said with a sincere smile while approaching the famous evangelist. He shook Allenby's hand in a robust handshake. "It's an honor to finally meet you."

"Same here," Allenby replied with a subtle grin similar to his father's. "Thank you so much for agreeing to meet with me on such short notice." He saw that Matt had a head of thinning hair that was starting to turn gray at the temples. He also noticed that the lawyer appeared to be in good shape for a man in his forties.

After introducing Wingate to Matt, Allenby said, "Well, shall we go?"

Matt became aware of the reception area starting to fill up with employees eager to get a glimpse of the famous preacher. "Yes," he said while opening the glass door. "Follow me."

Allenby nodded goodbye to the crowd of onlookers as he and Wingate followed Matt out the door. A few moments later the preacher and the lawyer chatted on the sidewalk while Wingate called the driver to pick them up at the curb in the rented sedan.

Allenby and Matt rode in back while Wingate rode in front with the driver. The sedan pulled up to the front of the historic Drake Hotel in Chicago. Allenby and Matt climbed out of the sedan as Wingate stayed with the driver. The meeting between the preacher and the lawyer would be private.

The door attendant greeted them and ushered them inside where the Drake's concierge led them to the Palm Court, advertised as the *'best spot in the Drake Hotel'* for many decades. Famous for its afternoon tea, finger sandwiches, and live harpist, Matt had used the Palm Court many times to entertain clients over the years. It usually didn't get too crowded until later in the day, so for a while they would have some privacy.

They sat at a table on the far side of the room. After they had ordered coffee, Allenby got right into it. "So did you get a chance to read it?"

"I did," Matt replied. "Once I started I couldn't put it down."

"So what did you think of it?"

"It's incredible," Matt declared. "And even more incredible for me since I'm actually a part of it."

"Matt, the part about his abduction." he said. "The beings. Do you think my father was delusional when he wrote this?"

"No."

"So you believe him?"

Matt wasn't surprised by the question. He leaned close to Allenby across the table. "Not only do I believe his story," he said in a low voice, "it also answers questions I've had ever since that trip across Texas with your father when I was just a boy."

Allenby *was* surprised. He'd half expected the lawyer to suggest that his father had become a *little eccentric* while writing the manuscript. A waiter brought their coffee to the table and poured it into fragile china cups.

After the waiter left, Matt said in the same low voice, "I can even add a few events I experienced during and after the 11-9 trip that actually support your father's story. There's one event in particular during the trip across Texas that I don't believe your father was even aware of. Or Paul Stover."

"You knew Paul Stover well?" asked Allenby.

"Yes," Matt said. "He was more of a father to me than my own father." Some emotion came into his voice. "It seems I learned the most important things in life from Paul, including what little I know about God and religion."

Allenby made a mental note to come back to that later. "So you knew him when he was killed?"

"No," Matt said. "I just learned of Paul's death from your father's manuscript. Paul disappeared around the same time your father disappeared when they left Austin. From your father's manuscript, I now know what happened to both of them. My suspicions of my father's role in their disappearances seems to be confirmed as well."

Allenby knew there was a lot more to this story than he currently understood but he wanted to stay on course for the moment. "I'm sorry for interrupting," he told Matt. "You said there was one event in particular during the trip across Texas that supports my dad's story."

"Yes," Matt said. "I believe it was the first night of the trip. We were camping near a creek. I took the dirty dishes down to the creek to wash them. Your father's German Shepherd, Billy, went with me. While I was cleaning some plates at the edge of the creek I looked up and saw an unusual light in the sky. It looked like a green ball descending from the sky. Now you have to remember, this was right after 11-9 and there were no airplanes flying in the sky yet. Anyway, I watched this green ball of light for a moment until it suddenly disappeared. While looking for it in the night sky I noticed some trees across the creek beginning to sway. I also noticed that the trees on either side of those swaying trees were not moving at all, ruling out the possibility of wind causing the swaying motion. My heart started pounding big time when the ball reappeared across the creek, hovering about ten feet above the ground not fifty feet away from me. Here I was an eleven year old boy washing some camp dishes in the dark at the edge of a creek, all alone and scared. Your father had given me a flashlight. I remember aiming it at Billy and seeing him staring and growling at that ball of light, knowing instinctively there was something malicious about it. Anyway, I remember the feeling I got while staring at it. Its interior seemed to swirl with this green, tendril-looking mess. The description your father gave of the atmosphere where he was held captive reminded me exactly of those green tendrils. They seemed to be drawing me closer. I couldn't seem to look away although I wanted to more than anything in the world. As the ball got closer I remember thinking that I saw some type of face in all that green mess. A face of a snake or lizard or something similar." Matt paused to sip his coffee before continuing. "Then a voice in my head said, 'RUN! RUN! RUN!' Which I did. I was too scared to wait for Billy. As I ran back to camp I could hear him barking, wondering if he was fighting the thing inside the ball of light. By the time I reached camp all scared and out of breath, Billy came trotting up behind me as if nothing had happened. I tried to tell the grownups about what happened but as I starting telling the story I realized how crazy it all sounded. So I just told them about seeing a light and left off the part about the snake-lizard thing."

Everything was coming together for Allenby. *My dad's story is true,* he told himself. *Of course it is. He never lied.*

"I think the thing that hurt the most," Matt said while still reflecting on the event, "was my father not believing me. I don't mean just about the light, but just in general. He never seemed to believe me or support me when I needed his belief and support the most."

"I'm sorry for that, Matt."

Matt just shrugged.

Allenby waited a moment before asking, "You mentioned some other events. Did they occur after this time at the creek?"

"Yes," Matt replied. "The same ball of light but also a large craft hovering nearby."

"You're joking."

"I am not," Matt said with a serious tone. "I saw them together for the first time when my father and I were still at the safe house in Austin after everyone else had disappeared."

"Everyone else?"

"Yes. Your father, then Paul Stover and that weird doctor, the archeologist who appeared out of nowhere during our trip."

"Dr. Robert Margolian?"

"Yes. He and Paul left to go hunt for your father, I think. Paul told my father something different but I don't remember what he said. Anyway, I saw the ball of light and a larger craft of some sort about a year later behind my father's big cabin in Gold Tree. I was inside the cabin and I heard my father in his office, talking and arguing with what sounded like more than one person. I heard their voices clearly yet as far as I knew no one had come in or out of the cabin. It was just me and my father, alone. I remember going outside to see if there were any cars parked nearby. That's when I turned and saw the same craft I'd seen in Austin. This time it was rising from the back of the cabin in a slow ascent. It kept ascending slowly until stopping into a hover as if it knew I was watching and wanted to give me a good look. All of a sudden it flew away, silently, so fast that all I saw was a green blur." Matt paused to sip his coffee. "When I went back inside, my father gave me a suspicious look and asked where I'd been. I brushed off his question and asked if he had guests in his office. He said he didn't but he'd been on a conference call with his high-tech speakerphone system. I knew that was a lie but I don't believe he knew that I knew, if that makes sense."

Allenby took a gulp of his coffee before leaning back in his chair with a loud exhale. "This is incredible."

"Yes, it is," Matt agreed. "And you can't imagine how good it feels to get it off my chest and share it with somebody."

Allenby smiled with a gentle nod of his head. He let another moment pass, sipped his coffee, then asked, "Is your father still alive, Matt?"

"No, he died years ago while I was attending the American University in Cairo, after the Middle East War. He lost his fortune in the war and I think that's what killed him."

Allenby nodded. After a short pause, "Are you married?"

"Divorced."

"Any kids?"

"No."

"Any close friends?"

"Not really. More like acquaintances, I suppose."

"Then you've really had no one to share anything with," Allenby said. "Right?"

Matt hesitated before saying, "Yes, you're right."

"Well," Allenby said. "I'm telling you that right now all that has changed."

Matt stared back at Allenby, his eyebrows slightly furled.

"Anytime you need to talk about anything," Allenby said, "and I mean anything, I'm here to talk to you and to be your friend."

Matt felt a wave of emotion rising from his chest. The feeling surprised him. The power in Allenby's presence was awesome. "I-I don't know what to say," Matt said.

"You don't have to say anything."

Matt seemed to be wrestling with his thoughts. He started to say something but hesitated. He tried again and said, "I have a question for you."

"Go for it."

"How do I become saved?"

"By faith," Allenby said without hesitation. "Like the faith of a child."

Matt thought for a moment. "Trust?"

"Trust is part of it," Allenby said. "Listen, Matt. You wouldn't believe how many people I've met who feel they were abandoned by their fathers when they were young. Abandoned either physically or emotionally. Extensive research into this subject has shown that many self-declared atheists admit to not having a good father figure in their childhood. That's not a coincidence, Matt. By rejecting the existence of God, the *Father* of the universe, they are perhaps subconsciously rejecting their own worldly fathers for rejecting them as children. In other words, they lost their *trust* a long time ago."

"So how do you change that?"

"By forgiveness," Allenby answered. "You must forgive your neglectful father, your abusive father, the father that you never knew, whatever the case may be. And listen carefully, Matt. You need to forgive your father for *your* sake, not his."

Matt tried to absorb this. A moment later he asked, "Then what happens?"

"It's a joyous thing when you come back to God," Allenby said. "Celebrate this reunion by giving thanks for the way he chose to reunite you, which came to you in human form through his son, Jesus Christ, who makes it possible for *all* to have everlasting life in the kingdom of heaven. Ask Jesus to forgive you of your sins. Accept that forgiveness. Now, let me ask you something, Matt: How can we accept God's forgiveness of our sins if we don't also forgive others for their sins against us?"

"What about people who have done *really* bad things?" Matt asked. "You know, like murder, rape, child abuse?"

"Anyone is forgiven if they *truly* accept Jesus as their personal savior and ask for his forgiveness. Their sins are not only forgiven but forgotten."

Matt's facial expression remained neutral. "Then it's about choice."

"Yes," Allenby said. "Choice."

"It's funny," Matt said. "I remember telling your father about this computer game I was trying to build when I was a kid. It was one of those civilization type of software games with little people and their towns, all of them trying to get along. I was trying to design the game where my characters had the ability to choose. Your father told me I'd probably make millions with it someday. He and Paul thought it was a great idea but my father thought it was a total waste of time." Matt smiled at some memory. "I realize now why choice was so significant in the game. Just like the real world, without free will or the ability to choose, we are nothing but robots."

Allenby sensed many things on Matt's mind. "You are a lawyer, Matt," he said. "You've been trained to be skeptical. Truth is the result of the proof you discover. The evidence. Correct? Now nobody, including myself, can *prove* the validity of the Bible with 100 percent accuracy, but in the same token, no one can disapprove it either, and that's saying a lot considering how many have tried to disapprove it for the last two thousand years. However, a huge amount of evidence is available for those who are honestly seeking the truth in Bible prophecy, archeology, science, astronomy, personal testimonies and the like. Keep in mind that we enter the kingdom of heaven with faith, not intellectual understanding, but many times intellectual people have stumbling blocks in the form of misconceptions and presuppositions about the evidence. If you make it your personal quest to find and sort the available evidence without any agenda other than finding the truth, you will find that the evidence *for* the validity of Christ and the Bible far outweighs the evidence *against* Christ and the Bible."

"Can you help me get started with that?" Matt asked.

"Absolutely I can," Allenby replied. "What's your biggest stumbling block regarding God?"

Matt though for a moment. "That if God created everything he must have created evil, too."

"Here's the problem with that," Allenby said. "God gave his creations the ability to choose. Evil is a choice."

Matt didn't respond.

"Here's a story that I think explains that matter the best," Allenby said. "Back in the middle of the nineteenth century, a brilliant young schoolboy was attending an advanced philosophy course at a university in Germany or Austria with students much older than him. The professor began class with this statement:

'If God created everything he must have created evil, too.'
The boy said: 'Professor, is there such thing as cold?'
'Of course there is,' the professor said. 'Haven't you ever been cold?'
'Actually, the first law of thermodynamics states that only heat exists,' the boy said. *'Cold is the absence of heat. Professor, is there such thing as darkness?'*

'Of course. Haven't you ever seen the dark?'

'No one can see darkness,' the boy said. 'You can only see light. Darkness is the absence of light. God is light. Therefore, God did not create evil. Evil is the absence of God.' Do you know who the boy supposedly was?" asked Allenby.

"No," Matt said with a shake of his head. "Who?"

"Albert Einstein."

"Awesome," Matt said with a smile.

"Here's something else," Allenby said. "I once debated a man who had absolutely no belief whatsoever in the Bible. He was a well-educated man yet he was ignorant of most scriptures in the Bible. He said the Bible was simply a book written by men, the same as any book. So I challenged him to what I'm about to challenge you. Are you game, Matt?"

"Yes, of course."

"Okay. I'm going to read you ten statements about someone," Allenby said while scrolling to a page on his cell phone device. "Just listen and then I'll ask you a question after I've finished. Understand?"

"Yes."

"I gave My back to those who beat Me, and my cheeks to those who tore out my beard. I did not hide my face from scorn and spitting.

"He was oppressed and afflicted, yet He did not open His mouth. Like a lamb led to the slaughter and like a sheep silent before her shearers, He did not open His mouth.

"He bore the sin of many and interceded for the rebels.

"They pierced my hands and my feet.

"Everyone who sees me mocks me; they sneer and shake their heads: 'He relies on the Lord; let Him rescue him; let the Lord deliver him, since He takes pleasure in him.'

"They gave me gall for my food, and for my thirst they gave me vinegar to drink.

"My God, my God, why have You forsaken me?

"He protects all his bones; not one of them is broken.

"They divided my garments among themselves, and they cast lots for my clothing.

"They made His grave with the wicked, and with a rich man at His death, although He had done no violence and had not spoken deceitfully.

Allenby leaned back in his chair. "Now who and what do you believe those statements were referring to?"

"Without any doubt," Matt said. "The Crucifixion of Jesus."

"That's the same answer the atheist gave me," Allenby said. "So I then told him that those ten scriptures were just a few of the many written in the Old Testament which were completed some four hundred years before Jesus was born. No critic or atheist or agnostic has ever claimed that those scriptures were written after his birth. In fact, all these scriptures were translated from Hebrew into Greek in Alexandria some one-hundred-fifty years before Christ's birth. So I asked him: 'If this is merely a book written by men, how do you explain these words being written?' He was speechless."

"So there is proof that they were written before Christ's birth?"

"Absolute proof," Allenby said. "Multiple copies of every scripture in the Old Testament except for the Book of Esther has been found in the Dead Sea Scrolls. Through paleography and radiometric dating they were all written over two hundred years before Christ. More than half of the ten Scriptures I read to you came from Psalms 22 and 69, most likely written by David a *thousand* years before Jesus came into this world, and the rest were from Isaiah 50 and 53, written seven-hundred years before Christ. And these are only ten of the hundreds of prophecies of the coming Messiah written in the Old Testament of the Bible. Matt, what do you think is the mathematical probability figure for these scriptures coming true?"

"Astronomical," said Matt.

"In fact," Allenby said. "Out of over three hundred Messianic prophecies made in the Old Testament that were fulfilled by Jesus Christ, the chances of one person fulfilling only an eighth of these prophecies is one in one-thousand-trillion! That's a ten with sixteen zeros. For one person to fulfill forty-eight of theses prophecies the number becomes staggering—one chance in 10^{157}—a number so large we can't comprehend it. Yet when you add the more than two-hundred other prophecies the number gets even larger! But one person, Jesus of Nazareth fulfilled them all despite the impossible odds."

"That's incredible evidence," Matt said. "I never knew any of that."

"You see, most of us can't understand numbers this large," Allenby said. "Even a mere trillion is so huge most people don't even think about it. Sometimes I explain it this way: A million dollars in evenly-stacked hundred-dollar bills is roughly four-feet high. A billion-dollar stack is four-thousand-feet high. A trillion-dollar stack is seven-hundred-eighty-nine *miles* high! And over here in Bible prophecy we're talking about odds of one in trillions multiplied by trillions multiplied by trillions!"

"Yes," Matt said. "That is astonishing."

"I can help you hurdle most intellectual stumbling blocks, Matt," Allenby said, "but you still have to come to the Lord in faith. Sometimes those intellectual stumbling blocks can prevent someone from exercising their faith. I've compiled massive amounts of research from some of the greatest minds in the world, including scientists in a variety of fields. For example, in one of the books in my series, I compare modern scientific discoveries in molecular biology and the Big Bang Theory to the world of largely unproved *facts* of Charles Darwin and the neo-Darwinists of today. Darwin's theory of life adapting within the species, *micro-evolution*, is seldom disputed by anyone, but Darwin himself had suspicions of his theory regarding one species evolving into another species, or what's referred to as *macro-evolution*. In the nineteenth century Darwin stated that when the paleontological record became complete it may prove his theory to be flawed. Well, the paleontological record has been considered complete for many years by virtually *all* paleontologists, believers and nonbelievers alike. And there is not one tiny iota of evidence to link one species evolving from another species. In fact, there is overwhelming scientific evidence to prove the contrary, DNA evidence that wasn't available in Darwin's day. The *Missing Link* we've been taught about for generations? It should be called the *Missing Theory*. And yet Evolution is still widely accepted by the masses and still taught in our public schools as it has been for more than a century." Allenby took a sip of coffee. "Have you read any of my books, Matt?"

"Sorry," Matt said with an apologetic smile. "I have not."

"Well, we'll fix that," Allenby said with a grin. "I'll also give you the names of many highly educated, intelligent men and women throughout the ages who have written about their turn to God through their journeys in intellectual areas usually reserved for nonbelievers."

"Thanks," Matt said. "I'd like that."

Allenby pushed his chair back and excused himself to go to the restroom. When he returned to the table he noticed that Matt's demeanor was much more upbeat, as if a long dormant fire inside of him had been suddenly rekindled.

"Thank you so much, Zeke," Matt said. "I don't think I've ever felt so optimistic, with so much hope for the future."

"That's wonderful," Allenby said, "because I want to make you a proposition that requires a lot of hope and optimism from both of us."

Matt seemed eager to hear the proposition. "Okay, let's hear it."

"Here's the deal," Allenby began. "For the last year or so the *ZAEA* has been trying very hard to take the *Awakenings* into Eastern Europe, Africa, Asia, and other difficult to reach parts of the world. We've made some progress, preaching in the Balkans, Romania, Bulgaria, even parts of Russia with the same results everywhere. Wherever the Gospel is preached the results are the same: many come to Christ no matter their cultural or religious background. So I want to take the Gospel everywhere I can as quickly as possible. What we need is someone who has international political connections. We also need someone who can help build the type of relationships needed to take the *Awakenings* to every reachable location on every continent on the planet."

"I'd say that's an ambitious goal," Matt said with a smile.

"Don't take this personal, counselor," Allenby said, "but our team did a little research on your talents. Not in your personal life but in your vocational accomplishments. We know of your success in brokering deals in much of Eastern Europe and the Middle East. We know you speak four foreign languages and have several one-on-one relationships with various Heads of State in some of those countries I mentioned. I believe God has brought us together for a reason, Matt. There's also something else . . ."

While Matt waited for Allenby to finish, he watched the famous preacher reach into his jacket and remove a folded piece of paper. "This is a letter from Dad that was at the end of the manuscript," Allenby said while holding the handwritten letter. "Since we are the only people in the world who has read Dad's manuscript, I think it only appropriate that you read the letter that went with it."

Matt took the folded paper from Allenby and opened it. He began reading. He stared at the letter after reading it, going back to several spots in the letter and reading them over. He finally finished and handed the letter back to Allenby. "As incredible as it sounds, it makes sense." There was a moment of silence. Then Matt asked, "Are you going to preach this in your sermons?"

"I have a lot of praying to do to get the answer to that," Allenby said. "But if I am meant to preach this warning along with the Gospel, I am confident that the Holy Spirit will guide me. So far I believe I've been guided in that direction. Before I left my office yesterday I watched an old video clip of a Billy Graham Crusade during the mid 1970s. I was looking for something in my desk when I heard Graham say something that took me by surprise." Allenby pulled his cell phone device from his jacket pocket and loaded the video clip onto the screen. He pressed *play* and handed it to Matt.

Matt watched the clip on the small screen where Billy Graham was preaching: *"Thrones, dominions, powers! Yes, there are thrones, dominions, and powers not only in this world but other worlds! Do I believe that other planets are inhabited? Yes, I do!"* Graham took a long pause to let his audience absorb this before continuing: *"I believe that there are angels! I believe there are demons! And the demon world is highly organized but so is the angelic world highly organized, and in my study of angels this year I've come to learn something about these wonderful beings with their tremendous power that are agents of God, that are to minister to the heirs of salvation."*

The clip on the cell phone device stopped automatically. Matt handed it back to Allenby. "It sounds like he was speaking directly to your situation, doesn't it? Is that what you are thinking?"

Allenby put his phone back into his pocket. "Yes, I believe it was meant for me to receive this message of encouragement from across the expanses of time, seventy-five years ago to this exact moment in time." Allenby paused before adding, "I also believe that *you* are the man for the job I described earlier. We'll be generous financially, but even more generous with sharing our love and joy with you, Matt. We are a family and you are welcome to join this family."

"What do I have to do?" Matt asked with a chuckle of disbelief.

"Make the choice," answered Allenby with a big grin. "Come share a life of adventure serving God Almighty, or stay here with the life you have now. It's your choice."

Matt laughed, trying to hold back his enthusiasm. "That doesn't sound like much of a choice."

Allenby just stared back with the same grin while waiting to hear a decision.

"It's a no-brainer for me," Matt said. "I'm in."

Allenby's grin grew into a large smile. He stuck out his hand for a big handshake to seal the deal. "I'm really excited about this," he told Matt. "There's so much I want to do and I can't wait to get started and get your input."

"Same here," Matt said. "Where do we begin?"

Zeke Allenby began explaining problems the *ZAEA* had in taking the *Awakenings* to one particular province in India. He knew Matt had handled some affairs for a major capitalist invested heavily into the Indian government. Maybe the investor had a few connections over there, connections that could possibly remove the roadblock which seemed to be preventing the ministry from reaching this particular province in India?

And this is how it started. How it all started. How along with the Gospel, the warnings of the nephilim's grand deception were taken to the entire population before the end days, probably saving countless souls from following darkness into eternity. By one bold decision made by two men inside the Palm Court of the Drake Hotel in Chicago, Illinois. One bold decision made over coffee sipped in fragile china cups. A decision to move forward. A decision to choose light over darkness. A decision to choose faith over fear. A decision to choose love over hatred. A decision to *choose* to serve God instead of self. A decision to make a choice . . . .

*   *   *

HAYDEN NICHOLAS has written over twenty top ten country music hit songs, fourteen reaching number one on the music charts. He has won numerous songwriting awards from the CMA, ACM, Grammies, and even a Tony Award for a collaborative work of music on Broadway. He currently resides in Austin, Texas with his wife and son. He still performs as lead guitarist for country singer Clint Black, a position he has held since 1986. This is his first novel in print.